"DO YOU ALWAYS ORDER EVERYTHING ON THE MENU?"

Jess flashed those dimples again. "Only when I want to spend a lot of time here. With you."

"You ordered all this just so you could spend time with me?" *Talk about stupid . . . but talk about sweet, too.*

"I didn't know when I'd see you again, and this was the only way I could think to make our time last."

Don't be sweet. Please don't be sweet. The Major's gonna kill me if you're sweet.

Corrie tallied up his bill. "It's going to cost you."

"You're worth it." He extricated one of her hands from her order pad.

"I am?" *I'm worth it?* Corrie had never been worth anything to anyone.

Raising her hand, Jess pressed his warm lips to the back of her fingers and lingered there a shade too long. Or a shade too short. Her heart rate didn't know which—it raced along on a hormone hurricane.

"Definitely." He rose, still clasping her fingers. "But I think I'll satisfy this particular appetite another way and another time."

"B-beg pardon?" she stammered. What did he mean by that? And damned if he wasn't making her knees weak.

"Next time you won't be working"—he caressed the back of her fingers with his thumb—"and we'll be alone." Gently, he released her hand and strode away, his long legs carrying him quickly to the exit.

She leaned both hands on the table and blew out the breath she'd been holding. Her resolutions to avoid Jess shredded like a dust bunny in a tornado.

Weak, Webb, definitely weak.

Dear Romance Reader,

Last year, we launched the Ballad line with four new series, and each month we'll present both new and continuing stories set everywhere from medieval England to the American West—the kind of passionate, romantic stories you love best, written by the most gifted authors. At the back of each book, we'll tell you when you can find subsequent books in the series that have captured your heart.

This month, Martha Schroeder and her passionate *Angels of Mercy* are back! In **True to Her Heart,** a beautiful but penniless young woman finds that her sojourn in the Crimea has discouraged wealthy suitors—and that she wants the one man she fears she can never have. Next, the fabulous *Hope Chest* series continues with Paula Gill's **Fire With Fire** as a woman travels back in time only to meet a rugged lawman who sets off an irresistible flame of desire.

In the next entry of the breathlessly romantic *Once Upon a Wedding* series, Kelly McClymer offers **The Unintended Bride.** A shy young woman longs for true love—and when a family friend must offer for her out of obligation, he longs to prove to her that he is the dashing hero of her dreams. Finally, talented Sylvia McDaniel concludes the fresh and funny *Burnett Brides* trilogy with **The Marshal Takes a Wife,** as a female doctor returns to her hometown and discovers that the man she left behind might be the only man to steal her heart.

Kate Duffy
Editorial Director

HOPE CHEST

FIRE WITH FIRE

PAULA GILL

ZEBRA BOOKS
KENSINGTON PUBLISHING CORP.
http://www.zebrabooks.com

ZEBRA BOOKS are published by

Kensington Publishing Corp.
850 Third Avenue
New York, NY 10022

Copyright © 2001 by Paula Gill

First Printing: July 2001
10 9 8 7 6 5 4 3 2 1

Printed in the United States of America

Where do you start passing around the "Thank yous" when it's your first published novel? I'll just stick to the basics. . . .

First, to my fellow WYRD Sisters: Karen Fox, Pam McCutcheon, Mo Webster, and Laura Hayden, who are in this with me, Von Jocks, who opens our eyes, and Deb Stover, whose idea this series was and who never flagged in her faith in my writing, even when I was ready to throw in the towel.

Second, to Mickey, who is my own personal Zelda. Love ya, Mom.

Last and always, to Charlie, my inspiration for every kiss. Without you, I would never have known the beauty and bounty and tenderness of love. Every waltz is yours, hon.

ONE

Charles Dickens should've died a lot younger. Corrinne Webb didn't know when old Charlie had penned his sappy *Christmas Carol*, but whenever it was, she wished he'd died before then.

Corrie hunched a shoulder and dropped a touch of lime into the chipotle mango salsa destined to top the sea bass on the grill. *Just because I'm not all nice and chirpy about Christmas . . .*

Paul LaDue propped one hip against her prep table. Without looking up, she shot out, "What?"

"Still in Scrooge mode, huh?" Immune to her mood—no, emphatically unaffected by it—he crossed his arms. No doubt about it, Bistro Terre's owner could outwait boeuf à la bourguignonne.

"I am *not* a Scrooge just because I don't want to attend the staff party tonight."

"Everyone's coming."

"But—"

"I've known you more than five years and you've always had an excuse for why you can't attend. Face it, Webb, you don't like Christmas."

"Why wouldn't I like Christmas? Of course I like Christmas. Nobody doesn't like Christmas." She realized she was ranting and gave the salsa a vicious stir. "The thing is, I'm very busy right now. Working."

"*Making* work, you mean."

"Wha—? But . . . I . . ." Corrie faltered to a stop as Paul waved his hand to encompass the kitchen.

The restaurant's core usually throbbed with the drumbeat of hurrying feet, the staccato chop of knives, and the soprano whine of Cuisinarts. At the moment, however, the prep person dozed in the corner and the grill chef concentrated on catching the tongs he tossed into the air every few seconds as he waited for the bass to cook.

"You're not working tonight. No one is." Paul took her by the arm and led her to the door into the dining room. "What do you see?"

"The same burgundy walls I told you two months ago would be more elegant if they were deep green. It still looks like a whorehouse from some old Western. You'd think a gay guy would have better taste."

"Besides the decor, Webb." He grinned. "Save the sarcasm for someone who doesn't know you."

Corrie resisted the temptation to goad Paul more about his misguided decorating and looked around the spacious room, her gaze pausing at each cozy dining alcove, each meticulously dressed table. As usual, the crystal sparkled, the china and silver gleamed, and the tablecloths were immaculate. In honor of the holiday season, fresh holly and pine festooned the tables and walls. A fire crackled merrily in the fireplace, a blue norther had blown through Dallas yesterday and the extra heat was a welcome addition in more than just aesthetics.

"What exactly am I supposed to be noticing?"

"You're never going to make it when you own your own restaurant if you don't see it." Using both hands to turn her head toward the dining room, Paul gave her a little shake. "Count the customers."

It didn't take long. "Two tables of two couples each equals eight customers," Corrie recited like a kindergartner answering a math question. Returning to her usual tone, she asked, "Your point is . . . ?"

"We only had three other reservations the whole night. And no walk-ins at all." He sighed. "That doesn't pay your salary for the night, much less all the others'."

"Oh."

"Yeah, oh." He shook his head as he walked her back to her station. "Anyone who runs a restaurant has to look at the bottom line. If you ever want to own your own place, you have to start paying attention to stuff like this."

Corrie fiddled with her knives, upset with herself for putting her dread of Christmas ahead of her dream—a café of her own. If she was ever to realize that dream, she had to concentrate on the business aspect of the restaurant as well as the food. In her head, she knew about customer load versus overhead balance, but in reality, it had never sunk in. But then, she'd never paid much attention to people—just work.

Only work.

Which was how, at the age of twenty-six, she'd risen to head chef at the prestigious Bistro Terre, one of the most highly acclaimed five-star restaurants in Texas.

She replaced her prized chef's knife in its slot and looked up at her boss. "I guess I didn't notice. . . ." She almost reminded him of the reason she was acting like a turtle, head pulled in and shell protected. Almost.

Paul scraped a hand over his face. *"I noticed."*

"And?" Something in his expression made Corrie dread the answer.

"I'm closing the restaurant."

"Closing the Bistro?" *No, you can't.* If she was the crying type, she would've broken down right there and flooded the city. But Corrie hadn't cried in more than seventeen years. A wall rose around the memories and she stiffened her spine.

Her fist closed around Paul's coat sleeve. "You can't. You can't close it. Not now. Not at Christmas."

"Hold on—"

She shook his arm. "What about all the employees? What'll they do? It's Christmas, for gosh sakes!" Her coworkers were the one thing that might make Paul change his mind.

"I said hold on." Paul pried her fingers from the fabric and brushed out the wrinkles. "I'm closing Terre until New Year's Eve is all. Not for good."

"But how will people pay their bills?" *How will I get through Christmas without distraction?* If she couldn't work herself into exhaustion, the nightmares might return.

"If you'll give me a chance to explain—I'm giving everyone two weeks' paid vacation. It's going to put a strain on the budget, but I want to be fair."

You had to choose now *to act like Santa Claus?* "Two whole weeks?"

"What's the problem? Everybody else is happy as clams."

"Ever hear of clam chowder?"

"Come on now, Scrooge. What's your problem?"

Corrie could stand sarcasm, but not Paul's concerned tone. She thumped him on the shoulder with her fist—not in anger, but defeat. Then she pressed her forehead against the place she'd hit so she wouldn't have to see his expression.

"Why the attitude, Corrie honey?" Paul squeezed her closer, like the big brother she'd always wanted and never had.

Because he was the only one she trusted, she couldn't help admitting, "If I don't have to be here, I don't have to be anywhere."

"But that's the good part. You can do whatever you want. Go see your family."

With her head close to his chest, Corrie heard his sharp intake of breath as he remembered. Her answering sigh trembled a bit.

His grip tightened. "Shit, honey, I'm sorry. I forgot."

"Can't say but what I'd like to sometimes," she mumbled into his coat.

"So . . . spend Christmas with me and the family. You know you're welcome."

Yeah, welcome and as comfortable as a duck in a tux. She'd never gotten the hang of families and holidays. How could she, when she never really belonged? And the enormous LaDue clan, all chattering in Cajun patois, would only emphasize that fact, no matter how much they tried.

Giving him a hug, Corrie shook her head. "No, it's okay. I'll be fine." How, she didn't know, but it wasn't Paul's problem. She stepped back. "Really, I'll be fine."

"I'm not taking no for an answer."

"Listen, LaDue . . ."

"No one should be alone at Christmas."

"I'm used to it." *Amazing what you can get used to.*

"You shouldn't be."

Corrie let him rant a little more as she plated the

sea bass with the salsa and passed it, along with a London broil with béarnaise sauce, on to the prep person to garnish and finish the presentation. She turned her attention back to Paul as he snapped his fingers.

"I've got it."

She folded her arms across her chest and leaned against the counter. "What is it you've got? Rudolph in the closet? Or has he come out with you?"

"Christmas." He threw both hands up to keep her quiet. "Hear me out."

She arched one eyebrow. "Get on with it."

"How about you spend Christmas in Virginia?"

"Why would I do that?"

"Because my Uncle André has a cabin outside Roanoke in the Allegheny Mountains—in a little town called Hope Springs. You can hike, maybe ski, just relax. All by yourself. Free of charge."

"I couldn't." *But it does sound good.*

"Sure you could." Paul joined her at the counter, mirroring her folded arms but eyeing her with that stubborn look. "It's free. It's not being used."

"But—"

"Ski season isn't in full swing yet. You'll be by yourself. No one to bother you."

"Well . . ." *It sounds really good. But I shouldn't.*

"You'd be doing Uncle André a favor, making sure it's still in good shape."

"Well . . ."

"Go on—do it. You haven't taken a vacation since this place opened."

Corrie studied his face and detected only what she always found—honesty and friendship.

"You could leave tomorrow morning and—the way *you* drive—be there by dark."

"Get real. It's two or three long days' drive to Virginia."

"You have two weeks."

"But—"

"Do it. It'll be fun."

"Well . . . all right." Maybe it *would* be fun.

"Great." He brushed stray parsley off his jacket and headed for the dining room. "I'm putting up the closed sign, then I'll write out the directions for you."

"Thanks," she called after him. Maybe being in a strange place would make the two weeks fly by.

Paul stuck his head back in. "Then we'll go to the party as soon as these customers leave."

Corrie gritted her teeth until her jaw cracked. What was it Scrooge said? Oh, yeah.

"Bah humbug."

A few days later Corrie anticipated surviving Christmas in rather better shape than usual. The nightmares that usually accompanied Christmas hadn't happened. And, as a tourist, she wasn't exposed to the incessant holiday wishes—or worse, pity—of coworkers.

Every night she built a fire and sipped vintage Bordeaux while consuming romance novels by her favorite authors, with an occasional foray into *The Complete Works of Shakespeare*. By day she explored Hope Springs, with its quaint stores, and even ventured up the hill to the abandoned Victorian-era resort called the Chesterfield. Something about the ramshackle "old lady" called to her.

This morning she was breakfasting at the Coffee Cup Café in the old Morris Mercantile building as she planned her day. A map of the area covered most of the table. She felt comfortable, having eaten here several times since her arrival. While the menu couldn't be called gourmet, the cook had a definite way with French toast.

"More coffee, hon?" The bee-hived waitress in the turquoise uniform set the pot down to straighten the load of dirty dishes on her arm.

"Thanks." Corrie's eyes never left the map as she forked up another piece of syrup-soaked bread. If she didn't strike up conversations, folks didn't get involved in her life.

"You surely do enjoy Joe's French toast," the older woman said and turned away.

Thinking she was safe, Corrie laughed. "It's threatening my waistline. But then, resisting temptation has never been my forte."

"Why, honey, you're too young to be worryin' about resistin' temptation." The woman's Marlboro-roughened laugh ricocheted off the ceiling as she placed the dishes on a vacant table and picked up the coffeepot. "You oughta be chasin' that sucker!"

Uh-oh. Why couldn't you keep your mouth shut, Webb?

"Here now, where ya tryin' to find?" An ample polyester-covered hip blocked escape from the booth.

The café was empty, so Corrie couldn't expect any distraction there. She shrugged, resigned to the inevitable. "There's supposed to be a waterfall up past that old hotel, but I can't find it on this map."

"Shoot, it ain't hard to find." Without a glance at Corrie's cup, the waitress—her badge identified her as Alma—filled it to within a quarter inch of the rim. One red talon tapped the map. "Right along here is the old railroad spur—used to serve the Chester-field back before it closed."

"So I follow the spur and then what?"

"About halfway up the spur, see that little blue squiggle right there?"

Corrie peered over the talon. Sure enough, a faint blue line traced its way past the end of the black-hatched marking of the railroad. She nodded.

"Just follow that up about a half mile or so, and there you'll be. But you gotta be careful . . ."

The waitress was obviously winding up for a long spell. Now came the difficult part—how to get Alma to leave her alone. Corrie knew the woman was only being friendly, but she never made friends easily. Short-term stays meant short-term relationships.

Fortunately, rescue came in the form of several squad cars of police officers. As a sheriff, two Hope Springs policemen, and a pair of Virginia highway patrolmen filed past, Corrie sighed in relief. She wasn't the only one addicted to Joe's cooking, and these guys were a heaven-sent reprieve. Alma followed them, deftly filled their cups, and jotted down orders, all the while keeping up a steady flow of banter. All aimed at the cops, not Corrie.

Which gave her time to finish her meal without further interruption. When Alma dropped her check on the table, Corrie glanced up. "Thanks for the directions."

"You just be careful up around the Chesterfield, honey. There's tell of people goin' up there and not comin' back." She dropped her voice to a whisper. "And today's the winter solstice."

"Now, Alma, don't go scaring the girl with your old wives' tales. No more people disappear at the solstice than any other day." One of the patrolmen swiveled in his chair to face Corrie. "But you watch the sky, little lady. I wouldn't be surprised to see a snow squall any time now."

Corrie glanced out at the clear azure sky, then mouthed a silent "Thanks" to the law enforcement table as she hurried out to her beat-up Corolla.

The wind tugged at her jacket and rattled the Christmas lights on the towering bare trees in the parking lot. Corrie paused, her hand on the car door, and scrutinized the mountains. Not a cloud in sight.

"Snow squall, huh?" She got into the car and headed for the trailhead about three miles down from the abandoned hotel. "Keep your day job, Officer. You're no weatherman."

Corrie squinted against the wind-whipped snow and hunkered farther into her coat. "Okay, Officer Whoever-you-were. I take it back; you *are* a weatherman."

By her reckoning, she should have already reached that damned waterfall. In reality, she hadn't even seen the railroad spur where she was supposed to bear left. She pulled out the map and studied it, turned it ninety degrees right, then one-eighty left.

She pivoted to stare down the trail she'd just climbed. At least it looked like the right one. But there were more than half a dozen others she *could* have come up. Somehow, in the snow, she'd become disoriented.

Footprints weren't any help. The unusual powder-dry snow was blowing so hard, it wasn't even sticking.

It was, however, bringing an early dusk.

"I *knew* I shouldn't have taken that old house tour

before heading up this way," Corrie muttered. "Or stopped for lunch."

A shiver unrelated to the cold traced its way down her spine. Her backpack was loaded, but that bottle of '96 Californian Cabernet wasn't going to help her see her way down this mountain. Still, she shucked off the pack and burrowed through the contents, just in case. . . .

It didn't take long to determine that a slice of pâté, a baguette of French bread, an apple, a bottle of 1996 California viognier wine, a pair of hiking socks, and six unused condoms—from a hopeful but disappointing, camping trip several years earlier—did not equate to one flashlight.

"Think, Webb. Which way is Hope Springs?"

No matter which way she turned, all the trails seemed to go uphill. A particularly brutal gust reminded her of the sodden state of her jeans and her lack of gloves or hat. Even her long, thick braid offered little protection from the cold or wet.

"Make up your mind or you're going to end up one ugly ice sculpture." With that, she shouldered her pack and started along the trail she hoped led to town.

The snow increased in intensity with each step. Corrie was tempted to take shelter under a tree, but her legs were already going numb. Without a heat source, she risked frostbite over a major portion of her anatomy. She pushed on even as her lungs labored to get oxygen to her muddled mind. Each breath was a gasp, each step torture.

I knew I should have kept up those aerobic classes.

She didn't see the railroad tracks until she tripped over the rail. By the time she felt herself falling, all she could do was go with it.

"Bah humbug," she said when she could breathe again.

Geez, I'm beginning to sound *like Scrooge.*

Tentatively, she eased each extremity into motion. Besides skinned palms and one bruised knee, she wasn't too bad off. She sat up and tried to see through the blinding snow. Getting back to town was no longer her goal; finding shelter was. Preferably with heat. There was a slightly darker, large shape a short way along the tracks.

The old, tumbledown Chesterfield.

" 'Be it ever so humble . . .' " Corrie sang under her breath as she ouched her way to her feet.

In order not to lose her way again, she decided to walk between the rails, even if it meant stumbling over the crossties. The track would lead her directly to the hotel.

"Okay, Webb, just a few more feet and you're safe." Her gaze dropped to her shoes. "Feet . . . come on, feet. I can't feel you, but I know you're there."

Her legs were cement stumps. Her hands were icicles. But she hadn't fought the odds all these years to succumb to a little weather.

"Corrinne Webb doesn't give up," she mumbled through chapped lips.

She lurched across a railroad tie and barely caught herself. Her vision blurred as she squinted toward the hotel again. Had it moved?

Tucking her hands under her arms, Corrie surged forward.

"Where're the rails, feet?" She floundered to the right—where the building ought to have been but wasn't. Or . . . it might have been, but she couldn't see it.

Panic rose, a bitter acid in her throat. She could die out here. Alone.

As always.

"Corrinne Webb doesn't give up." She wanted to shake a fist at the clouds but couldn't seem to make her hand close. For that matter, she couldn't really feel her hands.

Her left foot—or maybe it was her right, she couldn't feel either—slipped off the crosstie, plunging her headfirst to the ground.

She groaned and rolled to her hands and knees. Her head swam, and shaking it did nothing but scramble her brain more. But beneath her hands she could make out a walkway, veering off to her right. Hope cleared her head enough to send her half-stumbling along the walk, certain it would lead to the old hotel. Or at least some sort of structure.

The sound of the wind changed in pitch, whining around a building instead of through trees. Eyes squinted against the snow, Corrie forced her gaze upward and saw a sign above a gaping doorway, THE CHESTERFIELD HOTEL.

"Might as well say Pearly Gates," she breathed in relief. Then another gust stole her breath as snow pelted her through the holes in the roof and she changed her mind.

She floundered through the lobby and, by instinct, found the kitchen. The stove flues must have acted as supports because here the roof was, mostly, intact. Corrie stamped her feet and clapped her hands together, but the cold had penetrated too deep.

She needed a fire. Fast.

"Too bad you don't smoke, Webb."

When a search of the kitchen failed to turn up any matches, she extended her investigation to a hallway off the kitchen. Hurriedly, she rummaged through the rooms along it.

Other than a few rodents' nests and more beer cans than she could count, they were all empty. Corrie cupped her hands over her mouth and blew warm air over her fingers. All she felt was a vague tingling.

Not good. Not good at all.

"Paul LaDue, you owe me. You owe me big time."

Corrie closed her eyes. She was so cold. Too cold. Deathly cold.

Her eyes shot open. No way was she giving up.

She pushed on around a corner and continued her search. At least she was out of the wind here. Other than a few broken chairs and tables, she found little furniture—which made the big wooden chest in the corner room conspicuous.

Dropping to her knees in front of it, Corrie fumbled with the clasp. *Maybe someone left a blanket in here. Or an oil lamp. And matches.*

Unlikely, but hey, she could hope.

The wind howled around the corner of the hotel. Somehow the windows in this room had survived the years, and it wasn't as cold as the rest. The little light coming through revealed an odd assortment of items in the bottom. But nothing she could use in her current situation.

Just old, rusty, and broken things—a necklace, a pair of handcuffs, a nameplate—and a barely dusty antique dueling pistol like ones she'd seen in movies. Knowing she had to find something to make a fire with soon, still Corrie reached into the chest and brushed her fingers over the items. Frostbitten, she couldn't really feel anything, but a compulsion built within her to touch . . . something.

The pistol tilted beneath her numb fingers, revealing a tarnished sheriff's badge with one point missing. An odd sensation tingled up through her fingers to her arms as she lifted the badge.

Her head swam again, but this time everything felt . . . different. On unsteady feet, she lurched upright. She glanced down at the badge and closed her hand around it.

The world tilted. Corrie plunged toward the floor. But the floor didn't arrive.

A gray, swirling mist enveloped her. Calm. Quiet. But her stomach and inner ear informed her that she continued had falling. In desperation, she twisted around.

Light gleamed in the distance. A flashlight beam? Had someone found her?

Corrie struggled to reach a hand toward the brilliance. For a moment, her fall slowed to become a peaceful motion toward the light. Then she looked behind her. Darkness.

Her fall resumed—tumbling, rolling, out of control.

Whatever was happening—frostbite-induced delusion or snow madness—lasted way too long. Corrie tightened her grip on the badge. "All right, already. Hit the floor, Webb." Then pain slammed through her as she landed. Another lousy Christmas.

She struggled for a breath and wheezed, "Bah humbug."

Grit filtered under Corrie's eyelid. She didn't blink—it would've hurt too much. Breathing hurt, too, but she didn't have a choice about that.

"Knocked the stuffing out of you, did it?"

The proper English tones accomplished what pain hadn't. Corrie opened her eyes. Dark cloth filled her field of vision. Slowly it resolved into a skirt—a floor-length skirt with highly polished, old-timey black boots peeking out from the bottom.

With a groan, Corrie rolled onto her back. Mary Poppins gazed down at her—Gibson Ggirl hairdo, high collar, and all.

Hallucinating. Corrie closed her eyes against the figment of her injured imagination. *No question—a concussion.*

"Come, my girl. We'll have you fit as a trivet in a trice."

Trice? What sort of person uses a word like trice? Corrie managed to bring her hands up to rub her face. This would all make sense in a minute.

"None of that, now. You need a good wash first."

Figment here was becoming quite a nag.

Cool hands gently pushed her hands away and a warm cloth replaced them. Obligingly, Corrie wiped her face, then squinted up at the woman, about the same age as herself or maybe younger, kneeling at her side. "Thanks."

"You're quite welcome." The woman—she was awfully solid to be a hallucination—helped Corrie to her feet. "Now let's draw you a bath and see what we can do."

"Wait a minute." Corrie waved a delaying hand as she turned in a circle, surveying the room.

The nice, intact, fully furnished room. With a fire in the fireplace. And curtains. And a woman dressed for a costume party.

"I'm certain you have questions, Miss," Figment said as she ushered Corrie into an adjoining bathroom. Turning some ornate handles, she began filling a huge claw-footed tub with steaming water. She poured in scented bath salts and faced Corrie. "But they can wait until you've bathed and warmed up. Your fingers are freezing."

The adrenaline that had kept Corrie moving ebbed away with the rising steam, and she had to admit the woman had a point. A good soak sounded too good to pass up, even if this was all a dream, or a hypothermia-induced coma. She pulled off her coat and reached to untie her shoelaces. "Oh, why not? What have I got to lose?"

"Nothing, my dear. And everything to gain," Figment said with an enigmatic smile, closing the door behind her.

Blearily, Corrie stared after the strange woman. This would make sense in a minute; she knew it would. But in the meantime, warming up—even if only in a dream—seemed the sensible thing to do. Dropping the rest of her gear on the floor, she crawled into the tub, fingers and toes pinching from the sudden heat. Yes, this was the only sensible alternative.

Until she'd thawed out about ten minutes later.

Corrie's eyes flicked wide open and she surged to her feet, water splashing across the tile floor. What in hell was she thinking? This place was a derelict. Abandoned, dilapidated. How could she be taking a hot bath?

Her gaze darted around the room. This didn't look like the broken-down hotel she'd stumbled into in the snow. Gleaming tile and porcelain reflected the soft illumination from the light fixtures by the mirror. Corrie squinted at them, then crawled out of the tub and padded across to them.

"*Gas*lights?" With trembling fingers she reached

up and turned the knob at the bottom of one. The flame inside the globe flared brighter. And hotter. Gaslight. She'd heard about it but had never seen it in person. "How can the gas still be on?"

A brisk knock on the door sent her scurrying for the towel on the rack by the tub. Once she'd covered the essentials, Corrie faced the door and said, with just a slight quiver in her voice, "Come in."

Figment peered around the edge of the door and beamed. "Feeling better, are we?" She seemed to understand Corrie's confusion, silently ushering her out to a chair in front of the fire and bundling her into a cozy chenille robe.

Corrie rubbed her eyes and stared at Figment. *I'm dreaming. I have to be.* She flexed her fingers within the robe's folds. *At least it's a warm dream.*

The woman placed a plate of sandwiches on the table between them, then poured two cups of tea from an ornate teapot and handed one to Corrie after dropping in two sugar cubes and a dash of milk. "I don't know how you take your tea in the ordinary way, but I believe you need a touch of sustenance." She dropped one cube into her own cup, stirred it, and savored a sip.

The tea's aroma tempted Corrie to follow Figment's lead, and an involuntary sigh escaped as she swallowed the soothing brew. *Heaven.*

She shot a glance around the room. *Or the funny farm.*

"You have questions, of course."

Corrie jumped. "Questions?" she squeaked. She turned her attention to Figment, catching the maximum force of the fully furnished room. Her mind backpedaled—the room swirled in a maelstrom of colors and fabrics and Victorian clutter. This wasn't real. Couldn't be real.

"Breathe," Figment instructed in a no-nonsense tone.

Corrie breathed. Once. Twice. She placed her cup carefully on the table between them. She closed her eyes. *Wake up, Webb. You're going over the edge.*

"That won't help, you know."

Her eyes shot open to stare at Figment. "Won't help what?"

"Closing your eyes won't change the room and won't change how I look." Figment lifted a dainty shoulder. "It won't change where you are."

"And where *am* I?" Maybe she'd been rescued and taken somewhere. Yeah, that would explain things. Sort of.

"Why, my dear girl, you're in my room at the Chesterfield Hotel."

"That's impossible." Unable to contain her tension, Corrie rose to pace around the room. "The Chesterfield is deserted. It's falling down. Just a shell's left."

A sad sigh acknowledged Corrie's words. "Dreadful, isn't it? She is such a magnificent resort now. Terrible how she'll go downhill later."

Corrie slowed her pacing. "Is . . . now? Later?" Being rescued and transferred to another hotel didn't explain *this.*

"Let me explain."

An explanation—that's what I need. Then everything will make sense. She gulped. *I hope.*

Figment raised one hand, and Corrie halted in front of her. Somehow she knew this woman had the answers. Answers to questions Corrie wasn't even sure how—or what—to ask.

Rising, the woman grasped Corrie's hands in a gentle grip. "This is not easy to explain. . . ."

"Just tell me who you are, where I am, and how I got here." Hairs prickled on the back of Corrie's neck. "Straight out."

"All right, then. Straight out, as you say. First, who am I? My name is Miss Esmeralda Sparrow and I'm the head housekeeper in charge of the female staff." The woman looked deep into Corrie's eyes and said, "Where are you? As I said before, in my room in the Chesterfield Hotel."

Corrie tried to look away. *The woman's crazy. She has to be.* But for some reason, Corrie didn't break eye contact with her.

"And as for how you got here . . ." Figment—no, Sparrow—tightened her hold. "You rummaged through a chest—my hope chest—and found something."

For just a second, Corrie glanced away—to the chest, the warm-toned wood new and shining with polish. She returned her gaze to Sparrow. "I found a lot of stuff—nothing to keep me warm, by the way—but when I picked up the broken badge . . ."

"You fell . . . back here."

"Back. Here." The air in Corrie's chest refused to move, stifling her. "Back here."

"That's right, my dear. Back here to The Chesterfield Hotel." Sparrow flashed a bright smile. "To Eighteen-eighty-six."

TWO

An hour later, Corrie still wasn't too sure about having traveled back to 1886, but she *was* sure she wasn't wearing the getup Sparrow laid out on the bed.

"These should fit well enough," the Mary Poppins look-alike said, giving the mound of ruffles a delicate pat.

Not in this lifetime, sister.

Returning to their previous topic, Corrie asked, "I can't just pick up that badge again and walk through this time portal anytime I want?" She looked around the room. "And where did the badge go?"

Sparrow resumed her seat by the fire. "You will be able to return at the next solstice. In June." Only her fingers, restless in her lap, revealed an inner distress.

"What about the badge?"

"Oh, that isn't relevant."

"It is to me." Corrie plopped down in the other chair. That piece of tin was apparently essential to her getting back to her own time. Which made it damned relevant. "Where's the badge?"

"It . . . will appear at the proper time," Sparrow said, not quite meeting Corrie's gaze but primming her lips into a stubborn line. "That's all I can tell you at this point."

No use pursuing that line—Corrie could tell Sparrow wouldn't give in. So she backtracked to another one. "This has happened before?" Maybe someone else had figured out a way around this loony business.

"Yes." A smile flitted across Sparrow's now placid face. "But I cannot disclose the names, as I—"

"As you said before," Corrie completed and shoved her hands in the pockets of her borrowed robe. Her temper unraveled a bit more. "Is there anything you *haven't* said before that I should know? Or is that not allowed by your rules?"

"Sarcasm is unbecoming in a lady, Corrinne," Sparrow said in an injured tone.

Exasperated, Corrie rose to prop a foot on the hearth. "No one ever accused me of being a lady."

Sparrow sat up even straighter, her eyes wide and worried. "Oh, my. You don't mean you're a . . . a wh"—she swallowed loudly—"a woman of loose morals, do you? That would not do, would not do at all."

"You mean a—what do you call them in this time—a whore?" Corrie laughed—the first time she'd done so since this nightmare began. She shut her mouth when she realized the laugh threatened to become a wild, lost thing. "Good God, no."

A bitch maybe, but not a whore. Her stomach clenched as she thought of Paul, the one who'd last called her that—in fun and laughing with it. Would he try to find her? Would he miss her? No one had ever missed her. Did she have to get lost some hundred-plus years back in time in order to be missed?

Back in time.

A continuing shiver of disbelief and something else, something scarier, coursed through her. Had she really traveled to 1886? The chenille robe was soft against her skin, the fire warm, and the floor hard. Her heart raced. This was real.

But in spite of her alarm at actually being in 1886, Corrie stiffened her spine. Corrinne Webb never caved in. Not even when she was alone. More alone than she'd ever been before.

Sparrow seemed relieved with Corrie's response and her silence and rose to pace the room, startling Corrie and dragging her chaotic thoughts back to the matter at hand. Finally, Sparrow paused in front of her and cleared her throat. In a ladylike way, of course. "I *am* pleased you are of good moral character. . . ."

I've been called a character before. But moral? Oh, all right. I'm not a bad person. So she kept quiet and let Sparrow talk.

"Because I could never hire anyone who wasn't."

Corrie straightened. "I didn't think about needing a job. I just supposed you . . ." She let the thought trail off hopefully.

"Oh, no. I haven't the funds to support you for six months." Sparrow placed a slim white hand over Corrie's on the mantel. "I do have enough to start you with a small wardrobe appropriate for your station."

Can't blame me for trying. "I guess I should be thankful I won't go naked."

A blush flew up Sparrow's neck to redden her cheeks and ears. "I'd never—you wouldn't—oh, you're funning," she finished, catching the grin on Corrie's face. They shared a laugh—some things didn't change from century to century.

Corrie sobered as she thought of the next six months. What could she do to support herself? Did they have chefs in this time? Without a reference, how would she find a job? Who would hire a woman who walked in off the street and asked for a top position in a restaurant?

And what do they eat nowadays? Nouvelle cuisine is years away.

"You look worried, my dear."

With a start, Corrie realized the woman had been studying her. She shrugged. "Just wondering how I'm going to make a living."

"Well, the season is slow at present, but I think enough of the staff will want time off for the holiday to make an opening for a new person." Sparrow eyed her. "That is, unless you have some religious convictions that would preclude your working on Christmas."

"You mean work here at the Chesterfield?" Excitement scurried through Corrie. As a derelict in her time, the place had been awesome; what a palace it must be in this one.

"Of course."

"Well, working Christmas has never been a problem." Making it through Christmas sane had been. But the distraction of the Chesterfield, not to mention going back in time to 1886, would probably make this an easy holiday to survive.

"Excellent. Now, let's get you dressed and I'll introduce you around." Sparrow tilted her head to one side. "We're fortunate your hair is beautifully full and long. A rich color, as well. Styling it shouldn't present a problem."

Unaccustomed to compliments, Corrie ran her hand over her waist-length braid. Her ego didn't rely on her looks, but her long dark-brown hair was a point of pride nonetheless. Meekly, she allowed Sparrow to brush it out, braid it again, and twist it into a chignon at the back of her head. The natural curl kept the style from being too severe, and tendrils curled at her nape and around her face, softening the effect still more.

Sparrow rubbed her hands together, then picked up the frilly tank top from the bed. "Here, put on this chemise."

Corrie turned her back, shucked off the robe, and dropped the thin cotton over her head. It hung to mid-thigh, and she felt decently enough covered to face Sparrow without embarrassment.

"Now the drawers, then the petticoat."

The chill of the room made the baggy underwear welcome, and Corrie wondered what came next. She turned. Sparrow held an instrument of torture—about a foot and a half of steel rods encased in cloth with an obvious cinch of the waist. Corrie had seen *Gone with the Wind* and *Titanic;* she knew what came next.

And wanted no part of it.

She backed away. "Oh, no, you don't. I'm not squeezing into that thing."

"But you must wear this in order to wear the clothes." Sparrow glanced down at the corset. "You are accustomed to much freer movement. But in this time, you will not be called upon to be so active."

"No."

Sparrow held out the corset. Corrie retreated. Sparrow followed. Corrie cringed.

"No," she repeated.

She was still muttering refusals under her breath five minutes later as she hugged the bathroom doorframe and Sparrow tugged at the corset strings. When the woman placed one foot on the doorframe and yanked again, Corrie protested louder. "Is that really necessary? I can't breathe as it is."

"If you can talk, you can breathe," Sparrow gasped out.

"I'm talking, all right. Just two octaves higher."

"Only one that I notice." Sparrow laughed. "There. Finished."

Corrie caught a glimpse of herself in the bathroom mirror. Cleavage spilled out of the top of the torture apparatus, and her waist curved sharply inward, accentuating her bust and hips. It wasn't comfortable, but she couldn't deny it made her boyish figure very . . . womanly.

Sparrow approached from behind and tied a cord around Corrie's waist. Immediately, a rear weight dragged Corrie backwards.

"What is that?" She skewed around, trying to see behind her. It looked like the woman had strapped a birdcage to Corrie's butt.

"A steel-cage bustle support. The newest design. It will make a nice line for your skirt." Sparrow turned in a circle to display her own rear contraption, with yards of fabric billowing behind. "Yours is narrower than mine, and your skirt is narrower also."

"Thanks . . . I think." She took a few steps and tried to twirl as Sparrow had just done. Halfway through, the bustle took off on a tangent with a mind of its own.

And intent on escape.

Sparrow rescued her from the corner where the bustle had thrown her and tied the thing down more tightly. "Try that. Carefully, my dear."

Corrie maneuvered around the room. If she thought of the bustle as a backpack—just lower down—she could manage it. As soon as she thought of it any other way or tried to forget it entirely, she became hostage to the damned thing and ended up wherever it carried her.

After the corset and bustle, the high-collared, starched blouse and heavy, navy woolen skirt were a breeze. The skirt's train was something else again. If the bustle was heavy, the skirt was a drag.

Literally.

Who needs to dust the floors? Just walk around and swish your hips, and tada! Clean floors. With practice, Corrie was at last able to navigate dressed in the idiotic outfit. As long as she didn't turn. Then she and that dreaded train clashed.

Again and again, she strode around the room. Again and again, she turned . . . and fought the train.

The train won.

As Corrie landed in the potted palm in the corner for the umpteenth time, Sparrow's patience snapped. Lips thin and tone brisk, she said, "You will simply have to become accustomed 'on your feet,' as it were." Grasping Corrie by the arm, she steered her toward the door.

Corrie froze a few feet from it. She stared at the wood and imagined what lay beyond: 1886. The past.

Her future.

Her heart climbed into her throat, making breathing questionable. For as long as she stayed in this cozy room, she could shut out this twisted reality. Once she stepped into the rest of the hotel, she would have to accept that she would spend the next six months here. In the past. The shakes started at

her feet and traveled at warp speed up her body until
they threatened to undo the bun at the back of her
head.

"Miss Webb?" Sparrow's voice softened, and she
gave Corrie a hug. "Corrinne, are you all right?"

From one day to the next, few people touched
Corrie, much less hugged her. Paul LaDue was about
the only one, and even his hugs were rare. Sparrow's
tender concern threatened to breach Corrie's mental walls—walls she'd spent years constructing. Rein-
forcing. Making impenetrable.

Walls that kept her safe.

"Corrinne?"

Corrie dragged in a ragged breath and eased out
of Sparrow's hold. Her hands trembled as she wiped
her eyes. "The lamp smoke is irritating, y'know?"

Perceptive brown eyes studied her. Corrie lifted
her chin, daring the woman to challenge her.

Sparrow glanced at the gaslights, which showed
not a trace of soot, studied Corrie for another minute, then gave a little nod. "Quite." She raised one
hand as if to cup Corrie's cheek, but stopped as Corrie flinched. Changing the gesture to flicking lint off
Corrie's shoulder, she asked, "Shall we go?"

One breath made it into Corrie's lungs, then another. The shaking eased. The breach in her protective walls repaired itself. Almost. That *almost* made
her plaster a smile on her face and resolve to do the
best she could to make Sparrow proud of her. After
all, it would only be for six months.

Corrie squared her shoulders and waved a hand
toward the door. "After you."

"You're a strong young woman, Corrinne Webb,"
Sparrow said with a solid pat on Corrie's shoulder.
Head high, back straight, and skirts flowing grace-

fully behind her, Sparrow exited her room and sailed down the hallway.

Corrie raised her chin, shifted her corset with both hands, and sailed after her, shutting the door with a brisk click.

Two steps brought her to an abrupt halt.

Her train—blast the thing—was caught in the door. With a furtive glance at Sparrow's receding figure, she scuttled backwards and released the yards of fabric, then ran to catch up. Shops flew by on the left while bright sunshine filled an inner courtyard on her right.

The hallway opened onto a massive lobby and Corrie, her jaw dropping in awe, skidded to a halt. Marble floors covered with brilliant-toned Oriental rugs stretched for hundreds of feet, and thick white columns rose two stories to a coved ceiling with dozens of chandeliers. Victorian-garbed men and women strolled and chatted among ornate wicker chairs, attended by an army of maids and other uniformed hotel employees. Corrie wouldn't have been surprised to see the cast of *My Fair Lady* wander through.

Sparrow turned and snapped her fingers. In a low but penetrating tone, she said, "Don't dawdle, Miss Webb. The manager will want to approve your employment."

A job interview. That brought Corrie back to earth with a jolt. Her last real job interview had been with Paul LaDue—a soft touch, for sure. What would the Chesterfield's manager think of a chef with no references? Her stomach threatened to rise again, but Sparrow gave it no chance. All Corrie's breath was needed to keep up with the rapid tap-tap-tap of Sparrow's shoes across the lobby. Two bellhops—an older one with a quick grin, a younger one with curious eyes—snapped to attention as Sparrow strode past the front desk to a carved door labeled MANAGER.

Her knock was answered by a curt, "Enter."

When Corrie lagged behind, Sparrow grasped her hand and muttered under her breath, "Courage, my dear." Opening the door, Sparrow raised her voice, "Good day, Major. As I informed you earlier, I have an addition to the dining room staff."

A man in his early fifties with salt-and-pepper hair was bent over an old-fashioned ledger book. With meticulous strokes he made an entry, then replaced his pen in the elephant-shaped holder to his right. Only then did he look up.

Corrie stifled a snicker. Groucho Marx would've envied the man's very black, very stiff mustache. Before rising, he stroked it. Twice. His dark blue long-tailed suit and starched white collar—or rather, the way he wore them—gave the impression of a military uniform rather than of a hotel manager's clothes. No wonder Sparrow called him Major.

"Major Payne, may I introduce Miss Corrinne Webb?" Sparrow urged Corrie forward with one hand, at the same time lifting the top of Corrie's corset through the back of the dress so that she had to stand at attention or have parts of her anatomy severely squeezed.

The Major eyed Corrie with ill-disguised dubiousness. His gaze traveled over her hair—she repressed the urge to check her chignon—then down her entire body, inch by everlasting inch. All without the least sign that he saw the woman under the clothes.

Not that that was a bad thing—she would've decked him if he'd made one risqué comment or even raised one of those carefully trimmed eyebrows.

Which he didn't. Until he ended his perusal by staring at her feet.

After several minutes, he raised both eyebrows and lifted his gaze first to Corrie, then to Sparrow. "What are"—he sniffed and his mustache quivered—"those?"

Corrie looked down at her feet and raised her skirt. Rocking back on her heels, she surveyed her boots. They had cost more than two hundred dollars and fit like a dream. Even trudging around in all that snow on the way here, she hadn't had cause to complain about her feet hurting.

"I asked, what are those *things* on your feet?"

"Ecco hiking boots," she said with pride. "From France."

"I don't care where they're from. They are not acceptable at the Chesterfield." Major Payne scowled at Sparrow. "I expect anyone you present for employment to be properly turned out. These 'hiking' boots, as Miss Webb calls them, are not part of our waitress uniform."

"Who said anything about being a waitress?" Corrie interjected.

Overriding Corrie in volume, Sparrow said, "An oversight, Major. Easily rectified."

Forget the friggin' boots. "Who said anything about being a waitress?"

"I'll fit her from the uniform storeroom before I take her to the dining room." Sparrow raised the back of the corset another inch to keep Corrie quiet. "I plan on training her myself."

"Very good." Major Payne jerked a bow at Sparrow and resumed his seat. "I rely upon you to adjust the waitress schedules accordingly."

Indignation rose like bile in Corrie's throat. "You expect a *chef* to wait tables?"

Beside her, Sparrow fidgeted and sputtered.

Major Payne—and a major pain he was, too—twitched his mustache. "A chef?" His gaze flicked toward her shoes again before turning on Sparrow. "You mentioned nothing about a chef . . . a *female* chef."

Sparrow's grip tightened on that damned corset and Corrie stifled a gasp of discomfort.

The woman cleared her throat. "Miss Webb is from Texas, Major. It's true she was a cook there. A good one, I understand. If they choose to allow a woman to call herself a chef, surely we can understand their . . . desperation."

"Desperation?" *I'll 'desperation' her.*

"We have enough cooks, Miss Webb, and an excellent chef in Vladimir Sashenka, from the court of Russia." He picked up his pen and tapped the end on his blotter. "If you desire a position at the Chesterfield, you will wait tables."

"But—"

Sparrow jerked her back. "Waiting tables it is."

"No—"

Major Payne tapped the blotter again. "Which is it? Waitress here? Or work somewhere else? You're wasting my time."

Corrie's options slapped her in the face. In 1886 she had no work record, no references. She hadn't the slightest idea what jobs were available down in the town of Hope Springs. And if women couldn't be chefs, what else couldn't they do? No telling what she'd be reduced to.

A vague recollection of a tour she'd taken of a historic district floated to the surface. The only occupations she knew were open to women at that time had been as teachers, shop clerks, or prostitutes. Her heart began to pound. She didn't have any qualifications to teach, and she didn't know the shops *or* their merchandise. That left . . .

Oh, shit. Waiting tables suddenly sounded good.

"Well?" The Major's tone had a certain finality to it.

Corrie tugged at her high collar with one sweaty hand. "Well, if you promise to consider me for the next chef's—I mean cook's—opening . . ."

"Corrinne, please," Sparrow whispered as Major Payne scowled again.

"Oh, all right. I'll wait tables." Under her breath, Corrie muttered, "For now."

The man nodded. "Luncheon is already being served. I suggest you go to the dining room directly."

Pulling Corrie with her, Sparrow headed for the door. "Thank you, Major. I'm certain she will justify your faith in her."

"On the contrary, it is your faith in her that I value, Miss Sparrow." Major Payne harrumphed and turned his attention to the ledger book.

The door was almost closed behind Corrie and Sparrow when he added, "And don't forget the shoes."

Jess Garrett doffed his freshly brushed bowler hat to the ladies waiting for their carriage at the Chesterfield Hotel's colonnaded entrance. The two oldest stared down their noses at him and shepherded the three young ladies to the side. Resplendent as his new Harris tweed sack suit and starched collar were, he nevertheless looked what he was—a policeman.

And a policeman—even the chief of the Hope Springs Police—ranked well beneath these particular flowers of society.

Not all were so choosy. He usually had his pick of the debutantes.

Ignoring the cut, Jess shot a wink at the brunette with her hat ribbons tied rakishly under one ear. She giggled and blushed but trailed after the rest with only a brief backward glance when the doorman escorted them out.

"Flyin' too high for the likes o' you," a rolling Irish voice observed from behind a wall of potted palms. "Ye'll nivver catch one o' that, boyo."

"Ah, but would I *want* to catch that, is the question, Jack." Jess laughed and tucked his hat under his arm and strolled into the high-ceilinged Great Hall of Hope Springs's premier hotel. He flicked a final glance at the bustled posterior of the brunette and shook his head. "When I set out to catch a lady for my own, it'll take more than a fashionable gown and a Parisian hat to win my heart."

"Yer heart, is it?" the gnarled, balding little Irishman surveyed the lobby, then spat into one of the palms. "I were thinkin' a bit lower."

"Now, Jack, you wound me." Jess mockingly placed his bowler over his heart, then dropped it briefly to the front of his trousers before restoring it to its proper place under his arm.

"G'wan, ye daft copper," Jack said, fighting a grin and turning back to the mound of luggage he was supervising. "Have yer bit of fantasy in the high-and-mighty dining hall. When all's said, ye'll still be dirt 'neath some of them's feet."

"But well-groomed dirt." Jess brushed an imaginary

spot from his lapel, then smiled at his old friend. "When all's said."

His saunter through the lobby was met by friendly nods from the staff. He was a regular visitor, although he'd never been an overnight guest. Several times a week, he indulged his taste for fine food by dining at the Chesterfield. Even a bachelor police chief had to eat. If he preferred to fill his belly with a better grade of food than he could produce at home, who was to say no?

A frosty shiver ran down his back. Mama. *She'd* say no in her usual direct way. Three years had passed since he'd last seen her or the rest of the Garrett clan except one, but he could hear Mama clearly in his mind: "Any child of mine who cannot cook a meal, change a baby, or milk a cow should just live in the stable, for they're no better than animals if they cannot perform these basic tasks."

Well, he could do all those things; she'd made certain of that. But as a man on his own, he chose to hire others to do them for him.

Putting his outspoken mother from his mind, Jess skirted the open atrium in the center of the main building and made his way past the stockbroker's office and a row of shops. The sun might be bright this December morning, but he knew from experience that the atrium walls would retain the cold for hours yet. And the dining hall, cavernous though it was, would be warm and inviting. He quickened his pace, eager for Chef Sashenka's cuisine. A breakfast of burned coffee and charred toast had left him peckish.

The luncheon crowd was sparse this time of year, and he had no trouble obtaining a table by the bank of windows that offered a panoramic view of the

Allegheny Mountains rising from the rear of the hotel. Only a month ago, the forest had blazed with autumnal color; now barren trees stood sentinel over Cottage Row and the railroad station. Nothing outside held his interest, so Jess studied the dining room inhabitants.

He recognized the older Mrs. Vanderbilt, a couple of relations of the banker Mellons, and an assortment of minor European aristocracy whom he'd met previously. With Christmas a couple of days away, he assumed more family would be joining these to celebrate here rather than at their homes. With any luck, his own family wouldn't hear of this trend and descend upon him for a holiday visit. Jess suppressed an instinctive shudder. He loved his family, but their ways and his had diverged years ago.

By the time he finished his cold slaw with fried oysters and was savoring lemon custard and coffee, Jess had exhausted his curiosity about the diners and moved on to the staff.

Jack's daughter, Bridget, waited on his table, as usual. Jess wouldn't put it past the old man to scheme to link the two of them. *He can scheme all he wants, but I won't be part of them. The girl I marry will be . . .*

What? What exactly did Jess Garrett want in a wife?

He scanned the ladies in the room—society and staff both. None attracted him. Not for a permanent liaison. They were all pale of cheek and pallid of personality. Afraid of their own shadows. Of course, the current fashion for constricted, corseted waists, bobbing bustles, and tripping trains deterred them from adventure.

Adventure—an intriguing thought. *Maybe that's*

what I want—an adventurous girl. One who won't faint at the hint of hazards.

A particularly pretty waitress passed by, her skirts whispering, her feet tapping a steady rhythm on the oak floor. Jess followed her with his gaze. Was she adventurous? A starched white blouse tucked tightly into a navy skirt rustled faintly as she poured tea for the ladies at the next table. She blushed and almost overturned the cups, obviously aware of his scrutiny.

No adventuress there.

The rest of the staff swept through the room with the same practiced ease . . . and the same consciousness of their blasted femininity. Jess finished his custard and leaned back. Maybe he was being unreasonable. Maybe he *should* want a quiet, well-behaved, proper girl.

A movement at the door to the kitchen caught his eye. *Now there's proper and well-behaved,* he thought as Miss Sparrow entered the dining hall. But the young woman, clad in navy with starched white cuffs and collar, stirred not a string of his heart nor piqued his interest in any way but curiosity. While she had elicited his history during their occasional discussions, hers remained unknown.

As Miss Sparrow continued across the room, an object of definite curiosity followed her. A new waitress. Unusual to bring one on staff during the slow winter season. Doubly unusual to hire one so patently awkward. She jerked and lurched along, treading on both her own gown and that of Miss Sparrow, and twisted her neck to and fro like a boy in his first starched collar.

A duck had more grace.

The small procession ended at his table and he

rose—for Miss Sparrow. One didn't rise for a mere waitress, after all.

"Mr. Garrett," she said and extended her hand.

"Miss Sparrow." He gave her hand a brief shake, then raised an eyebrow at the new girl. In spite of his earlier assessment of her as a duck, he examined her with interest. It surprised him to see she was doing the same to him.

"Mr. Garrett, may I present our newest waitress, Miss Corrinne Webb?" Miss Sparrow, looking a tad harried, urged the girl forward. "Miss Webb, Mr. Garrett, our police chief."

Before he could react, Miss Webb grabbed his hand in a surprisingly strong grip and shook it with some force. Direct brown eyes set in a freckled face scanned him. "Just call me Corrie, Chief. But I won't be waiting tables long. I'm a chef."

"A chef . . ." The seriousness with which she said it prevented Jess from laughing. A girl . . . a chef? Impossible.

As if she could read his mind, Corrinne Webb bristled. Her chin lifted and her mouth firmed. "A chef," she repeated in a tone that brooked no rebuttal.

"But a girl—"

"I haven't been a 'girl' for years, buster." She shoved one tanned finger into his shirtfront. "And I'll have you know that back in Dallas I was the best dam—"

Miss Sparrow stepped in. "Corrinne is new to the area, Mr. Garrett." For once, she appeared flustered, her gaze darting between Jess and Corrinne. "She hasn't made Chef Sasha's acquaintance as yet."

"That explains it." It didn't, but Jess rarely argued. He turned a condescending glance on the impertinent chit. "You may *cook* after a fashion—most women do—but Sasha creates masterpieces."

"Like that artery-clogging mess that just went by?" Miss Webb gave an unladylike snort and placed both fists on her hips. "Bistro Terre's cuisine—"

Miss Sparrow shook the girl's arm, interrupting what looked to be a tirade. "That will do, Corrinne. I'll show you how to clear Mr. Garrett's table properly, and we'll let the good man be on his way."

"But I was simply telling him—"

"Enough, I said." Miss Sparrow nodded to Jess as she loaded her subordinate's arms with dirty dishes, then escorted her to the kitchen.

Running a hand through his hair, Jess exhaled sharply. To think he'd wished for an adventuress, a young lady who didn't blush or stammer when he spoke to her. In Corrinne Webb he'd found just such a girl.

Prim, proper, blushing, and shy suddenly sounded grand.

THREE

The first day of the last six months of Corrie's life in 1886 started early. The idiot ringing a handbell in the hallway woke everyone before the roosters crowed.

Shoot, the roosters haven't gone to bed yet.

With a groan, Corrie burrowed her head farther under the covers and ordered, "Shut up that racket."

"Up ye get now," a cheery voice with a hint of Irish said. "Don't wish to be late for the Major's muster."

Corrie flipped onto her back and squinted against the light from the lamp between her and Bridget O'Riley's beds. Then her gaze moved to the window. "It's still dark." She pulled her pillow over her face. "Go 'way."

"Miss Sparrow said ye'd likely be unaccustomed to our hours." Bridget whisked Corrie's blanket to the foot of the bed. "Up now, lass. Muster's in half an hour."

Lifting the pillow, Corrie asked, "What in the name of Pete is muster? And why can't it wait until a reasonable hour?" She had an almost overwhelming desire to yell "humbug."

"To be sure, ye wouldn't know the Major's ways, now would ye?" As Bridget brushed out her hair, she explained. "Muster is where Major Payne inspects all of us—the hotel morning staff, that would be. Afternoon staff sometimes are mustered, sometimes not. At such a fine resort as this, guests expect us to be well turned out."

"You mean I have to wear that . . . corset again?" Corrie restrained herself, having been chastised about her use of curse words last night. Repeatedly. "And the bustle?"

"Oh, not just that, although I shiver to think what the Major would do to a female staff member who did not wear them."

Give me a few days, sister, and you'll have a chance to find out. Corrie was certain that once she earned a spot as a chef in the kitchen staff she'd be back in her comfortable pants and chef's coat.

Then she would burn that damned corset and bustle. Under a chef's coat, who would know?

A gasp from Bridget dragged Corrie to an upright position. Seeing the woman bent over in the corner, Corrie crawled to the end of the bed. "What's wrong, Bidgie?" she asked, using the nickname she'd learned the girl went by.

"Your uniform. It's nothing but wrinkles from laying all night on the floor." Bridget held the navy skirt and white blouse up for Corrie's inspection. "Ye'll never iron it in time for muster."

From the woman's shocked expression, Corrie figured this muster was a big deal. She scrambled out of bed and took the offensive articles from her roommate's hands. "Don't worry. I'll just wear another one and toss these in the washer and dryer."

"Washer? Dryer?" Bridget gave her a blank stare. Too late, Corrie remembered 1886's technological handicap and Sparrow's warnings to keep her own origin secret. "The washerwoman?" she suggested with her fingers crossed that such a person existed at the Chesterfield.

"She's fearfully dear. Most of us prefer to save our money by doing our own laundry. Major Payne allows us to use the resort's laundry." Bridget splashed her face with water from a pitcher on an antique—no, new—washstand. "Very kind, he is."

"I don't call rousting us out of bed in the middle of the night kind," Corrie grumbled as she started to follow suit. However, when her hands touched the water, she swore.

"Whatever are ye grinching at now?" Bridget's tone made it clear that she was rapidly losing patience.

"This water's freezing."

"Ye're exaggerating. There's nary a crystal of ice on it," Bridget said in a reasonable tone.

Corrie was beyond being reasonable. First, she'd been thrown back to this godforsaken century; second, she'd been forced to take a job as a waitress; and third, she'd been awakened at an ungodly cold hour in a room with no bathroom. She needed to pee in the worst way. Then she wanted hot water, lots of it, preferably in a big, steamy shower.

A cold basin in a chilly room—shared, no less—just didn't cut it.

Fortunately, as a child she'd been forced by circumstances to get along with others, and now that training came to the fore. Corrie dried her hands on a skimpy linen towel and released a deep sigh. Alienating her roommate would do her no good. No good at all.

Instead of more complaining, she forced a pleasant tone to ask, "Where's the closest hot water?"

Bridget raised her head from buttoning her boots

to smile, obviously glad that Corrie was making an attempt at reasonableness. "End of the hall, but the line's always fierce long. Besides, my mother always preached the benefits of cold water." Her smile faded. "Had the skin of a lass when she died last winter of the influenza. Just after Christmas it was."

The pang of compassion that shot through Corrie stole her breath. This young woman with the irrepressible smile and seemingly carefree disposition had experienced the same thing Corrie had at a younger age—the loss of her mother. Of course, Bridget's mother had died of the flu while hers had—she shied away from the memory, throwing up her emotional walls again. But the loss would cut just as deeply at Bridget's twenty as it had at Corrie's eight.

Even at her current age of twenty-six there were no answers for the inevitable question, "Why?"

Never good at dealing with emotions, Corrie shoved her memories away and settled for patting Bridget on the back. She would have left it at that, but Bridget turned and buried her face against Corrie's side and burst into tears.

"I miss her so much, Corrie. At Christmas and all, I miss her more than ever. It's as if there's a gaping hole in my heart."

Corrie remembered that hole. She'd filled hers with walls and work. And avoiding holidays. She didn't even have a heart to hurt anymore.

But if that was true, why were her eyes tearing up? And why had she wrapped her arms around Bridget? Why was she rocking the younger woman like a baby, making soothing sounds?

Corrie raised her eyes to the ceiling and blinked

rapidly. She wouldn't let this happen. She wouldn't let Bridget penetrate her defenses.

Once you care for one person, others wiggle their way in. Then you start caring, they leave, and you're left with a hole in your heart.

Well, Corrinne Webb already had one hole in her heart. She wasn't going to have another. She stopped patting Bridget's back and tried to extricate herself. The girl only clung tighter. *Aw, hell.* Traveling back in time apparently had turned her emotions to mush.

"Shhh, Bidgie, shhh. You'll be all right. You'll see her again. In heaven." Corrie wasn't too sure of her theology, but she remembered people telling *her* that. She tightened her grip, then eased back to wipe Bridget's eyes with the end of the sheet. "And she's not sick up in heaven."

Bridget sniffed and swiped at her eyes with the heels of her hands. "Oh, Corrie, I'm so sorry to be blithering at ye. But with Christmas . . ."

"You don't have to tell me about Christmas and . . . stuff." Corrie wasn't ready to share her own loss. Sharing wouldn't help Bridget, and it certainly wouldn't help Corrie.

"Still and all, I thank you." Bridget rose and splashed water on her face again.

"It's okay. Really." And somehow it *was* okay.

After all the tears, Corrie couldn't ignore her body's needs any longer, and she scurried down the corridor, hoping for a short line at the ladies' room. Either Bridget was wrong about long lines or Corrie was running late. Returning to her room, she realized *how* late as women in various uniforms streamed past her. Several urged her to hurry.

In spite of her dislike of the waitressing job, Corrie

did hurry. It was better than nothing, since nothing could lead to a life of prostitution here. With Bridget's help, she donned the dreaded uniform again and sped down the stairs into the dining room.

Major Payne gave them the evil eye as they scooted into line with the other waitresses. Pulling out his pocket watch, he pointedly checked the time. "Miss O'Riley and Miss Webb, muster is at seven, not seven twelve."

Beside him, Sparrow closed her eyes and sighed. She said something to him and he grunted an acknowledgment.

Fifteen minutes later, Corrinne knew she was in big trouble. The Major had sent half a dozen employees back to their quarters to rectify minor infractions of the dress code. Mostly they needed to polish their shoes.

What is it with this guy and shoes? Does he have a fetish or something?

Not everyone had shoe problems. One had a stain on his collar and was sent to change; another hadn't shined his buttons sufficiently. What would Major Pain have made of her chef's coat at the end of the day? Probably would've had a coronary.

At last, he approached her end of the line. She tugged at her blouse to pull more wrinkles out, but that helped very little. Corrie needed a lot more than a little.

The Major stopped at Bridget, started to say something, then seemed to take in her tearstained face. A flush rose up from his collar and he smoothed a hand nervously down his coat front. "I believe your father has the day off, Miss O'Riley." Bridget nodded, and he continued. "Perhaps you would like to visit with him this morning? I'm certain the rest of the staff can handle breakfast without you. However, be prompt for the luncheon shift."

Corrie stared at him. *The Major has a heart? Who woulda thunk it?*

Dipping a quick curtsy, Bridget thanked him, then squeezed Corrie's hand. Corrie's gaze followed her out the door, then returned abruptly to the Major, at attention in front of her. She resisted the urge to fidget and stared straight into his eyes. She had no illusions that he would take it easy on her. She gritted her teeth and stared directly ahead.

Give it your best shot.

He scanned her up and down, then lifted one of those eyebrows in evident disdain. With one finger he indicated her entire costume. "Dare I ask, Miss Webb, did you sleep in this?"

"No. Sir." Growing up in Texas had taught her one thing if nothing else: "sir" and "ma'am" could sometimes ease one out of trouble. She grinned and lifted the hem of her skirt. "I changed shoes though. Shined and everything."

"So I noted." He sighed and waved Sparrow forward.

Her expression was distressed as she took in the totality of Corrie's outfit. "Oh, my. Miss Webb, whatever have you done to your uniform?"

Before Corrie could answer, Major Payne held up a hand for silence. He fidgeted with his mustache a second, then said with military sharpness, "She is your protégée Miss Sparrow. I relied on your recommendation in hiring her." He wiggled his fingers in Corrie's direction. "I rely on you to rectify the situation before I lay eyes on her again."

Sparrow paled and quickly ushered Corrie out of the dining room and into the cozy room where Corrie had landed yesterday. Had it been less than twenty-four hours since all this had started?

Time flies when you're having fun. Corrie gave a rueful snort of laughter—nothing, absolutely nothing, had been fun about this whole adventure.

"I do not understand what you have to be mirthful about," Sparrow said. "Your appearance is disgraceful. No self-respecting Chesterfield employee would think of going on duty in this state."

Corrie smoothed her damp palms over her skirt, wrinkling it more. Continuing to deplore Corrie's appearance in minute—and very vocal—detail, Sparrow roamed the room for several minutes.

It had been years since Corrie had worried about disappointing anyone. If you didn't care about anyone, you couldn't be held responsible for their feelings. Her desire for Sparrow's approval rocked her. She didn't care about the woman, did she?

When Sparrow ran down—or maybe she'd stopped for breath—Corrie cleared her throat.

"You wish to offer an excuse?" Sparrow asked.

"Well, not really an excuse," Corrie said, then added, "but maybe an explanation."

"Go on. I'm listening."

"Well, it's like this." Corrie took a big breath, then rushed to explain how rotten a morning it had been, from being awakened too early to needing to console Bridget. She finished with a hopeful glance at Sparrow. "I'm really sorry, and if you'll show me what to do, I'll be spit-and-polish proper every day. I won't disappoint you again."

Sparrow sat in her chair by the embers in her fireplace and rubbed her forehead. "You haven't disappointed me, Corrinne."

"Oh, yeah?" Corrie asked as she plopped into the chair across from her. "Sure looked like it to me."

"Actually, I'm disappointed in myself." Sparrow cradled her cheek in her hand and gazed directly into Corrie's eyes. "You see, I'm not very good at helping you people from the future adjust to this time. I forget you have so much to learn, that so much is different between your time and mine. I'm quite a failure, really."

"Don't be so hard on yourself," Corrie said, squeezing Sparrow's hand reassuringly. "You'll teach me how to spruce myself up to suit the Major, and I'll sail through these next six months."

Sparrow returned the squeeze. "You are most kind, my dear."

Corrie glanced down at their joined hands. She couldn't remember the last time she'd reassured one person with physical contact; now she'd done so twice in one day.

Before breakfast, to boot.

Jess studied the remains of his luncheon and wished he had ridden up to the Chesterfield instead. Dining there two days in a row would have been self-indulgent, and he did plan to dine there tomorrow in celebration of Christmas Day. However, the pickings for meals were slim in Hope Springs. Only Mrs. Warshoski routinely delivered good, solid meals.

Too solid, he thought, and patted his stomach. He wouldn't be able to mount his horse if he ate her potato dumplings every day.

Not to mention mounting something much more desirable.

That thought brought to mind the Chesterfield's

new waitress, Corrinne Webb. Of course, if he ever
dared pluck one of Miss Sparrow's chicks, he knew
she would take him to task in a manner all too remi-
niscent of his mother. But this particular chick, this
little brown duck, tempted him more than any of
the others before her. Odd, since his taste ran more
to the buxom and elegant, and Corrie, as she insisted
on being called, was neither.

Which made his contemplation of her doelike
brown eyes and her lustrous hair, with its ginger-col-
ored highlights, more of a puzzle.

Shaking off this peculiar train of thought, he paid
his bill and donned his overcoat and hat. Winter had
settled in over the mountains, bringing a damp cold
that bit through even his good wool coat. He looked
to the west. If those gray clouds cresting the Alleghe-
nies didn't bode snow, he'd eat his fine new bowler.
A gust of wind reminded him to snug said item
tighter on his head.

Pedestrians jostled past him on the sidewalk, most
greeting him by name and wishing him a happy
Christmas. He returned the holiday wishes with alac-
rity. This was his town, and he took great satisfaction
in that fact. The town leaders might have originally
offered him the job of police chief because of his
family's reputation, but they had kept him on due
to his own merit. Under his supervision, Hope
Springs had become known as a safe and honest
town. And he had become a well-respected local figure despite the fact that—or maybe because—he
never drew his gun.

Jess tipped his hat to the town doctor's wife as he
caught up with her. "Happy Christmas, Mrs. Jones."

"And a happy Christmas to you, Mr. Garrett." The
woman, laden with packages, gave him a broad grin

and continued her steady stride. "Will we see you tonight at church, or will you be patrolling our fair city?"

He smiled and relieved her of the heaviest parcels, for which she nodded her thanks. "Do you take me for a heathen, to miss Christmas Eve service? I see little need to keep an eye on Hope Springs on such a night as this. Any man of sense will be inside, locked tight against this frigid breeze."

"Ah, but are criminals men of sense?" she asked and came to a halt.

With the free fingers of one hand, he scratched his chin and weighed her question. Her intelligent eyes twinkled as she realized she had stumped him. Temporarily. He snapped his fingers as an answer came to him. "Criminals may not be men of sense, dear lady, but even the meanest of animals have enough sense to seek shelter from the cold and wind."

Her full-throated laugh joined his own. "Well said, Mr. Garrett. How lucky for you to realize that. Otherwise, you might have had to patrol tonight, cold or no."

He agreed with her assessment and they spent a few minutes catching up on the Jones brood. While she reported on her youngest son's run-in with a goat, he studied her slender but sturdy figure in its serviceable brown wool coat with a modest bustle, and was reminded of Corrie Webb. Except for coloring and size, they looked little alike. But something about Mrs. Jones's direct, no-nonsense speech and straight bearing called to mind the young waitress.

A waitress he was thinking entirely too much about.

He gave himself an internal shake and interrupted

Mrs. Jones, suggesting she complete her story on their way to her home.

"Indeed, I will not take you so far out of your way, sir," she said and pointed to the door where they had stopped.

With a jolt, he realized it was his own office. She insisted on taking her packages back and strode away. Jess wondered if she had ever been adventurous.

Somehow, he thought she might.

The train to Hope Springs from the Chesterfield was too cold and too crowded for Corrie's taste, but Sparrow had made it clear that everyone was expected to attend Christmas services—evening or day, as long as one was attended. Special trains for the occasion were even scheduled to handle the crowd of guests and employees to shuttle between the hotel and town.

No one but Corrie seemed to mind the wind that whistled around the edges of the windows and found its way down her neck and up her skirt. The car she rode on was occupied entirely by resort staff, all excited at the prospect of an extra evening off. They sang unfamiliar songs, increasing her sense of isolation. Corrie hadn't made any friends other than Bridget, who would take the later train as she attended the Catholic church.

A couple of the staff members made overtures, but they were easily rebuffed. So, surrounded by her fellow workers, she was alone as she disembarked in Hope Springs.

The town was achingly familiar, yet unfamiliar at the same time. Some of the storefronts were the

same, and the park in the center of the town square
was there as well, but much of the town was different.
Over the next few weeks, she planned on discovering
more about *this* Hope Springs. She had an uncomfortable feeling the Major wasn't pleased with her
performance as a waitress, so she'd better scope out
other employment options.

Through the blowing snow, she could make out
the fact that all the shops were closed. That meant
no shelter was available except the church. Townspeople joined the procession, drawing the resort per-
sonnel into their conversations with much laughter
and friendly greetings. Slowly, she followed the
crowd to a large white building with a tall steeple
reaching for the lowering clouds. Icy fingers closed
around her heart.

As she reached the door, Corrie tried to hang
back, planning to remain in the anteroom, but was
swept by the crush into the sanctuary. At the first
chance, she swam out of the main flow and sought
refuge behind a pillar. She looked around. Her foster
mothers had taken her to church, but the focus of
the teaching had been so much on families that Corrie hadn't wanted to keep up the habit once she'd
left their domain. She hadn't seen the interior of a
church for years.

In fact, she hadn't been in an old-fashioned one
with a steeple like this— She shoved the memory
behind her mental wall and sought distraction amid
the crowd.

Her gaze landed on a large family a couple of pews
in front of her. Try as she might, she couldn't look
away. Norman Rockwell had painted just such families—the loving parents, smiling and laughing as
they corralled their children into a pew where they

all knelt, heads bowed and hands clasped together in prayer.

Corrie had no memory of her mother in a church. No memory of her praying. No memory of her laughing. No memory of much at all.

Tears threatened to spill over and she blinked them away. She hugged up against the pillar and willed herself into a state of numbness. Surely the service wouldn't last longer than an hour. She could handle anything for an hour.

But time travel, in addition to being in a church, must have weakened her defenses, because her emotional walls crumpled.

The choir filed into the sanctuary and hymns rose to the rafters while Corrie stared unseeingly at the candles on the altar and her mind tumbled into a maelstrom of memories.

Bitter, painful, searing memories of abandonment and loss. Memories that paralyzed her as emotions replayed themselves over and over in her mind.

Memories that overwhelmed her.

FOUR

From his place at the back of the transept, Jess scanned the crowd for friends. Something in the far back corner drew his attention—the hotel's new waitress clung to one of the tall columns as if to a lifeline. He had never seen anyone more alone. Hemmed in on all sides, she radiated a palpable isolation.

The cold had left a hectic color in her cheeks, but her lips, which had been rosy when she'd waited on him at the hotel, were so pale as to be almost invisible. Her eyes wrenched at his heart. They were the eyes of a lost soul—a soul without hope.

What in heaven's name had stricken all life from that vibrant young woman?

As the Christmas litany progressed, Jess eased his way through the crowd toward her. She never glanced his way. Never dropped her gaze at all, but stared fixedly at the altar, as if that kept her upright. Close to, he could see the tears swimming in her eyes.

And the effort she exerted to keep them at bay.

From the pulpit, the preacher announced, "Please kneel and pray."

The people around Corrie shifted and knelt, leaving her the sole person standing except Jess. Her fists clenched as those around her tried to help her kneel.

In the silence, a soft mewling sound escaped her lips, and he increased the speed of his approach. Another minute and she would be crying. A proud woman like Corrinne Webb shouldn't have to suffer the pity of strangers. He didn't know the cause of her agony, but agony it obviously was. Jess would not be able to look himself in the mirror tomorrow if he failed to intervene.

Only seconds passed before he reached her side. Those pale, full lips trembled as he turned her into his embrace. Her gaze drifted past him, then locked with his, and a tear coursed down her cheek. A frightened, lost, wild animal stared out at him from her eyes.

"It will be all right," Jess whispered, wiping the tear away. "Just hold on to me and it will be all right."

She clutched at his coat, her fingers blanching with the intensity of her grip, and nodded. He pushed through the crowd to the door. The parishioners, apparently believing the woman to be suffering the vapors, parted before him, asking if he needed assistance.

Reassuring them that he had everything under control, he swept her out into the cold night air and around the corner, away from prying eyes. There, in the dim light through the stained-glass windows, he made her face him.

Tears streamed down her face and she trembled like a leaf in his loose embrace. A low moan issued from her lips. Dante, writing his *Inferno,* had never imagined such a forlorn sound.

The moan became a question. "Why? Why did she leave me?"

He gathered her against his chest and rubbed her back. Dear Lord, who had done this to her? "Who left you, Corrie?"

She shook her head and burrowed her face into his lapel, repeating her anguished cry, "Why?"

Tremors shook her, shook him. Her legs seemed to collapse, and he caught her behind her shoulders and knees and lifted her high against his chest. Still wracked by sobs, she linked her hands behind his neck.

Where was he to take her? Certainly not back to his house. Her reputation would never stand against that. So where? He ticked off a short list of female friends—every one of them back there in the church.

A blast of snow-laden wind slapped him in the face. He had to find shelter for her now, not wait for the service to finish. Only one place was both public yet private enough—the police station.

Taking a shortcut across the park, he reached the station in minutes. He set her down against the door. "You keep holding on to my neck now, sweeting. Don't go falling down," he said against her icy cheek.

She didn't answer him. Didn't seem to hear him. But she kept her hands locked behind his neck as he fumbled to insert his key into the lock. Snow pelted him, melting in freezing rivulets down his collar, and he hoped his body was protecting her from the worst of the dampness.

Finally, the door opened, and he carried her into his office, where he settled her into his chair. She had stopped crying, but now her lips were blue and she shivered uncontrollably.

He was cold, and she was near frostbitten.

The embers of his office fire flamed to life with little effort. The Franklin stove warmed in no time, and Jess drew her chair close to it. Chafing her hands, he kept up a steady one-sided conversation.

"Your hands are like ice. Here, let me warm them. Everything's going to be all right, Corrie. Whatever were you thinking of back there to work yourself into such a state? Well, never mind that, you just worry about warming up. Yes, just warm up, sweeting. That's it, just warm up. Everything will be all right. Are you feeling your hands yet? Your fingers look pinker. Just warm up these hands, my sweet girl."

He forced her fists open and held her palms up to the stove. They were capable hands, with short-clipped nails and an earthy strength.

A shudder threatened to throw her from the chair, so he eased her to the floor. He removed her coat and wrapped his arms around her to share his warmth as best he could. Just so had he held his younger sisters when they had stayed too long on the skating pond.

But never had they stared ahead as if seeing the depths of hell.

The town clock had struck one some time past before her shivers ceased. Carefully, he shifted her so she leaned only slightly against his chest. He had thought her a little bit of a thing, but her form was firmer than he had expected. But soft nonetheless. A tremulous sigh signaled her return from wherever her mind had gone. Then he felt her straighten within his hold.

She croaked, "Where am I?"

"The police station. My office." Loosening his hold, he leaned back to study her expression.

Distressed, her gaze flew to meet his. "Am I under arrest?"

"No." Now why would she think he would arrest her?

"You're the police chief." Her tone accused him of unknown crimes.

"Guilty as charged," he answered with a chuckle. His mirth faded as he noted the wild animal remained within her eyes. "My turn to ask questions."

"I don't have to answer anything if I don't want to."

Ah, the spunk he remembered from the hotel was returning. He tucked a stray curl behind her ear. "Who did this to you? Who left you?"

Her pupils dilated and her breath caught. He had hit his target dead-on.

As if aware that her eyes revealed too much, she dropped her gaze to the fire. "I don't know what you mean."

With one hand, he lifted her chin so she had to meet his gaze. "You were crying as if your heart were breaking and asking, 'Why did she leave me?' Who hurt you so much? Who left you, Corrie?"

"I'm sorry to be such a bother." She wrested her chin from his hold and rolled out of his embrace and onto her knees.

"You're no bother, but you didn't answer my question. Who left you?"

A sigh from the bottom of her soul left her lips. "Doesn't someone always leave?" She covered her face with her hands for a moment, then gave herself a shake. On unsteady legs, she stood, then offered her hand. "Thanks a lot, Chief. I appreciate everything you've done."

"Corrie—"

"No . . . don't . . . just don't." She located her coat and buttoned it with fingers that shook. "I have to get back to the hotel."

"I'll escort you." Jess didn't want her to leave while she was still upset, but he feared for her self-control if he forced her to stay. The only thing to do, therefore, was to see her safely home.

"You don't have to do that." She peered out the window. "Just point me in the direction of the train station."

"The last train pulled out more than ten minutes ago." He had her there—she'd have to accept his help now.

Her cheeks paled and she swallowed. "I'm in big trouble. Or I will be when the Major hears about this."

"Not if we get you back soon." A plan coalesced in his brain—hooking up his surrey would take too long. They'd have to ride double on his big bay gelding, King.

"But it's two miles up the mountain," she said, an echo of her earlier wail returning.

"Come with me," he said and guided her up the street to the stables. Saddling King took but a minute, and before Corrie had time to come up with any new objections, he pulled her up behind him and set out for the Chesterfield.

A train whistle mourned down the valley as they started up a heavily treed path. Corrie lifted her head, which she'd kept bent until then. In the darkness, he couldn't read her expression.

He thought it best to assume she needed reassurance. "The train is just now arriving at the hotel station. We're only minutes behind it." He nudged King to a faster gait.

The truth of his statement became evident some minutes later when they approached the hotel station. Several people stood around in small groups. Laughter carried to where he had pulled to a halt in the trees.

"You had best walk from here. No one will guess you didn't come up on the train if you head straight to your quarters." He felt her nod and, reaching behind him, Jess helped her slide down.

As he started to dismount, she stopped him. "No, stay there." She paused at the edge of the trees and turned around. "Thank you, Chief Garrett. You can leave now." Then she stepped into the clearing and hurried toward the west wing.

He stared after her until he saw her open the door and slip inside. King nickered as a penetrating blast of snow and wind whipped around them.

"You're right, old boy. Time to go home." They headed back down the mountain, but Jess couldn't resist one final look back.

Somewhere, some time, someone had left Corrinne Webb and inflicted a devastating wound to her heart.

Absently, he rubbed the region over his heart. What sort of devil would leave a sweet child—a precious woman—like her?

Somewhere, some time, Jess would discover who.

Corrie raced up the stairs to her room and slammed the door behind her. Heart pounding, she closed her mind to thoughts of what had happened at the church with Jess Garrett.

I won't think about it. I won't.

Her fingers trembled as she turned up the gas jet

for more light and shoveled coal into the small stove where embers still glowed. Kneeling in front of the stove, she raised her hands to the warmth. She told herself they only shook from the cold and leaned closer.

But even when the heat made her shed her coat, Corrie continued to shake. She held up her hands and clenched her fists. It did no good. The cold was inside—deep in her soul. A sob tore through her, and she pressed a fist against her mouth to keep it from escaping. If she gave in to the pain, if she let her memories rise, she would be lost in them forever. No Jess would come to her rescue here.

Hot tears dropped onto her hand. *No*, she shouted in her mind. *No, I will not give in.*

At that, she strode to the washbasin and splashed her face with the icy water. As she dried her face, she looked at her reflection in the stand's mirror. Eyes, red-rimmed and forlorn, looked back at her. Her nose could've done a clown proud.

I look like hell, she thought, then chuckled. Vanity—vanity was good. It took her mind off . . .

Enough, Webb.

She scrubbed her face with the towel and turned away from the mirror, forcing a breath deep into her lungs and exhaling a bit of the tension that vibrated through her.

"Okay, pity party's over," she said to the empty room. Thank goodness Bridget had gone to a later service and would stay overnight in town with friends. Corrie couldn't have survived a sympathetic ear.

She gave herself a deliberate shake. Now to regain complete control. "Head up, back straight, breathe." She went through the motions and the shaking eased. She repeated them and it completely—almost completely—went away. In spite of her earlier distress, she grinned. "By golly, maybe the Major's on to something."

Once again, she checked herself in the mirror. "Well, you won't win any beauty contests, Webb, but you won't scare any children either."

Grabbing the pitcher, she visited the bathroom and returned without having to explain her reddened eyes and nose to anyone. After a quick sponge bath, she added coal to the stove, turned down the light, and climbed into bed.

Long years of practice clicked in to blank her mind of the memories. Whatever triggered her earlier anguish had been in the church—nothing else, nothing more. The sense of isolation all the families had provoked in her—that had nothing to do with it. Nor did the fact that tomorrow was Christmas.

The loneliest day of the year.

Well, Christmas would be over after tomorrow, and she wouldn't have to attend church since she'd gone tonight. If she didn't return to that church, she would be safe. Safe from embarrassing herself.

Safe from remembering.

Resolutely, she pulled up the covers and curled onto her side. As she drifted off to sleep, Corrie could almost hear a deep voice calling her sweeting and assuring her that everything would be all right. She could almost feel his strong, warm arms around her, cradling her to his chest, keeping her safe. She sighed as a sense of peace settled over her.

Everything would be all right—she'd be safe.

With Jess Garrett.

* * *

"Humbug." Corrie slapped another order into the waiting hand of the kitchen boy.

"What's wrong, Miss Webb? Ain't got no Christmas spirit?" the boy asked, then ducked away with a laugh as she flipped the end of her apron at him.

"Oh, I have Christmas spirit, all right." She leveled her hand under her chin. "Clear up to here, I have Christmas spirit." She wiped her face with a napkin she'd stashed in her pocket and tucked her hair more firmly into its chignon. "I've had the blasted Christmas spirit since early this morning."

Not only had she handled the breakfast and lunch crowd, but she'd been assigned the dinner shift as well, to allow others to set up the ballroom. Her feet hurt, her back hurt, and that damned corset was wearing a blister in a sensitive spot.

But at least Major Payne had done nothing more than harrumph at her during morning muster. "For small favors be thankful," she muttered.

"Beg pardon, miss?" the boy asked.

"Nothing," she answered and tried to smile. "Just passing the time."

"Passing the time, is it?" Bridget asked from behind her.

Corrie whirled and was instantly enveloped in a lavender-scented embrace. The pleasure of it surprised her. She didn't like being touched. So why did she return the hug just as warmly as it was given?

"Happy Christmas to you, Corrie." Bridget released her.

Automatically, Corrie returned, "Merry Christmas to you." Then was startled to realize she meant it. She didn't even protest when the woman fussed with Corrie's hair and straightened her apron.

What in the world is happening to me? Has time travel scrambled my brain?

Her order came up, and Corrie lifted the heavy tray. "Back to work," she said with a rueful smile.

Bridget helped her by placing a fresh pot of coffee on the tray and balancing out the load. As Corrie prepared to return to the dining room, Bridget said in an excited voice, "I'll be serving at the ball tonight. Ye simply must take a peek. It's ever so lovely." Her lashes fluttered as she sighed. "Magical."

Corrie gave a sigh of her own, but hers held none of Bridget's girlish wonder. "I'm tired, Bidgie."

"To be sure, you're tired. But 'tis a ball, after all." A bell rang in the distance and Bridget turned to go. Over her shoulder, she called, "Seek me out after yer shift. There's a place I know where we can see everything." With that, she hurried out.

Through the doorway, Corrie saw the Major glaring at her. Quickly, she returned to her serving duties.

The dinner rush was shorter than usual because guests were eager to join the festivities in the ballroom, and Sparrow told her to take off early. Corrie didn't have to be told twice. She whipped off her apron and climbed the stairs to her room. By this time, her hair was all but falling down, so she pulled out the pins, then collapsed on her bed fully clothed.

Faint music drifted up from the ballroom and she dragged her pillow over her head. Shortly, one foot started keeping time with the beat. Corrie glared at it from under the pillow, but no sooner had she stopped one foot from tapping the air than the other one started.

She rolled into a ball—as well as she could, given she still wore her corset—and blocked her ears.

However, this wasn't conducive to sleep and she soon sat up.

"I give up. I give up," she groused as she ran a brush through her hair and gave her skirt a twitch to smooth it. "This is all an evil plot to make me meet Bridget downstairs."

The young Irishwoman would be disappointed if she didn't show up, and Corrie had begun to value her friendship. *So what if my feet fall off?*

Five minutes—ten at the outside—with Bridget, and Corrie would make her happy. Certainly Corrie could spare ten minutes for a friend.

A little uncomfortable and yet a little pleased at the warm reality of having a friend, Corrie made her way to the staff dining room. According to one of the bellhops, Bridget had just carried a tray of champagne glasses into the ballroom but would return as soon as she'd gotten rid of them. Corrie took a seat, propped her feet up in another chair, and closed her eyes.

"Here, can't have you starve."

Savory scents passed under her nose. Corrie opened her eyes. A bellhop held a plate loaded to the brim with all sorts of food.

"For you," he said. "Looks like you could use this."

Corrie sat up and lowered her feet to the floor. "Uh . . . thanks." A little flustered, she cleared her throat before she said, "I'm sorry, but I don't know your name."

"Rupert Smith, at your service." He clicked his heels and bowed, then let out a laugh that had her smiling with him as he filled another plate and joined her. "Eat up. The Major ordered Chef Sashenka to make extra of all the good stuff on the menu for us."

"Really? Major Payne did that?" Corrie added that tidbit of information to her observation of his kindness to Bridget—even his tolerance of her own deficiencies this morning—and came to the conclusion that the guy wasn't all bad.

Just saddled with a Napoleonic complex.

"He's not that bad if you follow his rules," Rupert said around a mouthful of veal cordon bleu. "My ma kept a tighter rein on my brothers and sisters than he does on the staff. I'm used to it."

While Corrie tucked into her own plate, he maintained a cheerful monologue about his large, obviously poor, family in Philadelphia and his plans to make his mark in the world.

"I keep my eyes and ears open around here. Never know when one of the swells will give me a stock tip." He polished his nails on his coat, then studied them in a worldly manner. "Own a bit of stock already, I do."

"You'll be living on that stock if you don't shake a leg," Bridget said as she snagged a chicken leg from his plate. "Major Payne was asking after you. I told him you'd been called upstairs."

"Gee, thanks for covering for me, Bidgie." Rupert wished them a happy Christmas and exited the room at a rapid clip.

Bridget took his seat and finished eating her chicken leg. Corrie finished her dinner and found herself with more energy than she would have imagined an hour earlier.

"Ready to spy on the ball?" Bridget asked as she wiped her fingers. " 'Tis truly splendid this year. The best yet."

Corrie rose. She needed some fun, some distraction. "You're the boss, Bidgie my girl."

After following Bridget up into the rafters of the theater that abutted the ballroom, Corrie was ready to demote her. In jeans and hiking boots, the scramble across the second-story rigging would have been a challenge. In a long skirt, it bordered on suicidal.

"We're here," Bridget whispered and pulled Corrie up next to her at a window that opened into the ballroom.

What breath the climb left her whooshed out of Corrie's chest. A Currier and Ives print had come to life.

The Christmas tree shimmered with silvery tinsel and hundreds of candles. The ladies shimmered as well, in diaphanous evening gowns and jewels. Their trains swept in sumptuous arcs as the gentlemen, clad in somber tuxedos with crisp white shirts, twirled them around and around the room in time to a waltz played by an orchestra. Corrie's eyes ached with the beauty of it.

The only thing that could have made it better would have been if she was one of that glittering company. A corset would be a minor discomfort if she could wear one of those beribboned and ruffled gowns and flirt with one of the delicate fans most of the women carried. Maybe one of the men, young and dark with eyes the blue of a Texas summer, would ask her to dance.

"Oh, Bridget, thank you. Thank you for bringing me up here."

"I knew you'd like it," Bridget replied. "I must be getting back. Miss Sparrow will be missing me. But stay as long as you like."

Corrie, mesmerized by the circling couples, nodded and leaned a little more against the window. It was Cinderella come to life.

Except I'm not Cinderella.

She sighed and tried to recapture the awe, but reality had slapped her in the face again. However, she had exerted so much effort to reach this window, she might as well stay awhile longer.

There was no harm in imagining she was that pretty blonde dancing with Police Chief Garrett. She could almost feel his strong hand at her waist as he guided her through the steps of the dance, his breath tickling her ear as he whispered compliments and his eyes warming as he flirted with her.

The dance came to an end and the blonde sank into a deep curtsy, her nose seeming to touch her knee. Corrie watched in envy as the woman held the position for two beats, then raised her head and smiled coquettishly before rising like a swan.

So much for imagining I'm that blonde. There's no way I could ever do that. I'd land flat on my face. Or get stuck in that position.

Oh well, back to the real world, she thought and released a resigned sigh.

As if he'd heard it, Jess Garrett looked directly at her. How he could think to do so was impossible. But he did. And raised a finger to his brow in salute.

Corrie stepped back. She was in for it now. The Major would can her for sure. Her knees felt like Jell-O as she inched her way to the theater floor. When she gained the main level, she retraced her steps to the staff hallway, intending to go straight to her room.

A waltz sounded from the ballroom to change her mind. Just one more peek, one more glimpse of the fairy tale wouldn't hurt. She slipped down the hallway and across the lobby, then onto the veranda. Freezing cold stabbed through her, but she continued around to the terrace and the ballroom windows. Up close, the scene was even more beautiful.

Where's a fairy godmother when you need one?

Corrie backed away, the cold overriding the dream. She gasped as a hard form blocked her retreat. Spinning, she came nose to shirtfront with a tux.

"Good evening, Corrie," the deep, well-remembered voice said.

His scent filled her nostrils and clouded her mind. All she could manage was to look up at his face and into those intense blue eyes.

"Ever been to a ball?" he asked, as if he met a waitress spying on a dance every day of his life.

"N-no."

"Ever danced?" He ran his hand down her arm and placed her hand on his shoulder.

"Not like this." A thrill of heat zinged along her veins. Her corset would burst if her heart pounded any harder. Was he asking her to dance?

"Then let me show you." He gave her no time to protest—not that she would have—before swinging her into the triplet rhythm of the waltz. When she tried to watch her feet, he drew her closer and spun them around and around so all she saw was a blur of light and shadow.

One-two-three, one-two-three. The rhythm and the music became one with the beat of her heart. The only way she could keep from being dizzy was to focus on his face, so close to hers, and his eyes, blue as a Texas summer.

Her feet barely touched the ground. She swayed in concert with Jess with a grace she never knew she possessed. She was lithe and elegant and as far removed from Chef Webb as she could be.

Just so must Cinderella have felt when her prince danced with her. Bridget had been right—the ball was definitely magical.

As long as the orchestra played, they danced. When the orchestra paused, Jess whistled a waltz under his breath. They circled and dipped and whirled, first on the terrace and then into the shadows of the front veranda, away from any prying eyes in the ballroom.

Corrie had never been to a prom. Never been asked to a dance. Now she was Cinderella and a fairy-tale prince swirled her in sweeping circles. Their silence—except for Jess's whistling—was part of the enchantment.

But even Cinderella had to leave the ball.

Several couples sought to cool themselves on the terrace only a few yards from Jess and Corrie. She stumbled to a halt, afraid of the consequences of what she had done.

A prohibition against consorting with the guests hadn't been specifically mentioned by either Sparrow or Major Payne, but Corrie figured the rule existed. The punishment could be anything, including termination.

Fear of being left without a means of support, without a roof over her head, chilled her more thoroughly than any wind could. "Let me go, Jess," she whispered, her throat tight. "Please, let me go."

"Corrie—"

His hold on her relaxed a little and she didn't wait. Twisting out of his embrace, she turned and ran away from the chattering guests. She reached the far door and glanced back. Jess stood, his arm raised as if to call her back. His eyes were shadowy, unreadable.

A tipsy voice called to him from around the corner. Jess hesitated, then lowered his arm slowly and backed away to join his friends.

The fairy tale had ended.

FIVE

Jess rubbed a hand over his face in a futile effort to ease the Sousa band marching back and forth in his head. What in hell had he been thinking to drink so much champagne? Raising both hands to his head, he pressed them hard to each temple. Maybe external pain would diminish the internal pounding.

And extinguish the image of Corrie as he twirled her in his arms the night before. The moonlight had kissed her hair with silver while the shadows had enhanced her magnificent eyes.

"What am I doing?" he muttered, releasing the pressure on his head. The pain returned like an avenging angel . . . or a devil. "As if I can't name a dozen girls with magnificent eyes."

In truth, he knew *more* than a dozen, each of whom could claim beautiful eyes. But none could claim Corrie's expression of delighted wonder or the breathless spell of enchantment they had shared while dancing. Others were certainly better dancers, but Corrie danced with an innate grace and an enthralling sense of oneness with him. Others performed the steps of the dance; Corrie breathed the spirit of it.

He squinted one eye open and blinked at the light streaming in his window. Last night Corrie's eyes had gleamed like a child's at a candy store window. Her yearning to be a part of the dazzling spectacle had been a palpable thing. To resist would have taken a hard-hearted fool.

"Fool, yourself," he said and forced himself upright. The little brown duck of a waitress occupied his thoughts entirely too frequently. And too thoroughly.

Without even closing his eyes, he could feel the silky fall of her hair across his hand, smell her soap, hear her little gasp as he pulled her closer for a turn. His right palm ached longingly for the supple bend of her waist. He ached . . .

A shaft of impatience shot through him. "You're nothing but a rutting bull," he told himself. "She's young, attractive, and available, and you haven't had a woman since the Contessa D'Angelo left. The girl's probably—certainly—an innocent. Not your style at all."

Head throbbing and eyes gritty, he shaved and dressed. As he gingerly donned his hat in preparation for his departure for the police station, he met his own gaze in the mirror. "Put her out of your thoughts. You have no future with her. Avoid her at all costs."

In spite of that resolution, Jess caught himself eyeing with interest every woman with curly brown hair as he strode down the street. He shoved his hands into his pockets and frowned.

Corrie Webb had burrowed under his skin like a nettle.

"God, I look like hell." Corrie rubbed a hand over her face and blinked at her reflection. Every sleepless

minute of last night had etched itself on her face.
Cold water from the pitcher erased some of the puffi-
ness but couldn't erase her memory. An embarrassed
flush burned her cheeks. How could she have
danced with *him?*

Jess Garrett was her absolute worst choice. First,
because he was a guest. *And what Sparrow and the
Major wouldn't say about that if they knew . . .*

Second, Jess had seen her Christmas Eve in all her
broken-down misery. Not even Paul LaDue had seen
her so vulnerable, so out of control. She had been
a child the last time her emotions and memories had
overcome her, paralyzing her like that—emotions
and memories she thought she'd forgotten.

No, I won't think about them. They're history.

She splashed more water on her face, then made
up the fire and crawled back into bed. No muster
for her this morning. She had the lunch and dinner
shifts, so she only had to report to Sparrow before
then.

The fire crackled and warmed the room. Corrie
pulled the covers over her head and curled up, slow-
ing her breathing and forcing her extremities to go
limp. Scenes from yesterday played upon the insides
of her eyelids. Her eyes opened of their own accord.
She flipped onto her other side. She rolled onto her
back. Nothing worked. Tired as she was, she couldn't
sleep. Her mind insisted on replaying the last two
days.

Christmas in her own time was trying—damned
difficult, in fact; this Christmas in 1886 was hell. Not
only had she embarrassed herself at the church in
front of many of her coworkers, she'd done it in
front of Jess Garrett.

Jess Garrett. The name conjured up his face—an-

gular and tanned and far too sweet for a cop—and
his body. Oh, yes, his body. Tall and hard in all the
right places. And those shoulders—strong and
broad.

And perfect for crying on.

Shit. She was becoming maudlin. Better to focus
on the guy's sex appeal than his sensitivity. His sex
appeal . . . now that was something to stay awake for.
A warmth that had nothing to do with the stove's
blaze oozed through her. Her skin heated, recalling
the strength in his arms as he'd held her last night
and swept her around and around—

Corrie dragged her mind to a screeching halt.
*There will be no more dancing, no more comforting, no
more anything with Jess Garrett.* He made her entirely
too . . . weak. That was it; he made her weak.

No way was she going to be weak. That meant she
had to become self-sufficient, and what better time
to start than now?

Throwing back the covers, she dressed in the
loose-fitting housedress Bridget called a Mother
Hubbard and placed irons to heat on top of the
stove. Bridget could do a better job, but Corrie
wasn't displeased when she surveyed the results of
her own efforts. By the time she was due in the dining room, she'd managed to press every item of
clothing Sparrow had given her.

When Major Payne passed Corrie's appearance
without a comment, Corrie couldn't help but feel
cocky. She was getting the hang of this century in
only a matter of days. Not bad. And not the charac-
teristic of a weak person.

Her self-confidence lasted through lunch and
most of the way through dinner. Her train stayed
away from her feet and her bustle only occasionally

threw off her balance. Then Sparrow seated Jess Garrett at one of Corrie's tables.

Corrie's confidence plummeted. She chased down Sparrow in a hallway off the kitchen. "You have to change Jess—uh, Chief Garrett—to someone else's station."

Without glancing up from the paperwork in her hand, Sparrow asked in a chilly tone, "Why would I do that, Miss Webb?"

"Because I don't want to wait on him?" Corrie replied, aware of how inadequate that sounded.

"Your wants have no place in the assignments." Sparrow raised one eyebrow. "Is there any *valid* reason for you not to wait on Mr. Garrett?"

How could Corrie tell this nineteenth-century woman that being near Jess made her nipples crinkle up and her blood turn to warm syrup in her veins? How could she tell Sparrow that simply the sight of him made her heart pound a waltz rhythm in her ears? How could she tell her that he made her think of sweaty sheets and long nights?

Corrie sighed. "No reason, I guess."

"Then take care of him, Miss Webb."

"Easy for you to say," Corrie muttered as she returned to the dining room. Every nerve recalled how he had taken care of her two nights before, not to mention dancing with her last night. Now she had to detach herself from that and serve him his dinner.

Steeling herself, she approached his table and cleared her throat. "Good evening, sir. What may I get for you?"

Crisp and impersonal—the perfect waitress.

He looked up and gave a start. An indefinable expression flitted across his features. "Good evening." He shot a glance around the room. "Busy tonight?"

She shrugged and repeated, "What may I get for you, *sir?*" Crisp and impersonal, no matter what. *Dammit.*

"Sir? Not Chief?" he asked with a smile. His smile could melt a glacier. It crooked up on one side, and dimples creased his cheeks.

Dimples, for Pete's sake. She hadn't really noticed them before; God knew how she'd missed them. Her breath whooshed out and she smiled back. "H-hi . . . Chief."

"That's better. After last night, formality would be superfluous, wouldn't you say?"

"Oh. Yeah . . . superfluous. Definitely." *So much for crisp and impersonal. More like lame and clueless.*

"I wanted to thank you for our dance."

"Our . . . dance?" *Not only clueless but mindless.*

Suddenly, Major Payne appeared at her elbow. "Is there a problem here, Mr. Garrett? Miss Webb, have you taken this gentleman's order?"

Clueless, mindless, and unemployed.

She wiped the smile off her face and gritted her teeth. "Not yet."

He picked up the menu from the table and placed it in Jess's hands. "Here you are, sir. My apologies for any delay in your meal." His mustache twitched as he frowned at Corrie.

"No delay, Major. We were just passing the pleasantries of the season." Jess grinned.

One dimple deepened, and Corrie's pulse accelerated. Aware of the Major's scrutiny, she lifted her order pad, pencil poised and ready. She flicked a patently false smile at the Major, which she then turned on Jess. "Your order, sir?"

As Jess reeled off the items he wanted, Major Payne wandered away, pausing at each table to greet the customers. Although he had his back to her much of the time, Corrie sensed that he was always aware of her—aware and waiting for her to screw up.

Resolutely, she carried out her tasks. Running a kitchen had honed her organizational skills. Waiting tables required organization, so she didn't do badly, as long as her uniform cooperated. But every time she went near Jess's table, her skin tingled and her blood pulsed one-two-three, one-two-three.

In her preoccupied state, she almost didn't notice when someone pinched her. A pat on her fanny—felt in spite of its bustled state—followed the pinch. Corrie whirled around and glared at the red-faced drunk at the table behind her. A scathing comment leapt to her lips, but one look at the Major's back only two tables away and she swallowed it. No reason to lose her job over some lush. Edging farther from the man's roaming hands, she finished clearing the salad course and returned to the holding area by the kitchen.

Bridget joined her with a worried look. "Whatever is the matter, lass? You look a thunderstorm."

"Do I? Well, there's a certain customer I'd like to strike with lightning." Corrie jerked her head toward the drunk's table.

"Oh, that one. Mind yourself, a right blighter he is. All hands."

"He patted me on my . . . backside," Corrie huffed, indignation still percolating hotly.

"He pats everyone's arse." Bridget shrugged, obviously not surprised. Or indignant. "We try to stay shy of his side of the table."

"You shouldn't have to 'stay shy' of him."

"He's a guest, Corrie, and rich. You'll gain nothing by challenging him." With that pronouncement,

Bridget picked up her tray and returned to the dining room.

Corrie fumed while she waited for her order to come up. So much for getting the hang of this century. The man's behavior was a slap in the face—not to mention a pat on the ass. And as a lowly waitress, she was expected to tolerate it.

Tolerate it, like hell.

She hadn't taken Tae-Bo classes for nothing. Her nostrils flared and she glared at the back of the man's head. "Next time, buster, I'll have a little slap of my own ready."

"What's that, Miss Webb?" the kitchen boy asked, loading her tray.

She shook her head and hefted the tray. For now, she would avoid the guy. He wasn't at one of her tables and she would be able to work around him.

But she couldn't work around Jess Garrett.

He ordered every course offered, and the Chesterfield offered more courses than the Culinary Institute of America ever dreamed of. She placed the final serving in front of him and stood back. He lifted a forkful, then lowered it with a muffled belch.

"Full?" she asked, beginning to suspect his appetite was as bogus as her 1886 work references.

Jess shook his head, then caught her grin and nodded. "I didn't think it possible to have a surfeit of Chef Sasha's cuisine, but it is."

"Do you always order everything on the menu?"

Jess flashed those dimples again. "Only when I want to spend a lot of time here. With you."

"You ordered all this just so you could spend time with me?" *Talk about stupid . . . but talk about sweet, too.*

"I didn't know when I'd see you again, and this

was the only way I could think to make our time last."

Don't be sweet. Please don't be sweet. The Major's gonna kill me if you're sweet.

Corrie tallied up his bill. "It's going to cost you."

"You're worth it." He extricated one of her hands from her order pad.

"I am?" *I'm worth it?* Corrie had never been worth anything to anyone.

Raising her hand, Jess pressed his warm lips to the back of her fingers and lingered there a shade too long. Or a shade too short. Her heart rate didn't know which—it raced along on a hormone hurricane.

"Definitely." He rose, still clasping her fingers. "But I think I'll satisfy this particular appetite another way and another time."

"B-beg pardon?" she stammered. What did he mean by that? And damned if he wasn't making her knees weak.

"Next time you won't be working"—he caressed the back of her fingers with his thumb—"and we'll be alone." Gently, he released her hand and strode away, his long legs carrying him quickly to the exit.

She leaned both hands on the table and blew out the breath she'd been holding. He resolution to avoid Jess shredded like a dust bunny in a tornado.

Weak, Webb, definitely weak.

Several days later, Jess turned up the collar of his coat and pulled on his gloves, stiff with cold, as the raw wind slipped under and around his coat. Ice rimed the bare-limbed trees glistening in the watery sunshine. He increased his pace—his detour to the bakery for hot cinnamon rolls was threatening to end in frostbite. With any luck, his deputy, Cyril, would have left the coal scuttles full, so Jess could build the office fire quickly. As he strode around the corner of the street onto which the police station fronted, he happened to glance up.

Smoke rose from the station's chimney. That could only mean that Cyril had arrested someone last evening and had spent the night at the station. Jess tucked the cinnamon rolls in his pocket. He hadn't braved an extra three blocks in this cold to share his treat with any stray rowdy. And Cyril could get his own on his way home.

The heady scent of coffee met Jess as he opened the station door, and he inhaled appreciatively. "Bless you, Cyril. Coffee's just the thing to thaw me out this morning."

He hung his hat and coat on the pegs beside the door and looked toward the cells—both of which were unoccupied, with their blankets neatly tucked in. He turned toward his office, calling, "Cyril, what are you doing here this time of the morning?"

A cheerful bass voice boomed, "Waiting for you, you shiftless layabout. What do you mean, dragging in to work this time of the morning?"

Jess laughed, throwing open his office door and taking in the sight of his oldest brother with his boots propped up on the desk. "Teddy, what brings you back so soon? I expected Ma to keep you dancing attendance on her until after the new year. How is everyone?"

While he didn't agree with his family in all matters, Jess loved each of his many brothers and sisters. The bonds of the Garrett clan were close. Fortunately for Jess, they were close-knit a couple of hours away from him. All except Teddy, who had a law practice in town.

Theodore Garrett shoved his hands into his pockets and rocked the chair back. "They're doing well and send their love. Ma sent a blackberry cake for you, but . . ."

"Don't tell me." Jess reached past Teddy's ample stomach to pour a cup of coffee. "You got hungry on the train."

"Exactly." Teddy beamed at his brother's understanding; then his face fell. "You won't tell Ma, will you? She made me promise to deliver it whole."

"Have I ever snitched on you?"

They shared a laugh and settled into savoring their coffee. As Jess retrieved the rolls from his coat, he hummed a waltz.

"Had a good time at the Christmas ball, did you?" Teddy asked with a knowing grin.

"Always do." Jess tossed one roll across the desk and bit into the other.

"Dance with Gretchen?"

"Yes." Jess shot his brother a sharp glance. "Something wrong with dancing with Gretchen?"

Teddy said with an attempt at innocence, "No, just wondering who you danced with."

"Just wondering what you're going to report to Ma, you mean." Jess gave an exasperated sigh. When he'd given Teddy permission to keep Ma updated on his doings in Hope Springs, it had been with the idea of keeping her off his back. He hadn't counted on her interest in his lady friends. *Though why I thought she would stay out of that part of my life, I'll never know.* "I danced with the usual assortment of girls—simpering and silly, without a thought in their heads but of fashion."

"If they're so silly, why do you bother?"

"Because they scratch an itch." That seemed to satisfy his brother, and Jess was left to ponder the dance in peace.

The society girls at the ball did indeed scratch the itch of polite and pleasant company. However, Corrie Webb was a new kind of itch. She was neither particularly polite nor excessively pleasant—in the way the other young women were pleasant—and heaven knew she wasn't society. But she was a bewitching, if nettlesome, armful.

Jess shifted as he felt himself go hard at the thought of her in his arms. Her hair had cascaded down her back and caressed his hand at her waist, creating images in his mind of her wild sorrel mane draped across his pillow. What man in his right mind wouldn't react?

Of course, she was prickly and obviously held to those women's suffrage ideas going around. Prickliness aside, Corrie was an itch he needed to scratch. Soon.

Never mind that when he'd dined at the hotel, he hadn't planned on seeing her. Dozens of waitresses served in the dining room. Why would he suppose Corrie would serve him? If anything, he thought she might avoid him after he'd swept her into that waltz with barely a word.

He hadn't planned to see her—to talk to her. Blast it all, he hadn't planned to kiss her hand. That would've been contrary to all his intentions. But he had seen her, talked to her, and kissed her hand, and none of these had eased his itch.

So, my intentions have changed. No harm in that.

In his mind, a voice very much like his mother's

queried, "What *are* your intentions?" sending a chill through him.

Try as he might, Jess had no ready answer.

He wrapped his fingers around the cup to warm them and only then noticed Teddy's furtive expression. Jess leveled a questioning gaze at his brother.

Teddy tried a seraphic smile. It failed miserably. His dark brows drew together in a worried frown.

"What else do you need to tell me, Teddy?" A finger of apprehension traced a chill down his spine. Was someone ill? Or worse, dead? In their youth, Teddy had been known to shield Jess from bad news.

With a family whose adult males were mostly lawmen, death was a possibility—a reality—they lived with every day. Jess dropped his feet to the floor and leaned forward. "Teddy, tell me. Has someone been killed? Uncle Pat?"

"Oh, no. Nothing like that." The worried expression remained. "As I said, everyone's fine."

"Then why the pallbearer's face?" If no one was ill and no one had died, the situation couldn't be too grave.

Teddy poured himself more coffee and studied the brew as if it offered an answer. Finally, he asked, "Did you know Ma's rheumatism is worse?"

"No," Jess said slowly. Ma's rheumatism worsened at times convenient to her and only her. No cause for alarm. He raised an eyebrow to prompt Teddy to continue.

"She says it hurts much more this winter than last, and she's seen the doctor about it." Teddy set down his cup and sighed. "He says she needs to take the cure."

That finger of apprehension changed to one of dread. Jess repressed a shiver. "The cure, you say."

"Oh, hell, Jess. Ma's coming to Hope Springs to take the mineral waters. The doc says it's the only thing to help her rheumatism. Says she should stay until at least spring . . . or that's what she convinced him to say." Teddy clasped his hands in front of him on the desk and turned a pitying gaze on his brother.

Jess deserved pity. Zelda Garrett considered it her God-given duty to find mates for her children. Since Teddy had become betrothed, Jess was her last bachelor son of marriageable age. With sixteen-year-old Peggy next out of the nursery but years from marrying, Ma could turn her attentions entirely on him.

"She's going to need someplace to stay, Jess."

"The hotel is convenient for someone taking the cure." Jess knew this was a futile hope even as he offered it.

"Not as convenient as staying in town is, for interfering in your life." Teddy wagged his head in sympathy—he had been Ma's last project.

"But you can—"

"Not on your life," Teddy interrupted. "I'm the good, engaged son who went home for Christmas. It's your turn, little brother. Your house is bigger anyway."

The coffee had lost its flavor and Jess set his cup down. He made one last effort. "How about if I pay for the hotel? I can afford it, and heaven knows I would rather be out some money than have her riding herd on me."

"But think how it will look if she doesn't stay with her beloved youngest son while she takes the cure." Teddy held up his hand to silence Jess's protest. "That's what Ma will say, and you know it."

Jess did indeed know what his mother would say. He wiped a hand over his face. Months of his mother's focused attention and *he* would have to take the cure.

SIX

Corrie's days settled into a routine—up at oh-six-way-too-early on days she covered the breakfast shift, then crawl into bed too tired to worry about her past, her present, or her future. Although she thought she was doing an adequate job, she couldn't shake the conviction that Major Payne merely bided his time before he fired her. As for the cook's position he had said he would consider her for . . .

Get real.

And it didn't help her peace of mind that every time she turned around, Jess was there. Watching her, seeking her out, and striking up conversations. If he wasn't eating breakfast in the dining room, it was lunch. If not lunch, then dinner. If he didn't show up for a meal, then he appeared out of nowhere when she ran errands on the Chesterfield's grounds or simply took a walk. When did the man actually work?

Not that she didn't like seeing him. She did. Far too much.

No man before Jess had ever made her so aware of her reactions to him. Those reactions intrigued her at the same time that they disturbed her. More so when she realized she actively looked for the tall lawman when she entered a room, and worse, felt disappointment when he wasn't there.

Like this morning, on her half-day off.

The wind howled out of the north, biting her hands and face and adding speed to her hike down to Hope Springs while she berated herself for being all sorts of a fool for missing the police chief. As for the cold, she had only herself to blame. When she hadn't been able to tolerate a full morning of needlework and gossip, not to mention Jess's absence, she headed into town to buy something to wear besides a waitress uniform.

Wanting to find an attractive outfit had nothing to do with Jess Garrett. She scuffed the toe of her hiking boot into the matted leaves and muttered to herself, "Nothing whatsoever."

With her head bent against the wind and her mind elsewhere, she didn't notice the gathering of people around a campfire until she was into the clearing. Even then, she only looked up as wood smoke made her cough.

A number of black people rose from around the fire, their expressions startled. And fearful. Children hid behind the women's skirts and whimpered.

Corrie halted. "Excuse me. I didn't mean to intrude." She couldn't help eyeing the blaze as she blew on her hands to warm them.

One of the men said, "Didn't mean no harm, missus." He was tall and burly and looked strong enough to lift the boulder he'd been sitting on.

So why was he so wary of *her*? Corrie approached and held out her hands to the heat. "I never thought you did, sir. Do you mind if I warm up a bit? It's awfully cold."

The man glanced around the group, then back at her. "Yes'm. You go right ahead."

She got as close as she could without catching her skirts on fire and sighed as her fingers tingled with returning circulation. But the others remained at a distance.

Giving a nervous laugh, she said, "I don't mean to hog the heat. Please, come on back here."

Slowly, the group inched toward her, first the men, then the women with the children. As they held out their hands to the warmth, their lack of gloves and mittens was painfully apparent. What coats they had were threadbare as well. In spite of the cold, they kept a few feet between themselves and Corrie.

She glanced around and saw small packs stacked underneath the trees and a handful of rickety lean-tos. She looked at the first man and asked, "You live here in the woods?"

He licked dry lips and gave a reluctant nod.

"But why?" History wasn't her strongest subject, but Corrie knew that slavery had ended with the Civil War. Therefore, these weren't runaway slaves. So who were they and why were they out here in the cold? Homeless people weren't common in 1886 . . . were they?

"Can't find no work, missus," he said. "No work, no money. Can't pay the rent."

"What about up at the Chesterfield?" As the words left her mouth, she recalled that the only black person she'd seen since arriving in 1886 had been a servant of one of the guests.

" 's long as they can hire white folks, they ain't gonna hire the likes of us. Cert'ly not Big John." The man's shoulders sagged, and one of the women slid an arm around his waist and hugged him.

"That's right, ma'am," she said. "Any of us here

would be glad of work, but so far, it's only a bit here 'n' a bit there. Barely enough to feed our babies.''

Another man chimed in, "If we didn't catch a rabbit or two, all of us'd go hungry, ma'am."

"D'you know of anyone in need of a maid or laundry woman? I'll do anything," the woman said, desperation in her voice. "Anything decent."

"I wish I did. But no, I'm barely employed myself," Corrie answered.

Their plight tugged at her heart. These were good people—willing to work but kept from doing so merely by their color. They reminded her of the illegals she'd given jobs to at Bistro Terre—all of whom had been desperate to work, to make their own way in the United States.

Yet what could she do here in a time not her own? With her job so uncertain?

Corrie stared into the flames and shoved her hands into her coat pockets. Her fingers encountered the few coins and even fewer folded notes that comprised her wages for the last weeks, carefully hoarded.

She lifted her gaze and looked—really looked—at each individual. The men with their near-broken dignity, the women with the eyes of proud poverty, the children . . . Dear God, the children with the beginnings of hopelessness in their faces.

The vivid memory of her own hopelessness knifed through her. A memory of Paul LaDue's helping hand followed. At the least, she could help feed the kids. Fumbling, she emptied her pockets and placed the money in Big John's hands. "Here, you need it more than I do," she said, fighting the trembling in her voice.

He gazed down at the small pile as the others clus-

tered around him. Fingers, big as cigars, counted out
the money; then he looked at her. His gaze seemed
to pierce straight into her soul, and Corrie wondered
what he found there. "We can't accept charity, missus."

A questioning rustle whispered through the
group, but several nodded in agreement as John
tried to return the money.

"No, you need it. I don't." Backing away and stuffing her hands in her pockets, Corrie shook her head.
"Please, buy some food for your kids."

Big John surveyed his family and friends with a
gentle expression, then held out the money again.
"We don't want charity, missus. If you got some work,
we'd be most grateful. But this . . ."

His voice trailed off, and Corrie realized she had
insulted them. *So fix it, Webb. But how?*

One, she had to put them on equal footing, getting rid of that "missus" and "ma'am." Two, she had
to discover a way for them to keep her money and
also their pride. Digging the toe of her boot into the
loamy soil, she searched her mind for inspiration.
Finally, her gaze lit on a small kettle at the edge of
the campfire. *That's it.*

A smile rose from deep within, and she beamed
up at Big John. "Then let's call it a loan."

"A loan, missus?"

"A loan, sir. And my name's Corrie Webb, not missus." She stuck out her hand and, folding his fingers
over the money, gave his hand a shake. Turning to
his wife, she said, "And not ma'am either. Just Corrie."

The woman appeared puzzled but hopeful. "What
do you mean about a loan, m—Corrie?"

"What sorta loan?" someone else asked.

"What we gotta do for this here loan?" another one called from the back.

"You don' look like no bank," yet another joked.

"I'm not." Until she'd seen the kettle, Corrie hadn't realized what she planned to do if Payne fired her. Now she knew. And she wouldn't wait to be fired.

She scrubbed her hands together. "I'm a chef and I'm going to open a restaurant in Hope Springs soon. I'll hire you, and you can pay off the loan from your wages. Whoever made that wonderful smelling stew can be my assistant chef, and I'll need kitchen and serving help and . . ."

Her smile stuttered a bit, and she caught Big John studying her. Plans were cheap—opening a restaurant took money.

"That sounds mighty nice, but this's all you got, ain't it?" He held out his hand with the money in it.

"Yes, but—"

"Jus' like uppity folks to get us hopin'," a young woman said, setting a toddler on her hip with a frown.

"Now you be quiet there, child," Big John ordered. "Corrie's at least tryin' to be a help."

His wife walked up to Corrie and stared into her eyes. It took all Corrie's resolve to face the scrutiny. She jumped when the woman lifted Corrie's hands and turned them back and forth, running her long, slender fingers over the calluses on Corrie's palms and sturdier fingers.

Finally, the woman nodded. "These are working hands. And she has honest eyes. *I* think she means what she says."

Tension, palpable but a minute ago, faded, replaced with tentative optimism. Those who had held themselves aloof at the edge of the crowd shared a smile; then Corrie found herself in what amounted to a group hug.

Her nerves twanged like telephone wires in a hurricane as hands patted her shoulders and back. Even as she extricated herself, a twinge of regret wound through her.

"Well," she said, tugging at her gloves, "I better be going."

Big John blocked her path. "You best be takin' this." He handed her half the money. "The rest will feed us good 'nuf. Jus' you open that restaurant soon, y'hear."

She opened her mouth to refuse the money, then saw quiet dignity in his eyes. He was right. Taking the cash, she said, "I will. And you'll be the first one I hire." With a lighter step than she'd had when she entered the clearing, she departed, wondering what Paul LaDue would think of her opening a restaurant.

In her mind came the slow, bayou-tinged drawl, "Go for it, *cher.*"

Jess stamped along the sidewalk, head down and collar up against the cold, but paused at a flicker of surreptitious movement down an alley. He squinted into the shadows, but whatever—whoever—had been there was gone.

He muttered in a breath that frosted out white, "Blast those boys. Why can't they break windows on a day when I'm not like to freeze to death?"

Reaching the Morris Mercantile Building, Jess found only broken glass and bricks. From the accuracy of the breakage, he had an idea who to blame.

But—he glanced up the street—that could keep.

The sun, in the form of Corrie Webb, had appeared, strolling down the street and gazing into shop windows. He hadn't realized how unflattering her waitress uniform was until now—her deep green suit fitted her like a glove and sparked red fire in her hair above which a frivolous fluff of a hat perched at a coquettish angle. The cold branded a golden blush on her cheeks.

All in all, a delectable creature.

As if aware of his scrutiny, she glanced around. The smile that lit her face when she recognized him sped the chill from his bones and nearly had him loosening his necktie as heat raced through him.

"Hi, Chief," she called as she drew closer and waved a brown paper parcel.

"Good morning." He doffed his bowler. "Spending all your funds on fripperies?"

"Hardly," she said with a grin. "But I couldn't resist this outfit over at the secondhand store. It was a bargain. And look"—she twirled around, laughing at him over her shoulder—"no train."

Her throaty chuckle had him wiping sweat from his brow. When she lifted one gloved hand and brushed his hair, tossed by the wind, to one side, he stifled a groan.

The little brown duck was indeed making him itch like nettles under his skin. But somehow she was no longer a plain little duck. The woman he'd waltzed with was back. She walked with an unconscious grace and glowed with health, her freckles adding to her beauty. It was all that—and something more, something within her—that had drawn him day in and day out to the Chesterfield.

"Something wrong, Chief?" she asked, and he realized he had been staring.

"No, nothing's wrong." Not if he didn't count his body's immediate, throbbing response to her touch. He dragged in a breath and tried to think of something besides the sparkle in her eyes and the pulse beating at the top edge of her collar. The skin there was paler, softer, and begged to be tasted.

At that thought, he groaned aloud. Quickly, he covered it with a cough. *Get control of yourself,* he admonished himself, wondering at his response to this woman. One would think he was barely out of short pants, to demonstrate such lack of control.

Fortunately, Corrie merely shot him another grin and peered into the windows of the closed shop. "What used to be here?" she asked as she scrubbed a hand over the dusty glass.

Blessing his coat for covering his blatant physical reaction, Jess replied, "The bakery, but they moved when they purchased their own place a couple of streets over. Been vacant since then."

Her lips opened and her exhalation fogged the glass. "Just the ticket."

With difficulty, he focused on her words. "What do you mean?"

Gripping his arm in a surprisingly strong grasp, she escorted him across the street, then stood gazing at the empty storefront and up and down the street. After a few minutes, she turned that same assessing gaze on him.

His ardor cooled a bit under that stare. But it revived as she slid her hand into the crook of his elbow and asked, "Where can we get a cup of coffee?"

"Coffee?" It occurred to him that his brain had gone lacking, and he shook himself fully awake.

"Is there a café or some place we can get a cup around here?" She started off down the street, clearly unfamiliar with Hope Springs.

Belatedly, he recalled thinking she was a strong-willed woman, and he disliked strong-willed women. He hauled her around and headed for Mrs. War-shoski's—her coffee was always hot and strong and could be counted on to keep him dead sober.

Something he needed in Corrie's intoxicating vicinity.

They had traversed a couple of blocks when he asked, "What's all this about? What's so special about the old bakery?"

From the corner of her eye, she slanted a dubious look up at him. "I'd rather wait—" She jerked to a halt and yelled, "Look out!"

Years spent on the battlefield made him look, not at her, but in the direction *she* was looking. Those same years kept his gun in its holster even as he slung Corrie to safety in a doorway. His Uncle Pat was the gunslinger, not him.

Only a moment passed as Jess sized up the situation. The bank's massive oak door was still closing and the two bank robbers were backing away from it when, voice low and hard and not three feet behind them, he said, "That's far enough, boys."

They whirled as one, guns at the ready. Jess studied their faces above the handkerchiefs covering their mouths and noses. Not anyone he recognized. A familiar tingle of danger heightened his senses—the men's breathing came too fast, too jerky for them to be hardened criminals, and sweat beaded their faces despite the cold.

Hands out to each side, he observed, "First time for you fellows?"

The taller one gave a start and shot a nervous glance at his companion; then he looked back at Jess. His gun trembled. "W-what makes you think that?"

So he was right—raw, scared newcomers to crime. The tall man's gun shook a little more, and Jess decided he had better bring this to a close before someone got hurt accidentally.

With a deliberate movement, he tipped his hat back on his head. "Well, anyone but a greenhorn knows to steer clear of *my* town. I don't tolerate robbing banks . . . or anything else nefarious, for that matter."

"And who the hell are you?" the shorter of the two asked in a loud voice.

"You mean you don't know who I am?" Jess pretended to act shocked.

The guns wavered a little more, and the men were beginning to scan the area for an escape route. In his peripheral vision, Jess noted Corrie peering out from her shelter, her freckles in stark contrast to her white face.

"You ever heard of Billy the Kid?" He waited for their nods—everyone from one side of the United States to the other had heard of that infamous outlaw. "How about Pat Garrett, the lawman who killed him?"

Again they nodded.

Jess brushed a speck of lint from his lapel. "My name's Jess Garrett. I should warn you, my Uncle Pat taught me to shoot."

"Ohmygawd," the taller man intoned. "I heard tell of the Garrett clan." His gun drooped toward the ground as he turned to the other man. "They's

all sharpshooters. Kill a man at fifty paces with one
shot soon as look at 'im."

Jess waited for the moment when the shorter one
switched his gaze to the taller one. Seconds ticked
by. A minute. Every muscle twitched, ready to react,
whatever they did.

Finally, the shorter one's gun shifted as he looked
toward the other.

Jess lunged for the pair, catching their necks with
his arms and banging their heads together with a
satisfying clunk. They sagged to the ground, and he
stepped back, drawing a pair of handcuffs from his
pocket. He rolled the first one over and snapped the
cuffs closed.

The rustle of skirts, a muffled curse, and a gasp
sent him into a dive to the side, scrabbling to gain
his footing even as he landed. He rolled onto his
hands and toes, coiled to lunge . . . and subsided
onto one knee.

Corrie stood over the other robber, who was curled
around himself, cradling his privates with both
hands. She beamed at Jess. "He was reaching for his
gun. So I kicked him."

Getting to his feet and forcing a calm he didn't
feel, Jess studied the man. "You did indeed, my dear.
You did indeed."

Any other woman of his acquaintance would've
fainted—or at best cowered in the doorway. Corrinne Webb stepped up and kicked the guy where it
did the most good.

Then she smiled at him.

"Oooh, my nuts is broke," the man complained
in a tight, high voice. "The damned bitch broke my
nuts."

None too gently, Jess handcuffed him, then rolled

him over onto his back. Standing, Jess placed the heel of his boot on the man's windpipe, lightly, but firmly enough to get the man's attention.

When he was sure he had it, Jess told him, "More than your nuts'll be broken if you call this young lady any more names. Got it?" He exerted another pound of pressure.

The man's eyes popped wide and he struggled to breathe.

"Got it?" Jess repeated, teeth clenched.

"Got it," the man rasped, then wheezed thankfully when the boot lifted from his throat.

Jess hauled the bank robbers to their feet just as his deputy arrived at a run. Turning them over to the deputy and several of the bank employees who volunteered to help, Jess scraped a hand through his hair and buffed a smear of dirt off his bowler's brim. With deep breaths, he fought the familiar tension that gripped his gut.

He'd almost drawn his gun. In fear of Corrie's life, he had—in the split seconds while he'd been scrambling from the line of fire—almost drawn his gun on another person for the first time in seven years. If he *had* drawn his pistol, he didn't doubt the bank robber would now be dead. Nausea rose, bitter in his throat. Not since that last battle, that last massacre . . .

Jess wrenched his mind from the memories. He refused to remember that day.

"Are you okay?" From her tone, Corrie was as shaken as he.

He couldn't let her know how scared he had been—not for himself, but for her—and judging by the tremors that shook her, she needed comforting.

He caught both her hands in his and yanked her into his embrace.

Only then did her composure break, and she trembled like an aspen leaf. Tears formed in her eyes and she struggled to blink them away. "You could've been killed," she whispered.

So could you, sweeting. So could you.

Muttering a curse on the robbers' heads, Jess tucked her head under his chin and held her tight as he rubbed her back. "Shh, it's all right, sweeting. I'm all right."

Jess caught the disapproving glare of one of the town nosies and returned it with interest. The biddy huffed off and others took the hint, giving Jess and Corrie their privacy. The wind whipped around them, cutting like knives through Jess's coat, and he hugged Corrie closer to his warmth.

At last, she let out a shuddering breath and lifted her head. Trying to smile, she said, "Thank you."

A fist of desire belted him in the gut. Her lashes were spiky from tears and her lips swollen with crying. Even so, she had not only warned him of danger but had probably saved his life. Then his plucky little duck resurrected the sunshine with her smile.

Jess thought he'd never breathe again if he didn't kiss her. Now.

Her pupils dilated so only a rim of gold-flecked brown remained as he dipped his head and laid his lips against hers. After that his own eyes closed, and Jess concentrated on the intoxicating taste of her, the heat of her. He'd never kissed lips so hot, so soft, so sensuous before.

He rimmed her lips with his tongue and was undone when she opened to him, drawing him in, stroking his tongue with hers. She clutched at his coat as if unable to support herself, and Jess tightened his hold. Even through his coat and hers, he felt the thunder of her heart.

Or was it his?

The world went away. No horses passed in the street, no pedestrians strolled by them. No winter wind whistled around them and no leaves rustled along the sidewalk. Silence enveloped them like a fog, muffling reality.

All that existed were her lips and his, her breath and his, her body pressed against his, almost one.

He was hard. And ready. And from the soft, eager moans issuing from her throat, Corrie was ready as well. He left her lips to trail kisses down to that erotic pulse point above her collar. She arched toward him and fisted one hand in his hair.

"Sweeting," he murmured against that pulsating, hot skin. "Oh, sweet Corrie."

"Oh, my," came the awed British voice of reason.

SEVEN

Uh-oh. Corrie's eyes flew open. Still in lip lock with the lawman, she turned her eyes to meet Sparrow's astonished gaze. *Busted.*

The Englishwoman stood, slack-jawed, in the middle of the sidewalk. From her hat, a long, slender feather extended skyward, trembling with her obvious indignation. Her jaw closed with a snap. "Corrinne! Mr. Garrett!"

Jess broke the kiss and lifted his head, sending a tracing of loss through Corrie. As if nothing out of the ordinary had happened, he tucked one of her hands into the crook of his elbow, then tipped his hat. "Good day, Miss Sparrow."

As he drew Corrie past Sparrow and down the street, she could have sworn the proper head housekeeper's indignation changed to a grin.

Two blocks down, Jess turned into an alley. "Did you see her face?" He collapsed into rollicking guffaws. "Priceless. I—we—actually surprised her."

Corrie stared at him, uncertain whether to hit him or laugh along with him. Sparrow, at least, had seemed genuinely shocked, and Corrie had to admit that everything she knew of Victorian times said she'd been completely beyond the bounds of proper behavior with that kiss. That kiss . . .

A sigh rose within her. Oh, yes, that kiss. She wasn't sure why he'd done it, but she couldn't deny she was happy he had. She could still taste Jess on her lips, feel his restrained power, his tenderness. His heat. And while it had pretty much knocked the terror of Jess facing down two armed robbers from her mind, it hadn't knocked out the sense of sheer stupidity he'd displayed.

Macho twit.

He was still chuckling when she pressed both hands against his shoulders, pinning him against the building and glaring at him. Laughing blue eyes stared back at her and one quizzical dark eyebrow rose.

"Don't give me that innocent what-did-I-do look."

"Now what's got you so upset?" His dimples flashed beside that wayward mouth.

Before she could control herself, she fixated on his mouth, those mobile, seductive lips, and her pulse kicked up. His grin widened and she had to remind herself, *Don't think about his mouth.*

She gave him a shove and said, "You know perfectly well what's got me so upset. Why in hell did you take those two on by yourself? And you had—what's it called?—the drop on them. Why didn't you use your damned gun? What sort of lawman doesn't use his gun?"

His expression sobered and sorrow flickered behind his eyes, sharp and painful. She knew that expression, saw it in her own mirror more than she cared to admit. Because she was familiar with it, she also knew when Jess shut the sorrow away.

The pang it gave her—for him not to share the reason for that look—surprised her and made her blunt. "What are you, a coward?" And hurtful.

Pride flared in his expression at that. His breath quickened. "Is that what you think? I'm a coward?"

"No, absolutely not. I'm sorry. That was a stupid thing to say," she replied and wished she had never made the accusation. "But I really don't understand—"

"Good. Leave the law enforcement to me." Suddenly, his expression shifted and mischief coaxed his dimples to reappear. He reached for her and spun her around, reversing their positions. Her back now rested against the wall and his arms bracketed her on either side. Heat rose in his eyes as his gaze skimmed over her, top to bottom and back again. "You stick to being beautiful."

"B-beautiful?" Her mind blanked except for the thought, *He thinks I'm beautiful.*

His gaze met hers, then dropped to her mouth. Corrie ran her tongue over her dry lips. Only when Jess, breathing harder, pressed her more firmly against the wall did she realize what she had done . . . and what his reaction was.

She brought her hands up to his lapels and felt his heart pounding beneath her palm. Lifting her gaze to his, she marveled at the power she held over him. This magnificent hunk desired *her*—the prickly chef.

Even more surprising, *she* desired *him.* Couldn't resist touching him. Had wanted to touch him since the first time they'd met. And wanted him to touch her.

As if he read her mind, Jess stroked the back of his hand along her throat, from ear to collar and back, tucking a stray tendril into her chignon. The caress sent her own heart racing to match his and set her breasts to throbbing, eager for his touch. Her nipples tightened and swelled against her corset, heightening her awareness of their ache.

"Beautiful," he whispered, his breath soft across her cheek. His eyes burned like a hot Texas sky as he dipped his head and feathered a kiss across her lips.

Her breath caught and fled.

"Beautiful and brave." Again, that imagined kiss.

"Jess, please . . ."

His chuckle rumbled through his chest. "Polite all of a sudden? You must want something." He kissed her left temple, his breath tickling the tendrils there. Her right temple received the same gentle treatment. "What is it you want?"

"I want . . ." If she had room to sway, she would have, but the wall held her steady.

"Tell me what you want, Corrie." His expression intent, Jess stared into her eyes.

"I want . . ." She dragged in a breath. "I want you."

Between one heartbeat and the next, he took her lips and plundered her mouth. His lips crushed hers, burned hers. They lit a fire within her that scorched a sweet ache along her nerves. No one had ever made her feel this way. Never. She wasn't a virgin, but Jess created sensations Corrie had only read about—had only imagined and never believed she would experience.

Somehow she found her arms around his neck, drawing him closer. She, who pushed people away, who avoided physical contact, wanted him closer. *Needed* him closer.

Jess left her lips to trail kisses along her jaw and down her throat to where her pulse throbbed above the damned high neckline. Corrie would gladly have ripped it open to allow him further access, but some noise made them both turn their heads toward the alleyway's opening.

One of the spinsters-on-the-make from the hotel—Miss Barrington . . . Carrington . . . Something-ton—gaped at them.

Jess muttered a curse under his breath and eased away from Corrie, placing himself between her and the indignant woman.

"Excuse *me,*" she said in a tone as frosty as the north wind.

"You *are* excused, madame," Jess replied in a voice that sent her scurrying away.

By the time he turned around, Corrie had forced herself to think rationally. With rational thought came dread. It was only a matter of time before the Major heard about this.

"Corrie . . . sweeting," Jess began, taking her hand in both of his.

His lips were swollen from their kiss, and Corrie fastened her gaze on his shirtfront to push away the memory of it. Was it only a short half hour ago that she had planned to talk him into backing her restaurant scheme? True, she had been attracted to him during his forays to the Chesterfield. But today they had acted on that attraction, and seeking his assistance after kissing him reeked of . . . payment.

Revulsion made her pull her hand from his grip. She couldn't ask him for help. Not now. Not when it would look . . .

She stepped back. "I have to go."

"Corrie—"

"No." Fighting the urge to return to the solace of his embrace, she took another step back and raised her hands to ward him off. "I have to go. I can't—I need—"

"You have nothing to be ashamed of." Jess swallowed. "It was my fault. I should never have—"

"Ashamed?" Corrie gave a brittle laugh. Brittle like her heart. "Ashamed? Lord, Jess, I'm not ashamed."

"Good, then—"

"But—" She bit off her near admission of how much she had wanted him to kiss her. "But I have to get back to the hotel."

"I'll escort you." He settled his bowler tighter onto his head and offered his elbow and a sexy grin.

Oh, no. He's being sweet again. Please don't be sweet.

"No, thanks," she answered with a resolution she hadn't known she possessed. As she passed him, Corrie could have sworn the only thing keeping her upright was that damned corset.

"Corrie—" His voice was tight. And wounded.

Without turning around, she said, "Not now, Jess. Not . . . now. I have to go." At a pace that would've done a power walker proud, she retraced their route, brushing past a man who gave her an intense look.

Reaching the square, she hurried across it but came to an abrupt halt as her gaze encountered the white clapboard church with its steeple shrouded in fog. Through the open door, candles flickered at the altar.

Bile rose in her throat. Roaring thundered in her ears. A memory tried to surface, soaking her in sweat. Convulsively, she swallowed and gulped for air. Almost, she could sense the heat. Almost, she could taste the fear. Almost, she could feel the hands. . . .

"No!" she cried and tore across the remainder of the square at a dead run. Figures flashed past her as she sprinted out of Hope Springs and into the

woods. Leaves and twigs, dry and sharp awaiting
spring's softening, slashed her face and throat. On
up the hill she ran, away from Hope Springs. Away
from the threat of memories.

Only when the stitch in her side robbed her of all
breath did she stop. Then she sank beside a sturdy
grandfather oak and lost her breakfast.

Jess stormed past the bank robbers in the jail cells,
slammed his office door behind him, and jerked to
a halt. "Don't you ever stay in your *own* office?" he
growled at his brother. If ever he wanted to be alone,
this was the time.

Teddy eyed him over the rim of his cup. "What's
put a burr up your butt?"

"For a lawyer, you have an amazing grasp of the
English language." Jess ripped off his overcoat and
tossed it at the hat rack. It missed and crumpled to
the floor in a heap. He dropped into his chair and
began slamming drawers open, then shutting them
just as sharply.

Teddy ignored the jibe and rested the cup on his
round stomach. He studied the mound of fine English tweed in the corner. "Well, something has you
madder'n a wet hen."

"That would be 'madder than a wet rooster' in my
case, you lack-wit. At least get the gender right."

"Ah, female trouble."

The smug tone stung. Jess knew he had a damned
fine poker face when he wanted, and his brother's
easy identification of the problem grated. He
snapped, "What would you know of female trouble?
Your betrothed is meek as a mouse."

Coffee splashed from Teddy's cup as he shot upright and wheezed in horror, "Don't tell me Ma's arrived?"

"No." Only that could make Jess's day worse. Her delayed arrival had been a daily reprieve.

Teddy gave a gusty sigh of relief. "Then what's wrong, baby brother? The fair Gretchen?"

Jess had to pause a moment to even remember the young woman's face. Then an impression of blond hair and an insipid personality arose in his mind and he shook his head.

"The waitress, then."

That snared his attention. Jess shot a sideways glance at his brother. "What do you know about a waitress? Who's been gossiping?"

"So it's true. You're smitten with a waitress up at the hotel." A smug smile spread across Teddy's face. "Ma will—"

"Ma will know nothing about her . . . for now." Jess stopped in midthought. Where had the concept come from, of a future time when his mother and Corrie might meet?

"If she knows what's good for her, she'll run the other way when Ma arrives. I know *I* would if I wasn't related."

Jess cringed at the thought of the two headstrong women clashing; then a reluctant grin tugged at his mouth as he envisioned Corrie giving as good as she got. Still, she was a vexing dichotomy—strong and outspoken, yet vulnerable and troubled. And he'd be damned if he'd let his mother wound his little brown duck.

Teddy rose and retrieved his coat and hat from the rack and silently hung up Jess's coat before hugging his brother farewell. After he left, Jess sank his head in his hands and pondered his morning.

If he denied wanting to kiss Corrie, he would be lying. Too many mornings he awoke hard and ready with dreams of her fresh in his mind. Afterward, he vowed to forego seeing her.

But each day found him at the Chesterfield on some pretense or other.

Self-honesty obliged him to admit that he enjoyed simply watching her work, but that kissing her had rocked him to his foundation. Moreover, the lightest touch made him ache to possess her, no matter her outspokenness. No matter the pain she hid behind the facade of strength.

No matter the secret that lurked in her troubled eyes.

Exasperated that he actually *cared* about Corrinne Webb's troubled eyes, Jess slammed the last drawer shut and joined his deputy in the other room. The bank robbers would be easier to handle—and much easier to comprehend—than his growing concern for the little brown duck.

The hands reached for her, their nails grimed, with ragged calluses that scratched her as the hands ripped at her. From a throat raw with silent screams, she croaked, "No! No!"

As the hands drew closer and almost enveloped her, her resistance flagged and she whimpered, "Mama, help me. Mama?"

The hands grabbed for her. She flailed at them but knew the futility of resistance. They were stronger. Soon they would—

"Wake up, Corrie. Wake up, lass." The Irish lilt jarred her a little.

The hands dragged at her, pulling her down.

"Corrie lass, wake up now. It's a dream." Gentle, warm arms encircled her, rocked her like a baby.

Her eyes flew open. No hands. No grimy fingers. No—She shied from the thought and raised her head to see Bridget's worried face.

"There, lass. You're back now. You're safe," Bridget crooned as she pushed Corrie's sweat-dampened hair from her face.

Heart still pounding and breath rasping, Corrie scooted back and wiped at the tears on her cheeks. She hadn't had the nightmare in years. To have it witnessed mortified her. Her foster parents had learned to ignore it when it happened. And she had always denied any memory of specifics.

She tried to speak but could only cough. Bridget went for a glass of cool water from the bathroom down the hall, and Corrie scrubbed her face with the sheet, removing the final residue of moisture. By the time her friend returned, Corrie had regained her composure.

"I'm fine, Bidgie. Thank you." Corrie let the water trickle down her parched throat. "Go back to sleep. I'm sorry I woke you. It's nothing. Really."

The young Irishwoman solemnly studied her. "You were keening as if the devil himself was after you. I don't call that nothing."

"It was just a dream."

"A nightmare, more like."

"Whatever you want to call it, it's over." Corrie forced a smile. Unfortunately, it wobbled a bit.

Bridget muttered under her breath as she made up the fire and tucked Corrie's blankets around her, but she didn't pursue the matter. After Bridget had crawled into her own bed and was sleeping, Corrie lay, staring at the ceiling, and considered what could have triggered the nightmare's return.

Her nerves continued to jump and twitch as she turned over in her mind the events of the last few days, refusing to even touch on her past. That was forbidden territory.

Careful review led her to focus on Jess and the kisses they'd shared as the problem. No, that wasn't right. The Major's *reaction* to Corrie kissing the police chief in the middle of Hope Springs would be the problem—that and how she was going to open a restaurant when she had ruined her chances for financial backing by kissing Jess. Who else would give her a loan? A bank? Yeah, right.

He had been her only hope. If she hadn't kissed him, she could have asked him for the money to back her.

Although if she *hadn't* kissed him, she probably would have ended up in the funny farm from frustrated desire. She chuckled at that. *Overdramatizing, aren't we, Webb?*

With the memory of Jess as he'd looked as he gazed down at her, just before he'd kissed her the last time, filling her thoughts, Corrie drifted to sleep, a smile on her lips.

The next morning, smiling was the last thing Corrie had on her mind.

The gaslights, dim in the early morning dark, flickered in the drafts from a late winter storm. The glass panes rattled with the wind, and smoke billowed from the fireplace as gusts shrieked down the chimneys. Cold seeped into the silent employees as Major Payne blasted the unfortunates who didn't meet his standards. And his standards were higher than usual this morning.

He circled Corrie, giving little snorts every so often, and quivered in frank disgust. Even his mustache vibrated like a guitar string at a Megadeth concert.

Corrie set her jaw. This would not be pretty. She could almost feel curls springing from her chignon as he made another circuit behind her.

"Frankly, Miss Webb, I don't know where to begin."

His voice made her jump. The certainty that he had heard about her kissing Jess in the middle of the street and was going to fire her anyway loosened her tongue. "Oh, just start at the top."

"I beg your pardon?" Now his voice quivered as well as his mustache, and his face flushed scarlet.

Rather than meet his gaze, Corrie focused on the waxed curlicue. "I said you should start at the top."

The mustache vibrations reached riff proportions.

A collective gasp down the row of employees told her that she'd overstepped her bounds. *Now you've done it.* She closed her eyes, reminded herself that she needed this job, and added, "Sir."

The scent of bay rum filled her nostrils and she snapped open her eyes. Narrowed brown eyes glared at her from two inches away.

"I will start wherever I please," the Major said through gritted teeth.

Her stomach made a foray up her esophagus, but she swallowed it down. Visions of homelessness played across her mind. She wet her lips. "Sorry."

"You had best be, miss." Somehow *miss* in that tone sounded like a curse. He took a step back and glowered at the others. "Dismissed."

Corrie sidled away, then stiffened in place at the Major's growled, "Stay."

Somehow it no longer seemed worth the strain. Maybe Big John and his family would take her in. Under her breath, she muttered, "I'm not a dog, you asshole."

"*What* did you say?"

On second thought . . . Within the folds of her skirt, she crossed her fingers. Maybe he really hadn't heard her. She sneaked a glance at him. "Nothing."

One of his eyebrows lifted so high, it threatened to leave his forehead.

She gulped. "Sir," she said in a meek tone.

He strode to a window and gazed out for a few minutes while she did her best not to fidget. Major Payne detested fidgeting. He'd told her so . . . in excruciating detail . . . repeatedly.

The other employees scurried away before becoming contaminated by proximity to her, and Corrie couldn't blame them. She had never seen the Major this bent out of shape before, but she figured it could have only one origin.

The kiss.

Before she could reminisce, a cold draft swept the room and goose-bumped every inch of her—even under her corset. Then Major Payne turned his flinty glare on her and the goose bumps froze. And so did she.

His approach reminded her of a rattlesnake closing in on a field mouse, hypnotizing the rodent before the final strike.

Just call me Mickey.

A nervous giggle escaped her and was quickly subdued when the Major's glare sharpened.

"You find something amusing, Miss Webb?"

"No, sir." A U.S. Marine couldn't have given a more crisp response.

"But you *have* found a way to amuse yourself in town, haven't you?"

She could almost hear the rattlers shaking. *M-I-C,* she sang in her head.

"Did you think no one would hear of your behavior?" Major Payne paced back and forth in front of her.

"No, sir." Less crisp this time. *K-E-Y* . . .

"Scandalous! Embracing in public. On Main Street!" He seemed unable to form a complete sentence. But that changed. "There can be no excuse for such conduct, Miss Webb."

"I'm sure *you* don't think there is." Corrie's heart pounded in her head, but the song stayed with her.

He threw up his arm and pointed an irate finger, barely missing her nose. "You're fired."

M-O-U-S-EEE.

EIGHT

Her stomach did a three-sixty, then sank to her toes. For all her flippancy, Corrie was aware that she was not only out of a job but homeless as well. Where was she going to live? She considered swallowing any pride still hanging around and groveling to the Major.

One glance at his ramrod-straight, retreating back killed any hope of a rehire. Her behavior in Hope Springs had trashed any chance there.

Way to go, Webb.

Moisture gathered in her eyes. Dang it all, she'd become a freaking leaky hose. Back in her own time, she never cried. Never.

Corrie gave herself a shake and straightened her shoulders. She'd been in bad situations before and survived just fine. *That's what I do. Survive.*

All by myself.

Her chin trembled, and she firmed it immediately. With her head high, she made for her room past the sidelong glances and hushed condolences of her fellow—former—coworkers. Her composure took another hit as she realized how much she would miss this group, how much they had become a part of her.

See what comes of letting one person in, Webb? See? It

*started with Bidgie. Now you have all sorts of people wea-
seling their way in. Damn.*

She stomped up the stairs to her room and slammed
the door shut. Otherwise, once word spread of her
termination, too many folks would stop by to console
her. While she changed out of her uniform and into
her green suit, she confronted the complications that
came with letting people become important to her.
Old Major Pain had done her a favor. Yeah, a favor.
Somehow during the last weeks she'd allowed her protective wall to be chinked at by various folks—Bidgie,
Rupert, even Sparrow. Well, she would have to shore
up that wall, and being away from the Chesterfield
would give her the chance to do so.

Then there was Jess.

He hadn't chinked at her wall. He'd rolled right
over it like it never existed. He was definitely a com-
plication, but one she would simply have to manage
until she returned to her own time at the solstice in
June.

Corrie finished buttoning her jacket and shoved
her meager belongings into a pillowcase. As she
turned toward the door, Sparrow opened it.

"My dear, I just heard." Her usually English-rose
complexion was pale and drawn, and she clasped her
hands together until her knuckles blanched white.

Corrie forced a nonchalant shrug. "Well, we both
knew it was only a matter of time before I rubbed
the Major the wrong way one too many times."

"But this is terrible!"

"I'll get over it."

"You *can't* be discharged."

"Tell that to Major Payne."

"You don't understand. This could botch all my

pl—" Sparrow broke off with a gasp and covered her lips with shaking fingers.

Eyeing her sharply, Corrie drew her down onto the bed. "I get the feeling this"—she pointed at Sparrow's tightly clasped hands—"has more to do with you than me. What I don't understand is why."

Sparrow tried to disentangle her fingers but quickly reclasped them in her lap.

"Come on, Sparrow. Give."

With a sigh, the Englishwoman said, "It's complicated."

"So's truffle sauce."

Sparrow recovered enough to raise one eyebrow in admonishment.

"I'm not leaving until you tell me what's upsetting you so much. It's not just my being fired." Corrie's patience wore thinner as Sparrow chewed her lip. "Dang it, you're hiding something."

"I am not," Sparrow began, then sagged in defeat. "No, that's not true."

Corrie popped the top button of her high collar and settled back against the headboard. She motioned for her to continue.

"I *am* upset that you've been sacked." Sparrow relaxed a little and rested one shoulder against the footboard. "But I'm also upset because I haven't told you everything about . . . returning to your time."

That seized Corrie's attention. She sat up and fixed her gaze on Sparrow's face. "What exactly haven't you told me?"

Sparrow shifted her eyes away. "What do you remember about being transported here?"

"Not much." Corrie closed her eyes and tried to visualize the old, dilapidated Chesterfield. "A falling sensation and roaring, but quiet, too. And the badge." A strong memory of the old Marshal Dillon badge with one point broken off rose in Corrie's mind. She could almost feel the rusted remaining points where they'd scraped against her palm.

"Yes, well, the badge belongs—belonged—drat!" Sparrow sprang up and paced the small room. "This confusion of past and future and present will have me seeking out Drake Manton, the mesmerist, to treat my deranged mind."

Corrie snorted. "You think *you* got it bad? How about me? I have all that *plus* living in the past. You try that for a while and see how deranged you get."

Pausing with her hands clasped on the iron footboard, Esmeralda Sparrow studied her. Corrie's head, normally held so high and proud, drooped, and her shoulders slumped as if in defeat. *What have I done?* she thought. She released her hold on the cold iron, then rushed to Corrie and hugged her. "My dear, I do apologize. My difficulties are nothing next to yours. It is simply the sense of responsibility I feel. . . ."

In her grasp, she felt Corrie shake her head and stiffen slightly. The withdrawal was less than previous encounters, and Esme smiled to herself. She'd be willing to bet a month's wages that Corrie didn't withdraw at all from Jess Garrett's embrace.

Easing back so she could watch the time traveler's expression, Esme said, "Allow me to be the judge of the scope of my responsibility. And allow me to tell you the scope of yours."

Corrie's brown eyes widened. "What do you mean?"

"You, Corrinne Webb, have a responsibility in this time. One you must complete."

"I can't go back without doing something? What is it?" A note of fear crept into Corrie's voice.

Odd, that phrasing of "go back" instead of "go home." Esme would have thought only of going home.

"Sparrow?"

Corrie's voice recalled Esme to her current predicament—how much to tell her. "It isn't that you *must* perform a particular deed, but that you *can* perform it, and therefore save someone from danger."

"I'm a chef, not a superhero," Corrie quipped.

"A super hero," Esme repeated slowly, at a loss as to the added meaning she was certain existed.

"Never mind," Corrie said, then frowned. "Let me get this straight. I don't *have* to do this in order to go back."

Esme repressed a shudder at the thought of what it would mean if Corrie shirked her duty. "Correct."

"But I can do it and save someone from being hurt."

"Correct."

"Okay, that's clear enough." Corrie glanced up. "Who am I supposed to save?"

Esme knew that if she revealed the whole situation-to-come, Corrie would either run the other way or would tell the victim-to-be, which could really throw a spanner in the works. *Oh, Lord. Listen to me. I'm* thinking *in hyphenation*.

"Sparrow?"

"Oh." Esme straightened. "I'm certain that will become clear. Later."

"You have to be kidding. You want me to wait around until I just stumble across this sheriff's badge? Get real."

"I promise it will show up without exertion on your part."

"Well . . . okay." Corrie met Esme's gaze with a serious expression. "Just understand that I won't let this get in the way of going back to my own time."

"Understood." Esme gave herself a shake and rubbed her hands together. "Now, let me see what I can do to help you."

"The Major's not going to hire me back."

"No," Esme agreed. Major Payne's fury over Corrie's behavior brooked no argument or quarter. So what to do with her? She looked at the girl. "Do you perhaps have any ideas as to what else you might do in Hope Springs? I'll assist you any way I can."

The laugh Corrie gave was bitter. "My assumption is that if the Major won't hire me because I kissed Jess, no one else will either."

"You are probably correct," Esme said. She'd called him Jess and their kiss was more than a friendly peck. That was a bit of all right. "So what shall you do?"

Corrie scowled for a second. Suddenly, she snapped her fingers and a big smile lit her face. "For a moment there I completely forgot."

"What is it? What shall you do?"

The smile turned a tad wicked, and Esme felt a tremor of disquiet. What was she planning?

"It's better if you don't know," Corrie said as she stood, tied on her hat, and picked up the pillowcase containing her few possessions. "Even if it *is* fitting."

Fitting?

Corrie opened the door and turned to glance back at Esme. "See you later."

Esme watched her stride down the hall and heard her clatter down the stairs in those odd, waffle-soled boots. Only when she heard the outer door slam shut did she shut the door to Bridget's room and proceed to her own. There she pondered Corrie's words and wondered what her protégée's plan might be.

Whatever it was, Esme had the uneasy feeling it would raise eyebrows.

Jess laid down the pistol he was cleaning and took a slug of his second cup of coffee. He needed it to stay awake. His nights had been disturbed enough by his army memories; now dreams of Corrinne Webb—much more pleasant, but disturbing nonetheless—made him restless.

"Damn," he muttered and picked up the pistol again.

" 'Tis a foul morning and fouler head I'm havin'," Jack O'Riley groaned from his bunk in the closest cell. "But I'm thinkin' ye're havin' one just as bad, boyo."

"Not so bad as you." Rising, Jess poured a cup of coffee, spooned in some sugar, and stirred it as he strolled to Jack's cell. "Here, this'll help, old man."

"Who're ye callin' old?" Jack protested as he shot to his feet. He grabbed his head and fell back on the bunk, then covered his face with the pillow. "Ow, me head."

The unlocked cell door opened easily with one nudge of Jess's foot, and he leaned against it as he held out Jack's cup with one hand while he drank his own down. "Drink this, O'Riley. It'll clear those whiskey fumes from your brain."

Jack pulled the pillow off his face long enough to ask, "Ye wouldn't be havin' a bit o' mother's milk around, would ye?"

"Not a drop. Wouldn't give it to you if I did. Whiskey's what put you here in the first place."

The pillow was returned to Jack's face. " 'Tis a hard man ye are, Jess Garrett."

"If I was a hard man, I'd have written you up in the record, and the *Hope Springs Times* would've published your arrest in the morning edition, where the whole town could see it." Jess placed the steaming cup on the floor by the door and returned to his desk, where he poured another cup before settling into his chair.

Grunts and muttered curses testified to Jack's efforts to reach the coffee. Jess snapped the paper open and pretended to read while he anticipated the usual complaint. He didn't have long to wait.

"What in the name of the Blessed Virgin did ye put in this swill ye're callin' coffee?"

"Sugar," Jess said, trying not to let his grin show in his voice. "It'll help your hangover."

"Hangover, is it? No Irishman gets a hangover, ye daft copper." Jack muttered a few more imprecations under his breath as he staggered across the room to plop into the chair across from Jess. "Jaysus, but the way ye dose this up, ye'd think I was a bluidy Englishman drinkin' tay."

"Sorry, O'Riley," Jess said and lowered his paper to reveal a contrite expression. Patently false, of course.

"Sorry, he says. Every time 'tis the same. Sugar in me coffee and an apology." In spite of his protests, Jack gulped down the coffee and stuck out his cup for a refill.

Silently, Jess swabbed out the gun barrel while Jack drank. The cup clunked a couple of times before the man was able to place it solidly on the desk.

"Ah, 'tis a bastard I am this mornin', Jess."

Jess directed his attention to the porter.

" 'S truth." Jack scraped a hand through his thin hair and scratched his head. "Here I sit, blitherin' about sugar in my coffee and ye've done me a fine turn."

"You forgot to mention calling me names."

"Oh, aye. Callin' ye names as well—the man who's saved me job."

Jess watched in fascinated silence as Jack contorted his face, ground his fists into his eyes, and yawned. Obviously, enough whiskey remained to numb Jack to the discomfort of pulled skin. Or maybe the hangover was worse.

"The Major'll can me if he finds out I've . . . indulged again. Not to mention the fit Bidgie will throw."

"They won't find out from me." Jess handed Jack his coat, tie, and hat. "If anyone sees you leaving the police station, tell them I asked you here to answer some questions about those bank robbers."

"Ye're a good man." Jack donned his coat and tie. "I must say, for a man who never draws his gun, ye spend an uncommon amount of time cleaning that thing."

"Habit, O'Riley." Jess gave a dismissive shrug.

"I'm thinkin' a certain colleen is becoming a habit." On that observation he departed, leaving Jess to wonder how many others were aware of his interest in Corrie.

And why *he* was interested in her.

Corrie paused in front of the former bakery and once again studied the space. It had a good exposure, and the sign painted on the front windows, even faded by age, was clearly visible from a block away. The inside looked spacious enough for an adequate number of tables, and what she could see of the kitchen looked good as well. There was even a small courtyard to one side with lots of trees lining it, perfect for outdoor seating when the weather improved.

Right now, the weather stank. Although she had been able to catch a ride on the train from the hotel, she was close to being soaked through, and her hat brim dripped cold rain onto her nose whenever she looked up. Catching sight of herself in the window, she thought she resembled nothing so much as a drowned rat. That thought diverted her from her wet clothes and the cold, and she grinned at her reflection.

Ever since she'd first started in the food service business as a dishwasher, she had harbored the dream of owning her own restaurant. Attending the Culinary Institute of America, then becoming a chef, had honed that dream, and now she could picture more than a generic restaurant.

Hers would be an intimate, inviting café serving only the freshest foods, exquisitely prepared. Not that nouvelle cuisine, with architectural shapes and tiny portions. No, she would serve satisfying portions of soul-pampering food in a not-too-big continental café where people lingered over glasses of wine and conversation. The café of her dreams.

Café of Dreams. That's what I'll call it.

Her grin widened. She would put all Paul LaDue's lessons to the test. She was about to make her dream come true.

All that remained was to convince Jess.

* * *

The station door banged open, followed by frigid wind and icy rain. Jess shoveled more coal into the stove and called over his shoulder, "Close the door."

Abruptly, the wind and rain were outside and silence filled the inside, broken only by the drip of water onto the floor. Lots of water.

He slammed the grate and dusted his hands together as he turned. Corrinne Webb stood in the middle of the station, water coursing off her hat and skirt. As he watched, she stuck out her lower lip and blew at the ribbon dripping onto her nose. No society lady would do such an inelegant thing.

But then, no lady of society—or otherwise, for that matter—had luscious lips that kept him awake or haunted his dreams. Jess felt himself harden and wondered what it was about this little brown duck of a girl that had him feeling like a randy adolescent instead of a grown man of sober occupation. Corrinne Webb went to his head like moonshine liquor and made him anything but sober.

She blinked at him, then flashed her brilliant smile. Lifting one hand, she waved. "Hi, Chief."

Then she sneezed, and Jess realized his little brown duck was near drowned.

"What in heaven's name brings you out on a day like this?" He clasped her hand and drew her close to the stove. Her fingers were like ice, but nevertheless they sent a surge of heat through him. Resolutely ignoring the heat, he tried to chafe her fingers, but she pulled her hand away.

She removed her hat and ruefully surveyed the damage. "A total loss, I'm afraid."

"Total," he said, taking in the ruined ribbons and droopy, shapeless brim.

"Maybe the suit can be saved. It's pretty sturdy wool," Corrie said, sluicing water from her skirts with her hands. She glanced up at him, raindrops dancing on her lashes. "What do you think?"

Beautiful.

"Chief?"

Jess forced his wayward mind back to the question. "Uh . . . the suit. Yes, it should be fine." Better than his brain would be if he didn't contain its meanderings. "But you should get out of those wet things as soon as possible."

As he helped her out of her jacket, he noticed the soggy pillowcase she had placed at her feet. A puddle was rapidly forming around it.

She caught his look and explained, "This is everything I own. And it's even wetter than what I have on. Not that I could be any wetter."

Why she carried all her belongings with her, he would find out in due time. For the moment, no gentleman would take advantage of a young woman in her condition, and Jess Garrett reminded himself that he'd been born and bred a gentleman.

Damn it.

He placed a teakettle on the stove to heat and rummaged in the storage cupboard for an extra cup and saucer. A cup of tea would warm her insides while he considered what to do with her outsides.

His manhood throbbed its idea and he sternly reprimanded himself. The girl had sought his help—that was what she would get.

That was *all* she would get.

She cleared her throat and squirmed in her chair. "You're probably wondering why I'm here."

Leaning against his desk, Jess crossed his feet at the ankles and nodded for her to continue.

She dropped her gaze to the fire, visible through the stove grate. "I—I've been fired."

"Fired." Miss Harrington's specter rose in his mind's eye. She had no need for that new invention, the telephone—she was much faster. His lips thinned as he bit off several scathing remarks. "Let me guess: Someone informed Major Payne of our . . . indiscretion . . . of yesterday."

"Got it in one, Chief."

Her words were odd and her pert tone surprised him, but that wasn't important. "What will you do?"

Chewing her lower lip, she rose and paced across the room before she answered. Something about the sidelong glances she shot him put him on alert.

Finally, she came to a halt in front of him. "It's not what *I'm* going to do. It's what *we're* going to do. Together."

"Together." Jess had some ideas along that line, but he doubted they were what she meant.

"Yeah. Partners."

"Partners," he repeated slowly. He was beginning to sound like a simpleton, but damned if he knew where she was heading with this talk of partnership.

"In a restaurant." In a rush, she added, "Where the bakery used to be. I'll be the chef. You'll be the money. I can live on the second floor. Big John and his family can work for me—us. It'll be . . ."—she took a breath—"perfect."

Only one explanation occurred to him. "The cold has muddled your brain."

"It has not. I've given this a lot of thought. Even before I was fired."

"Why would you even think about me as a partner?"

"Well, I don't have enough money to get started, and you seem to eat out a whole lot."

He couldn't deny that, but she still didn't make sense. "What about the bank?"

"That's where I was yesterday morning before I ran into you. Today, too." She shrugged, making an annoying squishing noise as she did so. "They turned me down. Rudely, too."

"I would have been surprised if they hadn't." In fact, he would have called Dr. Jones to examine the bank manager if he *had* given Corrie a loan. The man was adamant in his denunciation of women in the workplace, besides being a dyed-in-the-wool misogynist.

"So I'm asking you. At least you won't be rude."

"Why should I lend you anything?"

Corrie dropped her gaze to her strange boots. "Well, it was sorta your fault."

"Mine?"

"You were the one who kissed *me."*

Jess might have owned to a little guilt about her predicament, but now, he protested, "I seem to recall you kissing me back."

"I did not," she said, but the rosy blush that flushed her cheeks and ears said otherwise.

"Now we're sounding like my siblings when we were children." *But thank goodness you're not one of my sisters.*

"I never had any sibs." So wistful was the tone of her soft statement, he was uncertain whether she spoke to him or to herself.

Then her head snapped up and she plastered a smile on her face, ignoring the drop of rain on the

tip of her nose. "We were discussing why you should
be my partner." She rubbed a finger along the edge
of her cup. "It's because you have vision."

"What does my sight have to do with backing your
restaurant?"

"No, no. Not that type of vision. Entrepreneurial
vision." She took a sip of tea, then put the cup down
so she could wave her hands in sweeping arcs. "What
Hope Springs needs is a good, bistro-type café. Not
to disparage Mrs. Warshoski, but you can only eat
heavy Eastern European food so many times before
you get tired of it."

"The Poles in town would take exception to that."
Jess stifled a grin. She'd infected him with her enthusiasm, but he couldn't resist goading her.

"You know what I mean. Now *my* food"—she
tapped herself on her chest, and Jess had to remind
himself that he was a gentleman when he noted how
transparent the wet cloth had become—"is some of
the best in Dallas—a tough town on restaurants."
She paused, as if this was something monumental.

"Dallas? Where no one has the sense to build away
from the river, so it floods every spring? *That* Dallas?"
He'd ridden through parts of Texas and rested for
a couple of weeks with his troop at Fort Worth, but
Dallas was the last place he would visit.

"I suppose, but never mind. Just accept that I'm
good. Really good. My London broil with béarnaise
sauce was judged the best at—well, it was the best,
anyway. Take my word on it. My cooking will knock
the socks off this town. Chef Sashenka has nothing
I can't make better. And I was the youngest head
chef ever . . ." she faltered, "in Dallas."

Her bravado was amazing. Who would've thought

his little brown duck could be so passionate about cooking? So passionate when she kissed?

"So how about it? Will you back me?"

"I'm almost convinced, but I have to ask how you chose me. Besides the fact that you've seen me dine in the hotel restaurant nearly every day." Not everyone knew he came from a wealthy family, and frankly, he preferred to keep that fact as quiet as possible—the fewer husband-hunting debutantes thrown at him, the better.

"Oh, that was easy." Her grin convinced him of her veracity. "O'Riley told me you have money."

Jack, you ass. "And you believed a drunken Irishman?"

She laid one hand on his sleeve, and the heat jolted him again. "I believed your friend."

"But—"

"You were the one who kissed me. You were the one who got me fired."

Raising his hand in admission of the hit, he said, "All right, you win. I have enough cash to back this venture. But on one condition. No, two."

Wariness clouded her eyes, and he hurried to erase it. "One, you have to prepare some meals for me to taste before I ante up any money. Two, I'd like you to wait in my office while I ride over to Covington. Shouldn't be too late returning, but I agreed to meet the county sheriff there."

"Sounds fine to me, but I wanted to make an offer on that bakery property today so I would have somewhere to sleep tonight."

"You mean Major Payne kicked you out completely?" Jess and the Major weren't what was called friends, but he hadn't believed the man heartless.

"Let's just say I really, really pissed him off."

The mischievous glint in her eyes convinced Jess that he probably shouldn't inquire for details. She might give them, and he'd never look at the Major the same way again.

As quickly as he considered the housing options in town, he rejected every one. If he paid for Corrie's room or was seen escorting her to a hotel, her reputation would be even more tarnished than their kiss had made it. It would be beyond redemption and she would never be accepted in this town.

Only one choice remained—*if* he succeeded in sneaking her in and out unobserved.

"I have a third condition. You spend the night at my place." He was going to regret this.

NINE

By the time Jess returned that evening, Corrie could have told him exactly how many paces it was from anywhere to any anyplace else in the police station. Or how many bars made up the cell fronts. Or how many planks made up the floor. Or dozens of other bits of trivia . . . like his deputy's complete life history.

If Jess had asked. Which he hadn't.

All he did was walk into the place and growl at Cyril. "What are *you* doing here?"

Her relief took a nosedive. From Dopey to Grumpy—how had Snow White endured it?

The deputy took a huge breath—a *really* bad sign, she'd learned—and started in. "Well, it's like this. When I opened the door this afternoon, here sat this lady who said her name was Miss Corrinne Webb— she didn't say 'miss,' but I gather she's not married, not wearing a ring—and she was supposed to be here—which you hadn't told me, but she was awfully nice, so I let her stay—and then she said you had gone to Covington—which you *had* told me you were going to do but not when to expect you back—and that you would be back this evening—but not exactly when, and you really ought to let me know, sir, and not just today but whenever you go—"

Corrie shot to her feet and grabbed Jess by the arm. "Yeah, well, he's back now, Cyril, and I have to talk to him. Now." All but dragging Jess, she hurried him into his office and shut the door.

As she released him, she sagged against it and exhaled sharply. "Doesn't Deputy Dumber every shut up? Or at least give the short version occasionally?"

His dimples flashed and her nerves unwound a little. "You mean you think Cyril a tad discursive?"

"Discursive? Ha!" She crossed her arms and glared at him. "Try long-winded."

Jess held his hands to the stove. "You're right— Cyril could confuse Walt Whitman discoursing on Lincoln."

"You mean Walt Whitman the poet?" Lit classes had never been her strong suit, but the name rang a distant bell.

"Yes, that Walt Whitman." He glanced at her over his shoulder. "I heard him speak in Philadelphia. Have you had the pleasure? I wouldn't think Texas is on the usual tours."

"Nope, never had the chance." *By about a hundred years.*

His boots made a squishing sound as he shifted, and Corrie realized Jess was soaked. Not surprising, since rain had fallen intermittently all day. But he hadn't uttered a word of complaint.

"Hey, Chief, you need to get out of those wet clothes." She had merely meant it as an innocent observation, but the heat in Jess's eyes imbued it with a meaning she couldn't deny and triggered memories of her recent dreams.

Jess, naked and hot and ready. Her—oh, hell—her exactly the same.

Corrie's heart thudded against her corset stays.

She fought to maintain her sanity as his gaze rekindled more memories . . . of his kisses. Jess kissed better than he looked. Kissing him was better than her culinary masterpiece, halibut in puff pastry with three-wine sauce. And that had pretty near brought her to her knees with its exquisiteness.

No one had ever warned her that men—actually, one man in particular—could make her forget all the great sauces, all the great meals she had prepared. Could make her forget the best chocolate soufflé in the world.

If his kisses were that potent, what would making love with him be like?

A blush seared its way from her toes to her face, and she tore her gaze away. *He's your partner, Webb. Think of him as your partner. Like Paul.*

But Paul was gay. Jess blatantly was not.

She looked at him again and met that melting intensity. *Oh, no. Not gay. Not that Paul wouldn't appreciate him . . .*

Jess coughed and raked his hand through his hair. "It's getting late. We need to be going."

Going? Oh . . . to his house . . . to sleep. Corrie swallowed. As Sparrow said, "Oh, my."

She stifled the urge to tug at her corset—or was that tug *off* her corset?—and plopped her ruined hat on her head. Maybe the cold rain would cool the heat in her veins.

If she didn't steam off her clothes first.

As he scanned his neighbors' windows for possible witnesses, Jess unlocked the back door of his house and motioned Corrie inside. On a miserable night like this, he doubted anyone would be watching, but he hadn't spent all day worrying how to protect Corrie's reputation to risk it now.

They had departed the police station separately and met in the alley, where Corrie had kept to the shadows in silence. She broke that silence now with a heartfelt curse as she stood shivering in his mudroom, the pillowcase with her belongings streaming water onto the floor. Her pitiful hat provided no protection whatsoever, but merely directed moisture down her neck. She gazed around the room with eyes smudged by fatigue.

His little brown duck looked like nothing so much as a drowned rat.

"Here, let me carry that," he said, relieving her of the pillowcase. Even with the added weight of the rain, it amounted to a pitifully small bundle. He handed her the covered supper plate his housekeeper had left for him and motioned for her to precede him.

"I hope you've got central heating, Chief," she said over their soggy footsteps. "I'm c-c-cold."

"Where have you seen central heating? The Astors are planning it for their next house, but I haven't personally seen it." The pillowcase slopped against his leg and he shivered. "Sounds like a good idea."

"Trust me, it's wonderful." She climbed up the stairs to the second floor and reached one hand out along the wall, as if searching for something—no, *expecting* it to be there. She stopped when he joined her and shot him a guilty look as if he had caught her pilfering from the poor box.

"Wh"—she cleared her throat—"which room?"

He gestured toward the last door down the dimly lit hallway. "That one."

In only a few minutes, he had a fire crackling in

the fireplace and the plate of supper on a small table near it. With a smile, he drew up a chair and intoned in his best imitation of Major Payne, "Dinner is served, mademoiselle."

"What're you eating?"

"I have already dined."

"Oh." Corrie removed her ruined hat before taking her seat. A tired grin answered his attempt at humor. "Thanks."

"I'll leave you alone now. It's been a long day for both of us." He removed the napkin covering the plate and nudged the fork toward her. "Eat."

"I will." She picked up the utensil and waved him toward the door. "You don't have to fuss over me. I'll be fine."

From her tone, he doubted many had ever fussed over her, and something made him pause at the doorway and wait for her to start eating. Her shoulders drooped with obvious exhaustion and a forlorn sigh made its way past her lips. She laid her fork down. Apparently unaware that he hadn't left, she placed her elbows on the table and rested her forehead in her hands.

Tendrils of hair hung damply over her shoulders and down her back where the wind had dragged down her bun. The fair, tender skin of her nape glistened in the firelight. He told himself to look away. He told himself he should leave.

As if sensing his gaze, she looked up at him with an expression that started with a question and ended with an invitation. He told himself to think of something other than her inviting eyes.

"J-Jess?" she whispered, her eyes full of wondering surprise as he returned to her side.

Softly, with one forefinger, he traced her chin,

then her lips, and brought the dampness to his own, where he licked away the moisture. "You are so beautiful."

He told himself to keep her at a distance.

But he couldn't.

Dragging her up into his arms, he kissed her. Hard and fast. She gasped, and her eyes flew open. She drew her head back, and for a moment, her gaze searched his face; then she sighed and kissed him in return.

She tasted of rain. And need.

Her tongue mated with his in an ancient dance. He grew harder and pulled her more firmly against him, seeking the solace of her body. Her skin, cold at first, warmed within his embrace. Her breasts swelled against his chest, and he knew the peaks would be turgid and ready for his mouth.

Slipping one hand between them, he began unbuttoning her jacket. Corrie quickly freed her arms from around his neck to assist him, then shrugged out of the confining garment, all the while maintaining that mind-numbing kiss. Then she broke for air, only to transfer her lips to his chin and jaw and nibble his ear while she popped open his waistcoat buttons.

What was it about this girl—this woman—that rendered his control nonexistent? Whenever they were in the same room, it was as if fate itself compelled that they be together.

He pulled the pins from her hair and sifted through the strands with his fingers as she fumbled with his collar. He reached up and removed it. Then his breath caught when she kissed the skin he'd just bared.

Throbbing with need, he unbuttoned her blouse

and shoved it off her shoulders. Distantly, he registered an odd pattern of sun-touched skin, but her breasts, golden in the firelight, beckoned. He dipped his head and kissed first one, then the other, lingering and trailing kisses toward one pebbled nipple that spilled from the edge of her corset.

"Sweeting," he murmured as he took a rosy peak in his mouth.

She arched toward him as he drew her deeper into his embrace. His name trembled on her lips. She pulled his shirt from his pants and her hands, hot and eager on his back, urged him closer.

Just as eagerly, he returned to her lips as he lifted her against his arousal. She rocked against him, raising one knee to bring him closer still. With one hand, he captured her nipple and rolled it.

Her breath shuddered out. "Oh, my."

Against his lips, he felt her grin, and he grinned in return. He wasn't certain what she found amusing, but he was willing to go along with her for the moment.

"If you don't take me to bed soon, Officer, I may have to drag you to the floor right here." She nipped his lower lip.

Trust Corrie to make him laugh. He chuckled and lifted her tighter against him. "I'll let you land on top of me."

"Well, whaddaya know." She transferred her attention to his earlobe and nibbled there for a second before adding, "An officer *and* a gentleman."

A gentleman. *Damn.*

Jess lowered her until her feet touched the floor, then moved his hands to her waist and eased her from him. When she fanned her hands over his chest, he wanted nothing more than to bury himself in her.

But he had been raised a gentleman, and Corrie was under his roof, under his protection. He would protect her, even from himself.

She stroked her hand down his chest to the top button of his pants. He gripped her hand above the wrist and pulled it away.

Hurt overlaid the puzzled expression in her eyes, and he hated what he was about to do. He couldn't even stay and explain himself, because if he did, he wouldn't be able to keep his hands off her.

Drawing her hands together between them, Jess gave her a shake. Through a throat roughened by need, he said, "We can't do this, sweeting."

"It's okay." She chewed her lip as she dragged in another shaky breath. "I'm not a virgin."

The jealousy that smashed through him with that revelation shocked Jess. He never tampered with virgins—and Corrie's behavior in the last five minutes was anything but virginal. But the thought of another man touching her, even kissing her, roiled his gut.

No judgment of Corrie clouded his reaction. It was the other man—any man but him—he wanted to eradicate.

"Jess?" she said with a quaver. Then she raised her chin defiantly. "If you can't handle me not being a virgin—"

Too sharply, he said, "That's not it."

Corrie recoiled, drawing her blouse around her and clutching the front closed.

"Ah, hell, Corrie," he said in a quieter tone. "I can't explain right now." If he stayed any longer, they would be back in each other's arms. "Let's just say I'm a gentleman and leave it at that."

With the best of intentions, he couldn't resist touching her once more. It was the merest brush of his fingertips along her cheek, but it scorched the texture of her skin into his brain.

Even as he closed the door behind him and marched to his own room, he felt her heat singing up his arm.

Corrie stared at the closed door as she sagged into the chair. What had just happened?

One minute she was exhausted to the bone; the next, every nerve in her body blossomed into molten life. Then someone—Jess, dang it—had doused her with cold water, so to speak.

In spite of his desertion when things were getting really interesting, she believed him when he said he didn't care if she was a virgin. So if it wasn't that, what was it?

Exhaustion fogged her mind, and arousal was rapidly being replaced by the need for sleep. The bed beckoned a few feet away. Jess obviously wouldn't be back—not tonight anyway. Corrie undressed, located a spare nightshirt, and crawled into bed.

She wasn't certain whether she wanted Jess in her room—or her bed—but she *was* certain that tomorrow was soon enough to worry about that. On that thought, she drifted off.

No nightmares disturbed her sleep.

No one had rung a bell in the hallway to roust Corrie out before dawn, and she rose to bright mid-morning sunshine and the promise of spring in the air. Yesterday's cold rain had yielded to a warm southerly breeze. Robins hopped across the yard and loads of other birds warbled in the trees and bushes that had budded overnight.

The world was new again, and Corrie felt renewed as well. Running her fingers through her tousled hair, she shoved it behind her ears as she studied the room in the bright sunlight. Last night by firelight and in near exhaustion, she hadn't examined her surroundings. Now she did.

When Jess had ushered her up the stairs, she'd had an impression of restrained Victoriana with a heavy dose of English gentlemen's club and leather. This was the complete opposite.

Lace covered the windows, but restraint had not been in the decorator's vocabulary. No fewer than three different curtains bordered the windows, each caught up with gargantuan ties. Burgundy predominated, but the mad decorator's palette included every color imaginable. Jack O'Riley on a bender couldn't have done worse.

Knickknacks cluttered almost every surface and photographs carpeted the rest. She picked up one of the photos, probably hand-tinted by its colors, in an ornate, dust-catching silver frame. More than a dozen faces gazed back in frozen regard, but the stamp of blood relation manifested itself clearly— this was a family. With one fingertip, she traced each face. They all shared the same dark hair and fair eyes, and the same dimples lurked in their cheeks. Some bore the softer chin of the mother, front row center; others the sharper nose and sculpted jaw of the father beside her.

What was it like, growing up in a household where you saw yourself in others? Where you obviously belonged? Where outsiders could tell, simply by looking, that you were part of a specific family?

Corrie had never resembled anyone, had never belonged anywhere, had never been a part of a real family. She didn't count the time before her mother died. How could she, when she didn't have a clear recollection of it? Not counting her nightmares—which weren't all that clear anyway.

"Getting maudlin, Webb?" she chided herself and looked again at the photo.

The teenager at the end of the back row drew her attention. Dressed in a gray uniform so new it almost crackled, Jess gazed out at her. But this was a different Jess. His eyes were serene, without the heartache that haunted the man she knew. Laughter lurked around his mouth, but without the sardonic edge the adult Jess sometimes displayed.

She lifted her gaze from the photo to ponder those changes and caught her own image in one of the mirrors on the wall. Funny, but she could make the same observations about her own face. Her mind skittered away from the cause of hers, but she wondered what life-altering experience had made the change in Jess.

She looked back to the family picture. She had always believed having a family—a normal, everyday family—protected you from that. But something had happened in Jess Garrett's life to transform him from this carefree young boy on the cusp of manhood to the complex man she was beginning to know.

Until she learned more about Jess, she would have no answers. And she wasn't certain learning more about Jess was a good idea. He rattled her in more ways than one.

She set the photo back on the shelf as her stomach

growled. Spying a robe on the back of the door, she donned it, then made her way to the kitchen. Thankfully, Jess had the "modern" convenience of indoor plumbing. A jaunt to the outhouse would probably undo all the careful intrigue to get her to his house unseen.

A note on the table told her that he was at the police station and would be back at lunch, and to make herself at home. She savored the warmth his note produced and set about making breakfast. The stove was her first objective.

Unfortunately, the controls proved elusive.

"Now where would I be if I were a knob?" she asked as she surveyed the black iron contraption for the umpteenth time. Running her hand over the stove, she found a different handle and opened the door to a wood . . . pit . . . or whatever it was called. The Bistro's professional equipment this wasn't.

No controls—just wood. This was not going to be easy.

Fifteen minutes later she had the fire going. It would have been ten, but she burned her fingers and wasted five minutes searching for nonexistent burn ointment.

Next up, coffee.

The coffeepot was obvious, but she had to grit her teeth to pour water over the grounds and put the whole shebang on to boil. *Starbucks, forgive me.*

With no refrigerator in evidence, she figured she had to venture down into the basement for milk, eggs, and whatever else she could scrounge up. Hadn't there been "cold boxes" before refrigerators were invented? Made sense . . . of a sort.

Reality was worse than she'd expected. *The health department would have a field day down here,* she thought as she searched through the shelves of covered but unrefrigerated meats. At least the bacon was dry cured and should be safe, as should the eggs. Then something scurried under the shelves and squeaked. Heart thudding, she raced back upstairs with a couple of eggs and some bacon clutched in her fists.

As she skidded into the kitchen, the odor of scorched coffee assailed her. Singeing her fingers yet again, she lobbed the coffeepot into the sink under the pump-handled water faucet. One day without coffee wouldn't kill her.

The bacon didn't fare much better than the coffee. One side of the stove was too hot; the other wasn't hot enough. She ended with a choice of raw or burnt. Goldilocks had had it easy.

By the time she worked on the scrambled eggs, she had reached a tentative agreement with the stove—it wouldn't burn her *or* her food, she wouldn't take an ax to it.

As she lifted the pan of eggs, from behind her a stentorian female voice challenged, "Who are you and what are you doing?"

The frying pan went flying and landed on the floor, scattering eggs as it went. Corrie hit the side of her hand on the stove as she whirled, squeaked at the burn, and slipped in the eggs.

Landing hard on her butt at the woman's feet, she gazed up at a face she'd seen in the photo. Navy blue and kelly green stripes marched up a tucked and bustled skirt in chevrons to a high collar stiff with braid. The spatula, glued to the woman's considerable chest by the eggs for a moment, slid to the floor as she exhaled gustily. A hat, resembling nothing so much as a dead but reconstructed pheasant, trembled atop dark brown hair just touched with silver, and steely blue eyes regarded her above a grim mouth.

Uh-oh. With as much aplomb as Corrie could muster, she smiled and said, "Hi."

The pheasant's trembles began to resemble an earthquake.

Corrie reached her hand up to the woman. "You must be Jess's mom."

TEN

"You sure you want to do this, Mr. Garrett? It's a powerful lot of money." The real-estate agent dipped the pen into the inkwell but held on to it.

Jess counted out the money for the year-long lease and grinned as the man's eyes widened at the payment in full. Nipping the pen from the man's lax fingers, Jess said, "I'm sure."

"But what are you going to do with a bakery?"

Might as well spread the word—it would do business no harm. "Open a restaurant."

"A restaurant, you say. Now what would a policeman want with a thing like that?"

From the man's tone, Jess might as well have said he was buying an elephant.

"Actually, I'm the financial backer. A chef will be running the place." Jess signed his name on both copies and returned one and the pen to the desk. "From Dallas."

The man eyed him as if he had lost his mind.

And maybe I have. Or maybe I haven't. Corrie seemed confident of her skills as a cook—a chef, he corrected himself. With that sort of confidence, he had no choice but to believe in her.

"You wouldn't know the lady, but Miss Corrinne Webb is recently arrived from Texas and has agreed to open another restaurant here," Jess explained, warming to the spiel. "She has quite a reputation back there as a fine cook."

"Webb . . . Webb . . . say, isn't that the trouble-making waitress up at the resort? I heard she got sacked for kis—"

Jess wasn't sure whether it was his own expression or the man's innate sense of self-preservation that silenced the agent, but just to make certain, Jess said, "Miss Webb is a fine woman of good character. I would hate to have to correct anyone's misconceptions. . . ."

He clenched his right hand and studied his nails.

The agent blanched at the sight of Jess's fist and hurried to deny any thoughts of Miss Webb's reputation at all. "None at all, Mr. Garrett."

As Jess folded his copy of the lease and stepped out into the street, he nodded to several upstanding citizens of Hope Springs. Would they judge Corrie on hearsay as the real-estate agent had? Or would they give her a chance to prove herself as a chef?

He scraped one hand over the knot in his neck and headed for the police station. The reaction of the townspeople if they found out Corrie had spent the night at his house wasn't something he wanted to contemplate.

Although disaster came to mind.

Approaching his office, he became aware of a rowdy group milling about down one of the side streets. His lawman's instincts alerted, he made his way to Mrs. Zimmerman's boardinghouse, where the stout German woman looked ready to commit murder. When he saw the object of her ire, he considered allowing it.

A face he had hoped never to see again glared at

the crowd, then back at Mrs. Zimmerman. A face he
had thought he had seen these last weeks yet convinced himself he was only imagining. A face from
the past.

A face from his nightmares.

Roger Laughlin. Sergeant Roger Laughlin of the
U.S. Army. *Damn his black heart.*

Mrs. Zimmerman shied the end of her broom at
the man. "I told you, get out of house! That means
off porch, too."

Laughlin brushed away the broom and knelt, stuffing clothing into a carpetbag. Apparently, the
woman had tossed the lowlife's belongings into the
yard.

Jess was familiar with the lady's temper, having
been called to arbitrate squabbles between her and
her boarders from time to time. He could only imagine what Laughlin had done to earn her ire.

Beside Laughlin, a curvy redhead from a different
type of boardinghouse taunted, "Hey, old woman,
whatcha so upset for? Just 'cause he wanted some
fun."

"Fun, she say. In my house, no fun. In *my* house,
no whores. You bring whore in, you do not live
here."

"Hey, honey, you can come on down to my place,"
the redhead said, tugging on his sleeve. "Whaddaya
say?"

Laughlin straightened and answered, "I say that
sounds fine with me. But I have to settle with this
bitch first."

Lifting the carpetbag, he started to swing it. His
shoulder almost separated when the bag stopped in
mid-arc. "What the hell?"

Jess released the bag. "I'd rethink that move, Sergeant."

Laughlin wheeled on him, trying to bring the satchel into play. Familiar with the man's underhanded tactics, Jess slipped to the side and watched the bag fly into the yard, break open, and scatter linen in the mud.

"Damn you, Garrett," Laughlin grated through clenched teeth. "What right do you have interfering?"

"Yeah, what right?" the whore taunted.

"This"—Jess dug out his police badge, which he carried in his inside pocket—"gives me the right."

Mrs. Zimmerman thwacked the sergeant in the back with her broom. "Try to hit me? Take that"— she raised the broom again—"and that."

The broom connected and Laughlin flew off the porch, landing on his hands and knees on the muddy walkway. Curses erupted as he regained his feet, and Jess stepped in front of him.

"Hold it right there," he said and stiff-armed the man's forward surge.

"Outta my way."

"I can't let you attack this woman."

"I said, outta my way."

If he hadn't been expecting a fight, Jess would have been knocked cold. As it was, Laughlin's punch rattled his teeth a bit, but Jess stayed upright. For an instant, he closed his eyes as stars spangled his vision.

When the stars cleared, he turned toward Mrs. Zimmerman. "Now, ma'am—"

Cold as only a lethal weapon can be, the gun barrel that pressed hard against his temple chilled Jess's blood. He had no doubt Laughlin was prepared to kill him—witnesses or no.

A severe miscalculation on Jess's part.

The man hadn't recoiled from maiming and murdering innocent Indians. Hadn't flinched as the men under his command butchered children. Why wouldn't he kill Jess while he had the chance?

Experience—bloody and bitter—told Jess he was going to die.

"I said, get outta my way."

Between one second and the next, Jess felt it when the bastard shifted his grip to cock the pistol. Now or never.

Jess's left fist knocked the barrel away while he punched Laughlin in the gut with his right—just as Mrs. Zimmerman made contact on the man's temple with her broom handle. Laughlin dropped like a sack of flour.

Jess nudged him none too gently with the toe of one boot. The cur didn't even moan. Catching the eye of the redhead, Jess motioned toward Laughlin. "You wanted him. Get him out of here."

"Are you not arresting him?" Mrs. Zimmerman raged. "He brought whore into my house. He tried to kill you."

Merely shaking his head, Jess picked up the gun and walked away. How could he explain that arresting Laughlin would mean more time with the scum, and Jess wasn't prepared to ruin the next few days with him cluttering up the jail until a trial could be set up? Any association with Laughlin would revive memories Jess preferred to remain forgotten.

Later he would find the bastard and warn him to clear out of town and never return.

Jess brushed off his bowler and resettled it on his head. He wished he could brush off Sergeant Roger

Laughlin as easily. Slowly, he made his way down the street toward his office.

From an alleyway, a rumbling bass voice said, " 'Scuse me, sir. Can you help us?"

Turning, Jess found a large number of blacks—men, women, and children—clustered together. The largest stepped forward and tugged off his cap, obviously the spokesman. He repeated, "Can you help us, sir?"

"If I can," Jess replied.

"Would y'know of a lady by th' name of Webb? Corrie Webb? She was up to the hotel, but they says she's not there no more."

Jess tipped up the brim of his hat and studied the group more closely. They ranged in age from babies to grannies and had a desperate hopefulness about them. "What do you want with Corrie?"

"See? I tol' you someone in town'd know her," the man shot over his shoulder. He turned his massive shoulders back toward Jess and realization clicked into place.

"You must be Big John." Jess shook his hand. "My name's Jess Garrett—I'm a friend of Corrie's. Her partner."

"In the restaurant, you mean?" a woman asked as she stepped forward and raked Jess with a penetrating gaze.

"She told you about that?" Somehow the knowledge that Corrie had spoken to someone else of her idea before him gave him a twinge of hurt.

"She did indeed, sir." The woman took his hand and laid it palm upward in hers. After perusing it for a minute, she smiled up at Big John. "Oh, my. Corrie found hersel' a fine partner—more ways'n one."

Jess jerked away his hand, uncomfortable with the knowing glance the woman turned on him.

"So where's this here restaurant?" someone else asked. "Cain't earn no money 'thout we work."

"Well, it's not open yet, but I can show you the place," Jess offered.

By the time they all reached the old bakery, he had learned more of Corrie's offer to employ members of the group, been introduced to Maisie Johnson, Big John's wife, and Lula Brown, who was to be Corrie's assistant. He also learned that they hadn't eaten since yesterday. Any thought of showing them the place, then leaving them to fend for themselves fled at that revelation.

Arriving at the door, he unlocked it and motioned them inside. Even though the day was sunny and warm, the walls exuded a dank chill, and the dirty windows allowed in little light. The group gazed around in dejected silence. Obviously, their hopes had been for a warm, welcoming café, not this dirt-encrusted expanse.

The extent of his involvement in this scheme struck Jess like Laughlin's punch. He couldn't simply turn the lease over to Corrie. No, his commitment entailed not only paying for the space, but also taking care of others in this venture. And Big John Johnson's coterie was a lot of others.

Corrie, what have you gotten me into?

Jess and Big John walked through the entire place, including the upstairs, which would become Corrie's apartment. Jess paused in the front room with its bay window. "Later, she can furnish this as her sitting room."

"Shore will be a fine place," Big John said. "Not like them leaky tents in the woods."

"Tents?"

"Yes, sir. We live up in the woods a ways." He breathed into his cupped hands. "Cain't seem t'get the chill outta my bones."

Mentally, Jess ran through a short list of boarding-houses who would take in blacks and settled on one. He pulled out his small notebook and jotted a message to the proprietress. Returning to the main floor, he gave the note to one of the youngsters, along with directions, and sent him off to reserve rooms for the next week.

As Jess closed the door behind the boy, Big John reprimanded him. "Thankee kindly, but we ain't got no money for those rooms. Least not yet."

"Consider it a—"

"Ain't takin' no more loans," Lula chimed in, and others nodded, their chins held high with pride.

With a quick adjustment, Jess responded, "It's not a loan, ma'am, but an investment on my part."

From their puzzled looks, he could tell they weren't sure what he meant—exactly as he'd planned. Who would have thought helping others could be such a difficult proposition?

Still, they voiced their reluctance to accept what they called charity, and Jess scrabbled for a reason for them to accept. Then a baby sneezed.

"There now," he said, taking the infant from its mother and bouncing it in his arms. "You don't want to make this little one spend any more nights out in the cold, do you?"

The young woman caught Maisie's eye and shook her head. Then she retrieved her baby and withdrew into the group with a murmured, "No, sir."

"We'll get this place clean as a new leaf. That's *our*

investment," Maisie said with a wink at Jess to show him that she took his meaning.

"That's settled, then." Jess motioned for her to join him. "If you'll come with me, I believe Morris Mercantile will be able to provide all the cleaning materials you need."

Leaving Big John to round up their belongings from the forest and Lula to exclaim in horror over the state of the stoves, Jess escorted Maisie next door to the general store and set up an account for the café under his name.

Mr. Morris turned the matter over to his wife, who gleefully rubbed her hands together, exclaiming, "Oh, my dear Mrs. Johnson. How I have wanted to take a broom to that place. And now it's going to be a restaurant, you say? Well, I do declare."

Jess escaped with a nod to Mr. Morris and made his way to Mrs. Warshoski's and the bakery, to arrange for deliveries of meals to the café for a couple of days. He set up other accounts at the grocer's, the butcher's, and the dairy, but placed no orders. He figured Corrie would want to do that.

The town clock chimed twelve as he exited the porch of the lady with the best laying hens. "Miss Webb will be calling on you to place a regular order. Just direct the bill to me until further notice."

"Certainly, Mr. Garrett. I look forward to meeting her. So exciting—a female chef," the woman said with her usual friendly smile.

"Tell your friends and neighbors to be on the lookout for an announcement of the opening." Jess grinned to himself. He was becoming quite the advertiser.

"What is the name of her establishment?"

One hand on the front gate, Jess paused, then gave a bark of laughter. "You know, I haven't asked."

Continuing to chuckle, he turned toward home. And his little brown duck.

Corrie perched on the edge of her chair in Jess's living room—the parlor, Mrs. Garrett had called it—and tried to look innocent. That her attempt was doomed to failure was a given. Running around in a man's nightshirt, in a man's robe, in that same man's house could only have one interpretation. Especially in these Victorian times.

Ah, heck, in any time. Her tea sloshed into the saucer as she took it from the imposing matron's hand. "Sorry."

"Quite all right," Mrs. Garrett replied, never indicating that the scalding tea might have burned her fingers.

"Mama's accustomed to things being spilled," Jess's sister, Peggy, chimed in. "What with my brothers and sisters and all."

"You have a lot of children, Mrs. Garrett?" Corrie had briefly met Teddy, and Jess had mentioned a large family, but this sounded like *Cheaper by the Dozen.* She had watched that old movie again and again, imagining being part of the large family.

The photo upstairs had shown a lot of kids, but surely they weren't all siblings. Some had to be relatives.

"I have three sons and eight daughters, Miss Webb." She turned to her daughter. "I believe you have some sewing to attend to."

"I do?"

Peggy's startled expression almost drew a chuckle from Corrie. The girl hadn't mastered subtlety yet.

"You do," Mrs. Garrett said in a meaningful tone.

"Oh, I do." Peggy jumped up, almost upsetting the tea table. She dropped a curtsy and backed out of the room. "If you'll excuse me, Miss Webb."

"Sure," Corrie said, then realized this left her alone with Jess's mother.

At least the woman had allowed her time to dress and comb her hair. She'd even fixed the tea while Corrie was upstairs. A real bitch would've insisted on duking it out with Corrie still half-dressed.

There was hope. *Maybe.*

Corrie glanced at Mrs. Garrett's set jaw. *Or maybe not.*

"I must inform you, missy, that I do not encourage my daughters to associate with women of loose morals. Nor do I encourage my sons to do so either."

Uncertain what to say, Corrie merely nodded. Made sense to her.

"Unlike many of my peers, I do understand that a man—especially a young man like Jess—has certain needs."

Not to mention a young woman having needs. Corrie bit her cheek to control her grin, and nodded again.

"But there are . . . houses . . . that cater to those needs. A gentleman does not bring that sort of thing into his own home." The woman's voice trembled with indignation.

He doesn't bring his sex drive home? Yeah, right. But Corrie nodded again anyway.

Mrs. Garrett inhaled sharply and glared at Corrie. "I am pleased to see that you agree with me so wholeheartedly."

Corrie withered a bit under that glare.

Without warning, Mrs. Garrett shot to her feet and pointed a finger at her. "Then what are you doing in my son's home?"

Fixated for a moment, Corrie stared at the finely manicured nail. Then it sank in; the woman thought she was. . . . She shot to her own feet and returned the glare. "Who do you think you're calling a whore?"

"Well, aren't you?" Mrs. Garrett swung her arm in an encompassing gesture. "Parading around in my son's nightclothes can only be explained by—"

"By your son taking pity on me and giving me shelter last night." Corrie pointed her own finger. "Last night when it rained and all my clothes got soaked."

"How convenient."

"No, it wasn't." Corrie whirled away before she laid hands on the woman. "It was cold and wet, and if Jess hadn't taken me in, I don't know where I would've gone."

"I'm sure a woman of your stamp would have found someone to take her in."

"If I was the type of woman you think I am, I probably could've. But I'm not."

"Are you saying you spent the night here with him and didn't—"

"I didn't spend the night *with* him. I spent the night in his guest room. You can go look for yourself if you won't take my word for it."

Mrs. Garrett opened her mouth but nothing came out.

Once launched on Jess's defense, Corrie was unstoppable. "I'm really sorry you don't realize what a wonderful man your son is. I mean, he could've taken advantage of me last night, but he didn't. He didn't have to provide a roof over my head last night, but he did. He could've left me to fend for myself, and I probably would've ended up the type of woman you think I am. But Jess didn't let that happen." Tears fogged her vision. "Hell, lady, you raised a damned fine gentleman and you don't even know it."

"I—I don't know what to say," Mrs. Garrett muttered as she sagged into her chair.

"An apology would be nice, Ma."

Corrie's heart skipped a beat. "Jess," she cried.

He strolled nonchalantly into the room and tossed his hat onto the top of the piano before leaning down to place a kiss on his mother's cheek. "Good to see you looking so well."

"Where have you been, young man?" Even caught at a disadvantage, Mrs. Garrett went on the offensive.

"Working"—he grinned at Corrie, his dimples flashing—"on an investment with my partner."

"Partner?"

Unlike Mrs. Garrett, Corrie knew immediately what Jess meant. She squealed and rushed to hug him. "You got it!"

"As you so eloquently put it—I got it." He withdrew the lease from his inside pocket and handed it to her.

She scanned the paper, then clutched it in her fist and danced around the room. "I got it! I got it!" Reaching him again, she grabbed his ears and tugged his head down to kiss him soundly on the mouth. "You wonderful, wonderful person. I love you."

As she danced away again, waving the lease in the air, Jess stood stock-still. Stunned.

Mrs. Garrett rose and, keeping one eye on Corrie,

approached him. Under her breath, she asked, "You really didn't sleep with her?"

"No." He felt a blush heating his cheeks. Trust his blunt-spoken mother to embarrass him within minutes of her arrival.

She observed Corrie's continued exuberance and a reluctant smile flitted across her lips. In one of the reversals of opinion that kept the Garrett household on its toes, she said, "I don't know why not. She's delightful. So different from your usual sort."

"Ma," he protested. "I don't sleep with every girl I meet."

"I should hope not!" The indignant matron was back. For a second. The smile returned. "But she is so—"

Corrie scooted by, singing, "Chacha-chacha-cha-CHA!"

"—so energetic. What is that document?" His mother turned an arch glance his way. "A marriage license?"

"No," Jess said, beginning to understand how criminals felt when he clamped on the shackles.

"Are you sure it's not a marriage license?" she asked again with a hopeful gleam in her eyes.

"It's the lease to her restaurant. Our restaurant."

"Too bad," she murmured, then raised one eyebrow—an action that had resulted in far too many confessions from him as a child.

"It's a long story, Ma. Right now, I'd like to take Corrie there and let her start setting it up." Not to mention separating the two women.

With a look that said she would have the entire tale in the near future, she stepped forward to intercept Corrie. In tones that would have done a stage actress proud, she announced, "My dear Miss Webb, please accept my apologies. How could I ever mistake you for anything but an upstanding young woman?"

"Well, I don't know about the upstanding part—"

"Say thank you, Corrie," Jess interrupted. Lord, what would she say next?

She twinkled a smile up at him, thought a second, then dropped an awkward curtsy to his mother. "Thank you."

As she turned back to him, he gave her a nudge toward the hall. "Fetch your hat and I'll escort you to your new café."

"Oh, Jess. Thank you." Like a child at Christmas, she beamed and flew up the stairs.

Peggy, who had been eavesdropping behind the door, followed her. "You mean you're not a fallen woman?"

"Margaret Michelle Garrett! You watch that tongue, young lady," Ma yelled, hurrying after them. Upstairs the three women gathered in the guest room, then began exclaiming over the sad state of Corrie's hat.

Jess leaned one shoulder against the doorframe and sighed. *Doesn't that beat the Dutch? Just like home— noisy, full of women, and more trouble than it's worth.*

The ladies reappeared with Corrie in the lead, eyes sparkling and cheeks flushed. Her smile set his heart to hammering.

Perhaps it *was* worth the trouble. . . .

ELEVEN

Two weeks later Jess knew it was indeed worth it. In spite of the strain of having Corrie in his house every hour she wasn't at the café, he had kept his desires in check. Or rather, his mother had—by sharing the guest room with Corrie and Peggy.

At last, the café sparkled with fresh paint and hard work. Even the ceiling had been scrubbed, patched, and painted a cheerful pale yellow.

His mother had questioned the choice of pale colors, but Corrie had been adamant, compromising only on the floral fabric to recover the chairs Ma had located in the Chesterfield's basement and sweet-talked Major Payne into selling them for a pittance.

Now, with everything in place, they all stood on the sidewalk and stared at the bare front window.

The sign painter Jess had hired from Lexington leaned against the wall and crossed his arms. "I gotta have a name to put up there 'fore I kin start, Mr. Garrett."

"It needs to be something grand," Peggy said, "like the Excelsior."

"Oughta say somethin' about the cookin'," Lula offered. "Seen a place called the Good Food Here down outside Charlottesville once."

Big John scratched his chin. "Could jus' name it Corrie's Café."

"How about Miss Webb's Fine Food?" Ma suggested. "That addresses both the quality and the proprietress."

The rest of the group chimed in with other ideas, but Jess could tell none struck Corrie as right. She merely stood there with her gaze fixed on the window and a silly grin on her face. Every time that he had asked her about the name over the past weeks, that same grin had appeared, usually with one of her charming blushes.

The thick, long braid she had let cascade down her back this morning brushed the small of her back when she tilted her head back, sending his thoughts elsewhere. Resolutely, he dragged his mind—and body—back to the matter at hand.

He tweaked the end of the braid and asked, "So what'll it be, Corrie? It's *your* place."

Bringing one finger to her lips, she dragged down her lower lip in a pout that made him long to be alone with her. Without taking her eyes from the window, she released her lip and said, "I've dreamed of this for a long time, but I never knew if it would come true. It still feels like a dream."

"What's it gonna be, ma'am?" the sign painter asked. "I kinda like the older lady's suggestion myself."

Jess hid a grin at his mother's reaction to being called older, and prompted, "Time for the chef to make a decision. What will this fine establishment be called?"

Corrie stepped forward and swept both hands in an arc that encompassed the entire expanse of glass, saying, "Café of Dreams."

"What an odd name, dear." Ma slipped an arm around her waist. "Are you sure?"

"I've dreamed and dreamed of owning my own restaurant." Happy tears glistened in Corrie's eyes as she turned to Jess. "It can't be anything else."

If he hadn't been inclined to accept whatever Corrie decided, those big brown eyes would have convinced him. Blood beat a tattoo in his ears, and only their audience prevented him from kissing her right there. Instead, he gathered her hands to his chest and nodded. "Café of Dreams it is."

One tear escaped down her cheek to be caught in her brilliant smile.

"Audience be damned," he muttered and dipped his head to taste her lips.

She laughed and threw her arms around him. "Oh, Jess. Thank you, thank you. It wouldn't be happening without you."

The Johnson clan burst into applause, joined by Peggy and Ma, who raised that blasted eyebrow at him again over Corrie's shoulder before smiling. She had plans, he could tell, but he pushed that thought to the back of his mind. Let her plot all she wanted.

He had made Corrie happy.

Peremptorily, Ma pointed her finger at the sign painter and said, "There you have it, my good man. Café of Dreams." Turning to face the group, she drew the same finger along the bottom corner of the glass. "With 'Miss Corrinne Webb, Chef' here, I think?"

Jess released Corrie and waited for her approval of the recommendation.

With more tears, she rushed to embrace Ma. "Oh, yes, Zelda. That's perfect."

"You'll have them lined up out the door waiting

to eat here," Peggy said and hugged Corrie as well. "Oh, I couldn't be prouder if you were one of my sisters."

Suddenly, Corrie stepped back, cheeks aflame and gaze averted. She dragged a finger around her high collar and tugged it away from her neck. "Yeah, well . . . we'll see," she said in a roughened voice.

Jess studied her for a moment before drawing her inside, away from the prying eyes of the others. "Are you all right, sweeting?" he asked as he brushed her cheek with the back of one hand.

His heart plummeted when she flinched away.

"It's nothing." She ran her hands down her skirt several times. "I—I don't like crowds."

"Then this"—his gesture encompassed the dining room—"isn't a very good idea."

"Not crowds like that." One shoulder hunched, she looked away, as if to hide her expression. "Crowds as in people getting close to me. I don't do the touchy-feely scene well."

"Touchy-feely?" What in the world was she talking about?

"Never mind."

Gently, he laid a hand on her shoulder and held on when she tried to shrug him off. "But I do mind, sweeting."

The shake of her head said no, but the droop of her neck said otherwise. He drew her against his chest, tucking her head under his chin and rocking her slowly from side to side.

"Tell me," he whispered.

Her sigh, tremulous and vulnerable, knifed through him. Once again, he knew something—someone—had wounded her deeply, to the core of her heart. She sighed again, and he could almost feel her lean into him, as if seeking solace. Then she straightened and wiped her eyes.

Holding on to her shoulders, he repeated, "Tell me."

In the depths of her eyes, a flicker of hope flared, then faded. She dropped her gaze. "Nothing to tell, Chief."

"When will you trust me enough to tell me the truth?"

"I am telling the truth."

With one hand, he lifted her chin until her eyes met his. "Sweeting . . ."

"Sometime, Jess." Tears rose in her eyes and her lips trembled. "Sometime I'll tell you . . . in the future."

Days raced by like the Indy 500 as Corrie devised a menu to tempt everyone from the man-in-the-street seeking a plain, filling meal to the gourmand, and tried to master the wood-burning stove. That had proven to be her Waterloo, and the Johnson clan had decided they would manage building and maintaining the fire if she and Lula would cook.

Corrie thought she would be ready to open right after they refurbished the café interior, but Jess protested that no one knew about her restaurant. She needed to advertise before the café opened.

He had a point.

And now, so did she. Right on the big toe of her left foot. She sat on a mounting block at the far end of town and pulled off her boot.

Should've worn my hikers instead of these Chesterfield specials.

Exhausted from hand-delivering a flyer announcing the opening of Café of Dreams to every house in town, and now in pain, she rolled down her stocking and surveyed the damage to her toe. A big, ugly blood blister covered most of the end of it.

"Miss Webb, a lady does not expose her bare foot in public," a familiar voice with a British accent admonished.

Corrie let loose a sigh of exasperation. "Haven't you ever heard of thongs?"

"Thongs?" Sparrow paused, as if considering the word. "You mean footwear such as the Romans wore?"

"Yeah, like that."

The young Englishwoman glanced around before she whispered, "You wear thongs in your time? Exposing your bare feet? In public?"

"I live—lived—*will* live in Dallas. Gets hot as the dickens there. So, of course I wear thongs or some types of sandals. All summer."

Sparrow rubbed her chin thoughtfully with her finger. Then a mischievous smile lit her face. "How delightful. And how cool they must be."

The amazed tone wrested a chuckle from Corrie. Maybe Sparrow wasn't as stiff-necked and proper as she'd thought.

"Nevertheless . . ."

Proper Sparrow's back, Corrie thought with regret.

"You cannot, here and now, flaunt your bare foot like that."

Corrie stuck out her foot and wiggled the injured toe. "I cannot, here and now, put my boot back on either. So live with it."

"Oh, my." Sparrow lifted the foot and inspected it closely. "No, you are correct. You cannot be expected to put your boot on that."

"Glad you see it my way." Corrie picked up the flyers she had sat on and eased her heel to the ground.

"Actually, I was thinking I should help you dress it."

"You mean put a corset on it or something?" Corrie joked.

"With a bustle on the back?"

Sparrow's laughter echoed against a memory in Corrie's mind, triggering a warmth in her chest. Years ago, she'd joked with her best friend—what was her name?—and they'd laughed and laughed until they had been too sore to laugh more, as only six-year-olds could. Then they'd lain on their backs and watched the sunlight sparkle through the leaves of the chinaberry tree until Mama called them in to lunch.

"Corrie?" Sparrow's arm clasped her firmly around her shoulders. "Are you all right? You seemed very far away."

"I'm fine." Corrie smiled up at Sparrow. "I was remembering something. Something from my childhood."

"It must have been quite a happy episode. You were smiling so sweetly."

Corrie felt tears form in her eyes and blinked them away. It *had* been good. She'd recalled a time before—the protective mental walls rose in her mind—well, a time before the pain, anyway. And her mother had been there, too.

Corrie's smile widened. "Yeah, it was good. Very good."

Sparrow waved her hand at someone down the street. "Well, you just keep that good thought, my dear, while I arrange for your transportation back to your café."

Corrie tried to hobble on her heel and other foot but was brought up short by Sparrow's hand on her arm.

"Enough of that, my dear. It's a long way back. Too far for you to walk." Sparrow slipped her arm around Corrie's waist and assisted her into a horse and buggy driven by Sean Quinn, the Chesterfield's stable master. "This gentleman and I will see you safely home, won't we, Mr. Quinn?"

"That we will," the affable man, smelling faintly of horses and hay, replied. He clucked to the horse and they headed for the café, but when Sparrow learned Corrie had no medical supplies whatsoever, Quinn took them to the hotel instead, against Corrie's vehement protests.

Drawing up at a side entrance not too far from Sparrow's room, Quinn called out to a very young maid, "Fetch someone to help me carry this lady up to Miss Sparrow's room."

"You really don't have to do this," Corrie repeated.

"You cannot expect to stand on that foot and cook without it being seen to," Sparrow answered, a bit of impatience creeping into her tone.

That much was true. In the course of the ride, the toe had gotten even bigger and had begun to throb as if it would burst.

Great. Just what I need—an infection, with the nearest penicillin in the next century.

Quinn climbed down from the driver's seat as Chef Sashenka arrived in the wake of the maid.

"This child"—the big redhead patted the maid on her head—"tell me you have need of assistance."

"Thank you, dear Chef Sashenka," Sparrow said. "Miss Webb has hurt her foot and I have offered to attend to it."

"I can handle this myself," Corrie muttered without hope of anyone listening to her. Neither Sparrow nor Quinn had listened on the way to the hotel. Why would the Russian be any different?

"But no need there is for you to handle it, little von," Sashenka said and lifted her from the buggy in a move that shot the air from her lungs.

Without apparent effort, he whisked her inside and up the stairs. Only as he placed her on Sparrow's bed did he let out a woof of liquor-scented breath. She studied the florid face with its tiny, broken blood vessels around the nose and realized the chef was more bourguignonned than the beef. Tippling too much was one of the downfalls the Culinary Institute of America warned against.

But then, he predated the CIA. And AA, for that matter.

"There, good Miss Sparrow, she take care of you."

"Thanks, Mr. Sashenka—"

"Sasha, child." He patted her hand. "I am Sasha."

"Thanks, Sasha," Corrie said with feeling. He really had been gentle with her, and her foot had hardly throbbed any extra at all during the rapid transfer from buggy to bed.

As Sparrow gathered some ominous-looking supplies, he studied Corrie, which had her shifting under his gaze and hoping he hadn't heard her maligning his cholesterol-laden menu.

"You," he finally pronounced, "da, you are young voman who dares to open restaurant in town."

"The Café of Dreams."

"Ah, dreams . . . dreams . . ." He shut his eyes,

and frown lines appeared around them. "I had dreams vonce . . . of beautiful *czarevna*—princess in your language." A sigh rocked him, sending more liquor fumes into the air. "But the czar, her father . . ."

He expelled another puff of air and opened his eyes, now moist. Taking a large red silk handkerchief from his inner pocket, he mopped at the tears and sniffed loudly. "Enough self-pity. I now am hugely successful chef at premiere resort in United States. What more could Sasha vant?"

That beautiful princess, Corrie answered silently. With a start, she recognized her own frequently stated assertion that, as the youngest head chef ever of a five-star restaurant, what more could she want?

Irritably, she shook herself. *Getting maudlin, Webb. All this Victorian melodrama is turning you to mush.*

Still, he seemed a person to pity, not ridicule. As Sparrow carried in a basin of steaming water, she said on impulse, "The grand opening of my café is Saturday night. Would you do me the honor of being my guest?"

The handkerchief made a reappearance, although he blustered a little about being very busy himself. Finally, with Sparrow patiently waiting for him to leave, he took Corrie's hand and bowed over it. "I vould be honored."

Sparrow shooed him out of the room, then turned to her. "Astute of you to make him your ally."

"I f-felt"—Corrie stumbled a little over the word—"sorry for him. He's lonely."

"He's a blustering bag of hot air most of the time," Sparrow said, perching on a stool at Corrie's feet. "Talks about being the favorite chef to the czar and czarina. But if he was the favorite, why did he leave?"

She prodded Corrie's toe experimentally, frowning when she jerked her foot back.

"Hey, that hurts," Corrie protested and tried to tuck her foot away under her skirts.

With surprising strength, Sparrow dragged it back onto the towel in her lap. "Be still, now. You're squirming like a monkey."

"You calling me a big ape?" Corrie tried to hide her grin but failed.

"Big ape—that would be a common insult in your time?"

"Before my time, actually, but I watch a lot of old movies." Corrie grimaced when Sparrow prodded her toe again.

"Movies?" Sparrow glanced up. "What are movies?"

Adjusting herself more comfortably, Corrie settled in to explain moving pictures to a woman unfamiliar with TV, film, or Hollywood. Then she related the plots of some of her favorites as she forced herself to remain immobile while Sparrow lanced and drained the blister.

"But all in all, I like the romantic comedies of the Thirties and Forties best. They're sort of like Shakespeare's comedies, but updated."

"Romantic comedies," Sparrow said and rose from the stool, carefully placing Corrie's bound foot on it. "Yes, I can see how someone with your rapier wit would like those."

Corrie blushed. "My tongue sometimes operates with a mind of its own. I'm sorry if I've said anything over the last months that offended you. People are a lot ruder in my time than they are in yours."

"Then I'm glad to live in my time. There's much to be said in favor of courtesy and polite behavior."

A vision rose in Corrie's mind of the blonde curt-
sying deeply as Jess bowed over her hand at the end
of the Christmas waltz. Of Jess offering his arm to
Corrie as they walked down the street, of him tipping
his hat to her as they parted.

Of Jess calling her "sweeting" in that tender tone.

Taking the hot tea Sparrow handed her, she stared
into its dark depths and said, "You know, you might
just be right."

Jess paused for a moment at the side entrance of
the Chesterfield's bathhouse to enjoy the view of the
full moon illuminating the valley. A soft, warm breeze
ruffled his hair, and he was glad he had left his
bowler at home. Surely this late no one would be
around to be offended by his bare head.

With another appreciative glance at the view, he
unlocked the door and entered the palm-ringed
lobby, then relocked the door. Certain now of no
one discovering him, he made his way up the stairs
to the lady's side, where Miss Sparrow had said he
would find Corrie soaking her foot.

The sulfurous smell of the hot springs that provided the bathhouse with its famed mineral water
increased as he advanced down the hallway. Many of
his friends swore by the healing properties of the
spring water, but Jess had never indulged in either
soaking in it or drinking it.

"J-Jess?" Corrie's unmistakable voice wavered, as
if she was frightened. And well she might be, given
the distance from the hotel and its nighttime soli-
tude.

"It's me, Corrie," he called to reassure her and

increased his speed, only to come to a jarring halt at the door of her room.

Steam filled the large open space over the ladies' bath—a fifty-foot-wide marble bathing tub. But the huge pool wasn't what deprived him of his breath.

It was Corrie.

One foot dangling in the hot water, she sat on the edge with her hair tumbled down in soft ringlets to her waist. The robe she wore had slipped down on one side to reveal her soft, flushed shoulder with its strange tan line. Vaguely, he wondered how her shoulder had been exposed to the sun. Then his attention was drawn to the moisture that glistened on her lips as she licked them with the end of her pink tongue.

His body reminded him emphatically that he'd had no woman in months. And he'd wanted no woman for months.

No one but Corrie.

Fearful of scaring her, he slowly walked to her side and knelt without touching her. Every nerve ached for the feel of her, every heartbeat pounded a message of need.

She raised her foot. "I walked a heck of blister on my toe, but this is helping."

Water glistened on her calf, and the robe opened to reveal an expanse of thigh, again with an unusually placed tan, darker below and creamy pale above.

"Sparrow drained the sucker and then helped me make it here after the baths closed." Corrie lowered her foot into the steaming water again. "She said she'd send a message for you to get me home."

Through a throat tightened as the rest of him tightened, he answered, "Yes. She said she has to work tonight. Something about the royal Karakovs arriving."

She sank her other foot into the water, and seemingly unaware that her robe had parted far up her thighs, offering a mesmerizing glimpse of dark curls. Aching to grab her and tumble her right there, he forced his gaze to her face.

That was a mistake, for more dark curls, touched with deep auburn by the light, adorned her cheeks and brow and haloed her deep brown eyes as she stared up at him. Those eyes, full of promise, issued an invitation his body demanded that he accept.

They swayed together and their lips touched, held, released. He caressed her cheek and she sighed in response, a sound that echoed through his chest and into his heart.

"Oh, Jess," she whispered, her head rolling back and offering her neck to his lips.

Her flesh was soft and sweet and tasted faintly of the sulfurous water, but mostly of pure Corrinne. Burying his lips against the base of her throat, he could feel her hammering pulse, a mirror of his own. Heat rampaged through him and he drew away to yank off his coat and waistcoat and rip off his cravat, aided by Corrie's eager hands.

As she worked at the buttons of his shirt, he tangled his hands in her wild mane of curly hair. He kissed her hair, her temples, the tips of her ears. At that, she giggled and lifted her hands to cup his face.

"You are so beautiful," he said, staring into her velvet brown eyes.

"I was about to say the same thing about you, Chief," she answered and lifted her lips to his.

The kiss began softly and tenderly, then, with a moan, she opened to him, and he deepened it, plunging into her mouth as he longed to plunge into her body. She arched against him, the tips of her breasts hard beneath the robe.

As hard as he already was.

He slipped one hand down and released the tie of her robe, then cupped her breast when it slid open. Her rapid breaths became ragged and she whispered, "Oh, yes."

Dipping his head, he took the turgid peak in his mouth and suckled, smiling to himself at her swift inhalation. Eagerly, she tugged off his shirt, his suspenders going with it. In the recesses of his mind, he recalled that he had once told her he was a gentleman.

Now, his intentions were anything but gentlemanly.

"Sweeting, I don't know how much more I can stand."

Her chuckle increased his heat twice over. "I don't see you standing, Chief."

He returned to her lips and kissed her with all the restraint he could muster. "You don't understand. I don't think I can stop."

She shifted in his grasp and rose to kneel across his lap, the robe gaping open and revealing her in all her naked beauty. "I don't want you to stop."

If she called a halt, he would stop. After all, he was—damn it—a gentleman. He had to be certain— any further in this and he wouldn't be able to stop. So he asked, "Are you sure?"

"Sure as taxes, Chief."

"Thank goodness for taxes."

As he leaned back to lie on the warm marble floor, he cupped her breasts in his hands, lifting their buoyant weight and rasping his thumbs across the pebbled brown peaks. Her breath shuddered in, then out, with a purr of desire, and he thought he would burst right then.

Burning to feel her weight on him, he dragged her down onto him, the juncture of her thighs cradling his hot, ready member. Her heat seared him, brought him to a throbbing state of need that brooked no denial.

Suddenly, she broke away and straightened—only to throw off her robe, then pinion his shoulders to the floor. Keeping her eyes locked with his, she lowered her head to take his nipple in her mouth. Her tongue circled it, laved it, flicked it, and he bucked in response.

Grinning, she kissed her way across to the other nipple and repeated the treatment. When he thought he could stand no more, she licked her lips and began a foray down the center of his abdomen to his navel. As she loosened his buttons, he marveled at this amazing young woman, so unlike the prim and proper chits thrown at him.

He had wanted an adventuress and he'd found her.

Surprisingly, he discovered he wanted an equal.

What sort of woman could meet him as an equal? He fisted his hand in Corrie's hair and gently lifted her head to stare into her beautiful and mischievous face. What sort of woman?

This sort. His sort.

Corrie, his little brown, lusty duck.

TWELVE

Corrie grinned up at him and continued unbuttoning his pants. Finally, she was getting somewhere with tall, dark, and hunky. When he'd pulled that "gentleman" stuff at his house the night before his mother had arrived, she had begun to doubt whether he really wanted her.

As he popped free of his trousers, she knew he really—*really*—wanted her.

His eyes deepened to a dark, stormy indigo as she took him in her mouth, and a groan rumbled through him. Oh, yes, he really wanted her.

Just as she wanted him. The velvety iron feel of him evoked a strong desire to have him filling her in other ways. So when his hands urged her upward, she complied and slid along the length of him, reveling in the hard strength of his body.

"You are amazing," he whispered before claiming her lips in a kiss that sent rational thought scurrying for cover.

How could a man have such tender lips? Do such sweet things with them? All without ever kissing anything but her lips?

But then, she knew he was tender. He'd sheltered her and protected her and treated her like a lady when she wasn't sure what a lady was. And not just her—witness how he'd taken care of the Johnson clan, providing them with food and shelter, yet having a care for their pride at the same time.

How did she deserve such a man?

Maybe it wasn't an issue of deserving. Maybe it was an issue of fate. Fate had thrown her back in time.

Fate had thrown her together with this man.

As he continued to caress her, she spiraled into a sensual fog of kisses and touches and hardness against softness. Her body screamed for release. She whimpered as her nerves threatened to go on strike if this continued.

Just when she was certain she could stand no more, he rolled her over and sheathed himself in her. From both came a sigh, as each completed the other, like two parts of a whole.

Her arms encircled him, clutching at his back and shoulders as he began the movement unchanged by time. Inside, the tension mounted, tighter and higher, demanding she submit.

Submit to Jess, to herself, to this power.

She locked her legs around his waist and watched his eyes widen; then that devilish grin with its dimples appeared.

"That's it, sweeting. Ride with me."

In reply, she arched up to meet him, thrust for thrust, her breasts crushed against his chest, the fine hair there abrading her nipples deliciously. She found herself whispering, "Yes, Jess," over and over.

Together they climbed higher, the blood pounding in their ears, their eyes locked as they tumbled over the crest, air tight in their lungs as release surged through them.

Only slowly did the real world intrude. Then, all she could say was, "Wow."

"I agree," Jess answered, his head pillowed on his forearm as he held most of his weight off her, "completely."

She took a deep breath and repeated, "Wow." It was all she could summon from the mush that was her brain.

His deep chuckle rumbled through her, sparkling along her nerves and creating havoc in areas recently abused in such a delectable way.

"Keep that up, Chief, and you better be up for a rematch."

"I'm doing my best to keep it up," he said and gave a throb within her, proving his assertion. He turned his head and captured her lips, just brushing them at first, then delving deeper as the kiss became hotter.

Muscles she'd thought in revolt revived, and she tightened in a move that wrung a gasp from him. She giggled, drunk with her power over him.

Over him. Now that's an idea.

Silently thanking her Tae Bo teacher for making her do all those squats and kicks, she squeezed her thighs around his waist and rolled them over so she sat astride him.

"Full of surprises, aren't we?" he joked and rose up to meet her as she settled farther down onto him.

"Oh, I have more surprises in me than you can imagine," she answered and tried an experimental figure-eight motion. The flare of heat in his eyes was answer enough, and she figure-eighted in the other direction.

This time was slower, less frantic. But sweeter, as they intertwined their hands and whispered wordless sounds in each other's ears. Once again, they became one, seeking release, seeking union.

Seeking home.

As need whirled out of control, Corrie reached for Jess and clasped him to her. Tight and hard.

He was her anchor. Her harbor.

Her home.

Together they reached climax and plummeted over.

As their ragged breathing slowed and Corrie slipped to one side to be cradled against Jess's chest, tears formed in her eyes.

June and the solstice loomed little more than two months away—two months before she must relinquish this home she'd found in Jess's arms.

A couple of hours later, Corrie protested in his ear, "I can walk," even as she tightened her arms around his neck. "You don't have to carry me."

"The quicker we are, the less likely we'll be caught." Jess didn't mention the real reason he carried her—his reluctance to deprive himself of her touch. He lifted her higher against his chest and continued his progress toward the side of the bathhouse, where he had left King tethered.

Corrie's hair tumbled down her back and over his arm, and her clean lavender scent enveloped him. Surprisingly, he hardened again. Had she bewitched him that he could respond again and again to her touch, her scent? He glanced down at her face, shadowed in the moonlight, and wondered how he could fail to respond to such an enchanting little duck.

They reached King and he let Corrie slip to the ground, placing her hand on the bay's neck for balance. As he cinched the girth strap, she gave King an awkward pat.

"Good horsey," she said in a tight, almost frightened voice. "Nice horse."

Jess looked up from buckling the strap and grinned. Judging by the tentative little taps she gave King, Corrie had no familiarity with the animals. And next to the bay, she looked like a slightly overgrown fairy.

"He's awful big," she observed with an attempt at nonchalance.

"Sixteen hands and a bit. Quit holding your breath, you big ox." Jess whacked King on the side, and the horse let out an explosive breath. In a flash, Jess pulled the strap up another two notches. "Been together a long time, King and I."

"Oh?" she asked and turned to look at him. "How'd you two get together?"

"The army."

"That explains a lot." She seemed to be doing sums in her head before she said, "You weren't in the Civil War—you're too young. So what war *did* you serve in?"

Jess kept his eyes on the task at hand. Somehow this woman could read more in his eyes than he wanted. "The Indian Wars," he said in a tone that invited no further questions, but surely the wars had been covered in the Dallas newspaper. "King kept me alive more times than I can count, didn't you, boy?" He stroked the horse's neck affectionately, and King ranged his head around to nibble on Jess's hair.

Then he started on Corrie's, and she let out a little shriek.

Shoving the gelding's ugly Roman nose away, Jess released a laugh as he allowed Corrie to burrow into his chest.

King chewed thoughtfully on the long strands he had captured; then, as if reaching a favorable decision, he whuffled against Corrie's back. She, in turn, jumped and started to pull away, but Jess stopped her.

"It's all right, sweeting." He grabbed the bridle and held King's head still. "It means he likes you."

She slewed around within his embrace and glared at the horse. "I can stand not being liked so much."

"Be nice, now. This old boy is going to make returning you to Hope Springs much easier." He scraped a hand down King's nose in a favored caress. "Or don't you remember your sore toe after all our . . . activities?"

Her elbow jerked back and caught him under the ribs. "Still sore, thanks to you bumping it on the side of the pool." But her voice smiled.

He slid his free hand around her waist and pulled her back against him. "And whose idea was it to investigate the possibilities of the mineral water? I seem to recall a certain young lady taunting that it would reinvigorate me."

She leaned her head back and lifted her lips to his in a butterfly kiss. "And I recall that it worked." A sigh, contented and self-satisfied, whispered from her lips. "Very, very well."

Her lips beckoned him, but he knew if he gave in to their invitation, he and Corrie would never make it back to town before morning. So he stepped away and reached for the bag she carried.

"This is a strange material," he noted as he fastened it to the saddle. It had an odd texture, and the fastenings were unlike any he had ever encountered.

"It's . . . imported," she said, then placed her hands on King's saddle. "We'd better be going, Chief."

His fingers stroked the bag again; then he dismissed the matter from his mind. He could always study it tomorrow. Leaning down and linking his fingers, he said, "Give me your foot."

A moment later, she was settled astride King and he joined her. Fortunately for him, the horse was big, as was the saddle, and her bustle was collapsed and packed in her bag, leaving her buttocks nestled sweetly against him.

Remember you're a gentleman.

But a gentleman certainly wouldn't have taken advantage of a lady soaking her sore foot, no matter in what state of *dishabille* that lady appeared. And a gentleman wouldn't nibble a lady's ear as they ambled homeward at a horse's lazy walk either.

Therefore I am not a gentleman.

Corrie wiggled pleasurably and relaxed against him. He couldn't think of anything more right.

Then gentlemanliness be damned. I'll just be Corrie's . . . lover.

No, that didn't sound quite right. It sounded crass.

But it's the truth.

Yes, it was. But it wasn't the entire truth.

Somewhere in the last few weeks, Corrie had come to mean more to him than a business partner, more than a friend. More than a conquest. Jess's heart pounded in his chest.

She was more to him than he had ever allowed anyone to be. His little brown duck had become a part of him.

A part he would not let go.

Laughlin lit his cigarillo and puffed consideringly. It seemed the little waitress had snared the interfering, lily-livered police chief, and snared him intimately, if all that smooching and rubbing meant anything.

And he'd bet a month's pay it did.

Roger Laughlin, informally retired from the U.S. Army after a disagreement with an officer led to a gunfight the officer had lost—permanently—studied the smoke rising from his cigarillo. No question about it, Garrett had fallen for the round-heeled bitch.

Now the question was, how to turn that to his own advantage. And how to make fancy man Lieutenant Jess Garrett pay for the time Laughlin had done at hard labor.

Hard labor for ridding the world of dirty savages. Ha! Shoulda given me a medal.

Instead, he had stripes from the whip. For every stripe, Garrett would pay, and pay dearly.

Laughlin toed out his cigarillo and took a slug of barleycorn from his flask to quench the smoke in his throat. The addition of the waitress—a loose woman, by the rumors going 'round of her kissing Garrett on the street—opened up the possibilities for revenge. Seemed he would have to spend some time in that eating house she'd been advertising.

If Garrett finds her worth screwin', maybe I will, too.

Slowly, he rubbed the erection stimulated by the thought of doing the bitch. Yeah, that'd teach the holier-than-thou West Point lieutenant a lesson.

Taking his cock from his pants, Laughlin rubbed harder and thought of screwing the lieutenant's woman—with him watching. Drool gathered on his lower lip and dripped unheeded onto his shirt.

* * *

Jess arrived home after settling Corrie into her quarters above the café and stabling King. On the porch, he pulled off his shoes and, with exquisite care to be silent, unlocked the front door.

From the parlor, his mother called, "I'm awake."

Embarrassment flashed through him. Damn it, he was a grown man. His mother shouldn't be able to make him feel like a boy with his hand in the candy dish. His steps reluctant, he stepped into the formal room.

"I just made some tea. Come join me."

Jess had already decided on an excuse for just this situation. "I had to work late. You shouldn't have waited up."

"I didn't. I wasn't able to sleep." Ma took a sip of tea and smiled at him.

A pleased smile, if he didn't miss his guess. But what did Zelda Garrett have to be pleased about?

"Did you take care of Corrie?" she asked, widening the smile.

An uneasy sense came over him that his mother knew every detail of his evening.

"Yes." He cleared his throat, aware of the guilty sound of it. "Miss Sparrow lanced and drained a blood blister on her toe, then had Corrie soak her foot in the hot springs."

"Really. An intelligent woman, that Miss Sparrow." Ma filled a second cup and handed it to him, studying him all the while. "Perhaps I have been incorrect in my course of treatment."

"Treatment?" Jess floundered to follow her thinking.

"My rheumatism treatment," she said sternly. When Ma chose to be an invalid, one had best treat her as the most infirm invalid ever. "I believe I have made an error."

"Oh, yes . . . I mean, no . . . I mean . . ." Jess tugged at his collar and prayed for heavenly intervention. Any intervention. Admit Ma had made a mistake? Or deny she could make a mistake? Either way . . .

"Tomorrow Peggy and I will relocate to the Chesterfield. I had Teddy make reservations this afternoon."

"Reservations?" he repeated, still at a loss.

"That nice Dr. Ziegler at the hotel counseled me last week that I would derive greater benefit if I was able to partake of the treatments two, three, even four times a day instead of once a day as I am doing now."

"You mean move to the hotel." Realization dawned and Jess began to hope.

"That's what I've been saying," Ma admonished him. "You should pay more attention when your elders speak, Jess. I do declare, you grow more and more like your father every year. He doesn't listen to me either." She tapped one finger against her cheek and a blush stole up her neck. "Or only when . . ."

Jess marshaled every ounce of self-control to prevent himself from laughing with relief. After tonight with Corrie, he knew he couldn't stay away from her, but he also knew his mother would notice if he didn't sleep at home.

And the thought of waking up with Corrie in his arms and spending the mornings making love with her was too much for him to forego, Zelda Garrett or no.

Ma rose and loaded the tea things onto a tray. As

she passed him on the way to the kitchen, she reached up and patted his cheek. "Try not to be *too* happy, dear."

"Happy that you're going to stay elsewhere?" He tried to sound innocent and disappointed, but he had rarely lied to his mother with any success.

"Happy that I won't know when you get home," she answered, "or even . . . if."

She shut the kitchen door behind her, and Jess heard her climb the back stairs to her room. His breath whooshed out in relief and amazement. Relief that she wouldn't be his guest any longer; amazement that she had tacitly given her permission for him to spend the night elsewhere.

With Corrie.

Dressed in a voluminous nightgown, Corrie hobbled downstairs the next morning in her bare feet, unable to bear the pain of putting a shoe over her swollen toe. While the soak in the mineral water had probably done some good, Jess thunking her foot against the side of the pool probably hadn't.

A grin started and she knew she was smirking like a smiley face. *Good—no, great—sex will do that.*

Her knees turned to rubber at the thought of what Jess had done to her last night. Then she blushed at what she had done to him. Old can't-be-bothered Corrinne Webb had done scandalous, wondrous things with Police Chief Jess Garrett last night and reached heights she had only read about.

At least I can't be arrested for indecent behavior. Jess was the only witness . . . or is that accomplice?

Her laughter echoed off the clean white walls of the café's kitchen and she spun around in pure joy.

She felt drained and sore and energized all at the same time.

Because of Jess.

Her stomach rumbled and she told it, "And because of Jess you missed your dinner, too. How about a big breakfast? I have eggs and Smithfield ham."

She stuffed wood into the freshly polished stove and looked around for kindling. Apparently, no one had cut any; the wood box was full of nicely split logs but no small pieces. However, someone had left some newspapers folded up, and she stuffed several pieces into the stove.

Striking a match, she lit the paper, but without kindling the logs didn't catch and the fire died out quickly.

"Well, shoot," she muttered and stuffed the firebox full of paper, top, bottom and in-between.

Upstairs, she heard the distinctive rattle that meant the water in the tank was hot enough for a bath. Getting hot and sweaty with Jess was fun, but after last night's calisthenics, she needed a bath.

Hurriedly, she lifted the top burner cover on the stove and dropped in a lit match. She considered putting the cover back on, but peeked into the stove at the small flame beginning to catch the edge of a paper and decided the cover might suffocate it.

The tank upstairs rattled again and she limped to the stairs. By the time she finished her bath, the stove would be good and hot and ready for her own breakfast in her new place.

As she hitched herself up the stairs, she wondered if that cast-iron tub waiting for her was big enough for two. From long habit of living alone, she locked the door to her quarters and added a reminder to her mental list to make sure Jess had a key.

Behind her, the papers caught fire and flame licked at the opening she had left when the café's back door clicked, then eased open.

Jess stepped out of the bakery and adjusted his bowler to a more rakish angle before he strolled toward the park. Making the rounds of businesses and being seen on the street and in the alleys was his major deterrent to crime. If the hooligans didn't know where he might show up, they tended to tread warily. If they were so wary they didn't commit any crimes, he didn't have to arrest them. A very simple plan and very boring.

Jess liked boring.

Boring meant he didn't have to draw his gun except to clean it and occasionally do a little target practice. Not that he wanted his entire life to be boring.

And not that his life—with Corrinne Webb around—*could* be. Last night had been anything but that, and he had a few ideas he would like to try out soon.

Absolutely not boring.

He smiled at the thought, and Mrs. Warshoski, sweeping the entrance to her restaurant, beamed at him.

"I'm going to have competition, I hear," she called in a friendly tone.

"No one can compete with your potato dumplings, ma'am," he replied. Pleased that she held no apparent ill will, he added, "And your strudel is beyond compare."

"Pshaw," she protested, then rested her broom beside her and advanced on him. "Actually, I'm happy to have someone else feeding this town. Some days I work from sunrise to dawn next day and never do I catch up."

"You're *happy* Café of Dreams is opening?" Jess's relief doubled with the anticipation of sharing that with Corrie. She had been so worried about how Mrs. Warshoski would be affected.

"Oh, to be sure, I will feel pinch in my pocket a bit"—she fluffed her apron—"but I make enough to stand a pinch, and even be thankful for easing of my load. You be sure to tell Miss Webb I wish her well."

"That I will, ma'am." He tipped his hat. "With my thanks to you, I will."

"I have tray of cinnamon rolls coming out of oven any minute if you care to take cup of coffee while you wait."

Jess considered the offer, then removed his hat. "That sounds de—"

"Fire! Fire!"

The call that struck terror in every townsman rang out. Down the street, Jess saw a boy dash across the park and up the bell tower. Seconds later, the bell clanged, calling the volunteers.

Jess was already in motion, heading back the way the boy had come. The fire brigade would assemble in a matter of minutes. After Hope Springs's last fire, most had rebuilt in brick, so the damage might be contained to a small area. Still, there was always a chance of injury. Even death.

As he made the turn, smoke curled out of the red brick building on the far corner. The Mercantile? All those fabrics and gewgaws would burn like kindling.

But wait—Mr. and Mrs. Morris were in the street, looking past their store entrance.

At the smoke coming from Corrie's Café of Dreams.

THIRTEEN

"Corrie!" Her name erupted from his very soul. Jess lengthened his stride, breaking into a flat-out run that carried him to the café's entrance in a few heartbeats.

He dragged Mr. Morris around to face him. "Corrie—Miss Webb—"

"I'm here, Jess." From behind Mrs. Morris, a smudged and precious face peeked out, wrapped in a quilt.

Ignoring the stares of onlookers, he dragged her into his embrace, then kissed her hard. "Are you all right?"

"Well, I know what a smoked trout feels like." Her trembling lips belied her jest, and a single tear coursed down her cheek.

He wiped it away with his thumb, leaving a clean streak in the soot. As Big John came running up, Jess tucked Corrie against his side. She sagged against him, a gesture of relief—and trust—he wondered if she would ever admit.

"The fire's out," Big John said in a rush. "Smoke and soot mostly all's left."

"Can you tell what caused it?" Jess, advancing toward the building, felt Corrie's hesitation and looked down at her. Fiery cheeks glowed through the grime. He looked back at Big John. "Well?"

Big John Johnson was no coward, but he backed away, saying, "Corrie, she tell ya."

Jess drew her a little away from the crowd and pulled her around to face him. He pushed back the quilt from around her face and nudged her chin up with his finger. "You *know* what caused this?"

Grimacing, she nodded.

The silence stretched. "Well? What happened?"

"I built a fire in the stove."

"If the fire was in the stove, how did this"—his gesture took in the column of dissipating smoke— "happen?"

"I didn't put the lid back on the top?" she offered.

Exasperation loosened his tongue. "What sort of chef doesn't know how to build a fire and keep it *inside* the damned stove?"

"A chef who's used to a gas stove with controls and electronic ignition and—" She broke off as he took a step backward. "Oh, never mind."

"That little two-horse town of Dallas had all that?" *Whatever "all that" was.*

Corrie dropped her gaze to the ground, then brought it up to stare past his shoulder. "Yes."

"And that's why you have no idea how to work this stove?"

"Yes," she repeated, her tone flat, with no invitation to further questions.

He studied her, taking in the droop of her head and shoulders and the stubborn set of her jaw. He also noted the occasional tremor that shook her from head to foot before she stomped off toward the café.

In his parents' household, all the children had

been expected to learn how to cook and clean and care for the younger ones. Maybe Corrie's parents hadn't had those same expectations. Maybe she really didn't know all the things that he—and everyone else he knew—did.

That electronic ignition she had mentioned fascinated him. Ignition of a flame made sense; it was the electronic—he rolled the word around in his mouth—part that sounded unusual. Electricity he knew about and had even seen demonstrated on his last visit to New York. But how that related to electronic and ignition wasn't apparent.

How would Corrie know more about such things than he did?

Mrs. Morris bustled over to him after poking her nose into the café. "There's just some smoke that needs scrubbing off the walls, and the linens will need washing. The stove will need a wire brush and lots of elbow grease, but nothing a little hard work won't fix."

"I'll do it," Corrie said from the doorway to the café. She hitched the quilt higher around her neck and clutched it tighter in her fist.

Jess wanted to hold his anger a little longer, but the bleak look in those brown eyes ripped it away. Behind her stiff behavior and caustic tongue, Corrie slipped closer to that quivering precipice of heart-wrenching pain he had witnessed on Christmas Eve. No one deserved that. Even the one whose thoughtlessness had caused the damage.

"I'll help you," he said as he joined her.

She lowered her gaze to her toes. "It's my fault. I should do it."

"It's my place, too."

"You didn't almost burn it down," she said in a

strangled voice. She trembled violently, and the haunted quality returned to her eyes for a moment.

"Give it time." Wrapping one arm around her shoulders, he directed her upstairs. "Haven't you noticed I never cook?"

Her watery chuckle rewarded him.

"Why do you think I dine out so often?" he added as he opened the windows of her apartment.

"I thought it was my company."

Good, the saucy little duck returns.

He watched appreciatively as she dropped the quilt on her way to the bedroom. She was stark naked under that quilt. He berated his body for its instant response to her state of undress, but her curvy little bottom jiggled ever so slightly as she walked away, enticing him, mesmerizing him, exciting him.

Through lips gone dry, he asked, "May I ask what you were doing when the fire started?"

"Taking a bath," she answered from the bedroom, her voice now back to its normal tone.

He hardened even more and had to stifle a groan of desire at the thought of water sliding in rivulets over her bottom and the pale globes of her breasts. Maybe he could talk her into another foray to the Chesterfield's bathhouse.

Dressed in a robe and wiping her face and hands on a towel, she entered the sitting room. Her expression sober, she walked up to him and laid her forehead against his chest. Somehow she didn't notice his aroused condition, but instead murmured a soft, "I'm sorry for the fire, Jess."

He sighed and pushed aside thoughts of taking her to bed, to bath, to anywhere. Once again, he was a gentleman.

Damn it.

"Now, no more of that, sweeting," he said, squeezing her shoulders and leaning back. "Apology given and accepted."

She looped the towel around her neck and lifted her head to meet his eyes square on. "I meant what I said. I'll do all the repairs. It's only fair."

"It may be fair, but it's poor business when you've just advertised the grand opening." With luck, the two of them could repaint by then.

"But—"

"No buts, Corrie." He pushed her toward the bedroom. "Get dressed so we can get started. I'll go change clothes and meet you back here."

At the bedroom doorway she paused. "You're a wonderful guy, you know that?"

"So you told my mother," he said with a smile and an odd kick to his heartbeat.

Twenty minutes later he entered the Café of Dreams to find the entire Johnson clan hard at work, mopping up the water on the floor and gathering up the table linens.

Eyeing the number of adults and children involved in the tasks, he approached Big John. "I don't think all these folks are on the payroll."

"Don' matter," the big man said. "The sooner the café opens, the sooner we pay back our loans."

"I tried to tell them they didn't have to do this, but . . ." Corrie said, coming through the back door.

Jess stared at her. "What are you wearing?"

Scandalous was the only word for it—men's trousers and a coolie coat such as he had seen the Chinamen wear on the railroad gangs out west. If not for her hair scraped back in a tight braid, she might have passed for a boy.

Though he knew no boy's body hid beneath those

garments. No, they concealed a woman's body, with warm recesses and curves that just fit his hands.

Corrie spared her attire a momentary glance, then gazed at him with a puzzled expression. "My usual chef's outfit. It's easy to clean and makes more sense than climbing ladders in that torture chamber you call a corset. And as for the trains on the skirts? Don't even go there."

"It's not decent." Dressed as she was, anyone could observe the seductive sway of her breasts beneath the loose coat. Jess sent sharp glances around at the men in the room. Although they all appeared engrossed in their various tasks, he disliked the possibility that any of them might notice—well, just notice—Corrie as a woman.

Corrie gave a bark of laughter. "Get real, Chief. You don't tell me what to wear. I'm my own boss now."

"And I'm part owner," Jess said, drawing her close and muttering in her ear, "and I say you wear a proper dress."

She jerked out of his hold and stepped back, hands on hips. "A proper dress will only cause a repeat of today's disaster or worse. What if I had been beside the stove in a dress when the fire escaped?"

That brought a slew of heads around, and the Johnson clan weighed in on the discussion. Pros and cons flew back and forth.

Finally, he could stand the arguments no longer and yelled, "Quiet."

Immediately, the room fell silent.

"I thank you all for your invaluable commentary, but now my partner and I must confer in private." He swept his arm toward the stair to Corrie's quarters. "After you, Miss Webb."

Corrie opened her mouth, then shut it with a snap. "Thank you, Chief Garrett."

She sashayed up the stairs ahead of him, and he strongly considered patting that sassy little bottom, so clearly delineated in the trousers. How could he remain angry when he wanted nothing more than to grab her, kiss her senseless, and remove the offending clothing? After which, the only thing to do would be to take advantage of her.

She glared at him over her shoulder, then quickly turned her head away. After that, the movement of her hips increased and her rapid progress up the stairs slowed. As they entered her quarters, she waved him in and shut the door.

Eyes downcast, she approached him. "Did you like the view?" Her pink tongue traced a languid circle on her lips, leaving a sheen of maddening moisture.

The unexpected reversal of attitude took him aback—for about two beats of his heart. Then it pounded a tattoo in his chest.

Her hands slipped inside his coat, the heat searing through the fabric of his shirt. She lifted her gaze and the velvety depths beckoned him. "Won't you reconsider?"

He slid his palms around her waist and down to cup her buttocks. Without the corset and bustle, she was a warm and inviting handful. He continued his exploration by stroking up her back and around to unbutton the coolie coat. As the front opened, only a thin singlet obstructed his view of her pebbled nipples.

"It certainly looks comfortable. Practical as well," he said, his teeth gritted.

She shrugged off the coat and let her suspenders fall down onto her arms. Stepping forward, she rubbed her thinly veiled nipples against his chest. "*Very* practical, wouldn't you say?"

Images rose in his mind of luring her up here—after breakfast, after lunch, after dinner, after everyone had gone home—and of removing her outfit just as they were doing now.

Maybe the rational dress movement had the right idea with its support of loose, unrestricted clothing. Who was he to go against progress?

Especially when progress led to such rewards.

Reaching behind Corrie, he released her braid and threaded his fingers into the clingy strands. Teasing the rim of her ear with his teeth, he whispered, "Very practical, very modern, and very enticing. I forbid you to wear anything else while working."

Then he captured her lips in a kiss that left them both gasping for air.

"I love the way you change your mind," Corrie said as she nibbled along his jaw and shoved off his coat. "I'll have to remember to walk ahead of you up the stairs more often."

Jess laughed, pressing her against the wall and catching her hands over her head. "As long as you're coming up here with me, you can walk ahead of me anytime."

She looked over his shoulder at the door. "Do you think they'll notice if we stay up here awhile?"

He considered that a moment, then grinned. "We can say the discussion was"—he nipped her lower lip with his teeth—"heated."

On a sigh, she opened her mouth and drank in his kiss. As they broke for breath, she chuckled. "You could say fiery even."

Nudging up her chin, he kissed the fluttering pulse at the base of her throat. Corrie let loose a loud moan and wrapped one leg around his, pulling him closer into her heat.

Rapid footsteps pounded up the stairs. Big John called through the door, "Corrie, you all right in there?"

Jess met her amused—and frustrated—gaze and laughed. "You were the one making noise," he whispered when he regained his breath.

"Don't try to weasel out of blame, Chief. You were the reason I was noisy."

The door handle rattled. "Do I need to break this down? Don' you go hurtin' Corrie, Garrett."

Jess inhaled deeply and then let the breath out with a smile as he stepped back and released Corrie's hands. "I'm the one hurting."

Corrie twinkled up at him, but said loud enough for Big John to hear, "I'm fine. We'll be down in a jiffy."

Quickly, she buttoned her coat and began braiding her hair while Jess walked to the window and endeavored to gain some semblance of control. Down on the street, the crowd was dispersing. Most of the ladies strolled along on gentlemen's arms. One of the waitresses from the hotel dallied under a tree with a young farmer—they would wed after the harvest, according to local gossip.

In the reflection of the window, he watched Corrie finish braiding her hair and tie it off with a ribbon. What would he and Corrie do after the harvest? Would they merely be partners in the café?

Just then, she looked up and flashed a smile at him and turned to leave. Beating her to the door, he opened it and, unable to resist, brushed his hand down her braid as she passed.

No, not merely partners in the café. But if not, then what *were* they?

Late that evening, after everyone left, Jess and Corrie surveyed the day's work. With one of his arms draped around her shoulders, she could tell Jess was trying to impart as much reassurance as he could, but the task seemed insurmountable.

Black streaks smeared the walls where they had tried to clean them. The only real progress was that the linens were ready for washing and the tables were clean.

"We'll make the grand opening," he said in a bracing tone that a child wouldn't believe.

Corrie eyed him tiredly and shook her head. In a month maybe, but in a week?

"Have a little faith, sweeting."

"Get real, Chief. My Café of Dreams is the Deli of Destruction." She bent and trailed her fingers over a chair cushion. Holding up her blackened hand, she gritted out, "It's all my fault."

The worst part wasn't that her dream of a café was slipping away like water through a sieve. No, it was the Johnson clan—or rather, the fact that she cared about the Johnson clan. She cared about the baby with the sniffles and the granny with arthritis. She cared if they had enough to eat and were dry and safe at night.

Damn it, what was it about traveling back in time that had made her start caring?

And now that she had started, how did she stop?

She studied Jess, who had wandered into the kitchen to examine the stove again. Worn out as she was, he still made her heart turn over in her chest

every time she looked at him. True, he was dead easy
on the eyes—not to mention incredible in bed—but
that wasn't the reason. She cared for him.

There I go again—caring.

Way too much—in a way she had never cared for
anyone else, and wasn't sure she could ever care for
another.

The thought of going back to a world without Jess
squeezed her soul. She closed her eyes and tried to
resurrect the emotional and mental walls that had
protected her most of her life.

But the barriers had been breached. Bidgie had
been the first to barrel through her defenses. Now
a whole gang of folks occupied what had once been
that cold, sterile place in her heart.

With Jess rising above them all.

*God help me, how do I go back? To the way I was. To
the place I was.*

Exhaustion trembled through her and she
thought her legs would give way where she stood.
Then she felt Jess's arms around her and gratefully
laid her head on his shoulder.

"Come on," he said, tucking her under his arm
and steering her toward her quarters. "You're too
tired to handle this. Morning's soon enough."

Slowly, they made their way up the stairs.

"It still smells so smoky," she protested.

Although no soot stained the walls, the smell per-
meated her rooms, so she opened all the windows
and threw an extra blanket on the bed for warmth
before changing into a nightgown.

"I'm too tired to take a bath," she said, flopping
onto the bed and curling onto her side.

Gentle, as if tucking in a small child, Jess pulled
the covers over her, then crawled in with her and

drew her against him. "Sleep, sweeting. Just sleep," he whispered.

In spite of her worries about fixing the café in time for the opening and the Johnsons and all the other issues in her life, drifting off in his arms was the sweetest thing this side of heaven.

The hands reached for her, ripping at her, dragging her down. Dragging her into the darkness. Into the hollowness behind.

Behind the candles.

She tried to scream, but the hands—hard, callused, dirty—covered her mouth. Her lips bruised against her teeth and she whimpered. Blood filled her mouth, gagging her with its coppery taste.

"Mama, help me," she called in her mind as the hands tore at her, hurting her, touching her.

Words—filthy words she didn't really understand—grated in her ear. Where was Mama? She would make the hands stop, make the words stop.

Make the hurting stop.

The hands blocked her nose. She struggled for air. The room blurred, and she blinked as she continued to writhe against the hands. They hit her. They ripped at her clothes.

They touched her. There.

Pain! Oh, Mama, it hurts. It hurts. Why did you leave me? Why?

Smoke filled the room and she pushed harder at the weight on top of her. Heat fell like a blanket around her.

"No!" she shrieked as the hand over her nose slipped. Again, "No!" Her scream tore from a throat raw with smoke. "No! Mama! It hurts."

The hands drew her down, down. Blindly, she flailed at them, shouting, "No! Mama! Why did you leave?"

The hands held her tight, pinioning her arms against her sides. The stench of smoke clogged her nostrils and she thrashed within their hold.

"Corrie," a voice called, "wake up. It's all right, sweeting. It's all right, sweet girl."

She blinked and kicked out at the weight.

"Corrie, shhhh," Jess whispered. "You're here with me, sweeting. You're safe."

Jess. Jess was with her. He would keep her safe.

Blinking against the lamplight, Corrie opened her eyes to find Jess cradling her in his lap, an expression of questioning worry drawing tight grooves around his mouth.

She tried to swallow, coughed, then cleared her throat, which felt as if she'd swallowed a sack of nails. "I'm okay." She coughed again. "The smoky smell must've gotten to me."

As he relaxed his grip, she drew in a shuddering breath and rested her head against his chest. The solid thump of his heart beneath her ear obliterated the last vestiges of the nightmare, and she sighed.

Safe.

"Do you want to tell me about it?"

"No." In order to tell him, she would have to remember. Remembering would hurt. In so many ways.

Rubbing his chin on top of her head, he said, "It might help."

"No." It would hurt. Hurt her. Hurt him.

"When are you going to trust me enough to tell me what hurt you so much?"

His wounded tone brought her head up. "I do trust you."

"Then tell me." His blue eyes burned with intensity.

"I don't remember." *I won't remember.*

"You do in your dreams."

"These aren't dreams." She buried her head against his chest again. If she could hear his heartbeat, she could forget.

His arms, strong and safe and warm, circled her shoulders. "Then what are they?"

A chill stole up from her soul and she shivered.

He rocked her back and forth for a minute, then asked again, "What are they, Corrie?"

"Pain," she whispered. "And betrayal."

FOURTEEN

For a long time after rocking Corrie to sleep, Jess leaned against the headboard with her cradled in his arms and watched her with the lamp turned down low. She trembled and twitched, a frown or an expression of alarm flitting across her face at intervals. Every so often, she whimpered wordlessly, and he feared the nightmare held her in its thrall.

At those times, he whispered in her ear, "Shhh, sweeting. Jess is here. I have you safe."

Then she quieted in his arms until the next time. Each time the agitation was slower to return, and finally she fell into a deep slumber.

Carefully, he eased her onto her pillow and covered her. He made his way to the window and stared out at the waning stars, as if they held the answers to his questions. These were no ordinary bad dreams. Corrie's nightmares were the product of something horrible—something she refused to talk about.

Judging by the lost look in her eyes, he doubted she had ever talked about it. She barely admitted anything had happened, much less discussed it.

From his experiences in the army, he knew that sitting around the barracks shooting the bull with fellow soldiers could ease a lot of what gnawed at one's soul. Bad as things had become during that time of his life, he still recalled how much talking with the others in his troop had helped keep him sane.

At least, until the last battle . . .

He scraped a hand through his hair as he spared Corrie a glance. Too well he knew the way nightmares preyed upon your mind, making you doubt yourself, even hate yourself.

Years had passed since he had awakened with the screams of death stabbing his ears. Yet that did not mean he didn't live with that sound, that guilt. Sweat stung his eyes and he wiped it away as he continued staring up at the stars. Oh, yes, he remembered it. Lived with it.

He had not forgotten the massacre, and neither had he forgiven those who had taken part.

Nor had he forgiven himself.

Corrie whimpered again and he left the window to kneel beside the bed. In the flickering lamplight, she had the smooth features of a child, yet no child should harbor the memories she did—whatever they might be. At least he had been a man grown when he had lived through his nightmare.

With a gentle hand, he snugged the blanket around her more tightly. As he rose to turn out the lamp, she moaned. The sound was that of a soul lost, without hope, and he sank onto the bed to gather her close.

"I'm here, sweeting. I'm here and you're safe," he whispered against her hair.

"Jess?" she croaked, obviously still mostly asleep.

"I'm here, love."

" 'Fraid I'd gone back," she murmured.

"Back to Texas?"

She sighed and slipped toward sleep, but she answered, almost too softly to hear, "Back to my time."

"Your time, sweeting?"

But Corrie was asleep.

What did she mean by back to her time?

Jess turned out the lamp and sat there, studying her in the dim light from the window. A child of sorrow. A woman of contradictions. Who was Corrinne Webb?

A question to be answered.

Two days before the grand opening, Jess still had not asked Corrie about her odd remark. But then, everyone had been so busy, he barely remembered it himself.

Right now, something even more odd occupied his attention.

Big John joined him with a puzzled frown. "Y'gonna study that stove much longer there?"

Jess squatted at the back of the stove and looked up the stained wall again. "I don't see it."

"Don' see what?"

"I don't see how a flame could hit the wall this far down."

"Whatcha mean?"

"See how far down this burn mark runs?" Jess pointed to the area that had confused him since the fire. "If only the front burner cover was off, there's no way for the flame to have spread downward like this."

Big John craned his neck to look where Jess pointed. "I sees what you means, but it weren't the front burner caused that."

"It had to be. Corrie said she lit the box through

the front burner, then left off the cover." Jess straightened and dusted his hands on his grimy pants.

"Weren't the front burner open when I got here, and I was the first 'un in."

"Corrie was sure—"

"She's wrong. It was the back 'un."

Cold settled in Jess's gut. "You're sure it was the back one? No chance you got mixed up?"

"No, sir. I'm sure." The black man strode to the back door. "I came in this way and saw the fire goin' up, outta that 'un."

From that angle, Big John could not have made a mistake about which burner was open. Jess doubted Corrie was wrong, but . . . He scanned the dining room until he located her, up a ladder and dressed in her now usual trousers.

"Corrie," he called, aware of how many heads turned and how many knowing grins formed before the owners returned to their tasks. "Could I see you a moment?"

"Sure thing, Chief."

He had to admit, the trousers made her descending the ladder much easier. And much more scenic.

"What's wrong, Chief?" Her eyes widened in alarm. "Don't tell me something's wrong with the stove. I have to have a stove to cook on."

"It works fine," he quickly reassured her. "But this burn mark has me stumped."

"Why you tell 'im you left the front burner open, Corrie, when I knows I saw the back 'un open?"

"But I didn't use the back one." Her gaze shuttled back and forth between Jess and Big John. "I wouldn't reach over the front burner if I didn't have to. I'm not an expert, but I'm at least practical."

The cold in his gut froze as Jess examined the back doorframe. "Jimmied."

Corrie had been upstairs in the bathtub. If a man had broken into the café, he could have broken into her quarters as well. Jess gathered her against his side. His precious little brown duck could have been . . .

"Jess? What does this mean?" Corrie gazed up at him, willing him to contradict what she feared was true. She shivered and snaked one arm around his waist, seeking his warmth against the chill of dawning realization.

"Someone deliberately uncovered the back burner and let the flames burn that part of the wall"—Jess tightened his hold—"and skim upward in this pattern."

"No one would come in here and try to—" She broke off, unable to put her fear into words. "That's impossible."

Even as she denied it, the thought arose, *Impossible like time travel's impossible, Webb?*

"On the contrary, arson's the only explanation," Jess replied, his tone serious and his arm hard as steel around her.

"But who would do something like that?" She ran over a list of people and came up blank. Major Payne was a major pain and he was the only person she had really ticked off, but he wouldn't commit arson to get back at her.

The door swung open and Corrie squeaked. When Zelda and Peggy Garrett entered the kitchen with baskets fragrant with the scent of hot bread, embarrassment flushed her cheeks.

Immediately, the older woman noticed Corrie's expression and asked, "Why, whatever is wrong, child? You're skittish as a colt."

Corrie shook her head, unable to get words past the constriction in her throat. Someone had tried to burn down her Café of Dreams. As Jess and Big John retold their stories, some wellspring of strength deep within erupted, and fear gave way to anger.

Somepne had tried to burn down her Café of Dreams, damn him. Someone had tried to rob her of her dream.

She whirled out of Jess's hold and smacked her hand against the wall, wishing it were the arsonist's face. "Damn it, someone tried to burn me down."

"That's what I was just saying," Jess said in the placating tone one used to talk a crazy person down from a ledge.

I'm not crazy. I'm not afraid. She smacked the wall again. *I'm mad.*

She fisted her hands on her hips and glared at the entire lot of them, all staring at her. "Well, it isn't going to work. We're going to open this place, and open it on time."

"Amen," Maisie Johnson said and slapped her own hand against the wall she was scrubbing.

More hands buffeted the walls, and soon the café resounded like a drum corps gone bonkers. If enthusiasm would open the café, the grand opening was a sure thing. Corrie banged a rhythm on the wall, relieving the bite of her anger and building the resolution it had spawned.

Into the cacophony trouped a band of women dressed in the height of fashion—or so they seemed to Corrie's eyes. Any female guest of the Chesterfield would have killed to be dressed so well.

With an embarrassed chuckle, Corrie stopped

pounding the wall and approached them. "I'm sorry, ladies, but the café won't open for two more days."

The room fell silent as the women exchanged looks among themselves. The tallest, topping Corrie by a head, folded her hands and pronounced, "We're not here to eat."

"I beg your par—"

"Messy!" a lady in peacock blue screamed, and made a dash past Corrie, her bustle creaking in her wake.

Two others chimed in and hurried past. Corrie swung around to follow their route only to find Jess surrounded by fashionable ladies, looking surprised and very pleased. A bone of jealousy sprouted in Corrie—one she would use to club the self-satisfied policeman to pieces.

The tallest woman paused beside Corrie and chuckled in a tone that carried the ring of familiarity.

Corrie shot her a searching look, then exclaimed, "I've seen a picture of you. You're Jess's sisters."

"Guilty as charged," the woman said, flinging up her hands in mock surrender. "I'm Abigail Andersen. Call me Abby."

Corrie shook her hand and introduced herself.

"Oh, I knew who you were the instant we opened the door. Mama described you quite well."

"Zelda wrote to you about me?" A pleasing warmth spread through Corrie's chest—Zelda had thought enough of her to mention her in her letters.

"Of course. Teddy, too." Abby slung an arm around Corrie's waist and walked toward the chattering horde. "It isn't every day that Messy becomes involved with a female chef and foots the bill for a restaurant."

"Messy?"

"Sorry," Abby said on another chuckle, so much like Jess's. "Our nickname for him. He was quite a dirty little beast of a brother until he went to West Point. The army gave him a taste for spit and polish."

They reached the noisy band, which proved to be only the three plus Peggy and Zelda. Each woman hugged her as they were introduced—Beatrice, Clarabell, and Diedre. Or Bea, Clare, and Deedee, as they insisted she call them. They clustered around Corrie, who didn't need to say a word. They said everything for her—and lots more.

Never having been around families much, the next step escaped Corrie. Given her druthers, she would have made a rapid exit. No one gave her that chance. At least one sister had her by the hand, the arm, the waist—in some way holding her within the group— the whole time.

And dang if it didn't feel . . . good.

Jess caught her eye over the plump one's head— Clare, it was—and winked. Peggy was almost jumping up and down with excitement, saying, "I have missed you all so much. It's just like home now."

"Except I seem to be missing my brothers-in-law," Jess countered with a strained laugh. Although he smiled, deep grooves bracketed his mouth and creased his forehead. "Where did you leave them? No, don't tell me—they're managing the mountain of luggage you brought."

An uneasy silence swept over the women, and they dropped their gazes, unwilling to meet his eyes.

Frowning, he turned to Abby. "Where's that over-grown Swede, Erik?"

She blushed and became engrossed in rubbing at a spot on her skirt.

"Bea, don't tell me Bertie was too busy to get

away." Strain tightened his joking tone as he caught Deedee's hand and asked, "Sven Andersen actually let you travel by yourself?"

"Oh, Jess," she answered on a sob.

Abruptly, Jess dropped her hand and stepped from the family circle. Zelda grabbed at his sleeve, but he jerked from her grasp. In a voice of ice, he muttered, "I see."

What's going on? Corrie searched the faces around her for an explanation.

Jess repeated, "I see." Then without another word, he stalked out, the glass rattling in the door as he slammed it.

Corrie rushed to follow, but Zelda stopped her with a firm, "Leave him be, dear."

"But he's hurting," she said.

"I know."

"But—"

"I'll explain, but not here," Zelda said with a jerk of her head toward the Johnsons. She gathered up her daughters with a single glance and shepherded them upstairs, along with Corrie.

There they perched mostly on window seats as the café had been her priority to furnish. Zelda lowered herself into the only armchair, and for the first time, Corrie noticed how old Jess's mother was. A gray pallor shadowed her face, and her hands trembled as she tucked in a stray hair.

An hour ago, Corrie would have expressed her concern. Now she glared at the older woman who had been a part of hurting Jess.

Stonily, she asked, "What was that about downstairs? Why did Jess leave? What did you do to hurt him?"

Zelda lifted unsteady fingers to her eyes and wiped

away tears. "I had hoped . . ." Her voice trailed off and she motioned for Abby to speak.

The eldest sister seemed to seek silent counsel from each of the others before she cleared her throat and said, "It's a private family matter."

"You hurt Jess," Corrie said, the accusation stark and harsh. The pain in Jess's eyes wrung tears from her heart. Families meant safety and a haven of comfort. She didn't remember those things—not really—but that was what families were for. Not this hurtful disaster of a reunion.

"Yes, and you should know why," Zelda said in an old-lady's voice. "Go on, Abigail."

"I'm not sure where to begin," Abby said.

"Out west, I know that much," Deedee said. "Everything was fine before the Indian Wars."

Wars? Wars were for politicians, for nations. Not for individual people. Corrie didn't see the relevance but nodded for them to continue nonetheless.

"That's when it started, yes," Abby said. "But I'm not certain any of us know exactly what happened out there."

Clare gave a little cough. "My Bill says Jess changed after that."

Abby looked at her sister. "Has he ever told you precisely what happened to Jess? Erik certainly hasn't told me, no matter how much I plead with him."

"Bertie hasn't told me either, even when I threaten to never make lo—" Bea broke off, cheeks flaming.

"Be that as it may," Abby said with a silencing frown. "We have scarcely seen Jess since he returned."

Bea scooted forward and began ticking off events

on her fingers. "Let's see, he came to your wedding, Deedee, and your last baby's christening, and—"

"Don't forget Christmas three years ago," Deedee added.

Bea nodded and opened her mouth to continue, but Corrie beat her to it.

"I don't care what wedding he went to. I care about why he left here like he'd been beaten." She had been leaning against the door and now straightened and pointed her finger at Abby. "You give me the straight scoop. Only you," she said with a warning glare at the others.

Abby shut her eyes tight and a tear streaked down her cheek. When she opened her eyes, Corrie saw a bleak uncertainty in them.

Ignoring the tears filling her eyes, Abby said, "When Jess returned from the war, he was . . . different. He left us, an eager young lieutenant fresh out of West Point and chomping at the bit to serve his country. He came back angry and bitter, and holding something in. He wouldn't tell us, his sisters, what had happened."

"Tell her about the meeting." Clare gasped as she realized she had interrupted.

"The meeting?" Corrie, trying to imagine what could have transformed Jess, prompted Abby to go on with a wave of her hand.

"Soon after he came home, Jess argued with our father. Papa sent for the men in the family—practically everyone came except Uncle Pat, who's all the way out in New Mexico territory."

"What did they argue about?" Corrie asked. This drawn-out explanation wound her tighter and tighter and gave her no answers.

Again, Abby glanced around, as if for consensus. "We don't know."

"What do you mean, you don't know?" Unable to contain herself, Corrie stomped around the room.

"Our husbands never told us." Abby fidgeted. "Whatever happened out there must have been horrendous, otherwise our husbands would have shared it with us."

"That doesn't explain why Jess asked where your husbands were and then shot out of here when they hadn't made the trip to Hope Springs. It's not as if he's got a fragile ego."

Blank looks and quizzical eyebrows followed her statement. Oops; Freud wasn't known here yet.

She inhaled sharply and rephrased, "It's not like he's easily insulted."

"No, but apparently, he insulted every one of our husbands. Even Papa." Abby scrubbed her hands down her face and stared at the moisture as if she didn't know where it came from. "Insulted them so badly that they cannot forgive him."

"But he's your brother." Family accepted you no matter what . . . didn't they?

"He's also a man who said something that hurt the others so horribly they won't discuss it with us, their wives. They refuse to speak to him at all." Abby withdrew a pristine white handkerchief from inside her sleeve edge and wiped her eyes. "The only man in the family who will speak to Jess is Teddy, and all I can get out of him is that Jess's remarks didn't bother him as he wasn't a lawman."

What in hell did being—or not being—a lawman have to do with anything? Corrie shook her head, trying to sort out the scant information she'd been given. And trying to reconcile this reality of a divided family with her images of how families worked.

"Leave It to Beaver" it's not. More like "Judge Judy."

"This makes no sense," she said. Nods showed their agreement. "But I can't just let Jess wander around out there alone."

She knew too much about being alone. No one deserved that, least of all a wonderful man like Jess Garrett.

"Where will you look?" Zelda asked, her face still gray but a spark of hope deep in her blue eyes, so like her son's.

"Everywhere." Corrie walked to the window and stared down at the street and off into the hazy distance of the mountains. Turning back to the assembled Garretts, she said, "I do know I'm not leaving him by himself. No matter what he said to your husbands, a family is supposed to forgive and forget."

And love you forever.

Jess crested another hill and pulled King to a halt under an ancient apple tree in full spring flower. The sweet scent drifted down to him and he inhaled, thinning the stench of rejection.

Seven years, he thought. *Seven years and I can't unsay my words. Seven years and they haven't forgiven me.*

Anger roiled in his gut. He swung out of the saddle and paced up and down through the old orchard. Insult and rage churned, screaming for release.

Without conscious thought, his Colt appeared. The grip itched in his hand, begging to vent his wrath. He leveled the gun at the town in the distance and sighted down the barrel. Just so could he kill.

Just so had he killed.

"No!" It was the howl of a wounded animal—his soul. He flung the gun to the ground, then hurled himself onto King, riding away from the past, from the killing. From himself.

FIFTEEN

Hours later, with the gelding lathered and blowing and barely able to stumble another step, Jess drew up at a deserted cabin and slid from the saddle. His own legs aching from the ride, he watered King and hobbled him within reach of the new spring grass.

Then Jess dropped to the ground beside the bay and stared up at the moon, eyes gritty with unshed grief. He had hoped that time away from the family would have blunted their anger. Each holiday had been an aching void—he, who reveled in being in the center of the garrulous, affectionate brood, had spent those family times alone.

And seven years after he had hurled insults at his father, his uncles, his brothers, his sisters' husbands, he remained the outcast. By his own actions, true, but still the outcast. Only Teddy had forgiven him.

Pride stood between him and the others. Their pride and the insults he had spewed. His pride and the rejection that followed.

His sisters and mother had never known the whole story and, to their credit, their men had never forbidden them to converse or correspond with him. A tightness encircled his heart at the thought. Much as he decried the female interference in his life, without it he would have been truly lost.

Perhaps, years ago, at the beginning, his words might have been forgiven . . . if he had asked. But he had been young, disillusioned, and sickened by the depths of hell he had witnessed. He had seen no way but his own. He had not asked then.

He could not ask now.

King nuzzled him, drawing him from the past. Jess stroked the horse's head, soothing his mind with the familiar ritual. A rift existed between him and the Garrett men, but the women and Teddy were willing to cross it. For now, that would suffice.

Otherwise, he was alone.

With an exhausted groan, he closed his eyes. An image rose in his mind of a pair of velvety brown eyes and a smile that woke the morning. As he slipped into sleep, the constriction around his heart eased.

No matter what came of the family schism, he would never be alone again.

"Jess," Corrie called for the millionth time from a throat gone hoarse. "Jess Garrett."

Buford the mule flicked his ears back and forth and snatched a mouthful of grass on the fly, sending Corrie over the saddle horn and almost onto the ground. Hauling on the reins to bring the animal's head up, she ground out, "Damn it, I told you to stop doing that."

She dragged him to a halt and dismounted, neither elegantly nor gently. Ladylike behavior had deserted her two minutes into this ride from hell.

Careful to keep hold of the cheek band—she'd spent a good half hour last night chasing Buford before she learned that necessary piece of mule trivia—

she stomped to his head to reason with him. Again. He curled his lip at her and brayed. By this time, Corrie *knew* he was laughing at her.

"Does the phrase 'glue factory' mean anything to you?"

He mouthed his bit and returned her glare with a satisfied *brrrtt* of his lips. Corrie jumped back. Too late.

Slimed again.

Buford, one eye on her, let loose a laughing neigh.

As she tied the comedian to a bush and dug into the saddlebag for a cloth, she muttered, "I don't know who's the horse's ass around here, bud, me or you, but I got a sneaking suspicion it ain't you."

She moved out of slime range and pulled the map Rupert Smith had given her from her pocket. The Chesterfield folks had been helpful—Rupert gave her the map, and Sean Quinn provided her with Buford, although that had proven to be a mixed blessing. Even the Major wished her the best. But once they learned that Jess had headed into the mountains of his own volition, none would join her search.

Unless she counted the slimer there, she had spent the previous night in the woods by herself, wrapped up in a scratchy wool blanket. Camping was for good old boys in gimme caps with coolers of Bud in the back of their dented pickups, not for a five-star chef. The closest she wanted to come to bugs was escargot.

Instead, she was up close and personal with bugs *and* mule spit.

The anxiety that had driven her from the café, up the hill to the hotel, and into the mountains had decreased during the cold, long hours of the night with all its creeping and crawling and—*oh, God*—slithering.

I'll never have rattlesnake on the menu again. Just don't bite me, she silently promised again.

But the memory of the sorrow in Jess's eyes drove her on, in spite of the cold and bugs . . . and Buford.

Laying down the rough map and weighting the corners with rocks, she walked around it and compared it to the terrain. She advanced up the trail a short way on foot and returned to study the map again. A compass might have helped, but since she didn't know how to read one, probably not. Slowly, she circled the map, finally squatting down and admitting defeat.

" 'Déjà vu all over again,' " she quoted. With an exasperated sigh, she folded up the map and tucked it back into her pocket. Not really expecting an answer, she yelled, "Jess! Jess Garrett!"

Buford snorted in response.

With another hard stare up and down the hill, she released and mounted the mule. No matter that her saddle sores had saddle sores, she would find Jess.

The mule turned his head and hawked a big one on her boot. "Son of a—" She dug her heels into the animal and directed him uphill.

Oh yeah, she was going to find Jess.

And give him Buford.

She stood up in the stirrups and called, "Jess. Damn you, Jess Garrett, where are you?"

Off to one side, she thought she heard something. She hauled at the reins. "Whoa," she commanded in a deep voice, as Sean had instructed.

Buford kept plodding along, oblivious to the human on his back. His need to stop didn't coincide with hers.

"Whoa, damn it," she said and kicked her feet from the stirrups. The animal slowed but continued up the trail.

Swearing under her breath—it was all she could manage as she had worked her way to drape belly down across the saddle—she slipped to the ground, where she raced to wrap the reins around a tree and braced one foot against it. This, too, she'd learned late yesterday.

Perpetual motion, thy name is Buford.

Coming to a halt and releasing a long-suffering sigh, the mule blinked at her.

"This"—she tugged on his rein—"means stop." Then she remembered her mission and stepped to the edge of the trail. "Jess?"

"Corrie?" Although far away, the voice was unmistakably his.

Heart tripping, she yelled his name again, then plunged into the trees. Her feet flew over the leafy ground and she arrived in a sun-drenched clearing as he entered it from the other side.

No one ever looked as good as he did at that moment, day's growth of beard and all.

In a breath, he crushed her against him, kissing her hair, her face, murmuring her name over and over. Arms around his waist, she drew him closer to reassure herself that he was truly safe.

Then she lifted her mouth to his and kissed him, imbuing the kiss with all the heart-wrenching fear of yesterday, all the relief of today.

Dear God, all the love of forever.

For love Jess she did. Completely. As she had never loved another.

As she had feared to love anyone.

Her mind retreated from the thought. She didn't

know how to love anyone, much less a treasure of a man like Jess. She didn't *want* to love anyone.

And certainly not Jess.

The summer solstice loomed like a tornado on the horizon. In only a couple of months she would be back in Dallas if Paul could forgive her for an unannounced six-month leave of absence. Jess would still be here in Hope Springs in 1887. How could she have forgotten that detail?

He lifted his head and gazed at her with those summer sky blue eyes, and her heart turned over in her chest. No, she didn't want to love anyone. But she did love Jess.

Only Jess.

"I—I—" she tried to get out the confession, but her throat tightened around the words. She had no right to tell him—not when she would be thrown back to her time in June and never see him again. *Oh, God.*

"Shh," Jess whispered and eased her down in the softness of the thick spring grass and framed her face with his hands. A nimbus coruscated around his head in the sunlight, which dazzled her eyes and provided an excuse for her tears.

With his thumbs, he wiped them away, then followed that with his lips. Heat shimmered through her as he stroked her face and neck with first his fingers, then his hot, knowing mouth. The very air in the meadow pulsed with their breathing, vibrated with her moans of pleasure.

Then the heat of the sun caressed her skin as he dragged her suspenders down her arms, capturing them against her sides while he unbuttoned her shirt and pulled up her undershirt. Arching upward, she begged, "Please, Jess. Oh, please."

In reply, he slid along her length until his mouth found her right breast and he drew deeply on its aching peak. Her core grew molten and she heaved her torso up to meet his, seeking the filling of her void, craving the precious heaviness. His erection brushed her inner thigh through their clothes and she strained to urge him closer, much closer to the ache building inside her.

He switched his attention to her left breast and drove her deeper into the spiral of desire. Wordless protests rose in her throat but died into whimpers as he suckled more strongly and his teeth grazed the tender tip. His hands gripped her arms, allowing his thumbs access to the sensitive undersides of her breasts. As the roughness of his fingers gently—maddeningly—added to the tumult of sensations, she flew closer and closer to climax.

When she cried out, "Please," again, Jess merely drew her more deeply into his mouth and flicked her nipple like a hundred hummingbird wings. Her core tightened and she cried out as she plummeted into a breath-robbing climax. Again and again the contractions rocked her until she thought they would never end.

And she never wanted them to . . . except to have Jess join her in this ecstasy.

Hazily, she opened her eyes and whispered, "Oh, my. That was *good.*"

With a laugh, he stripped off his clothes and tugged her pants down to her ankles, untied her hiking boots, then finished undressing her. Before she was able to draw more than a few recuperative breaths, he rejoined her on the grassy bed and settled his welcome weight upon her.

"If you thought that was good, this will be even

better," he said, easing into her as he once more possessed her mouth in a kiss hot and deep as their joining.

Finally, they broke for air, and Corrie said with a smothered laugh, "Mmm, mmm, good."

"Only good?" Jess asked with another thrust into her depths.

She rose to meet him, his hardness to her softness, and closed her eyes as they settled into the rhythm of give and take like old lovers, accustomed to each other and eager for more.

"Not just good—" she gasped as he stroked harder, deeper, driving her into the spiral again. "Better . . . much"—another gasp—"much better."

Clasping him tighter, she silently pleaded for completion, her muscles rhythmically tightening around his shaft as he plunged and withdrew and plunged again into her core. The dark curls on his chest abraded her nipples, already tortured so wonderfully by his mouth. Now the friction arrowed an exquisite tension to her depths. His lips added to the spiraling need with their mesmerizing glide over her neck and face, ending at one earlobe with a sharp pull and that hummingbird flicker.

His breath rasped in and out, then held as he moaned, the sound reverberating through his chest and driving her over the edge.

The heat of the sun and of their bodies united, the sounds of the forest retreated, the wind stilled. Their souls mated and became one.

Corrie whirled into the maelstrom where they were together forever in a love without place or time.

On a sigh of satisfaction, Jess raised his chest from hers and stared down at Corrie. Had she sensed the enormity of their joining?

Had she known how her touch had soothed his pain and quieted the ache of separation? And eased the torment that had sent him flying into the mountains?

Her eyelids fluttered, then opened to reveal golden-spangled depths of brown. She grinned, a slow, satisfied widening of her luscious lips that beckoned him, and he succumbed, taking her mouth again in a kiss that had his head buzzing for air.

Gasping, he lifted his head and said, "Wow."

Her laughter sparkled like diamonds in the glade as she echoed, "Wow."

He rolled to one side and tucked her against him, throwing an arm over his eyes and hers to block the sun. No fire could have been as warm as the sun, no bower so sweet as this bed of green grass, no wildflowers so fragrant as Corrie.

This was how he wanted to stay—with his little lusty brown duck. As long as they could be together, he could endure the Garrett men's ostracism.

As long as he and Corrie could be together . . . forever.

From under his arm, he studied her face with its sprinkling of freckles and dark lashes against golden cheeks. What had made her follow him into the mountains? None of his sisters had done so, which said something about the deterioration of those family ties.

Tracing her profile with one finger, he asked, "Why did you come after me?"

"I was worried," she said. "You shouldn't have left like that."

"I had to be alone for a while . . . to think things through." He dismissed the hours of soul-searching with a lift of one shoulder. "I'm sorry you were worried."

"I'm not good at this worrying stuff. I never had to before I came here."

"You never worry about your family?" Estranged as they were, he still craved news of his family members—especially all those men in law enforcement.

She shrugged. "No family, just the people I fostered with. And we don't keep in touch."

"Fostered? What's that?"

"You know—foster care. Folks who take in kids who don't have parents or family to take care of them. The court appoints them." Her tone made it sound routine.

"I don't think I've ever heard of foster care." He had not even heard of them in his law classes at West Point. "So you're an orphan."

"Used to be." Her chin firmed and a bleak expression appeared in her eyes. "Now I'm my own woman."

Masked by the glib phrases, a wounded heart dwelled, and his own heart contracted with grief for Corrie, the woman. And more for Corrie, the child.

"When did your parents die?"

"I was eight when my mother . . . died." She yanked up a handful of grass and sifted restless fingers through it. "My father wasn't in the picture. Apparently, he didn't see himself as the father type and split before I was born. No big loss, believe me."

"Split?" What did she mean?

"He left."

Several strands of her hair teased her face, and Jess curled them around one finger as he watched remembered pain flicker over her face. What sort of husband deserted a wife who carried his child?

"Your mother must have been a very strong woman," he murmured, "like you."

"I'm nothing like my mother," Corrie said and flung away the torn grass. An angry flush crept up her chest to her cheeks as she sat up and started dressing. "Her own family didn't even come forward to take me in after she . . . died. I was sent to strangers."

"This foster family you spoke of," he prompted to clarify his own jumbled thoughts as he also dressed. A family deserting an eight-year-old child tasted bitter in his mouth.

"More than one. Once they'd experienced one of my nightmares, a lot of them sent me back. They couldn't take my screaming, they said."

The sadness in those few words knifed through him, and Jess drew her into his arms, regardless of her initial stiffness. She struggled against him, then exhaled a tiny sob and clutched his waist with both arms.

In the few seconds they remained that way, Jess felt he came to know the true Corrinne Webb. His little brown duck had been deserted by all who should have loved her and grown up without the roots he took as his natural right. Despite that, she had emerged strong and loving—though she obviously did not see those qualities in herself.

He laid his cheek against her hair as she sighed. *Seems it's up to me to show her just what sort of loving woman she really is.*

And maybe show her what a family could be.

Determined to quell this growing tendency to leak like a sieve at every turn, Corrie allowed little time to elapse before heading back to town. The walk up the hill to the trail started out uneventful and quiet.

Until they reached Buford.

"I'm not riding that escapee from *Ghostbusters* even if I have to walk all the way back to Hope Springs." Corrie planted her fists on her hips and glared at Jess, who was holding his well-behaved King by the reins.

Buford aimed his evil eye at her and gave a loud *brrrrt*, narrowly missing her foot with more mule spit.

When she looked at Jess again, he was hiding a grin behind his hand. "This is not funny, Chief."

He dropped his hand and guffawed. "I'm not sure what a ghost buster is, but it *is* funny." He leaned his head back and howled. "I can't believe you have Buford as a mount. He's infamous."

"Well, since it's so funny, *you* ride him."

Instantly, he sobered. "Not if I had two broken legs and he was the only way home."

"Then you understand exactly how I feel." Corrie looped her arm through his and batted her eyelashes at him. What the heck, it had worked for the blond bimbo at the Christmas ball.

"No." Jess gave the animal a look of pure loathing, then frowned down at her. "And don't attempt to imitate one of those simpering society misses. It won't work."

Corrie stuck out her tongue at him, and his eyes blazed.

"That's the Corrie I know," he said and, giving her no time to protest, tossed her into King's saddle. With obvious distaste, he tied Buford's rein to the gelding's saddle horn and mounted behind Corrie.

After the mule's cantankerousness, King proved a

breeze to ride. Even Buford behaved while linked to the big horse.

Still, they were well on their way when Corrie finally eased her grip on the saddle horn and patted the horse fondly on his neck. "I don't know why I was ever afraid of this old guy. He's a pussycat."

"I wondered about that," Jess said next to her ear, sending distracting shivers down her spine.

"I'm not the country sort," she hurried to respond. "Not much call for horses in Dallas."

Then she kicked herself mentally as Jess straightened behind her in obvious surprise.

"How can that be?"

Uh-oh. You've done it now, Webb.

Corrie scrabbled for a reason. "I lived in town? Never went very far?" Even to her ears, the comments sounded tentative.

And lame.

"What sort of town doesn't have horses?"

"One with a really strong homeowners' association?"

Again, he puzzled over her flippant response and repeated, "Homeowners' association? Sounds like a union."

She shrugged and said, "Something like that."

They rode on in silence for a few minutes while she berated herself for her smart mouth. Reaching an old orchard, he slowed King to a stop and dismounted. The sun touched Jess with gold as he stood at her knee and gazed up at her with myriad questions in his eyes.

To her relief, he merely shook his head and turned away to search in the grass beneath the trees. A short time later, he stooped and picked up a gun. Distaste soured his features as he stared at it before sliding it into his shoulder holster.

When he noticed her scrutiny, he closed his jacket to cover the firearm, then strode back to where she waited with King and Buford, both lipping at the fresh spring growth. With an economy of motion that had him back in the saddle before she could ask a single question, Jess settled in behind her and directed King down the mountain to Hope Springs. The tension vibrating through his body communicated better than words his reluctance to discuss his find.

As they approached the café, she could stand it no longer, and slewed around until she could see his face. "You're not going to explain how you knew about that gun in the orchard?"

His gaze slid from hers, but not before she saw pain and regret cloud his blue eyes with gray. He pulled to a halt and released a pent up breath. "You have your secrets, Corrie. I have mine."

She opened her mouth, but she bit back her instinctive denial. Jess was right.

She had secrets best not revealed. To anyone.

SIXTEEN

Once Corrie climbed off King and entered the Café of Dreams, secrets were the last thing on her mind. Everywhere she looked, people scrubbed and painted and chatted at a volume to rival a Dallas Cowboys game. She spotted not only the entire Johnson clan but Bridget, Rupert, Sean Quinn, a whole flock of waitresses and maids and grooms from the hotel, Mrs. Morris, and Zelda, as well as the Garrett sisters. Soot and paint stained all their clothes, but none seemed to mind.

As she gazed at the activity and all they had accomplished, hope blossomed. Yesterday she had believed the grand opening would be a bust. Now it looked like a sure thing.

The sting of tears—once so foreign and now so familiar—made her bite her lip to hold them back. Instead, she blinked rapidly and laughed.

"Just look at all you've done," she exclaimed, running from group to group and thanking them.

In the excitement, she forgot the friction between herself and Jess and grabbed him by the hand when he appeared at the door. "Chief, it's like new."

He followed her from window to window and into the kitchen to survey the progress there. Returning to the dining room, she gave all the crew a round of heartfelt applause, which Jess seconded.

"My Café of Dreams." She leaned her head against his shoulder and sighed happily as the workers turned back to their tasks.

All those years in foster care, she had dreamed of being part of a big family. Her misty glance encompassed the dozens of people who had taken her into their world, into their lives, and now slaved to help her with no hope of repayment. Indeed, no question of any payment. Just her thanks was enough.

Family was like that.

Tears fell unchecked on her cheeks as she smiled and smiled some more. She'd had to travel back to 1886 to find a group of people to accept her and help her when she really needed help.

To find a family of sorts.

Jess tightened his hold around her waist and grinned down at her as she raised her head. Oh, yes, a family of sorts. But there were all kinds of family, and she wished . . .

Corrie's breath hitched in her chest. She wished for a family—a family with Jess—but summer would be here soon. Only a handful of weeks. Then she would be pulled back to the twenty-first century and away from the man she loved.

With a different kind of sigh, she laid her head against Jess's shoulder again.

If only . . .

An excited Lula Brown appeared at the door to Corrie's quarters. "The delivery boy just arrived with the chickens."

"Thank goodness. I was beginning to worry." Corrie

glanced up from where she hovered over Sparrow's shoulder and motioned her assistant over. "Take a look at these menus. They're gorgeous."

Sparrow made a deprecating movement. "Just my little contribution to your Café of Dreams."

"They sure is pretty, ma'am." With a sidelong glance at the other two, Lula picked up one of the pieces of vellum. Upside down.

A brick of understanding slammed into Corrie, explaining several miscommunications over the last few days. *She can't read.*

Smoothly, Corrie lifted the paper from Lula's fingers and displayed Sparrow's fine calligraphy, rotating it in the process so it was right side up.

"See how beautifully all the courses are laid out?" she said, and read off the selections, from boeuf à la bourguignonne, chicken marsala, and roast pork to apple pie and flan, pointing out each word as she named it.

"Flan," Lula repeated, running her finger under the short last word on the list. "That's that puddin' you've been makin'."

"It's not 'pudding,'" Corrie protested. "It's flan. It's eggs and sugar and . . ." She trailed off as she met Sparrow's amused gaze and Lula's puzzled one. With a resigned sigh, she nodded. "Okay, you win. It's that pudding I make."

"Well, it's mighty tasty, whatever you calls it," Lula said. "I'm gonna go make sure that boy put those chickens where I told him to."

Corrie waited until she heard Lula's voice downstairs before throwing up her hands and pulling at her hair. "A five-star chef doesn't make pudding."

Sparrow rose and, laughing, gathered the menus into a stack. "The Café of Dreams is not a five-star restaurant, my dear. It is a small-town restaurant in Eighteen-eighty-seven. That makes your fine dessert exactly that—pudding, delicious though it may be. And it most definitely is."

"At least you like it, whatever it's called." Corrie laughed as well. Leading the way down the stairs, she asked, "You will be here tonight, won't you?"

Sparrow was the only one who knew how Corrie endured the trials of a twenty-first-century woman coping with a nineteenth-century kitchen. Without her, Corrie wasn't sure she would have the guts to open the doors at six tonight.

"Oh, my, I wouldn't miss this," Sparrow assured her. "Chef Sashenka is to be my escort. He is very much looking forward to a delightful evening without having to worry about the food."

A shiver of anticipation ran through Corrie. Sasha was the closest thing to a competitor—and a peer— she had. If *he* was pleased . . .

"Well, bring him on. Maybe he can learn a few things." *Like cholesterol is not a food group.*

"I am certain he will be content with simply a night off from his own kitchen. And of course, he is aware of Mr. Garrett's sophisticated wine palate, so he has no concerns in that area."

"I still think the French wines are overrated. Just you wait until the vintners discover California. Then you'll see a revolu—" Corrie screeched to a halt inside the kitchen. "Oh. My. God."

Sparrow leaned around her to see what transfixed Corrie. "I take it not what you expected?"

"They're chickens."

"So they are," Sparrow answered and closed the door on Lula's interested expression.

Corrie turned and gripped Sparrow's shoulders. "They're . . . alive."

A cacophony of cackles seconded her statement.

"They usually are, my dear." Sparrow steered her to a table. "Sit," she ordered, "while I make a pot of tea. That will set you to rights."

As the Englishwoman bustled off, Corrie laid her head on the tablecloth and rolled it back and forth. *Just when I think I'm getting the hang of this nineteenth-century shit, wham! Chickens. Live ones.*

Visions of her pouring marsala wine over squawking, flapping chickens and tossing them onto plates festooned with mounds of parsley filled her mind's eye. When Sparrow returned, Corrie had descended into giggles of hysteria. No amount of tea would cure crates of live chickens.

"Here," Sparrow said in a bracing tone, "this will set you up nicely."

Dutifully, Corrie sipped the dark brew. And wheezed as the burn of rum stole her breath.

"I like a little tot in my tea in times of stress," Sparrow said, sipping hers with relish.

Corrie tried to speak and finally squeaked out, "A tot?"

Sparrow sipped again and frowned. "Perhaps more than a tot this time, but I believe the situation calls for it."

The situation—oh, yeah. Forget the tot—bring on the whole bottle.

Through the kitchen door, squawking reached Megadeth decibels. *Sort of sounds like the band, too,* Corrie thought on another hysterical giggle.

Straightening to even more than her usual rigid bearing, Sparrow placed her cup and saucer on the table and folded her hands in her lap. "Control yourself, Miss Webb."

The formal address jerked Corrie out of her nervous outburst, and she drew in several deep breaths to calm herself. Thank goodness she wasn't wearing a corset under her chef's outfit or she never would've made it. When the urge to break into insane laughter passed, she folded her hands in imitation. "Controlled, Miss Sparrow."

Grasping Corrie's hands in her own, Sparrow ordered, "You must become adept at these sorts of things if you are to make the café a success."

Corrie cringed. "These sorts of things don't include a squealing pig or mooing cow, do they?"

That elicited a chuckle from the proper head housekeeper. "No, they do not."

"Then why did I get live chickens?"

"Surely even in your time chicken meat does not keep as well as pork or beef?"

"You're right," Corrie agreed, relieved that some things were constant—even if it was only the problem of obtaining fresh chicken.

"That's my girl," Sparrow announced and rose, pulling Corrie with her through the kitchen and out the back door. "Lula has begun dispatching the fowl you will need for tonight's dinner, and I have sent for more helpers to pluck and gut them. Now, which would *you* rather do?"

Corrie watched as Lula opened a crate, snatched out a chicken by its neck, and spun the bird around in a circle with a snap of her wrist.

And a snap of the chicken's neck.

"I'll do whatever you don't wanna." Lula dropped the bird into a pile of its dead fellows and reached for another. "What would you like to do?"

Corrie's stomach made a mad dash up her esophagus. She swallowed it down and said, "Die."

Fortunately, the Johnsons responded in force and Corrie was able to concentrate her efforts on fixing the grand opening feast. The limited produce available—as opposed to the produce imported from all over the world in her own time—had dictated the menu, but nevertheless, pride filled her as Maisie threw open the front doors at six o'clock and escorted the first party to its table.

Jess hovered in the kitchen, apprising her of the arrival of their friends and making wine suggestions to the wait staff as they handed in their orders. But when he began tasting the sauces and adding salt, she flipped.

"When you spend years at the Culinary Institute of America and Escofier in France, then you can *suggest* adding more salt," she gritted out, barely able to restrain herself from reenacting the chicken strangling. On Jess. "Until then, keep your fingers out— repeat, *out*—of my sauces."

He laughed and apologized with a mind-boggling bit of tonsil hockey. Unable to resist him, she succumbed and almost scorched the hollandaise for the baby asparagus.

"Out," she commanded, tempering the order with a caress below his belt that had him limping from the kitchen and muttering about sweet revenge.

Lula clucked her tongue and withdrew a roasting pan of chickens fragrant with herbs from one of the wall ovens. "You two smells of April and May."

"All I smell are those chickens," Corrie replied

and turned to carve several servings of the pork roast being held at a lower temperature in another oven.

"If you says so, but all us is waitin' for a weddin' invite."

Corrie froze. A wedding. Dear Lord; what she would give for that to be true. Loving Jess logically led to marrying Jess.

But marriage wasn't an option.

In less than two months that talisman would show up and she would be returned to her own time. End of story. Fate. Destiny. Heaviness settled over her heart and she shuddered out a breath.

Why had she let herself care? Why had her emotional walls failed her when she needed them most?

Why had she fallen in love with the sexiest, tenderest, tremendous gem of man? In the wrong century?

"Corrie, you all right?" Lula asked from behind her, and Corrie hurried to quell her pity party.

After that, she concentrated only on the food and the service. Nothing else was allowed to intrude upon her thoughts.

Nothing.

Late that evening, as she realized the orders had stopped some time before, the door into the dining room flew open. Sasha sailed in, flushed with wine, judging by his breath as he tiptoed to a halt in front of her, smacked his heels together, and lifted her hand to his lips.

"Bolshoi, bolshoi!" He tilted precariously, his head heading for his knees . . . or the floor.

Corrie shot out a hand to steady him and helped him straighten. "What does the Russian ballet have to do with anything?"

"Pardon? Ballet?"

"Nothing. Ignore me, I'm just . . . tired." Giving

herself a mental slap, she backtracked. "You were saying?"

"Ahh, little Corrie, forgive. But ecstasy overtake my English."

He staggered to one side, and she hurried to ease him away from the stove.

"Bolshoi in mother tongue of Russia mean superb." He exhaled another wine-laden breath. "Magnificent."

Her spirits rose as she helped him into a chair and poured a cup of coffee from the pot at the back of the stove. "Your praise means a lot to me, Sasha. Thank you."

"No thank me, little von. Thank *you* for best meal I not cook for self."

Corrie muffled her chuckle in a cough. *Oh, well. Second place when he thinks he's better than the best . . .*

In deteriorating English, he continued to praise her menu, item by item. "Pine nut in vilted spinachk—ve vood not do."

"But it was an interesting contrast of taste and texture, wouldn't you agree?" she asked and refilled his cup.

"Da."

Hoping his monosyllabic answer meant he was winding down, she signaled for Lula to have Sparrow join them. The housekeeper would see he reached the hotel safely. Otherwise, Corrie was sure the large chef would wander off the closest cliff and hurt himself.

Jess arrived with Sparrow. "I have my carriage parked outside, and Miss Sparrow has promised to see our friend here home."

"I will have Mr. Quinn's staff return it tomorrow," Sparrow said as she slipped an arm around Sasha.

"With my thanks, and I am certain Chef Sashenka's as well."

Jess lifted her arm from the chef and replaced it with his own and motioned for Big John, who had followed them in, to take the other side. With much grunting and swearing under their breaths, they heaved Sasha to his feet.

Sparrow took the lead and called sharply over her shoulder, "Come, Chef Sashenka. We must be leaving. Now."

Her tone seemed to pierce his fog, and he docilely followed her, with Jess and Big John steadying his erratic progress. As they proceeded through the dining room, Corrie saw that all the customers had left and the staff was clearing the tables while Maisie tallied their take.

"I'd say we're a success," Maisie said and held up a stack of money that would choke King.

Or Buford, if I'm lucky.

"Looks like we'll all be able to pay back our loans in no time." Corrie smiled at Jess when he glanced at her over the Russian's shoulder. "I've always said, provide fine food and the public will come."

Reaching the outer door, Sasha shot out a hand and snagged the frame, effectively stalling his exit. "Food, da, *bolshoi* food."

"Thanks, Sasha." Corrie patted him on the back. "You already said that."

Sasha twisted around, slinging Jess against the door and dislodging even Big John's hold. As the men grabbed him again, the chef leaned down and waved one finger at her and whispered, "But perhaps soupçon more salt, da?"

* * *

Roger Laughlin lurked in the shadows of an alley down the street from the Café of Dreams and puffed his cigarillo. The sight of Garrett in evening attire, looking the coddled blue-blood, riled him.

Back when they'd been scalping Indians, Garrett hadn't been dressed so fine. Not that the coward had sullied his la-di-da fingers doing any of the dirty work. Nosiree; he puked his guts up and whined about the army's honor.

Honor, shit. Ain't no honor nohow. Leastways, not in the damned army.

Laughlin rubbed the shoulder that still ached these seven years after lick-spittle Garrett had run him through. Taking a drag of tobacco smoke, he gave a bark of laughter that ended in a cough.

Didn't stop me, though. Got me more'n a dozen afore the day ended.

He inhaled the smoke again. He liked tobacco smoke, liked watching the paper and leaves catch fire. Liked watching nearly any fire.

Especially one he set.

Too bad about that stove fire at the café. Should've stuck around and made sure that the walls caught good, but the noise upstairs had scared him off. Didn't want to screw the job he'd set for himself, so he'd skedaddled.

Garrett's strumpet appeared at the café door and helped load the tub of lard from the hotel into the buggy. Them trousers sure did make a man horny, cupping her butt like that.

Just get an eyeful of that tight little ass she got on her. Do her that way, too, afore I'm finished with her.

He puffed faster and imagined screwing the lieutenant's woman. Hell, he hadn't been allowed to so much as look at an officer's woman back in the army.

Before he left this town, he'd have one. He'd have one good.

His cock hardened and he stubbed out his cigarillo. The redheaded whore waited for him back at the bordello. Again, he thought of Garrett's woman and her round little ass and walked faster.

The redhead's gonna earn her pay tonight.

Jess finished loading Sasha into the phaeton. "Are you certain you need no assistance, Miss Sparrow?"

"I am a woman of many talents," she replied with a grin. "I have driven a variety of conveyances. This one is not difficult." She lifted the whip and expertly caught the end of the lash.

"A woman of many talents indeed," he said and grinned. After assisting Corrie down from where she had been tucking in the chef, he stood back and bowed to the Englishwoman.

"Thank you, Mr. Garrett," she called as she set the vehicle in motion.

He watched her drive away, impressed by the crisp turn at the end of the street. "Drives as good as any man."

"Why do you sound so surprised?" Corrie asked and knuckled him in the ribs.

Laughing, he jerked to the side, then caught her and drew her into the café, away from prying eyes. Maisie Johnson had dropped a hint that others were noticing the frequency with which he visited Corrie.

And left late, if at all.

While she professed not to pay heed to such gossip, she had wanted to inform him in order to protect her friend's good name. Unsaid was an "or else," with Big John being a hell of a lot of "or else."

With any other woman, Jess would have been more discreet. With Corrie, discretion wasn't part of his thinking. From the first he had sensed a difference, and since their first kiss, he had known she was different. This was the woman he would spend the future with. He had not mentioned marriage yet because of Corrie's fierce independence and need to establish her Café of Dreams.

So he would wait. The summertime ball would be soon enough to propose.

Still, discretion was sharp in his mind as he helped Corrie close up while the kitchen crew finished washing and drying the dishes and Lula supervised the storage of the leftover food. Once the cash was locked in the safe, Maisie excused herself with only a single admonitory glance. The rest finished quickly and said tired but happy farewells before heading to their boardinghouse.

As she turned the key in the back door, Corrie released a contented sigh. Then she walked into his arms and laid her head on his chest. Surely she had to hear how his heart pounded in response to the sensation of her soft curves against his body.

"Thank you, Jess," she whispered. "You've made a dream come true."

Carefully keeping his arms by his sides, he said, "You were the one who worked so hard. I only supplied the money."

"And the inspiration." She raised herself up and nibbled his chin.

Every instinct screamed for him to tell the gossips to dance a jig in their underclothes, but he couldn't ignore what their allegations could do—would do—to Corrie herself and her Café of Dreams.

But neither could he ignore what her embrace did to him. Nor what she meant to him.

One kiss. Just one taste of her lips. He deserved that much, didn't he?

Catching her to him, he pressed his lips to hers and delved deeper. Her whimper of need fueled a fire within him, and he fisted one hand in her hair to gather her closer. She looped a leg around his thigh and rocked against him.

He groaned. How was he to deny this enticing woman?

Raining kisses across her cheek and into her hair, he inched away from her. "Sweeting, I have to go."

By the light of the single remaining lamp, her brown eyes beckoned to him. One word whispered from her lips. "Stay."

"I can't." He stepped back and straightened his attire. "We can't give the biddies in town any grist for their gossip mills."

"Then when?"

"Soon." *Not soon enough.*

She lowered her gaze and wiped her hands on her tunic. "I . . . I sleep better when you're here."

The simplicity and vulnerability of that revelation—that trust—nearly unmanned him, nearly broke his resolve. But Maisie had reminded him and he would heed her warning.

He was a gentleman.

Damn it.

SEVENTEEN

Corrie crawled out of bed late the next morning after a night of dreams of Jess and the café, and nightmares of fire. Fortunately, she had decided to close on Sundays, so no one was around to notice her shlepping around in her robe.

The Major would be appalled.

That brightened her outlook, and she made a scrambled egg and cheese sandwich and carried it up to her apartment, where she ate it with relish while perusing the latest edition of the *Hope Springs Times.*

By noon she was dressed and raring to go . . . somewhere . . . anywhere. But Jess didn't show. They hadn't made any solid plans, but after last night, she had expected to at least see him.

Finally, she stomped downstairs and pulled the coffeepot off the stove; Lula had drilled a lot of nineteenth-century survival skills into her these last few days. She ran upstairs, perched another of her secondhand hats on her head, and set out for Jess's house.

If Muhammad won't come to the mountain . . .

Glaring over her shoulder at the bustle that made her rear view look like a mountain, she barreled into a man on the sidewalk. She stumbled back and said, "I'm sorry. I wasn't looking where I was going."

Beady black eyes roved over her from hat to boots and back, leaving the sensation of dirty fingerprints on her skin. Smoke from his dangling cigarette made her cough.

She stepped to one side to pass, saying, "Excuse me."

The man sidled over and blocked her way. "Goin' someplace?"

"Yes, and I'm in a hurry." She moved to the other side and started past him, suddenly aware of how much she had come to expect the common courtesies of the Victorian age.

"I'll come along, if it's all the same with you."

While the words themselves were innocent enough, his tone and his continued eyeing of her made Corrie vaguely uncomfortable. He looked familiar, but she had seen so many people while waiting tables at the Chesterfield, she couldn't be sure.

His hand snaked out and grasped her upper arm. In an instant, discomfort morphed to alarm and defense training kicked in.

Literally.

She left him leaning against the wall, curled around her target. If this was some upstanding citizen of Hope Springs, she was in for it, although she figured Jess would understand. If he didn't and she ended up in jail, maybe she would see more of him there.

Briskly, she turned a few corners, relieved when she didn't see old beady eyes following her. Arriving at the corner of Jess's street, she spied his carriage headed her way.

"Stop the buggy," Zelda said with enough volume for Corrie to hear her clearly.

Corrie saw when Jess recognized her. As his dimples appeared and his white teeth flashed in a smile, her anxiety about his absence last night and this morning retreated. The expression in his eyes when he drew to a halt beside her revealed his own restless night.

And his own need.

Good, she thought with satisfaction, then directed her attention to his mother. "Hi, Zelda. How was last night? I'm sorry I didn't get a chance to visit while you were at the café."

"Oh, Corrie, the meal was wonderful. Such flavors. Such odd—umm, interesting—combinations."

"Just using what I could get my hands on." She winked at Jess to let him know what—who—else she wanted to get her hands on. "Where are you off to?"

"Your place," Jess said, trying unsuccessfully to keep a straight face. "Ma wanted to thank you by taking you to luncheon at the Chesterfield."

"Yes," Zelda said. "The idea came to me during the sermon this morning."

"Doesn't say much for the sermon," Jess teased.

Zelda rapped him on the arm. "You weren't even there, boy. So none of your sass."

Jess climbed down and assisted Corrie into the buggy. Rather than wait for Zelda to question why she wasn't in church either, Corrie asked, "Where are Peggy and the rest?"

"I sent them back to the hotel. The walk is a stimulating constitutional. I highly recommend it for young ladies." Zelda skimmed a glance down Corrie. "Do you take regular exercise, my dear?"

Cornered, Corrie did what she could—told a partial truth. "Every chance I get." Zelda didn't need to know the exercise Corrie referred to was the horizontal cha-cha with her son.

Jess gave a strangled cough and changed the subject. "Ma tells me that royal family causing such an uproar at the hotel is going to throw a party later this week. They're inviting all the hotel guests and anyone the guests wish to invite."

Zelda patted Corrie's hand. "You, of course, will attend with the family."

The warm fuzzy of family warred with the panic of going to a formal affair. Panic won. She gulped and clutched at Jess's arm. "I can't go. I have to cook. The café . . . and all that."

I'm babbling. Babbling is not good.

"Lula, while not the talented chef you are, seems quite the competent cook." Zelda patted Corrie's hand again with a finality like Doomsday. "You will attend and that's the last I'll hear of it."

Jess shot Corrie a look of resignation. "I've received my own orders. My presence is required also."

"But I—never—I don't—" Corrie's words jolted out as anxiety escalated.

"Now don't be concerned. The Karakovs are quite pleasant and stand on little ceremony. True, Prince Dimitri is a trifle stiff, but the Grand Duchess couldn't be kinder."

"Dress! I don't have a dress to wear," Corrie blurted, becoming desperate.

"Nonsense. You may wear one of my daughters' gowns. Heaven knows they packed enough of them." Zelda dismissed Corrie's last protest with a wave of her hand.

"Surrender, Dorothy," the wicked witch had screamed in *The Wizard of Oz.* This should teach Corrie to be careful what she wished for. She wanted to belong to a family. Zelda had taken her under her wing and was giving her a dose of belonging.

Corrie blew out a breath and glanced at the older woman.

Zelda smiled. "It will be such fun. You'll see."

She might as well have said, "Surrender, Corrie," and cackled.

In spite of her growing sense of dread, Corrie enjoyed the afternoon at the Chesterfield. Cholesterol-laden as usual, the meal was still delicious, and the wine Jess chose sparkled on the tongue.

Sasha bustled out to greet them and personally directed the waitresses. "Such vonderful little chef deserve vonderful service, no?"

Embarrassed by all the attention, she muttered under her breath, "No."

Jess kicked her skirts under the table. "We are overwhelmed by your care for our enjoyment," he said and covered her fist with his hand. "Aren't we, my dear?"

She twitched her hand from his and rose. "Excuse me, folks." Before anyone could object, she hurried across the dining room and lobby toward the ladies' room.

Reaching it, she swept through the door only to be brought up short by her train being caught. "Why anyone in their right mind would ordain that women sweep the damned floor with their dresses, I'll never know."

A warm chuckle answered her, and Corrie jerked around, heart racing at being caught voicing such a non-Victorian sentiment.

From around the corner appeared a pretty, dark-haired, and definitely pregnant young woman. "I quite agree," she said and flipped hers to one side with an experienced hand while she studied Corrie with a peculiar avidity.

"I'm not from around here," Corrie improvised. "That's why I'm not used to wearing this thing."

There, that ought to explain things.

Seconds inched by as the woman gazed at her. Then, checking her hat in the mirror, she said, "No, I can see that." With another chuckle, she passed Corrie but paused in the doorway. "Tell Esme I said hello."

Corrie stared after the strange individual. Odd that a hotel guest would refer to Sparrow by her first name. Even more odd was the woman's breeziness. Very un-nineteenth century.

Deciding that Sasha would have returned to his domain by now, Corrie exited and started across the lobby. Rupert relaxed in a hidden alcove between some palms and a pillar, and she stopped beside him, pretending to study the plant.

"Rupert," she muttered.

"What can I do for you?" the bellhop answered sotto voce.

"Did you see the lady who just came by here? Dressed in a bronzy color."

"Yes, ma'am." Suddenly, Rupert appeared behind her, cap in hand.

"Do you know who she is?" If anyone would, the nosy kid would.

"Of course. Gina used to work here but lives in Richmond now." Rupert made a face and donned his cap. "Married Drake Manton, the mesmerist, a year or so ago. He's giving a show the night before the Karakovs' fête at Miss Sparrow's request."

She had been right—Rupert knew everything, or almost, about everyone. *Except me,* she added gratefully.

Since she had left her purse back at the table, she had nothing to thank him with. "I owe you, Rupert."

"I won't let you forget that," he answered with a grin. At the desk, Major Payne frowned at them, and Rupert tipped his hat good-bye. A few steps away, he paused and turned. "Something else about Gina."

Corrie stopped. "What's that?"

"She was another of Miss Sparrow's special projects, just like you."

He turned and hurried to the desk while Corrie puzzled over that last piece of information. Way back in December, when this adventure had just begun, she remembered Sparrow mentioning that this had happened to another person.

Could Gina Manton be that other? Not likely. Not probable.

But if Gina Manton had traveled back in time like Corrie, what was she still doing here? And if she was still here . . .

Corrie's heart skipped a beat. Was it possible?

"I don't think this is a good idea," Corrie protested an hour later in Zelda's suite. Jess had wisely taken himself off somewhere, leaving her to his family's full attentions.

Blast him.

"Nonsense, my dear. It fits you."

"Not very well, Mama," Abby said as she tugged

at the gaping bodice of the gown Corrie had been laced into.

"The color is good for her complexion." Zelda twitched back a curtain and raked her gaze over the gown again. "Whatever possessed you to have a gown made in that shade, Clare? It would look positively hideous on you."

"Bill bought the fabric as a gift," Clare objected. "I couldn't tell him I wouldn't wear it. His feelings would be hurt."

"Mama's right. The color is all wrong for you." Abby glanced around the room and pounced on a pair of stockings. "Here, these should help."

As she started stuffing them down the front of Corrie's corset, Corrie batted away her hands. "Wait just a darn minute. What on earth are you doing?"

"Giving you a bosom."

Peggy circled them critically. "You don't have much of one, you know."

Heat flashed into Corrie's cheeks. "What I have is mine. I don't want falsies."

The sisters stopped their chatter and stared.

Corrie fluffed her hands in front of her bodice. "You know . . ."

"I understand what you mean, but if you are to wear this gown, you need a little something to round out the fabric." Zelda snatched the stockings from Abby's limp fingers and handed them to Corrie. "So stuff. We'll sew in the ruffles later to fill out the dress."

Stretching her arms to their limit, Corrie began yanking at the strings closing the dress in the back. "Thanks, but if I have to pad my bra—"

Another set of blank looks told her she'd goofed again.

"Anyway, if I have to pad my bosom, I'd rather buy a different dress."

Bea came up behind her and helped her with the laces. "Store bought? I'm not certain. . . ."

"I am." Abby caught Peggy by the waist, then drew Corrie into an impromptu hug, with the rest joining in. "We'll go shopping tomorrow and find Corrie a suitable evening gown."

"I have to work tomorrow," Corrie said as the sands of protest slid from under her feet like the California coastline in the rainy season.

"You have to rest sometime." Bea squeezed her shoulder. "We'll do it then."

"Why, we can have breakfast at the Café of Dreams, then wait for the crowd to thin." Clare grinned at her.

Peggy chimed in, "That way we can wait all day if we must."

All day. Right.

She had always envied the girls at school who shared clothes and shopped together. She was about to get a crash course in being a sister.

Before Corrie had time to concoct an excuse, the night of the fête arrived. Jess, resplendent in black tux and high starched collar, picked her up at the café. His eyes widened for a second; then he offered his arm with a studiously bland expression.

Corrie felt her cheeks heating and plucked at the emerald green ruffles that covered the dress. "It's pretty horrible, isn't it?"

Jess cleared his throat and started, "Well . . ."

"The truth, Chief. I look like a QVC collectible doll."

"Q.V.C.?"

"Never mind. Just tell me the truth. The dress is . . . ?"

He puffed out his cheeks and motioned for her to turn around. "A bit overdone."

"I knew it." She stalked back to the café. "Let's just call this whole evening off."

"We can't do that," Jess said and grasped her arm to lead her out to his carriage. "This is royalty. We accepted their invitation; we have to attend."

"Humbug," she muttered as she hauled the yards of frills and train and bustle inside. She continued muttering under her breath all the way up the mountain.

They reached the edge of the hotel clearing and Jess pulled the carriage to a halt. He laid one arm along the back of the seat and stroked her nape with his fingers until she ceased her complaints and sighed.

"That's more like it," he said in a satisfied tone.

"Sorry for the attitude, Chief."

"You're a little nervous."

He massaged her neck and she leaned into his fingers. "More than a little."

"Just remember that no matter how overblown your gown, you will still be one of the loveliest ladies present." He lifted a curly tendril and twisted it around his finger. "I personally am acquainted with at least three matrons who would sell their souls for your hair."

That elicited a chuckle, and she pulled his head down for a kiss. "I can always count on you to make me feel better."

"Glad to be of service." He tipped his top hat, then clucked to the horse to go forward.

Entering the Chesterfield at night as a guest sent shivers through Corrie. Waiting tables had never been this exciting. The gaslight chandeliers suffused the lobby with a golden, magical glow.

Zelda discreetly motioned for them to join her and the Garrett sisters in the receiving line outside the ballroom. She clasped Corrie's hand warmly and drew her into the chattering group. "Now never you worry, my dear. Simply concentrate on your curtsy and worry about anything else later. I will keep my eye on you, and if you have any questions, just look to me."

Corrie welcomed her reassurances, but the true reassurance came from Jess's hand at her back, his breath teasing the tendrils of hair that had escaped her chignon, his mere presence at her side.

Too soon, her turn to be introduced arrived. Major Payne announced her name and Jess's, and she walked into the presence of royalty. As she approached, she studied the tall, dark-haired young man and the kind-faced old lady beside him.

He could do with a little less starch, but she looks like a grandmotherly sort.

Beside Corrie, Jess bowed deeply. "Your Imperial Highnesses."

That was her cue. Abby's voice played over in her mind: *head up, back straight, small smile, and dip, bowing your head at the same time.* Corrie had stunk at this curtsy business all week.

She still did.

As she sank down on her right knee, she overbalanced and keeled over into Jess. Only his strong grip kept her from total disaster, and he raised her upright by sheer force.

Heated embarrassment raced through her, and

she wanted nothing more than to sink through the
floor and never be seen again. She couldn't bear to
look at Jess. He must have wanted to disavow any
knowledge of this klutz at his side.

Then the Grand Duchess stepped forward with a
smile and took her hand. "Careful, my child. I believe there is a slippery spot on the floor just there."

Corrie managed to get out a disjointed, "Thank
you, ma'am," before being directed away from the
royal pair. When she and Jess joined the remaining
Garretts farther into the ballroom, she glanced back
at the duchess. "That is one nice lady."

"I told you," Zelda said. Tapping her toes in time
to the music of the string quartet in the corner, she
craned to see the line of those waiting their turn.
"Unfortunately, no one may dance until everyone
has been introduced and Prince Dimitri opens the
ball."

Recalling the intricate steps of the dances she had
observed, Corrie said, "Well, the only dance I know
is a waltz. So if they play anything else, I'm staying
right here."

"A waltz!" Zelda flashed a broad wink at her
daughters before clasping one of Corrie's and one
of Jess's hands together in hers. "I so want to see
you two waltz. I do like the pairing of a tall man and
a smaller woman, don't you? And such a romantic
dance it is."

A sensation of being driven—or stalked—settled
over Corrie. Zelda had plans with a capital *P.*

Those plans nosedived when Sparrow appeared
and requested Corrie's presence outside the ballroom. Jess frowned as she followed the woman into
the hall.

"I am desperate, Corrie," she said in a breathless

voice, more distraught than Corrie had ever seen her. "It's Chef Sashenka."

Corrie's first thought was that the cholesterol had finally killed him, but Sparrow didn't seem *that* upset. Her second thought was the one she voiced. "Plastered?"

"All to pieces."

"I suppose he hadn't finished the meal preparations before sucking on the bottle." The lack of items prepared ahead of time had seemed strange when she worked at the hotel. It was about to bite the Russian in the butt.

"No, and his assistants are no help at all. Without his direction, they are no better than silly geese." Sparrow wrung her hands. "Forgive me for being so forward, but do you think you could help?"

Corrie glanced down at her dress. It was frilly and not her style, but it was her first evening gown. Music drew her gaze back to the ballroom.

A waltz.

One-two-three, one-two-three. The rhythm echoed within her, and she sighed. Her first prom and she wanted so badly to dance again with Jess.

Sparrow's face fell, and she stepped back. "I was presumptuous. Of course you cannot—"

"Of course I can," Corrie said firmly and gripped the Englishwoman's hand and headed toward the kitchen. She looked over her shoulder as the dancers whirled onto the floor with the prince in the center of the circling couples.

Her heart plummeting to her feet, she said, "There'll be other balls."

But not for me.

EIGHTEEN

Corrie had only been gone a moment when Jack O'Riley came to Jess in the ballroom and informed him that she had been asked to fill in for Chef Sashenka. Jess quickly made his apologies to his sisters and mother and sought out the kitchen. The staff scurried past, their expressions frantic and their voices raised in distressed panic.

"Sasha is really drunk?" Jess asked.

"As an Irishman," Jack quipped and dodged a waitress with a tray of pitiful-looking beef.

"You should know." Jess winked to take the sting from the insult, and Jack responded with a hearty chuckle.

They pushed through the swinging kitchen doors into a hurricane. Pots clanged and cooks screamed at one another—and no one in particular. Completed meas congealed unheeded on the counter.

In the midst of this, Corrie had planted herself, fists on hips and fire in her eyes. A waitress hurried past with clean linens, and Corrie snagged a tablecloth off the top. Tying it around her waist and tucking one end in the neckline of her gown, she yelled, "Quiet! All of you shut up!"

The chaos continued.

Grabbing an empty pot, she banged on it with a

ladle and, in a voice that would have done a master
sergeant proud, yelled again, "Quiet!"

The staff halted where they were and stared at this
madwoman in their midst. As they recognized her,
several smiled and nodded greetings. The only
sound was a trumpeting snore from the corner—Sasha passed out on the floor.

Corrie trained an exasperated glare on the Russian, then clapped her hands together sharply. "Attention, everyone. Sparrow has asked me to step in
for Chef Sashenka. You"—she pointed to a rotund
blond man—"oversee the beef and the pork. You"—
her finger rotated to a slim dark man—"see to the
vegetables."

Jess crossed his arms and leaned against the wall,
for the first time observing Corrie in her element.
She had insisted that she was accustomed to managing a large kitchen staff. It appeared she had not
exaggerated.

In a matter of minutes, calm was restored. Everyone had an assignment, and plates of food began to
exit on the waitresses' trays in good order. The staff
bustled around, obviously busy but with direction
and intent.

"Congratulations," Jess said as Corrie spied him
and strolled over. "No general could have done it
better."

"No general has my training," she retorted with
a grin. "I can't believe I've missed this. I must be
crazy."

"You don't miss it now?" Strange, given her delighted expression.

She glanced around, then tucked her hand into
the crook of his arm. "No. No, I don't. The Café of

Dreams is so much more rewarding. It's me cooking there, not this army of people."

"So you're content with your café, then?"

"Content?" She gave a sigh and squeezed his arm. "It would take only a little more to make me completely and totally content."

"Me?" he asked with a lift of one eyebrow as hope swelled. Although she gave herself freely to him physically, she had never articulated her feelings for him. Did she—could she—love him as he now realized he loved her?

Her gaze slid to one side and she disengaged her hands. He could have sworn he saw a tear slip down her cheek. But he had no chance to pursue the matter.

Corrie approached the passed-out chef and nudged one of his feet with the toe of her shoe. "Someone get him out of here and sober him up before someone trips over him."

No one else volunteered, so Jess stepped forward, commandeering a couple of sturdy cook's helpers and removing Sasha from the kitchen. In the hallway, they ran into Miss Sparrow, and she directed them to a vacant room close to the kitchen. Getting him up the stairs to his own quarters would have been impossible.

"I am afraid for him to be alone," she said. "He is quite despondent."

"Don't worry. I'll stay with him." Jess thanked the helpers and shut the door behind them after requesting a pot of strong coffee and a couple of sandwiches. Even if the Russian wasn't hungry when he awoke, Jess already was. No reason for him to go hungry. He relieved Sasha of his shoes and cravat and sat back to await the man's return to consciousness.

As the coffee and food arrived and the chef continued to snore, Jess untied his own cravat and relaxed in a chair by the window, his feet propped up on a stool. Music from the ballroom drifted into the room, and he ached to twirl Corrie around and around, displaying to the world that she was his.

So what if her frilled and furbelowed gown was a terror of design? She was the most beautiful belle at the fête. And for the Midsummer Ball in June, he would make certain her gown was as lovely as she was. Perhaps a gossamer silk like the whisper of a butterfly wing. That would suit her.

He must have dozed off dreaming of dancing with Corrie, because he roused abruptly when Sasha gave a sharp yell.

"Katyuska! Katya!" The words seemed wrenched from the man's soul.

Jess lurched to the bed and shook him. "Sasha, wake up. Wake up, old boy."

The chef opened bleary eyes and blinked. He whispered, "Katya?" Then tears rolled down his cheeks as he sat up.

Jess let him cry it out, occasionally patting his back and assuring him that all would turn out right. Finally, the man seemed to be nearing the end of his outburst, and Jess poured them both a cup of strong coffee.

Shaking, Sasha took his. "You are wrong, my friend. Nothing ever be right again."

"Why is that?" Jess took a seat and cradled his cup in both hands. "You called out a name. Katya? Does all this have something to do with her?"

"Beautiful czarevna—princess." Sasha released a

liquor-soaked sigh. With only a little prodding from Jess, Sasha related in surprisingly few sentences how, as a young man, he fell in love with a Russian princess and was exiled from the St. Petersburg court.

Jess could only imagine the anguish of forever being separated from the woman he loved. "But what brought you to drinking yourself into a stupor on an important night like this one?"

"Grand Duchess Karakova bring this." Sasha removed a folded piece of fine stationery from one of his pockets and handed it to Jess. "Read."

Opening the missive, Jess stifled a chuckle. Strange letters dashed across the page, like nothing he had ever seen before. "Uh, Sasha, I think this is in Russian."

"Vot?" The chef grabbed the paper and stared at it. "Oh, sorry. I translate." Squinting, he started to read from it but gave up when he was unable to focus. "Bah, I tell you." His lips trembled and he exhaled again as he laid down the letter. "Czarevna Katyuska, my little Katya, is married. To Prussian pig."

"She called her husband a *pig?*" In spite of himself, Jess was drawn into this sad story, so beyond the realm of his life, but he doubted a royal princess would put such an insult in writing.

"No, I say pig." Sasha collapsed back onto the bed and mumbled, "All Prussians are pigs."

He rocked the room with a raucous snore, ending the tale. Jess arranged a blanket over the chef and turned down the light before he left him to sleep off the alcohol, certain Sasha intended himself no harm.

Jess turned toward the kitchen and Corrie. Sasha

had lost the woman he loved. Jess didn't intend to allow the same thing to happen to him.

Corrie wearily accepted Jess's assistance from the buggy as the town clock struck one. She turned her head toward the sound and flinched—over the tree-tops, the church steeple gleamed in the moonlight.

Well, so much for sleeping tonight.

Jess escorted her to the café door and unlocked it with the key she had made him accept as co-owner. Arm in arm, they made their way across the dining room and through the kitchen to the stairs leading to her apartment. If only he would stay . . .

If only she could. Forever.

But that was impossible, and every day that passed dragged her closer to her return to her own time. Though until then, she would savor each minute with him and store up memories.

She turned and burrowed her head into his shoulder, wrapping her arms around his waist and wishing she never had to let him go. "Stay with me. Just for tonight."

His hand on her cheek was gentle and warm as he whispered, "I can't. The gossips—"

"The gossips be damned," she said, firing up, and leaned back in his embrace. "If I don't care, why should you?"

In the dim light from a low-turned lamp, he studied her, and she returned his gaze unflinchingly. "Stay," she whispered. "Please."

He cupped her face with both hands and continued staring into her eyes, as if he read the secrets of her soul there. Finally, he nodded. "I'll go stable the horse and carriage and be back."

"Promise?"

He brushed a kiss across her cheek. "I promise."

As the door closed behind him, she walked up to her apartment and undressed. Opening the door of the armoire to hang up the fluffy green dress, she jumped as her backpack fell out upside down and spilled its entire contents onto the floor.

"Shoot," she muttered as she knelt and started gathering up the items. She paused as her hand encountered a mound of small, square packets—condoms. She had stashed them there years ago for her last vacation, a camping trip on which they had been the last thing she needed.

Unlike her "vacation" here in 1887. Safe sex had completely slipped her mind with Jess. All she had thought of was being with him—becoming one with him. So much for being a careful, twenty-first-century woman. How would she explain introducing them to Jess now?

Deciding that Sparrow must have disposed of the food while she was storing the backpack for her, Corrie stuffed it into the armoire and propped it up with the bottle of wine to keep it from tilting over and falling out again.

By the time she pulled on her nightgown, she heard Jess's step on the stair and hurried to the door, but he was already there, his dark hair gleaming in the lamplight and his eyes alight with desire.

Her pulse accelerated. "You came back."

"I promised I would," he said and opened his arms.

As she walked into his embrace, the sense of coming home overwhelmed her and she clutched his lapels with both hands, afraid to let go. Afraid to let him go.

"What's the matter, sweeting?"

She shook her head, only mumbling, "Hold me."

Jess drew her tighter against him and pressed her head to his shoulder. Corrie sighed. This felt right as nothing had felt right in all her memory. If only they could stay this way forever.

If only the future never came.

Slowly, they walked into the bedroom and crawled into bed, too tired to make love. Jess cradled Corrie next to him and studied her profile. A pressure welled up in his heart, demanding release. Never in his thirty years had the urge to profess his devotion taken such hold. But this was the time.

And this was the woman.

He feathered a kiss across her temple and whispered, "I love you."

Her breath caught, so he knew she had heard. As she kept her eyes closed, doubt burrowed into him. Had he misread her affections? Did she not love him as he loved her?

Tears trickled from the corners of her eyes when she opened them and turned her gaze toward him. Pain clouded them—a pain from deep within her soul, deep within her past. Her lips quivered and she drew in a trembling breath as she whispered almost too softly to hear, "God forgive me, but I love you, too."

She rolled to a sitting position, clasped her arms around her knees, and buried her head against them, shoulders shaking in silent torment.

Jess rose and pulled on his trousers with an abrupt economy of motion, the tension of his movements mirroring the tension in his depths. Why would loving him engender such despair?

With another woman, he would have left. With another woman, it wouldn't have mattered. But this was Corrie, the woman of his heart.

He wetted a cloth in the bathroom, then took a seat facing Corrie and wiped her drawn face, the freckles stark against her pallor. And he waited.

At last, a shuddering breath racked her body and she laid her head on his shoulder. "Sorry I'm such a watering pot," she said in a strained little voice.

"I didn't realize that loving me would cause you such distress."

"Oh, Jess, it's not that," she answered in a rush. "Loving you is . . . wonderful."

But her lips quivered again.

"Then why the tears, sweeting?" He looped an arm around her and drew her closer with a tender kiss in her hair.

"I . . . it's . . . I don't . . ."

"If you're worried about your reputation, you needn't." With one finger, he forced her head up until she met his eyes. "Marry me. Today, tomorrow, whenever you say."

Happiness flickered across her face, too soon replaced by an expression of despair as she shook her head. "I can't."

Doubt gnawed at him. "Don't tell me you're already wed?"

"No way."

"Then why not?" He pressed a kiss to her lips. Her instant response garnered hope. "I love you, Corrinne Webb, and I want you to be my wife. I want us to be a family."

"I don't know how to be a family." She shifted her gaze to one side. "I don't know how to love—really love."

A chill ran down his soul. How could she not know? "It's easy, sweeting."

"Not if you've never—" She broke off and abruptly stood and strode to the window.

"Never . . . ?" Jess prompted.

Keeping her back to him, she reached out a tentative hand and fingered the lace curtain. "I've never been part of a family, Jess. Not one that I can remember, anyway. Or not one that I can claim as my own."

"You told me you're an orphan. But being an orphan shouldn't keep you from loving me."

"But being a reject who doesn't know how to love anyone does." Her hand fisted in the lace, and she seemed to stay upright only by that tenuous hold.

"You're not a reject, Corrie." Every impulse cried out for him to drag her into his embrace and kiss sense into her, but he feared rejection himself.

"What do you call a kid no one wants?"

A pang of sorrow speared his soul. He touched her shoulder with the lightest of hands and she sagged against him. Encouraged, he said, *"I* want you."

She barked a bitter laugh. "I'll grant you I'm a good lay."

Angered now, he spun her around, grabbed her by both shoulders, and shook her. "Never say that. Never. I love you, you stupid girl. Yes, I love making love with you, but that's not where it ends. I love *you.*"

Dropping her head to one side, she stroked her cheek against his knuckles, tears spangling his hand. "I love you."

"And I want to marry you and make an honest woman of you, damn it." Being a gentleman no longer mattered. Loving Corrie did.

"No." Just that, a flat statement.

"Why?" *Give me a reason before I go mad.*

Her breath shuddered out. "Because I don't have a choice. I have to go b—" She stopped.

"Go where, Corrie?" Taking another step, he was close enough to feel her breath, smell the scent that was hers alone. "It doesn't matter. I'll go with you."

She stared up at him with wide, frightened eyes. "You can't."

"Then stay here and marry me." He shifted his hold and pulled her against him, tucking her head under his chin. "Say you'll marry me, Corrie."

"Jess, I—I can't. Not now."

"At least promise me you won't go away."

She tensed within his arms.

"Corrie, promise you won't leave."

Against his shoulder, she hitched in a breath. "Ask me"—again that shuddering breath, but this time she returned his embrace—"ask me after the Midsummer's Ball."

Hope surged in him. "Is something special about that date, sweeting?"

She lifted her hands and cupped his face. "Very special." She wiped her eyes with the heels of her hands and stepped away. "Now, not another word about marriage until then, understood?"

He studied her as she tucked her hair behind her ears. While he wanted to believe they had reached an agreement, the odd reserve in her eyes belied that and twisted his gut with misgiving.

"There's something else we need to discuss, and now's as good a time as any." Corrie led the way into the parlor and he followed. After she emptied the bottle of wine from the liquor cabinet into two glasses, she took hers and dropped onto the settee with a wave of her hand to indicate that he was to join her.

"What is it?" Infected by her restlessness, yet puzzled by her serious expression, he perched on one end and sipped his wine.

Her gaze pinned him like a bug on velvet. "You never got around to explaining your jaunt into the mountains."

His gut clenched, and he placed his wineglass on the table with care. "An old family disagreement. Nothing to be concerned about."

"I put up with mule spit for that 'nothing.' You owe me an explanation." Her eyes gleamed fiercely in the lamplight. "It had something to do with your sisters' husbands not coming with them. What gives with that?"

"What gives . . . ?" Sometimes she used the strangest phrasing.

"Why did that upset you?"

He picked up his wine and drank deeply, avoiding her gaze.

"Give, Chief. Family's important—without a family, you can't know who you are. Believe me, I know." She swallowed the remainder of her wine and leaned forward. "Yours let you down and I want to know why. Heaven knows, your sisters and mother weren't exactly the worldwide web of information."

Trying to stall her, he shrugged. "A minor disagreement. Nothing—"

She rolled onto her knees and captured his face in her hands. "Don't tell me it's minor, Jess. God knows I'd give everything I own to have a family who loves me as much as yours loves you. Abby told me something happened out west to change you. What was it?"

How could he tell her that he still awoke some nights with the screams of the dying stabbing his ears and heart? How could he tell her what he had done?—what he could never forget?—why he could never forgive himself?

Those probing brown eyes gazed into his, then drifted away for a second. Suddenly, she gasped. "The gun in the orchard—that was part of it. Then there's that episode at the bank. You didn't draw your gun." She released him and paced around the room. "What sort of lawman doesn't draw his gun during a bank robbery?"

Ah, she had reached the periphery of the problem. Jess exhaled a breath he hadn't realized he held. "A lawman whose family considers him a disgrace to the profession."

"That's it? You won't use your gun, so the men in your family won't talk to you?" She whirled to a stop in front of him. "Hell, I know that's stupid and I don't even have a family."

If only it was as simple as that, Jess thought, his chest tight with remembered insults and accusations.

"Chief?"

Who would have guessed she would be so tenacious? Jess dropped his gaze to his clenched fists. If she was going to be his wife, she deserved at least some explanation of his rift with his family. "Years ago, I vowed never to shoot another man. When I told my father of my decision, he took great exception and called a family meeting."

"All the lawmen in the family."

He grimaced. *Abby's been busy.*

Jess reminded himself that Corrie would soon be his wife—or so he hoped. She should know the reason for the estrangement. Or the part of it he was willing to share. He motioned her to be quiet and continued. "When they arrived, I informed them of my decision to never draw my gun on another man. They thought I had gone mad."

And maybe he had, in a way.

"Can't say but what I don't agree with them, Chief. After all, a policeman who won't use his gun . . ."

"Put that way, you're right. It sounded insane, but remember, I wasn't out west or in the big city. I was back in small-town West Virginia—the town where I'd grown up. Not a hotbed of violent crime."

Corrie plunked herself beside him on the settee and drew her knees beneath the hem of her nightgown. "You're not telling me everything. Give."

Stomach knotted, he said, "To a man, they told me that if I refused to draw my gun in the line of duty, I was writing my own death warrant. And rather than wait for me to be killed, they would consider me dead from that day forward."

"Men!" she exploded and threw up her hands. "You mean you haven't spoken with them since because of *that*?"

He nodded. That and much more.

"Of all the stupid, pigheaded, testosterone-poisoned"—she slapped the cushions with both hands and glared at him—"*male* things to do."

Although he did not understand all the insults, he bridled anyway. "It was a point of honor on both sides."

"Well, I give up." She flounced up and retrieved a bottle of wine from somewhere in the bedroom. As she opened it and refilled their glasses, she muttered under her breath. Then she resumed her seat and said, "I can't believe they would break off contact with you for something as lame as that."

Not so lame after he added that when they killed a man in the act of apprehending him for a crime, they were no better than murderers. Just like the army.

Just like him.

NINETEEN

The remainder of the night passed in tense silence. Although they returned to bed, Jess kept to his side, wounded by her refusal to consider his proposal and by her not always clear insults. And by his own memories.

When the alarm clock rang only a couple of hours later, Corrie dressed without a word. He felt her pause beside his side of the bed before leaving but resolutely feigned sleep, unwilling to risk the resumption of their argument. Later, after he had time to consider all they had said, then he would be ready to talk.

Exhausted, Jess slipped into a restless sleep. Bright sunlight filled the room when he roused to the smell of coffee beside the bed. He opened his eyes, hoping to find Corrie, but instead, one of the Johnson boys grinned back.

"Miss Maisie said you'd need this," the youngster said and held out a cup. So Maisie Johnson, not Corrie, had been the thoughtful one.

He thanked the boy and saw him out before sitting down to drink his coffee and think. Once he started on his second cup, he realized he was being too harsh on Corrie. Why should he expect her to be sweet and thoughtful after their argument when he was still bristly as a porcupine? Hadn't he pretended to be asleep rather than talk to her?

His parents had not only drilled being a gentleman into him as a child but had also loaded him with a hefty dose of self-honesty. Jess could expect nothing more from Corrie than he was willing to do. In spite of himself, he grinned. Ma would be proud of him if she knew how fresh her lessons remained in his mind.

And what better way to apologize to Corrie than to arrange for her to truly shine at the Midsummer's Ball? Of course, any garment would ostensibly be a gift from his mother, but Corrie would know. Ma would make sure of that.

With that decided, he dressed and slipped out the back door so as not to be observed.

However, Jess's exit did not go unnoticed.

Roger Laughlin lounged at the corner table of the Café of Dreams and sneered as Garrett, unshaven and baggy-eyed, slipped from the alleyway. Here he'd thought the high-and-mighty lieutenant had begun to tire of the brown-haired bitch. Staking out the café was proving to be worth the time.

"Is everything all right, sir?"

Laughlin jerked, instantly on guard in case his surveillance of Garrett had been noticed. Looking up at the black waitress, he scowled. "Go away."

The waitress eyed the empty plate and asked, "Can I get you anything else, sir?"

"Pie." He hadn't seen the whore yet today. Maybe he should hang around some more. "And get that coffeepot over here, bitch. A man could die of thirst in this joint."

Turning on her heel, the woman flounced off, her backside wiggling under all those clothes. Laughlin felt himself harden as he watched her retreat. That gal had seemed awful friendly with Garrett's whore. Maybe he'd do her, too, when the time came.

The kitchen door swung open and the cook entered, carrying a coffeepot. Hell, if she wasn't wearing men's clothes again—and putting all the biddies' noses out of joint, to judge by the raised eyebrows and whispers that followed her.

One leg flung out and an arm draped over the back of the chair, he waited for her to reach his table. Her breasts bounced beneath her shirt and his cock throbbed. When the time was right for him to take his revenge on Garrett, he wouldn't have a hard time undressing her—just a quick rip and she'd be naked and ready for him. Just like those Indian squaws.

She plowed to a stop in front of him. "You wanted coffee?"

He nodded and let his gaze travel from her face to her toes and back with stops in between. Any woman but a whore would have blushed to high heaven; she only glared at him.

Corrie ran her gaze over him, recognizing him for the lech who had accosted her on the street. Leaning over, she filled the bottom-feeder's cup and in a low voice vibrating with anger, she said, "The next time you call one of my employees a bitch, you're going to get this pot of boiling coffee in your lap. You got that?"

His beady black eyes burned angrily as he straightened, protecting his prized possessions from any stray splash. "Don't know what that nigger told you—"

"That *woman*," Corrie said, with emphasis on the noun, "is to be treated like anyone else. With respect."

"I don't take orders from no policeman's whore—"

Corrie stepped back, motioning for reinforce-
ments and wishing desperately that she and Jess
hadn't argued. Otherwise, he would be around to
handle this asshole. "Get out of my café now."

"It's a free country, bitch," the man said and
sipped his coffee while he glowered at her over the
rim of the cup.

Nearby customers whispered among themselves,
and several men rose and asked if they could be of
assistance. Thank goodness for Victorian manners.

"I said, get out of my café and don't come back."
She raised the coffeepot in mute threat.

From the corner of her eye, she saw several of the
Johnson men slipping through the kitchen door. Obviously, the man saw them, too, and he brushed past
her to the exit.

But not before he muttered in passing, "Gonna
get you, bitch. Gonna get you good."

Every nerve twanged in alarm, but Corrie forced
her voice to a low, calm tone as she said to the room
at large, "Please forgive the disturbance, folks."

Maisie arrived and relieved her of the coffeepot.
"I'll do this for you, honey. You go on back and work
your magic in the kitchen."

As Corrie passed through the dining room toward
the back, several customers stopped her and spoke
kindly. Even Mrs. Harrington, seated with several of
the women from the hotel, said, *"Brava*, Miss Webb.
I have seen that ne'er-do-well lounging about the
streets and warned my girls against him. A particularly unpleasant sort, I fear."

More like a bastard, but Corrie gave Mrs. Harrington the benefit of better breeding—not something Corrie was burdened with. She could call the
asshole whatever she pleased. At least silently.

Instead of sharing her own feelings about the man, Corrie smiled. "Thank you for your support, ma'am."

She returned to the kitchen with an urge to giggle. What was this world coming to when the starchy, proper Mrs. Harrington came down on her side?

However, considering the choice was between her and a sleazebucket . . .

I wonder if he's in the market for a mule?

No, even Buford deserved better.

Jess paused to study the upturned faces of his sisters and mother and made his concluding plea. "So I figured who else could I turn to but the Garrett women to outfit Corrie properly this time?"

Ma shot a knowing glance around the group, then clasped his hand and squeezed it warmly. "Who else indeed?"

"I know just the dress. I saw it in *Harper's Bazaar.*" Abby rose to rummage through a stack of magazines in the corner of the suite.

Ma pulled him down beside her as the rest gathered around his oldest sister and discussed fabric and color. "Jess," she said in a voice that would not carry to the group, "what are your intentions toward Corrie? She has no family here, and I feel it my duty to inquire . . . even of my own son."

"Don't you mean *especially* of your own son?" he teased.

With a playful slap on his arm, she reclined in the chaise. "She's a fine young woman with a good heart. Not quite up to snuff, no matter how much she tries to cover it with a show of bravado."

Jess nodded. That was his little brown duck—bluff and bravado and a warm heart beneath it all.

"You are aware she's been hurt badly, aren't you?"

Startled, he met his mother's direct gaze. "Yes—yes, I am, but I didn't know she had told you."

"She didn't." Ma shrugged. "You don't raise the brood of children I have without learning a thing or two. One of those is being able to recognize the pain they try to conceal."

Just then, his sisters descended on them, squealing with delight over the dress design they had found. After Ma sent them to the other side of the room to look at it in a better light, she pinned him with a glare. "Do you intend to marry the girl? Or just bed her?"

"Ma!" The exclamation escaped, sounding like his protest when, at the age of twelve, he had been caught playing hooky although he knew there was no way she could know.

"Well?"

"You are the darnedest mother a man ever had."

"Thank you, my dear. I appreciate your circumspection in your relationship with Corrie, but answer my question."

"You raised me, Ma. What do you think I'm going to do?" He shoved his hands through his hair. "I've already asked her."

"Good." A smile twitched the corners of her lips. "Have you set a date?"

"She hasn't said yes . . . yet." And her reluctance gnawed at him. "Told me to wait until after the Midsummer's Ball."

"Odd."

"Demoralizing, if you ask me." Jess buffed his nails on his lapel with pretended indifference. "Any number of women would jump at the chance."

"But . . . ?" Her comforting hand closed around his arm.

"But it's Corrie I love." There, he'd told Corrie and his mother. No backing out now.

Ma gave his arm another pat and closed her eyes. Dimples flirted in and out of her cheeks. "I know."

Theodore Garrett settled himself into a corner table and sighed. The scents wafting through the Café of Dreams set his mouth to watering. If Jess didn't marry Corrie, he would.

If I wasn't already engaged that is, he thought with a guilty start. Oh, his fiancée knew how to *cook.* But Corrie created masterpieces.

He placed his order and sipped a glass of wine while he perused the latest legal journal. Only when a steak nestled in a bed of tender baby asparagus and a beurre noir sauce appeared did he look up.

Corrie arranged his plate just so in front of him, then perched on the chair opposite. Torn between his upbringing and the call of his stomach, he gave a jerky bow from his seat and picked up his napkin.

"Don't worry about being polite, Teddy. Eat." Corrie flashed a grin that made him realize again how lucky his brother was. "A chef is insulted if you don't eat her carefully prepared meal while it's at its best temperature."

A woman who understands. Teddy returned her grin and cut off one tip of the steak and dipped it in the sauce. The flavors exploded in his mouth and he couldn't contain his moan of pleasure. "Oh, God, this is superb."

"Eat."

He savored a few more bites before noticing how

she pleated the tablecloth with her fingers. Uh-oh, he recognized that fidgeting from his sisters—usually when they wanted a favor.

"Teddy? Can I ask you something?"

"Depends. Confidentiality and all that." The succulent steak lodged like a cannonball in his stomach. He smelled trouble.

"It's personal." She kneaded the table linen into a knot. "Or rather, it's about your family."

"Why don't you ask Jess? He's a good man, Jess is. Much better to ask him." He paused for breath and caught her expression—resolute. So much for shuffling whatever it was off on Jess.

"I can't. This is *about* Jess." She leaned forward, spreading her hands and smoothing the tablecloth. "I have a plan."

As he expected, trouble. But how could he refuse a woman who cooked like Corrie?

Jess made his way up to Corrie's quarters that evening in excellent spirits. Not only would he be able to surprise her with a beautiful evening gown, but he had enjoyed being in the middle of his family again, even if only with his sisters. He shoved away the accompanying thought of how much he missed the same camaraderie with his brothers and the other Garrett men.

Not today. Today I apologize to Corrie.

Glancing around, he could tell she had spent the entire day downstairs in the café. Even their wineglasses from the previous night remained on the table, and the wine sat open beside them. The least he could do was straighten up. Corrie would be exhausted after all day in the kitchen.

Before placing the wine bottle in the liquor cabinet, he shoved the cork into its neck. The label caught his eye and, expecting a French appellation, was surprised to see it was from California. A back label—odd in itself—carried a lot more information than he had ever seen on a wine bottle before, and he read the description of the vineyard and region with interest. He turned the bottle over and read the front again.

Then he read the vintage a third time, and icy fingers closed around his heart.

There it was. No mistake.

The vintage clearly read: *1996.*

Corrie hurried up the stairs to her apartment. Big John had reported Jess's arrival, smiling and joking, over an hour before. Hopefully, he was as ready as she to kiss and make up. Funny how the mere thought of kissing Jess gave her a lift and kicked up her pulse. Skin tingling in anticipation, she reached the landing and opened the door.

Her heart plummeted to her feet.

Jess sat on the couch with a bottle of wine, the pile of condoms, and her backpack on the table in front of him. Grayness tinged his skin with a ghastly pallor. The eyes he turned on her shot ice into her soul.

He knew.

"I've been waiting for you. Come in, Corrie." His lips thinned. "If that really is your name."

"Jess, I can expl—"

"Shut up." His voice, the dear, deep rumble that stirred her insides to Jell-O, grated harsh and hard. "Don't try to tell me more lies."

Her knees almost collapsed and she sank onto the armchair facing him.

He knew.

Jess fingered the backpack. "I have studied this and studied this, and it's like nothing I've seen before." He inverted it and jabbed at the label. "Nor have I seen anything remotely resembling this from Japan."

"Please, just let—"

His glance silenced her like a slap across the mouth. Next he spread out the condom packages, one by one, then lifted one he had opened. "These I recognize. Whores call them French purses." A muscle popped in his jaw and his nostrils dilated as his breathing rasped in and out. "But I doubt any whore has a contraceptive like this."

Oh, God, help me. I've hurt him.

"This"—he hefted the wine bottle—"is what tipped me off first. Did you think I wouldn't look to see what wine I was drinking? Did you think I wouldn't read the label?"

"Jess . . ."

He shook the bottle in her face. "Did you think I wouldn't notice that this wine won't be produced for a hundred years? Well? Did you?"

Hot, burning tears cascaded down her cheeks as she shook her head. The thought of telling anyone about being from the twenty-first century had never crossed her mind. She had never considered telling even him the truth. Now the truth was destroying them.

If I had trusted him with the truth . . .

But trust was something learned from a family, and she'd never had a chance.

Steps leaden, Jess paced the room and spoke as if

to himself. "At first, I thought it some joke, some strange jest. The label might have been concocted to make me laugh." He inhaled deeply. "I could use a good laugh."

He paused beside her but she couldn't look up, couldn't face his anger. His pain.

"Then I found one of these in front of the wardrobe. It, too, had unusual writing on it, and an 'expiration date.' I opened it and knew immediately what it was, but in all my experience, I have never seen a French purse like that. But only prostitutes use them."

He paced to the window, slapping the bottle into the palm of his other hand. "After that, I searched your quarters."

"You had no right." The protest was more form than heat. There was no going back now.

"I had every right, damn it. I loved you and you've methodically lied to me for months."

Loved—past tense. Oh, God.

"Tell me," he said in a falsely inquisitive tone, "what are those strange fastenings called that have interlocking rows of metal? Ingenious."

"They're called zippers." No reason not to tell him. Not that it would help her cause. Or regain his love.

"Zippers." He tested the word under his breath several times. "It fits."

His calm unnerved her, and she lifted her head to watch him. "Jess, I'm sorry I didn't tell you."

"Tell me what?" The enraged heat in his eyes belied the mild tone.

"That I'm from the future." Strange how unreal it seemed when spoken aloud.

"The future." Again, that slow repetition of words.

"You believe me?" *Hell, I* didn't *at first.*

"I don't know what I believe." He pressed the bottle against his forehead. "But it would explain your oddities, like wearing trousers, and the strange things you've said. It would explain all that I found in your room. And not being able to build a simple fire in a stove."

"Yeah, well, we've made some advances in my time."

"What is your time? *When* are you from?"

"Two thousand one."

"Two . . . thousand . . . one." He closed his eyes. "Not just the next century, but the new millennium as well."

"Jess? Are you okay?" What if this knocked him over the edge into insanity? How would she live with herself?

"Okay? I find out the woman I loved is from the twenty-first century and I'm supposed to be okay?" The strain in his face tugged at her. "You admitted you weren't a virgin the first time we . . . our first time. You omitted the fact that you whored your way across time."

Suddenly, he launched the bottle at the opposite wall. Glass sprayed them both, but he never flinched, only stood there glaring at her. "How many men do you have waiting among all those years? Two? Ten? A thousand?"

"I don't—"

Lunging for the table, he swept the condoms off the table. "Just tell me one thing and I'll leave you alone."

"Jess, please—"

"One thing, Corrie. Tell me this one thing and I'm gone." He towered over her, shaking with obvious rage. "Did you deliberately set out to seduce me? To make me love you?"

"I never—"

He grasped her wrist in a crushing grip. "You never loved me. I know that. Everything you've ever told me is a lie." Giving her a shake, he dragged her up against him. "But did you deliberately decide to make me love you?"

"I didn't lie, Jess. I do love you." Each breath was an inferno of grief, yet she gasped for it. She was even thankful for his touch, no matter how brutal. "I didn't plan it this way—"

"It wasn't deliberate, then. That's all I wanted to hear." As if flinging away a piece of garbage that fouled his hand, he released her and slammed from the room.

She crumpled to her knees, cradling her bruised wrist in her lap. Tears flowed down her cheeks and onto her lap, unheeded. The only man she had ever loved hated her.

She had hoped for a few more weeks of heaven before she was thrown back to her own time. Now Jess had left, taking her heart—her very soul—with him.

Heaven had turned into hell.

The next hours were a blur. Jess knew he stalked around town in a daze until finally arriving at King's stall. Somehow, he managed to saddle the horse and ride hell for leather into the mountains. Maybe there he could think.

Think, ha!

Corrie traveled through time. She probably had a man in every year—decade?—century? In this one, he was the unlucky man of choice. He had fought believing that she came from another time, but the evidence was incontrovertible. No one could perpetrate such an elaborate hoax.

As he and King climbed higher into the cool of the mountains, he fought the memories of her. Her laughter. Her scent. Her touch. No, she shared those things with others. In other times.

But he drew to a halt as he remembered the haunted pain in her eyes as he held her after her nightmares. Surely, she had not fabricated that. No one was that accomplished an actress.

Could any woman lie so well when she said she loved him? Had her reserve in confessing her love resulted from her knowledge that she did not belong in this time? Or was it that she never loved him?

No, she had to be a liar. She had to be the heartless bitch he thought her. Kicking King into a canter, he let the wind sweep the confusion from his mind. The clear mountain air cleansed his lungs of the smoke of doubt.

Then he recalled her protestation: "I didn't lie. I love you." He slowed King to a walk and slipped to the ground to pace. What could he think but that she lied about everything if she lied about being from his time? What could he think but that she loved him when her voice, her eyes, her soul told him so?

Was Corrinne Webb a liar? Or was she the sweet little duck he had loved for months?

Damn her. Why hadn't she told him?

TWENTY

Spring eased into an early, mild summer as weeks crept along at the speed of snails, and with each passing day, the aching void in Jess's heart gnawed at him. He vacillated between anger at Corrie—her lies, her secrets—and anger at himself. In spite of this, he haunted places where she might go, the bittersweet sight of her adding to the ache. But he avoided the Café of Dreams. It held too many memories of their final argument . . . and of their nights together.

Too many dreams of what they had lost.

Jess slammed his hand on his desk. "I can't stand it any longer. So help me, I'm going to beard her in her den."

"Beard who, boyo?" Jack O'Riley asked groggily from the chair opposite. The Irishman was taking advantage of Jess's recent largesse with liquor and spent more than the usual time in the police station. As a guest, not an inmate.

"Corrie, damn her eyes." Damn her deep, velvety brown eyes and freckled nose and . . . Jess shot to his feet. "Sleep it off here, O'Riley. Don't want the Major to see you the worse for wear."

Jack drew himself up and glared at Jess with owlish eyes. " 'Tis worse for wear I am? I'll have ye know—"

Jess didn't wait to learn what Jack would have him know, but hurried out into the cool evening air. The Café of Dreams was only a few minutes' walk away—just long enough for him to reconsider his frontal attack. So, before entering, he paused outside the front window and perused the interior.

His mother and sisters occupied a large table in the center of the restaurant, chatting and enjoying themselves, quite unlike the solemn, condemnatory harpies they had been toward him these last weeks. He was son and brother, but they had taken Corrie, a lying, time-traveling whore, into their hearts and placed all the blame on him.

If he told them the truth about her, they would recoil in horror, as he had. Wouldn't they? But to do that was to deprive Corrie of much-needed support—the family she had never had and desperately wanted.

Still, they were his blood relations and, by damn, he had the right to dine with his family. The tightness in his gut was hunger, not nerves.

Nevertheless, as he entered, his gaze snapped to the swinging kitchen door. Was she there? Would she come out? Would she speak even a few civil courtesies to him? He had never known how she would act.

And didn't now.

These past weeks, all she had done was ignore him, even to the point of walking around him with her head averted rather than speak. As if he was the liar, not her.

"Why, Jess, whatever are you doing here?" His mother's stentorian tones overrode all other conversation, and the café dropped into relative silence.

Heat crept up his neck, and he resisted the urge to duck his head like a child. Approaching the table, he snagged an empty chair and placed it across from her, between Abby and Peggy. "Good evening, Ma." He nodded to the rest. "A man has to eat. Here's as good as any place."

Peggy shot worried glances between him and their mother. This estrangement over Corrie had been especially hard on her, torn between her new friend and her favorite brother.

He patted her hand, and a tentative smile flickered across her features. As he turned his attention from her to the rest, the disapproving silence intruded upon his awareness. That and his sisters' stony glares.

"Are you certain this is wise?" Abby asked.

Wise? No, but necessary. He shook his head and kept his gaze riveted on the kitchen door.

Maisie swept through, jerking to a halt when her gaze encountered his, then retreating quickly back the way she had come.

Shortly, a familiar figure appeared from the kitchen and stood, arms crossed over her chest, simply watching him. Had she always had that air of command about her? That aura of barely contained energy?

Had the lamplight always glinted off the auburn highlights in her braid quite that brightly?

Corrie let out a huff and strode across the room. Several diners stopped her and praised her cooking, but she kept her gaze locked with his. As she drew closer, he saw dark smudges beneath her eyes and a gauntness in her cheeks that he had never seen there before.

Was it possible she missed him as much as he missed her? His heartbeat accelerated. *Good.*

She broke eye contact with him when she reached their table. Turning a smile on the rest, she asked,

"How is everything, ladies? Did you save room for Lula's cherry pie?"

Bea, Peggy, and Deedee voted for dessert while the rest opted simply for coffee. Corrie studiously ignored Jess's request for pie and coffee and spun on her heel to go.

Jess leaped up and grabbed her arm. "Corrie, please, at least—"

"Let go of my arm." Ice held more warmth than her voice.

"Corrie, I—" He stopped, uncertain what he wanted to say. The reality of what she was—a time traveler—and what had passed between them—love and lies—silenced him.

Her gaze raked him head to toe, settling on his hand on her arm. "Let go of me if you want to keep that."

He released her as if he'd been burned. "If that's the way you want it."

Rotating her face away from him, she gritted out, "You were the one who left, not me."

She hurried across the dining room, then paused to look back for an instant. Her eyes glimmered in the light, awash with tears.

And a pain that mirrored his own.

Jess forced himself to stay through dessert—which he was never served—then bade his family good-bye, and made his way to Teddy's small house. While he waited for the door to open, he jammed his hands in his pockets, his mind roiling like his gut. And his heart . . .

Damn it.

"Come in," Teddy said with equanimity, not the

least put out by this late unannounced visit. Unusually perceptive, he made small talk as he poured them drinks and directed Jess to a comfortable chair by the empty fireplace. Silence settled on the room like a shroud, broken only by the clink of glass as Jess refilled his tumbler.

The second brandy burned away his reticence, and Jess exploded. "Why in hell did I have to fall in love with her?"

Teddy sipped his own drink and merely shrugged.

"It's not as if she's a beauty. A little, dowdy brown duck—that's all she is." Restlessness of mind spilled over into restlessness of body, and Jess rose to pace Teddy's study. "I can name a hundred girls far prettier."

"Mmm."

"And as for grace! Did I tell you she almost fell when she was presented to the Karakovs? She's beyond hope."

Teddy raised an eyebrow.

"Has no idea how to dress, and her hair—" Her hair was like silk in his hands as he plunged them through her curls when they made love. Jess subsided into his chair. "Oh God, Teddy, what am I going to do?"

The gas sputtering in the chandelier was the only sound as Teddy considered his answer.

Jess accepted his brother's slow, thought-out ways, but this was maddening. "Well?"

Teddy took another sip of brandy before answering. "What do you *want* to do?"

"I want to shake her senseless."

"Not very productive." Teddy raised his glass and studied the mellow golden liquid. "And not what you really want to do."

"You're right. Strangling her also comes to mind."

Teddy raised his other eyebrow. "If it moves *you* to contemplate violence, whatever she did must be all-fired unbearable."

Jess slugged down another mouthful of brandy. "It's unbearable, all right. And unbelievable."

"What's so unbelievable?"

Did he dare tell Teddy of Corrie's origins in the future? What would prosaic Teddy make of a time traveler? Would his brother believe him, or would he call Dr. Jones to give him a sedative? Damn it, why did Corrie have to complicate his life, not only with her own self but with her secrets and lies?

"I asked, what is so unbelievable?"

Jess emptied his tumbler and placed it on the table. "She lied to me. Kept secrets from me."

"She's not carrying another man's child, is she?" Teddy's voice held a note of reserve.

"What?" Jess scrubbed his face with his hands. "No, nothing like that."

"Then what's so horrible about keeping secrets?"

"It's the type of secrets she kept—the kind of lies she told." No, he couldn't share her story with Teddy.

His brother scrutinized the remaining liquor in his glass for several minutes before he lifted eyes full of gentle reproach to meet Jess's gaze. "Have you told her what happened seven years ago? During that last battle?"

Fire erupted in Jess's gut. "Hell, no."

"Then how can you expect her to share all her secrets with you? And why should she?"

Jess scrubbed his face again, then stood and wandered to the window so he wouldn't have to meet his brother's gaze. Was Jess being unreasonable to expect complete honesty from Corrie when he wasn't forthcoming himself?

How different were their two secrets? Time travel was certainly a momentous one, but was his any less so?

At least she's not responsible for anyone's death.

He heaved a sigh and turned toward Teddy, who waited with his accustomed patience.

With a benign gaze, Teddy asked, "If you want her to be honest with you, don't you think you should be honest with her? Can you really expect her to conform to a different standard of honesty?"

"Damn it all. You're right. I've been a fool." Worn down by the days of conflicting emotions, Jess sagged into the chair. God, he wanted to take Corrie into his arms and never let her go. "When did you get to be so smart?"

Teddy chuckled and slipped deeper into his chair. "Must have been when you weren't looking."

The next morning dawned way too bright for Corrie's comfort after a night of recriminations and nightmares. Two days remained—only two—until the summer solstice and her return to the twenty-first century.

The weather was becoming uncomfortably warm, especially given this damned corset and all these petticoats. She tugged at the high neck of her seersucker dress and squinted down the railroad tracks against the sun. Air-conditioning; that's what she wanted right now.

That and the biggest, most super-sized Coca Cola she could lay her hands on. With lots and lots of ice.

Shorts and a tank top sounded great, too.

A train whistle hooted in the distance, and she tilted the brim of her straw boater to better shade her eyes and stepped to the edge of the station platform at the same time she crossed the fingers of her other hand.

Please let them be on the train. Please.

She glanced over her shoulder at the massive burgundy and blue Chesterfield carriage with its three triple-seats and the baggage cart behind it. Would it hold all of them? Or would none of them show up?

See what caring gets you, Webb? Worry and wrinkles. And heartache.

She shoved that thought away as the train rumbled closer. Several men hung out the windows and the doors and looked toward those on the platform, but Corrie figured she wouldn't recognize anyone anyway, so she stepped back.

This had to be the most lamebrained, insane idea she'd ever come up with.

Amid much smoke and cinders and screeching brakes, the locomotive drew to a halt and disgorged its passengers. Uncertain down to her toes but knowing it was too late to back out now, Corrie held up a piece of paper with one word printed on it in block letters: GARRETT.

Almost every man who disembarked tipped his hat as he passed her but none stopped. She chewed her lip as the passengers slowed to a trickle. Damn it, they weren't coming. So much for her bright idea.

Then a cluster of tall men descended the steps of the next-to-the-last car and her heart skipped a beat. At least half sported the dark hair and blue eyes of the Garrett clan. All of them carried themselves like the cops back in Dallas did—proud and aware of their power. Yet, like the best of modern cops, these men also exuded a certain gentlemanliness, as if they were as accustomed to rescuing a child's kitten as catching the bad guys.

Very like Jess.

There was no need to lift the sign for them to read. These were the Garrett men.

The oldest, whose dark hair sported a liberal sprinkling of distinguished silver, moved to the head of the entourage and touched a finger to the brim of his hat. "Excuse me, but are you Miss Webb?"

Corrie raised the hand not carrying the sign. "Unfortunately."

Eyebrows climbed their foreheads.

Oops. "Sorry. I mean, that's me—that is I—oh, hell." She gave herself a mental thwap to the head and amended, "My name's Corrie Webb. You have to be the Garretts or I'll turn in my chef's knife."

"Some of us," the man said, dimples flickering at the corners of his mouth.

"You," she said, sticking out her hand to shake, "must be Zelda's husband, Max."

The smile widened, and his eyes twinkled as he grasped her hand with barely a beat of hesitation. "That would depend on what she has told you."

Chuckling, Corrie said, "Ask *her* about that." Her gaze drifted to the others in the group and she asked, "Now, who are each of you?"

A blond giant stepped forward and clasped her hand in a paw the size of a grizzly's. "I am Abby's husband, Erik. This"—he dragged a slightly smaller version of himself forward—"is my brother Sven, Deedee's husband."

"I'm Jess's brother, Patrick, not to be confused with my Uncle Pat," a somewhat softer version of Jess said.

"Charles Garrett here," one of the older men offered. *"Uncle* Charlie to most of these boys."

"Bertie Smith here," a gangly young man with a sweet smile said from behind the two blond bears. "I belong to Bea."

That caused a ripple of laughter to circle through the group, and soon she was acquainted with all of them and their relationships to Jess. A round dozen, all told.

"Is that our conveyance?" Max asked with a jerk of the head toward the carriage.

Corrie nodded. "But I don't think you all will fit."

"Not a problem, little lady," one of the uncles said and hefted his carpetbag and himself into the baggage cart. "A couple of us can ride back here. You soft-living dandies can have the coach."

In the good-natured ribbing that followed, Jess's father pulled her to one side. "I want to thank you for inviting all of us here. No one in the family has had the guts to try."

A blush heated Corrie's cheeks, but she notched her chin up a bit. "You might want to save the thanks until after you talk with Jess."

Max tilted his hat back on his head and shoved his hands into his pants pockets, very like Jess did. "Why do I have the feeling Jess is unaware of this reunion?"

"Because he is? Unaware, I mean."

He blew his breath out between pursed lips and ran an assessing gaze up and down her length. "Zelda said you have guts. She didn't say just how big a dose of them, though. Lord, girl, I know that stubborn son of mine. He's going to be ready to shoot fire when we show up."

"I'm sure he will." *And I'll be singed in the process.* "I'm counting on you guys to shoot some back."

Max guffawed and slapped her on the shoulder. "Zelda was right when she said Jess had caught him a bright one. You're going to be a fine addition to the family."

A chill settled over her. "I'm afraid Zelda misled you, sir. Jess and I—" Her mouth was dry as an overcooked filet, and she licked her lips with no appreciable improvement. "Jess and I aren't . . . together. We're not a couple . . . anymore. I just couldn't leave without trying to help all of you straighten out this rift with Jess."

"But Zelda said—"

"Zelda doesn't have all the info—information." Corrie firmed her quivering chin. "I'll be leaving in a few days. I hope by that time you guys will kiss and make up."

"Kiss and make up?"

There I go again. "You'll reconcile your differences. Make everything better between all of you and Jess."

"Hey, Max," Uncle Charlie called. "You can talk up to the hotel. Get on in here. I'm hungry."

"He's always hungry." Jess's father gave a sad shake of his head as he waved to his brother. "But I fear you bit off a hunk of hurt when you took on this mission."

"Probably." *Absolutely, in more ways than you know.*

"We wouldn't have made the trip if we weren't ready to extend the olive branch to my son." Max closed his eyes. "God knows, I've missed him."

"He's missed you, too."

"Has he?" Hope sparked in Max's eyes as he opened them. "Then maybe we *can*—how did you phrase it?—kiss and make up."

"I hope so," Corrie said as she walked with Max to the impatient group in the carriage and cart.

"Aren't you coming with us?" Max asked when she refused a hand up into the carriage.

She shook her head. "I've arranged with Teddy for Jess to meet you in a parlor in the hotel this evening at ten. Ask for Rupert Smith, one of the porters. He'll direct you."

"You won't be there, I take it?" Max kept her hand clasped in both of his.

"No. You guys have to work this out among yourselves."

"I hope we are worthy of your faith in us," he said, releasing her hand and sweeping off his hat to her. He stepped into the carriage and it lurched forward.

I hope so, too. Please, God, let it work.

As she waved good-bye, she fought to keep her stomach out of her throat. What made her think someone like her, with no family, could patch up a broken one? Who had made her Dr. Laura?

That evening Jess ambled up to the Chesterfield on King while Teddy plodded along on his latest nag. After Teddy shifted in his saddle for the tenth time and cleared his throat, Jess drew to a halt. He knew his brother too well to ignore the signs.

"Do you have a boil, or is there something you want to tell me?"

Teddy gave a start. "What? Why? Uh . . ."

"Not a boil." Jess leaned forward and asked, "What is it you need to tell me but don't know how?"

"Dang your hide," Teddy griped. "Can't a man adjust himself without you interrogating him?"

"If that was what you were doing, you would be going blind by now." Jess grinned. "So what is it?"

"Ah, hell, Jess . . ."

"Don't let Ma hear you swearing."

"She isn't who I'm worried about."

"Then who?" Jess stared at his brother, still shifting in his saddle. He jerked his thumb toward his shirtfront. "Me?"

Teddy would not meet his gaze. "Sort of."

"What would this 'sort of' have to do with me?"

Kicking his horse into a canter, Teddy shot ahead. King plunged after him with barely a nudge, but only caught up as they hit the graveled drive of the Chesterfield. By the time Jess dismounted, Teddy was running up the steps.

"Hold on there," Jess called, tossing his reins to a groom. But Teddy kept on at a near run through the lobby. While his brother skirted to the right toward the tower, Jess made a more decorous progress, pausing to nod and bow to acquaintances. He reached the newest addition to the hotel, the elevator, as it rose to the floor above.

Muttering a curse under his breath and following the elevator's sound from floor to floor, Jess hurried up the stairs. Finally, he heard the contraption stop and skidded to a halt in front of its doors as they opened.

"Jess!" Teddy had the temerity to sound surprised. "I thought you were dawdling far behind me."

"He's here, my boy. That's all that matters," a well-remembered, and well-loved, voice said.

"You never were a good liar, brother mine," Jess gritted between his teeth as he turned toward his father. Then he saw the others in the suite's parlor and swallowed the lump in his throat. "Good evening, gentlemen. What brings you here?"

They looked at each other, then at him. Together, they replied, "You."

Corrie released a sigh and desultorily helped wash the dishes after the café closed for the evening. Part of her mind registered how adept she had become at using nineteenth-century technology—or lack thereof—while the rest of her mind ran in circles of depression and pain.

Pain . . . and Jess . . . and memories.

Somehow, all this ordeal was triggering more dreams—no, the night terrors—of her childhood. The walls between memory and sanity that she had erected so carefully and with so much effort barely existed anymore. Sleep proved elusive night after night, and when she did sleep, she awoke sweat-drenched and trembling. She hadn't slept well since Jess had held her through the night.

Not much chance of him ever doing that again. Two more days to the solstice and wham! I'm back to the future. Her breath hitched in her throat. *Whether I want to be or not.*

But at least Jess would have a chance to make things right with the men in his family. She was able to leave him that. If she was lucky, someone might even remember to let her know how the reunion had gone.

"Corrie, honey." Maisie's voice drew her back to the kitchen and dishes. "You're all worked out, girl."

Corrie swept the damp curls from her forehead with her arm and dredged up a weak smile. "Just a few more and we'll be done."

Maisie took the plate from her and guided her toward the stairs to the apartment. "You're done now. Get on up there and get some rest." Maisie gave her a little shove. "And don't you be coming down to fix breakfast. We will handle that. You sleep in."

"But—"

"Go on, now. Upstairs. Right now," Maisie commanded.

"But—"

Maisie framed Corrie's face with her strong, capable hands and directed an assessing gaze at her. Gently, Maisie brushed her thumbs across Corrie's under-eye area and *tsk*ed a couple of times.

Warmth flooded Corrie's cheeks and she dropped her gaze. "Pretty ugly, huh?"

"Pretty pitiful, more like," Maisie retorted in a bracing tone, then nudged Corrie's head up. "Is he worth it?"

Tears, a frequent visitor, welled up and ran down Corrie's cheeks to be caught by Maisie's fingers. She had asked herself just that question a dozen, a hundred, a thousand times these last weeks. With the same answer.

"Do you love him?"

"Oh, yes." Corrie's lips trembled, and she gladly sank her face against Maisie's comforting shoulder when the woman pulled her into her arms.

"Then what's the problem, child? You love him. It's clear as day he loves you."

Unwilling to lie more than she already had, Corrie merely shook her head and pulled away to run up the stairs. She quickly undressed and crawled into her jumbled bed, clutching a pillow to muffle her sobs.

Why hadn't she told Jess the truth? If she trusted him enough to love him, to make love with him, to let him see her during her nightmares, why hadn't she told him about from where and when she came? If only . . .

You blew it, Webb. Irrevocably . . . for all time.

The hands dragged at her again, blocking her air, smothering her while the pain continued down there. She felt herself rip inside and screamed against the pressure on her mouth. "Mama, help me! It hurts, Mama. It hurts!"

Fetid breath filled her nostrils as the hand shifted a bit and she gasped for air.

"Got you now, little bitch."

The voice—she knew the voice. "Mama, help!"

"Your mama ain't gonna help you."

The pain almost made her pass out, but she struggled against the blackness of unconsciousness. Somehow she knew if she fainted, she would never wake up.

Never be allowed to wake up.

A loud sound, not of her nightmare, intruded, and Corrie, drenched in sweat and tangled in the sheets, fought her way out of the nightmare.

What's going on?

Her heart pounded in her ears as the knocking came again. Insistent. Urgent.

TWENTY-ONE

"Just a minute," Corrie called as she stumbled down the stairs in her bare feet and dragged on a robe, the nightmare receding with each step. The knocking started up again. The only one she could imagine that insistent this time of night was Jess, seeking revenge for siccing his family on him.

The door rattled with the next onslaught, and she yelled, "I'm coming, I'm coming. Damn it, Jess, can't you wait until morning to kill me?"

She yanked open the door. A scruffy-looking kid of no more than ten stood on the step and handed her a folded piece of paper. She eyed it, then the kid.

"The gen'lman said I's to give this to you." The boy barely lifted his eyes to peer at her through dingy reddish bangs. "If'n you's Miz Webb."

"You have her," Corrie said. The kid lingered for a second and sniffed the scents wafting from the kitchen. Much as she wanted to read the note, she couldn't resist the tug of his hungry gaze and the way he licked his lips. The note could wait a few minutes.

She held the door open and motioned him in. "Let me fix you something to eat before you go home."

Inviting a stranger—even if he is only a child—in for a midnight snack? The nineteenth century has completely fried my brain.

The kid scuttled in, obviously starved, and perched uncertainly on the stool she pointed out. As she sliced some bread and made a sandwich that would've fed the entire Dallas Cowboys team with some left over, she tried to draw him out.

He merely stared at her and nodded his head occasionally.

"You don't talk much," she observed before handing him the sandwich wrapped up in butcher paper.

"Best thing I kin do is keep my mouf shut." But that didn't prevent him from wolfing a huge bite and taking another before he headed out the door. As Corrie started to close it behind him, he paused and turned back to her. "You sure is a nice'n. Thankee."

"You're welcome," she answered and watched until he disappeared around the corner on seemingly reluctant feet. Only then did she take a seat on the stool and draw the lamp closer so she could see the writing on the note.

In a slapdash hand, it read: *Must see you tonight. Meet me behind church at midnight. Jess.*

She rubbed her thumb over his signature and considered his request—no, command. He told her what he wanted and expected her to comply. Well, she would just show him a thing . . .

Her mind slammed into park. *Wait a minute,* it screamed. *Don't you want to talk to Jess? Did you not a few hours ago wonder what could have been if only you had been honest with him from the beginning?*

Corrie folded the paper and laid it on the prep

table. She would go if only to set him straight about ordering her around.

And maybe . . . to say good-bye.

The town clock struck a quarter past midnight as Corrie approached the church. She had wasted more time than she had counted on when she changed into a pretty dimity gown she and Abby had picked out. She might as well get some wear out of it. Heaven knew she didn't wear it for Jess.

Yeah, right, she thought with a shiver. *I wear the lightest damned dress I own on the chilliest night in weeks because I'm—what?—certifiably insane? Get real.*

Shivers coursed along her arms and down her spine that had nothing to do with the cool mountain breeze. The church loomed over her, its steeple piercing the starry sky. She didn't like it here. Not one bit.

"J-Jess?" she whispered. "You here?"

Wind rustled the leaves in the tall trees and sighed around the church building. A scrape behind her brought her up short. Breath snagged in her throat as she whipped around.

A branch dragged across the clapboard again as the breeze captured it and pulled it over the boards.

Okay, no more Scream *movies for you, Webb, and forget renting any of the* Halloween *videos again. You can live without Freddy Kruger if he makes you jump at a piece of wood.*

A deep breath calmed her a little, and she slowly walked toward the rear of the church, stopping to listen every few feet. Normally, Jess wouldn't expect her to meet him somewhere like this, but the past few weeks hadn't been exactly normal. He'd made it clear that he hadn't wanted to be near her, so she hadn't expected an invitation to his house. But sheesh, he could've met her at the police station. This place gave her the willies—for more reasons than the obvious spookiness of a deserted building.

At night. Alone.

Stop it, Webb. You will not psyche yourself out.

A twig snapped under her foot and she jumped a mile out of her shoes.

Yeah, right.

"Jess Garrett, you get out here fast. I'm not—" The rhododendron bush next to her swayed and she whirled to check behind her.

A hand shot out from the darkness and clamped over her mouth. Corrie tried to scream, tried to breathe. She knew this. She had done this.

This had been done *to* her. Before.

Jess! Help me, Jess.

"Ol' Lieutenant Garrett ain't gonna be here, bitch." The cold barrel of a handgun nudged under her chin, forcing her to walk through the open back door of the church. "It's jes' you and me . . . and lots of privacy."

Her mind spun in circles of fear. Of memory.

The man—a part of her recognized him as the one who had insulted Maisie at the café—directed her into the church sanctuary. "Ain't nobody gonna disturb us here," he said, dragging her toward the altar, forcing her to the floor, and straddling her.

As his hold loosened, she gasped for breath and yelled, "Help me! Help me, somebody! Jess, help!"

His hand crashed across her mouth, and the coppery taste of blood gagged her. His gun to her head, the man ripped her dress, tugging down her corset until he freed one breast. Then he squeezed it until her eyes watered from the pain.

"Got me the lieutenant's whore and gonna have her." He traced the outline of her face with the gun's barrel. "You understand me, bitch? I'm gonna have you every way there is."

She could scarcely hear him for the bass drum pulse in her ears. *Oh, God, it can't happen to me. Not to me.*

Not again.

He forced the barrel into her mouth and chortled. "Then I'm gonna kill you, right here. But don't worry. Garrett'll know everything I did to you. Just like all those Indian squaws we killed back in the army."

"Oh, God, no," she whispered as he withdrew the gun and buried his face in her neck, licking and kissing it. She couldn't handle this. She couldn't. Her mind rebelled and memory claimed her.

Heaving upward with her chest, she tried to dislodge him, but he was strong. So strong.

"Been flaunting yourself in those trashy little dresses. Making me hot. Making me want you instead of your mama." His hands grabbed her flat chest and squeezed as he continued the assault, scraping her back on the floorboards.

"Stop it. You're hurting me," she cried and flailed her fists against his back and shoulders, the only places she could reach.

"Yeah, it hurts. You're tight, bitch. Good and tight." He bit down on her neck and she screamed again.

Her head exploded into a thousand pieces as it slammed into the wall. Blackness beckoned, but she dragged herself out of it. "Mama! Why did you leave me?" she croaked, unable to scream anymore, barely able to breathe.

The pain crescendoed.

"Mama, why?"

Corrie fought her way from the remembered pain to the present. She would not let this happen again. As the man let the gun drop so he could claw at her skirts, she heaved up with one knee and caught him on the thigh.

He reared back and socked her in the stomach. "Don't even try to stop me, bitch."

Wheezing, she fought to keep the blackness at bay. No way was she going to pass out and let this bastard rape her. She struggled against his weight, succeeding in dislodging him for a second. "Help!"

His arm came down hard across her throat, cutting off her air. "I told you, I'm gonna have you. It's useless to fight me."

The dim light of the altar candles flickered across his features—wild and demented and evil. She knew that evil. She'd seen it close up, just like this.

"Don't fight it," he said, tearing off her underwear. "Them Indian squaws did, and your lieutenant killed them." His hand closed over her mound. "Didja know he killed Indians? Braves, squaws, papooses. He killed all of them. Raped the squaws first, though."

Barely able to breathe past the pressure on her throat, she could only think, *Jess, a killer? A rapist?*

But that was impossible. Her gentle Jess wouldn't harm defenseless women and children. No, it was unthinkable. No matter what this bastard said, she would never believe it.

The man found her opening and jabbed a finger into it, laughing maniacally. Mind in rebellion and unable to stop him, Corrie relapsed into memory.

She clawed at the man's weight—oh, God, her stepfather's weight—on her, but he continued, her head slamming into the wall with each thrust. Something brushed her hand as she swung it back, and she grabbed at it. Cloth hanging from the table—no, from the altar. The altar of St. Andrew's down the street from her house.

God, where are you? This is your house. Why are you letting him do this? she raged within her mind.

He hit her again, and she yanked at the cloth, only succeeding in pulling the fabric over them and the candlesticks onto the floor. She heard them thud as her head exploded again.

Flame licked at her hand as the crumpled altar cloth caught fire. Oblivious, her stepfather kept up his steady torture.

Corrie roused, memory returning. Anger returning. She shoved at the man and caught him with her knee. He punched her in the stomach again as he wheezed for air.

No! I won't let this happen. Not again. Never again.

She forced a deep breath past the ache in her gut and made herself look around for something to help herself. Beside her outflung hand, the altar cloth dragged the floor. With a burst of energy from deep within her memory, she pulled it down, the lit candles rolling on the floor, the flames spitting and greedily sparking on the cloth. One rolled onto the draped end of a curtain, which immediately caught fire.

Maybe someone would notice. This time, maybe someone would notice.

Please, somebody see.

Up at the hotel, Jess sat in the corner of the smoking room, nursing a single shot of brandy. His meeting with his family couldn't have gone worse. They had ended tonight, as they had seven years ago, in curses and recriminations.

The chasm between them gaped even wider than before.

He still wouldn't draw his gun. They still resented the fact that he considered killing in the line of duty to be murder.

Stand off. Draw. No way out.

No way back into the fold.

Setting down his glass, he stared into the darkness outside the windows until a young rowdy from the wrong side of town appeared at the door. The boy's expression sent a shaft of alarm through Jess. When the boy jerked free of the restraining hand on his arm and ran to him, that alarm escalated.

Jess knelt on one knee so he was face-to-face with the youngster. "What is it, boy? Who let you in here?"

"I did, sir," Rupert said from where he hovered by the door. "He said it was urgent he speak to you. When I told him to wait until you were in your office tomorrow, he said you would want to hear what he had to say about Miss Webb."

"What about her?" His heart crawled up his chest and lodged somewhere in his throat.

"Maybe he'll tell you, sir. He wouldn't tell me."

Jess forced his tone and expression into mildness

while his heart threatened to choke him. "Well, boy? What is it about Miss Webb that you need to tell me so urgently?"

The boy had been ogling the parlor's opulence and returned his attention to Jess with some difficulty. "You oughta help her."

"Help her how?"

"Get 'tween the bastard and her."

"I don't understand." *God, help me understand.* "Tell me what you know."

"Well, I took the note to the lady, like the sharper tol' me. Said he'd pay me good," the boy said warily, as if he had done something that could earn him a beating. "But he rooked me—didn't pay me a penny."

"Who rooked you? Can you describe him?"

"Said he was in the army. A sergeant, I reckon he said."

With absolute certainty, Jess knew who the man was—Laughlin. Only by force of will did Jess remain still. He wanted to jump up and run to Corrie, but he needed to know where. *Where, damn it?*

"And the lady were nice—fed me, she did." Rubbing his stomach, the young hooligan eyed the leavings of the buffet table at the end of the room.

"You can have all you wish of what's left there if you'll tell me where the nice lady is. What did the note say?"

"G'wan, I don' read none." The boy sidled a couple of steps toward the table. "But I see'd her headin' for the church close on to midnight."

Jess glanced at the clock. Twelve twenty. His gut clenched. The scenario was easy to perceive once Laughlin was factored in. The former sergeant had lured Corrie to the church. What he would do with her there needed no imagination.

Giving the boy a shove toward the table, Jess rose, then wrestled with his conscience and pride for all of five seconds. *I can't do this on my own. I need help—more than Cyril can provide.*

With utter disregard for the other patrons, he barreled out of the room, across the lobby, and up the stairs of the tower to the suite where he had met with the Garrett men earlier in the evening. Not bothering to knock, he slammed into the room and strode to where his father sat.

"Pa," Jess said, "I know nothing has changed between us, but I must—*must*—beg a favor."

All eyes turned toward him as Pa set down his wineglass. "What is it, son?"

"My army past has come to haunt me—to get revenge. I'm going to need some backup. Will you come?"

On one side of Pa, Sven sat forward in his chair. "Serious business?"

"Very serious. An army sergeant from my platoon named Laughlin has Corrie, probably in the church in Hope Springs." Jess raked a hand down his face. "I don't have to tell you what he'll do to her."

That brought all of them to their feet with outbursts of rage.

"This doesn't change anything," Jess said over the furor, and the volume increased with protests.

"I mean it." Jess caught and held each man's gaze for the space of seconds. "We do it my way—no bloodshed—or not at all. Is that clear?"

"But this is Corrie," Pa remonstrated. "Surely—"

"My way or don't come with me." Jess headed for

the door. As he raced down the stairs, he glanced back.

The Garrett men—every one of them—followed.

Heat shimmered behind her, around her, suffocating her. Corrie coughed, throat irritated by smoke. The weight holding her down eased as her assailant raised up to cough as well.

Fumbling blindly with one hand, she located one of the altar candlesticks. Before he could stop her, she heaved it with all her strength toward his head.

He saw it coming and blocked it, so only a glancing blow landed. However, it knocked him off her, and she rolled onto her hands and knees and scrambled away.

A flaming curtain collapsed in front of her and she recoiled, throwing up a hand to protect her eyes. Quickly, she scooted to one side and regained her feet.

Not again. I won't let it happen again. The litany repeated itself in her mind and strengthened her resolve. No way was she going to submit to rape, and no way was she going to let him kill her afterward.

No way was she going to be left here for Jess to find—dead and used by this bastard.

Smoke hazed the interior of the church, and Corrie couldn't get her bearings. Which way?

As she paused to peer through the smoke, the man latched onto her skirts and dragged her back against him, his gun pressed firmly under her right breast. If he shot her, the bullet would go straight through her chest and into her heart. Mouth dry with fear and smoke, she swallowed. And froze.

"That's more like it, bitch."

Through her petticoats and bustle, she could feel that he rubbed himself against her. In spite of the revulsion that crawled up her spine, she almost laughed.

Never thought I'd be thankful for that damned bustle. Can't feel anything but vague pressure.

She shot the man a look of loathing. Good; he hadn't noticed she wasn't able to feel him.

Unfortunately, her relief was short-lived. The hand not holding the gun grabbed her breast and squeezed it like an orange. Corrie gritted her teeth and scanned the area again for anything she could use as a weapon.

Just then, the front double doors of the church sprang open and Jess, thumbs resting lightly on his belt, strolled in, followed by the Garrett men. They all looked a bit itchy, and Corrie noted their pronounced lack of visible firepower.

Great, the cavalry arrives and they're unarmed.

The man shoved the gun harder into her ribs.

Jess waved at the smoke that had dissipated a bit with the door being open and approached Corrie and her captor, stopping about halfway down the center aisle. His gaze skimmed her and the room. "Are you all right, Corrie? Has he hurt you?"

"She's mine, Garrett." The man scraped his fingernails across her breast, beads of blood pooling as he dug into the outer part of her breast.

Breath hissed between her teeth at the pain, but she wouldn't give the bastard the satisfaction of anything more.

"You don't want to hurt her, Laughlin. Your quarrel's with me. Let her go."

Laughlin shifted his gun to her jaw and placed his other arm across her chest, making her a human shield. "You got a soft heart, Lieutenant. I hurt your woman, I hurt you. Don't take a lot of brains—or an officer's commission—to figure that out."

From the corner of her eye, she saw the other Garretts fan out, but the fire in the curtains had spread to other parts of the altar and blocked their progress.

The gun at her neck shifted again; this time Laughlin pointed it at Jess. She was surprised that the hammering of her heart didn't bounce the man's arm off her chest.

Damn it, Kevlar hasn't been invented yet.

"Be careful," she squeaked past her abused throat. Then she saw it—a star gleaming on Jess's chest—and her breath stopped. He'd never worn a badge around her, and she had assumed his would look like the Dallas police badges: oval and shield-shaped.

But there it was—a five-pointed silver star like the one that had thrown her back here.

Jess was her ticket back to her own time.

"Your lover is always careful, you whore. Out west, he was always the last onto the battlefield. Kept close to the skirts of any damned colonel or general, so he wouldn't have to dirty his hands like the rest of us." The gun wobbled a bit, and Laughlin held it under Corrie's jaw again. "Bet he didn't tell you how he murdered innocent women and children, did he?"

The lines of tension around Jess's mouth and eyes blanched white, and Corrie was glad she wasn't the object of his wrath. How was she to keep her mind on the present situation when her own time-traveling predicament stared her in the face?

"He raped and killed, but when I did the same, he ordered a court-martial." Laughlin's foul breath enveloped her as he panted in anger. "Me! All I did was kill Indians."

Now Jess's knuckles whitened. "You didn't just kill them. You tortured them, and goaded others to do the same."

"I did to them what they did to the whites. No difference, Lieutenant."

"Very different. That last battle was against a tribe who had signed a peace treaty with us. We never should have attacked their village." Even half a room away, Corrie could see the pain flash in Jess's eyes. Then his gaze met hers and the pain receded. His blue eyes bored into hers, then into Laughlin's. "I tried to stop the massacre, but you had whipped the men into a frenzy. No one could stop that mob."

Laughlin chortled, an evil rumble. "Damn right, you namby-pamby officers couldn't stop us. The only good Indian is a dead one. Every enlisted man knew that. Doesn't matter if they signed a treaty or not. Ain't a single treaty they kept."

Corrie flinched as he jabbed her with the gun again. Jess dropped his gaze to his waist, and somehow she took the hint. She recoiled from the barrel, throwing Laughlin off balance just enough that she hoped he wouldn't notice Jess loosening his gun in his holster.

Was Jess finally going to wise up and shoot this bastard?

Laughlin's hold tightened, and Corrie fought to maintain her control. If she lost her cool, he'd probably shoot her, then Jess. She suspected he knew he would die, given all the other lawmen in the sanctuary.

But he seemed focused on her and Jess. It didn't take a rocket scientist to know he would have time to kill them before he died.

"Hold on, Corrie." Jess's voice drew her gaze back

to him. He cut his eyes to her left, and she turned her own to that side.

Max and Uncle Charlie had made their way from the rear of the church and now crouched behind a pillar just off the altar. Max pointed to Jess, tipped up his hat with one hand, then made a beckoning motion toward her. They had a plan . . . if she read Max's cryptic movements correctly.

Jess cocked one hip onto a pew and said, "I have to take exception to your accusation of rape, Sergeant." Before Laughlin could protest, Jess continued, "I never raped anyone, woman or child."

"You were there." Laughlin jerked Corrie around to her right as several of the Garretts eased forward. "Stay right where you are or I'll kill the lieutenant's whore where she stands."

Jess's face turned to stone, but he only said, "I never raped anyone. Unlike you. How many women did you defile, Sergeant?"

"Hundreds by last count."

The answer came too fast for Corrie's comfort. What sort of sleazebag kept track of how many women he raped?

Behind her, the fire spread to more curtains, and they caught with a loud *whoomph*. At that moment, Jess tilted his hat back with his left hand, drawing Laughlin's attention that way.

As Corrie twisted out of Laughlin's loosened hold, with a shove to throw off his balance, and lunged to her left, Jess drew his gun and pointed it at the man. Time slowed as Max and Charlie caught her and pulled her to safety behind the pillar, while Jess shifted his gun up a fraction and fired. She screamed as Laughlin's gun zeroed in on Jess, but her love was already rolling over the top of the pew to the protected floor behind as the chandelier over the altar crashed down onto the deranged sergeant.

The others swarmed the altar, leaping over flames to subdue the struggling Laughlin, then started tugging down the curtains before the ceiling could catch fire. Teddy ran to the door and yelled for the fire brigade, and Bertie hurried to check on Jess.

Only when Max draped his coat over her did Corrie realize that her breast poked out over the top of her corset. A blush heated every exposed part of her, and some parts that were covered. She shot a glance at Max and Charlie, but they proved Jess came by his gentlemanly behavior honestly; neither one showed by so much as the twitch of an eyelid that they had noticed her boob hanging out.

Then Jess was beside her and she was in his arms, and any concerns about her modesty flew out of her head. All she knew was the warmth of his lips on hers, like a part of her that had been missing now returned to make her whole.

His five o'clock shadow rasped against her skin as he covered her face with kisses, asking, "Are you all right? Did he hurt you? Oh, God, Corrie, did he hurt you?"

"I'm fine," she said, and pulled back to look him over. Not a bullet hole anywhere. She looped her arms around his neck and raised herself up to kiss his lips again in thanksgiving.

"Better move it outside, son." Max passed them carrying a pail of water. "Give us more room to put out this blaze."

Corrie's breath whooshed out as Jess picked her up and carried her out the door, only setting her on her feet when they reached the opposite side of the park. Inside, on the floor, she had thought the church an inferno. Actually, the fire brigade seemed to be getting things under control quickly.

"Are you certain he didn't hurt you?" Jess's voice was soft and gentle, but the true question remained unasked.

Drawing the jacket closer around her shoulders, Corrie captured his face in her palms and gazed steadily into his eyes. "I'm a little bruised here and there, but he didn't rape me. I'm okay."

He pulled her to him, tucking her head under his chin, and held her with arms that tightened spasmodically. "Thank God."

"Yes, and thank you and all your relations." She rubbed her cheek on his chest. "And through it all, you remained true to your vow to never kill someone you were trying to apprehend. Pretty fancy shooting, Chief."

His chuckle reassured her—the old Jess was back and held her like a rare antique.

"When he put that gun barrel to your neck . . ."

"Yet you didn't kill him." She rubbed her cheek against him again, savoring his heat and his scent. "Something to be proud of."

In a warped, altruistic way.

"My family thinks I should retire." He gave a rude snort. "They think I'm a danger to myself and others."

"They're just jealous, Chief." She turned her head and hugged him closer. Her cheek scraped against a piece of metal and she gasped. How could she have forgotten his badge?

In a matter of hours it would be her ticket back to Dallas, and away from the place she now called home.

And far away from Jess.

TWENTY-TWO

The feel of her against him was heaven; and having her safe with him was the answer to his prayers. Jess filled his lungs with the cool, moist night air and relished the warm weight of her in his arms.

Time traveler she might be, but she was also the woman he loved. He would make her give up all those other men in other times. If he kept her busy—and satisfied—in bed, he figured she wouldn't miss her own time.

Shadows masked her expression as she drew back and sighed. "I better be getting back to my place."

"You're coming home with me." After the horror of seeing her in Laughlin's clutches, there was no possibility of letting her out of his sight tonight. He offered his arm, and she placed her hand, trusting and small, in the crook, and they headed for his house.

"What about the gossips?"

"I care more about you than any gossip." *I care more about you than anything ever in my life.*

A sad smile curved her lips, and he wondered at the sadness. Then she seemed to shake off her subdued mood. "So, confronting the bad guy out in the open like that sort of blows your inhibitions out of the water, huh? And what was it with you just walking in like that? You could've been killed."

"I served with Laughlin for years. I knew he would have to speak his piece before he would pull the trigger. It's his nature. Sooner or later, we were destined to fight it out." Her hand gripped his arm harder, and he patted it reassuringly. "Besides, walking straight in was the fastest way to see you and assure myself that you were unharmed."

"It was also the fastest way to get yourself shot."

"But I had to see you, Corrie, right then. I thought I would die if I didn't see you." He drew her into the deep blackness of the oaks. "I don't know what I would do if I couldn't see you."

Corrie placed one warm hand against his cheek; then a sigh shuddered through her. "Your face is burned into my mind forever. I see you every time I close my eyes." Pulling his head down, she kissed him, her lips holding his for a space of two heartbeats, then opening and drawing him in.

Heat exploded along his veins, and he wanted to plunge into her right now. But he reminded himself that he was a gentleman by upbringing and reined in his rampant desire. Only moments before, Corrie had been manhandled and almost raped by a thug who wanted to hurt her simply because of his hatred for Jess. He eased away and stared down at her. "I know you can't want to make love right now. Not after what Laughlin did to you."

"You think because that bastard tried to rape me . . . ?"

He nodded. How could she think otherwise?

"Chief"—she stabbed him in the chest with one finger—"the mechanics of what he wanted to do and what we do together have a vague resemblance, but no way are they the same. No way!" She softened her touch and splayed her hand across his chest. "When we make love, it isn't like anything else that has ever happened before. It's . . . special."

Even in the dark, he could see the darkening of her cheeks. She wasn't prim and proper as he had once bemoaned—fool that he'd been—but she did blush. He tipped up her chin and kissed her softly. "It is special indeed." He rimmed her lips with his tongue and grinned. "Want to do something special?"

Her answering chuckle reassured him, and they hurried to his house, barely waiting until the door closed to start stripping. Then they tumbled over each other as they climbed the stairs, unwilling to break a touch or a kiss to do so.

Finally, they fell into his bed, and he lifted his head to gaze down at her. She was so beautiful in her own freckled, spunky way, with her sparkling brown eyes and sassy mouth. He kissed her eyes and the side of that mouth, and reveled in the hitch in her breath as his hand found her nipple and rubbed its peak to pebbled hardness. Replacing his hand with his lips, he suckled there, uncertain whether the pulsing thunder in his ears was hers or his.

He placed light, teasing kisses down the underside of her breast, to her stomach, and paused briefly at her navel to circle it with his tongue.

"Jess, you're driving me wild," she said, her voice husky and eager.

"Just a little more, sweeting," he murmured and drifted lower, darting his tongue into her shadowed recesses, and feeling her buck against him. She was hot and wet and musky with the scent of arousal, and he wasn't sure how long he could exercise control.

Corrie fisted her hands in his hair and lifted his head a bit. "Please, Jess, I want you in me."

"Good, because that's where I want to be." Placing a final kiss on her nether curls, he nibbled his way up her torso, then filled her tight sheath with his manhood. Her internal muscles drew on him, and soon they settled into the ancient rhythm.

Her hands were gentle on his cheeks and she whispered endearments and words of love as she kissed his chin, his throat, and nibbled his ear. He stroked in and out with exquisite hesitation, drawing out her pleasure and his. Her eyes glazed as her climax neared, her breath rasping in her chest, her hands clutching his body, her back arched.

He plunged into her faster and harder, driving them both over the edge as he whispered, "I love you, Corrie."

Slowly, their breathing eased and she drew him down on top of her. Beside his ear, he heard her whisper, "I love you, Jess. For all time, I will love you."

Later, he tucked her to one side and studied her as she drifted off to sleep. While relief was foremost in his mind for her safety and wholeness, unease remained. Their lovemaking was different tonight. Oh, she still aroused him as no other woman ever had. But her kisses held a new poignancy, a sweetness and desperation he had never felt before.

He had the unshakable feeling she was saying farewell.

Corrie thought the pain would kill her, but she struggled anyway. Why had Mama left her with her stepfather? She never had before tonight. Why, Mama? she raged inwardly.

Suddenly, the man stopped. He slumped over her, blocking her air. She shoved against him, her hands slicking in something wet and sticky on his neck and face. Then he was pulled off her and Mama was there, crying and holding one of the big altar candlesticks.

"I'm sorry, Corrie. Oh, God, I'm so sorry." Mama lifted her up. "Oh, God, I'm sorry he did this to you. I didn't know, honey. I didn't know."

Corrie clasped her hands around Mama's neck and wept, sobs wracking her body and robbing her of breath. "Mama, you came. You came, Mama."

"I'm here, honey." Her mother rose and, settling Corrie on one hip, turned.

The fire had leapt from the altar cloth to the carpet and the red velvet curtains to one side. Flames soared to the ceiling, casting a hellish glow over the body of Corrie's assailant. As Mama scooted around the altar and started down the stairs to the sanctuary, the man moaned. She stiffened and turned to stare at him. Then she laid her head against Corrie's before she hurried toward the outer door.

"You're going to be all right, Corrie. It will never happen again." Mama set her down outside the church and knelt in front of her.

"It hurt, Mama. A whole lot," Corrie sobbed out.

"I know, honey. But he's never going to hurt you again. I promise."

Mama kissed her on the cheek and hugged her tight. Corrie hugged her back, sure that Mama would make it better.

Then Mama rose and gripped Corrie's shoulders. "You stay here, Corrie. Understand? You stay right here. I have to go back in there, but you have to stay right here."

"Don't leave me, Mama. Please don't leave me!"

"I have to go back in there, Corrie. I have to make sure he never hurts you again. Then we'll go home and be safe—just you and me. Okay?" With another admonition for Corrie to stay there, Mama entered the church where she was silhouetted for a moment against the wall of flame.

Seconds later Corrie heard her stepfather curse and her mama yell something back. Then the roof collapsed, the force tossing Corrie back like a rag doll. Blackness claimed her for its own.

Corrie sighed and opened her eyes. She knew she had had the dream again, but this time she knew her mother hadn't deserted her, hadn't intentionally left her on her own. Mama had returned to the church to keep Corrie safe.

All those years, her memories had centered on her mother leaving her, interpreting that as abandonment—but what else could the child Corrie have thought? She had blocked out her stepfather's rape—had even blocked out the man's very existence. She had sought to explain what had happened in terms she could understand.

How was she to know they were wrong?

In erecting mental barriers against the remembered pain of the rape and the loss of her mother, Corrie figured she must have prevented any psychologist from reaching her and helping her. Sometimes being an independent kid wasn't the best thing. But again, how was she to know?

She had only been a little kid—abused and alone.

A heartbeat in her ear, with tickly hairs as well, reminded her that she was no longer alone. *Jess*, she thought with a surge of love. Jess had torn down every barrier she erected. He had shown her the power of love and shared his family with her.

She blinked away the tears forming in her eyes. He had given her memories to fill the rest of her life.

If only . . .

At her side, Jess cleared his throat, and she lifted her gaze to his intense blue ones. "You're going back tomorrow, aren't you? That's why waiting until the Midsummer Ball is so important." His tone was quiet and sad.

"I—I—" She stopped and snagged the breath he'd ripped away. She dropped her gaze. "Yes."

"Stay with me. Give up those other men. Give up your travels in time."

That elicited a snort of laughter. "You say that like I'm a professional. Chief, you're the only man in my life and this is the first—and last—time I do this."

"Then stay with me."

If only I could. She burrowed her head against his chest and sighed as tears bathed her eyes. "I can't." She breathed in his scent and let the tears flow. "I don't know any way I can."

When Corrie awoke the next morning, Jess had already gone. In a way, she was glad. If she had to spend this entire last day looking at him, knowing what she would lose when she went back, knowing there was no way out, she would end up screaming. That wasn't how she wanted him to remember her.

She made her way downstairs and paused at the kitchen door, the memory of her first attempt at cooking breakfast sharp and pungent in her mind. Laughter—and tears—tickled the back of her throat.

Jess must've been crazy to put his money behind a chef who couldn't cook an egg without burning it . . . or tossing it onto his mother.

Corrie stuffed her hair under one of his hats and let herself out the back way. Disguised in one of his old suits, she hurried to the Café of Dreams and slipped up the stairs with only the kitchen staff the wiser. No need to rub her and Jess's liaison in the gossips' faces.

Her apartment seemed abandoned already. Little bits and pieces of her life here littered the surfaces, and she trailed her fingertips over the daguerreotype of Jess she had taken from his guest room as waves of what-might-have-been crashed over her. She sank onto the needle-point footstool that Peggy had given her and laid her head on her knees and gave in to the sobs tearing at her chest.

The Johnsons must have sensed her need to be alone because Maisie didn't make an appearance until Corrie had bathed and was toweling her hair dry by the open window. Corrie smiled at her through the damp tendrils. "Come on in."

Her friend entered on hesitant feet. "Deputy Cyril came by this morning to tell us what happened. He said you were doing fine, so we—I—decided not to bother you until now."

"I'm fine, Maisie. Just a little tired." Corrie shifted a shoulder and winced. "And a little sore. But otherwise I'm okay."

"Thank the good Lord."

Suddenly, Maisie enveloped Corrie in a hug, and her tears escaped and blurred her vision. The woman had become a good friend, and Corrie would miss her gentle teasing and honest concern. Maybe when Corrie returned to her own time, she would be able to make a friend like Maisie, now that she had learned what a friend was and how to be a friend herself.

"Now, Corrie, you gotta get dressed," Maisie ordered and wiped her eyes. "Miz Zelda's carriage will be here soon."

"I didn't know they intended to come into town today," Corrie said and twisted the thin towel around her hair. "Maybe I'll fix them something special."

It's the only way I can say good-bye.

Maisie fisted her hands on her hips and stared at her. "You'll do no such thing, missy. You're going to that dance tonight, and Jess's sisters have a surprise for you. I've seen it and it's pure-dee beautiful."

The dance—the Midsummer Ball. Of course.

Corrie's hopes soared. At least she would be able to waltz with Jess one more time. He would hold her in his arms and swirl her around and around. One more time, she would be Cinderella.

And like Cinderella, midnight would come for her.

Corrie turned away to hide her expression until she could control it. Then she called Maisie over to her desk and handed her a folded document, closed with a wax stamp. "Keep this somewhere safe."

Maisie turned it over in her hands. "Looks important. What is it?"

"Just keep it safe," Corrie said, closing both of her friend's hands over it. "If something ever happens to me, open it. Understand?"

Puzzled, the woman studied the paper, then turned her too perceptive gaze on Corrie. Before she could ask another question, Corrie said, "That's all I'm going to tell you. Just keep it and open it if something happens to me."

The steady brown gaze held for a moment; then

Maisie nodded and tucked the paper in her bodice. "Nothing bad's going to happen to you."

"Well, if it does . . ." Corrie saw her out and leaned against the closed door. That particular item on her mental list of farewells was done—the Johnsons would have the Café of Dreams when she was gone.

Now to say good-bye to the Garrett women and make it through the Midsummer Ball. She dragged out her emerald green evening gown and made a rude noise.

So much for going out in style.

The sun was lowering toward the Allegheny Mountains, tinting the sky with a riot of pinks and purples, when Zelda tossed the offending gown into the corner. "That goes back to the secondhand store, my dear."

"But that's—"

"Repulsive, I'm afraid," Abby finished for her as she led Corrie into one of the other bedrooms. Her sisters, who had been standing in a row in front of the bed, stepped back with a flourish.

An ethereal creation, the shade of the palest yellow rose imaginable, floated on the bed. Tiny forest green bows peeked out where the flounce was tucked up in front and in the bustle.

"It's yours," Peggy said, pulling Corrie forward.

Afraid it would melt, Corrie hovered over it. Then she drew them all into a hug. "Thank you. Thank you."

Fairy godmothers really did exist—she had six of them.

Shimmering petticoats and a new corset, edged in

petal-soft lace, rested on a chair nearby. Abby lifted them and said, "Can't have you wearing your everyday underthings."

"Hurry, the ball begins soon," Zelda said, and handed the evening gown to Clare. "Deedee, you see her hair doesn't get mussed. We want those curls to cascade down over her shoulder to cover that bruise."

Just that easily, Zelda dismissed the terror of the previous night, and Corrie laughed. She would have one more evening with Jess, and because of the Garrett family, it would be perfect.

She gave herself a stern lecture about weeping willows and leaky hoses while they dressed her. She wouldn't cry tonight. She would have plenty of time for that back in Dallas.

Before she knew it, she had been laced into the silk corset—much more comfortable than her coarse cotton one—and stepped into the petticoats. They wouldn't let her see herself in the mirror until the dress was on, rosebuds were tucked into her hair, and a long silk, forest green ribbon was tied around her neck with the bow at the back and the streamers drifting down to her waist.

Then they stepped back and let her look.

All her resolutions crumbled and tears pooled in her eyes. *I'm beautiful. Really, really beautiful.*

The neckline dipped wide and low over her breasts and shoulders, held by little wisps of gathered fabric no wider than a couple of inches for sleeves. The color set off her skin and eyes, and the skirt, narrow across the front and releasing into a profusion of gossamer ruffles below the bustle to form a long train, gave her an elegant line she never knew she could possess.

Peggy circled her, eyes saucer wide. "I hope I look as beautiful as you do when I let my skirts down."

Corrie hugged her. "You will be—you already are."

The Garrett men arrived before they could all succumb to weepiness, and they made their way downstairs as a group. Corrie strained for a glimpse of Jess, but he wasn't present.

Chin up, Webb. He'll be here. And won't he be surprised, she thought with a grin. Crossing the lobby, she spied Bridget and several other friends, waving excitedly to her. She shot them a thumbs-up sign. She wouldn't think about missing them. Not yet.

Zelda held her back at the entrance to the ballroom. "Just a moment, my dear."

Obediently, Corrie halted and turned toward her. In the doorway, the Garretts seemed to be whispering a lot, but Corrie waited for Zelda to tell her whatever it was she needed to.

The older woman smiled and squeezed Corrie's hand. "You are indeed a beauty, my dear. In heart as well as in appearance." She kissed Corrie on one cheek and whispered, "I feel as if I have another daughter."

Heart overflowing, Corrie's throat clogged with tears. Blinking rapidly, she whispered back, "And I've found another mother."

They hugged, and Zelda used her handkerchief to wipe away their tears. "Thank you for bringing my boy back into the family," she whispered, then added in a firmer but still kindly tone, "Now you may make your entrance."

Corrie swiveled around to see the Garretts lined up on either side of the doorway inside the ballroom, framing Jess, elegant as always in his tuxedo. The

appreciative light in his eyes zinged straight to her
heart and she straightened, remembering all the lessons in the social graces that Zelda and her daughters had drilled into her.

Walking on air and never taking her eyes from
him, she approached Jess. The light gleamed on his
dark hair and she brushed his usual wayward strand
from his forehead as she reached him.

Her breath whooshed out as he captured her hand
and kissed her fingers, heat singeing her as his lips
caressed her through the silk of her gloves.

"You are the loveliest woman here," Jess said as
he straightened, "although I've had eyes for no one
but you since you walked in the door."

Move over, Cinderella. My fairy tale is coming true.

"Th-thank you," she managed to say. Then the
orchestra struck up a waltz and she knew the fairy
tale would last the whole night.

What happened after that, she would worry about
later. For now . . .

Her feet seemed to operate on automatic—or
maybe it was that Jess was such a wonderful dancer—
but she floated over the floor, barely touching
ground. They twirled and twirled, and Corrie giggled
as her train arced behind her in a bell shape, just as
she had witnessed others' doing when she had spied
on the Christmas ball.

The waltz rhythm swept her along, echoing the
triplet rhythm of her heartbeat. One-two-three, one-
two-three. Her vision blurred, and the room receded
to light and shadow.

All she saw was Jess—tall and dark-haired, with
Texas summer eyes. His dimples flickered in and out,
and she learned to anticipate a breath-robbing turn
when they appeared.

One-two-three, one-two-three.

They dipped and whirled, and Corrie longed for it never to end. But every dance has an ending, and Jess put them into a reverse turn as the concluding phrase sounded. Then he sent her in a final spin and stepped back, holding her hand and bowing.

Corrie's heart thudded against her corset. Now or never.

With a light grasp on Jess's hand, she sank down onto her back leg, and sank even more as she lowered her nose toward her knee. Abby had drilled and drilled her for hours, and a spark of delight filled Corrie as the practice paid off.

She held the pose for a beat. Two beats. Ah hell, why not trounce the blonde? Three beats. Four. Then, like the mist rising off the mountains, she rose, her eyes never leaving his.

In her mind, she pumped her fist and yelled, "Yes!"

As he widened his blue eyes, Jess let loose a laugh and caught her up in his arms and whirled her around, her feet never touching the ground. "My little duck is a swan."

"What?"

"Never mind." Then he whirled around again.

She threw out her arms and laughed with him. It felt amazing to be with him—to touch him, to dance with him. She never wanted it to stop.

Her return to her own time loomed, but she pushed away that concern. For now, she would enjoy the ball. And enjoy it she did. The Garrett men claimed her for every other dance—she kept the rest for Jess. His smile as he rejoined her after each dance apart sent heat coursing over her.

If only . . .

But too soon she noticed that time had run out—midnight loomed. Whether she wanted to or not, she had to take Jess's badge and return to her time. Otherwise, she would probably cause one of those time paradoxes or alternate universes, like on *Star Trek*.

As if TV has anything to do with real life.

Sunk in despair, she went to find Jess.

The moon cast a silvery light over the gardens, shadowing the darkness with a deeper shade of night. The gazebo gleamed eerily, but its cool interior provided a private refuge for them to catch their breath.

Jess drew Corrie into his embrace, inhaling the scent of roses in her hair, as well as the scent that was Corrie's alone. She molded herself to him and slipped her arms under his coat to encircle his waist. Minutes passed as they stood, quietly and desperately, making memories that would have to last them a lifetime.

He knew the time had come for her to leave and felt the future barreling at him like an out-of-control locomotive. A future without Corrie.

A future without love.

"Do you really have to go?" he asked.

She nodded and stepped back, leaving a Corrie-sized hole in his being. His only consolation was that the pain in her eyes echoed his own.

Her fingers lingered on his lapel. "I—I need your badge, Jess."

"My badge?" Confused, he removed it from the inner pocket where he kept it except for times like last night. He held it out on his palm, the silver catching the moonlight. "To remember me by?"

She lifted the tiny confection that was her evening bag. "No. I have a picture of you in here . . . to take with me."

"Then what do you need my badge for?" His mind yelled its confusion, and he fought to maintain control. He would see this done, no matter how much his heart pleaded for a reprieve.

"I'm not sure, but I think when I touch it"—she shuddered a sigh in and out—"I go back."

Hope reared its head. "You mean if you never touch it . . . ?"

"I don't think it works that way. I think—" She flung away from him and paced the perimeter of the gazebo. "Oh, hell, I think I can control the timing with it—only on this day—of when I go back. Otherwise, before tonight is over, I go back whenever the Powers-That-Be want to send me."

"I don't want you to go. I love you."

She clutched a post and sagged onto the guardrail. "I love you, too. I don't know why I had to travel a hundred years to fall in love, but I did."

He walked to within arm's reach of her and stopped. "I will always love you. I don't know how I will live without you."

She directed a steady gaze at him. "You have your family. They'll help."

He thought of the way his father and the rest had joined together to rescue Corrie and nodded. "Yes, they will. But they can't replace you. No one can."

"And there'll never be another man to compare to you." A sob escaped her and she stood on tiptoe to press her lips to his.

Then she whispered, "I'll love you forever," and pulled the badge from his hand.

A roaring like a thousand waterfalls assailed his ears and a hurricane wind pummeled him. Squinting his eyes against it, he saw a vortex form and sweep Corrie into it.

"No!" he shouted, and jumped into the vortex. He tumbled, and the roaring increased until, from one heartbeat to the next, he touched Corrie's hand and his motion calmed.

Her eyes were wide with fear but shone with love as she protested, "You can't be here. You can't."

"If you can't stay, I'll go with you." Better an unknown time with her than his own without her. "I want to be with you wherever—whenever—that is."

"I—I don't know if you can." She turned to look toward the darkness ahead, and they tumbled like logs caught in a spring flood, the thundering noise magnified.

"That's the future?" he yelled in her ear.

She nodded, and her grasp threatened to cut off circulation to his fingers.

He shot a glance behind him, but all he could see was a soft white light. Giving her hand a tug, he asked, "Then that's my time back there?"

As she looked back, their momentum slowed and silence settled around them. They seemed to float between their worlds. He took advantage of the calm to pull her into his arms, and their motion ceased altogether.

They exchanged a puzzled glance; then Corrie chanced a look toward the darker end of the vortex and the twenty-first century. Instantly, she regretted it, for they started the headlong, end-over-end rolling again.

Wait a minute. She grabbed Jess and managed to turn them toward the end of the vortex in his time. The calm returned and the noise abated.

"Notice something, Chief?" She nodded at the soft glow coming from the nineteenth century. "I noticed this when I came through before."

"Enlighten me," he answered, his tone as tight as his grip around her waist.

"When I fought moving from my end of the tunnel toward yours, there was all that noise and being battered against the sides of whatever this is." She risked a smile, wondering if she was right. Praying she was right. "It's as if someone was telling me in which direction I was supposed to be going."

"But it's only quiet when you—" Light sparked in his eyes as he stared at her. "You mean . . . ?"

"Maybe I'm supposed to stay in your time."

"Then what are we waiting for?"

"Hell if I know, Chief." She shifted her eyes to the shining white end of the vortex—toward family and friends. Toward the home she had craved for so long. "I don't have ruby slippers to click three times."

Jess laughed. "I have no idea what that means, but let's try something else three times." He cupped her cheek with one hand and pressed his lips to hers, released them, then did it again.

"Third time's the charm?" she whispered, and fisted a hand in his hair as he kissed her again.

As always, his lips were warm and tender, with a hint of power. She sighed and tangled her tongue with his, lost in the sensation of holding Jess and kissing him when she had been sure she would never see him again. His back was warm beneath her fingers, and his arms held her as if he would never let her go.

Never let me go. Oh, please, if only . . .

"Harrumph."

She clutched Jess closer. *Oh, please.*

"Harr-r-rumph." This time the sound was more pronounced.

And familiar.

Corrie opened her eyes and glanced its way. Major Payne glared at her from the steps of the gazebo.

Joy blossomed within her and she laid back her head and let loose a peal of laughter. "Jess, we did it. We're home."

Jess opened his eyes, then spun her in a circle. "You're right. We're home, sweeting."

"Actually, you are in the Chesterfield Hotel's gazebo, making a spectacle of yourselves." Major Payne pursed his lips and issued another "harrumph."

Reining in his exuberance, Jess shook his head. "Forgive me, Major, but you'll understand when I tell you the lady has just accepted my proposal of marriage."

"Jess—"

He gave her a surreptitious shake and whispered from the side of his mouth, "Shh."

Major Payne's features transformed into a smile. "Well, in that case . . ." He bowed and backed down the steps. "I'll order champagne immediately."

As his ramrod-stiff figure exited past the rhododendrons, Corrie whirled on Jess. "What was that about marriage? You haven't asked yet, so how could I accept?"

"I asked you months ago, remember?"

She grinned. "And I said to ask me again after the Midsummer Ball."

Solemnly, Jess dropped to one knee and gazed up at her, his Texas summer blue eyes shining in the moonlight. "Corrinne Webb, will you marry me and live with me for all time?"

"Oh, get up, Chief," Corrie said, but her heart threatened to burst. She finally had her fairy tale, complete with handsome prince and happily-ever-after ending.

Best of all, she had found her home . . . in his heart.

He kissed her fingertips before getting to his feet, then yanked her into his arms and said, "You belong here, with me, forever. Will you marry me?"

When she didn't answer immediately, he gave her another shake. "Say yes, damn it."

"Yes, damn it," she replied like a good nineteenth-century woman. Then laid a twenty-first century kiss on him that rocked them both to their souls.

EPILOGUE

The day after the solstice, Esmeralda Sparrow opened her door and beamed. "I thought you would be by today. Come in. I've just made tea."

Corrie, looking much more comfortable in her bustle than the last time she had stood in this room, hugged her and said, "Thank you, Sparrow. I don't know how you did it, but thank you."

"Whatever do you mean?" As if she didn't know.

"I wouldn't have met Jess if I hadn't come back in time." Corrie accepted the cup of tea and sipped before she placed the china on the table and clasped her hands in her lap. "I don't know how you managed it, but I met the only man I could ever love here, a hundred years before I'll be born. And almost as great, I have a family. The Garretts treat me like I've always belonged." Her gaze drifted to one side, and a sweet expression settled on her mobile features. "Belong—what a wonderful word, don't you think?"

"Definitely, my dear." Esme sipped her own tea and smiled. "As for the whys and hows, I find it best not to dwell overmuch on the business."

Laughing, Corrie agreed. They sipped in companionable silence until they emptied their cups; then

Corrie removed Jess's badge from her purse. "This is for you. I figured you would want it."

"Indeed I do." Esme's heart raced, and she rose to open the lid to her hope chest. "Would you care to do the honors?"

Corrie ran her fingers over the badge a final time and knelt to lay it in one corner of the chest. "If I hadn't come back in time, Laughlin would've shot Jess and hit this star over his heart, breaking off one of the points."

"You are correct."

"And Jess would be dead."

Lips tight, Esme nodded.

Corrie inhaled a shaky breath and touched the dueling pistol placed there but a couple of years ago. "There's a pattern—a plan—here. This is all part of a plan." She lifted her head and fixed Esme with her gaze. "You have a plan."

"Yes, I do have a plan." Esme, eyes filmed with happy tears, met her gaze without flinching. "I also have hope."

She closed the chest's lid and stroked her palms over the smooth wood. *Only three more left. But if a chef is as temperamental as Corrie, how much more so will an artist be?*

Dear Reader,

In *Fire with Fire,* love ignites between a nineteenth-century lawman and a twenty-first-century, time-traveling chef, and burns away the pain of their pasts. Without Corrie Webb, Jess Garrett would die. Without Jess, Corrie would live, but in a world without love.

Thank you for laughing and crying with me as these two found their way to a peace within themselves and a love that soared in the splendid Allegheny Mountains of western Virginia.

You've visited with some old friends from the first in the Hope Chest series, *Enchantment* by Pam McCutcheon, and some that you will see in future books in this series, *Grand Design* by Karen Fox, *Stolen Hearts* by Laura Hayden, and *At Midnight* by Maureen McKenzie.

I love to hear from readers, so you can e-mail me at *paulagill@aol.com,* visit *www.paulagill.com,* or write to me at 1042 West Baptist Road, #153, Colorado Springs, CO 80921.

Live always with love.

Paula

COMING IN AUGUST 2001 FROM
ZEBRA BALLAD ROMANCES

___WOLF AT THE DOOR: *Dublin Dreams*
  by Cindy Harris   0-8217-6913-8 $5.99US/$7.99CAN
Millicent is determined to become a "modern" woman—and her spirit intrigues Captain Alec Wolferton—a reputed scoundrel! Thrilled by her own passionate attraction to this blackguard, Millicent suddenly finds herself swept up in a romantic adventure.

___STRANGER'S KISS: *Midnight Mask*
  by Maria Greene   0-8217-7103-5 $5.99US/$7.99CAN
Rafe Howard returned to England after the war, but a head injury had erased any recollection of his previous life. Finding his estranged wife is the first step in reclaiming an identity he cannot remember. Does beautiful Andria Saxon hold the key to Rafe's past?

___GRAND DESIGN: *Hope Chest*
  by Karen Fox   0-8217-6903-0 $5.99US/$7.99CAN
Artist Cynda Madison wants more from life than restoring old paintings for the historical society. Then she begins working on the damaged portrait of the handsome Prince Dimitri; she is transported back in time to 1887 and meets the prince himself. Now Cynda must prevent the prince's death in order to return to her own life . . . but can she prevent herself from falling in love?

___LOTTIE AND THE RUSTLER: *Bogus Brides*
  by Linda Lea Castle   0-8217-6831-X $5.99US/$7.99CAN
Lottie is quite satisfied to live without a man. Taking the name Shayne Rosswarne from a wanted poster, she's invented a long-lost—and conveniently absent—husband. She is running her successful dress shop in peace, until the real Shayne Rosswarne shows up—and wants some answers. . . .

Call toll free **1-888-345-BOOK** to order by phone or use this coupon to order by mail. *ALL BOOKS AVAILABLE AUGUST 01, 2001.*
Name _____
Address _____
City _____ State _____ Zip _____
Please send me the books that I have checked above.
I am enclosing $_____
Plus postage and handling* $_____
Sales tax (in NY and TN) $_____
Total amount enclosed $_____
*Add $2.50 for the first book and $.50 for each additional book. Send check or money order (no cash or CODs) to: **Kensington Publishing Corp., Dept. C.O., 850 Third Avenue, New York, NY 10022**
Prices and numbers subject to change without notice. Valid only in the U.S. All orders subject to availability. **NO ADVANCE ORDERS.**
Visit our website at **www.kensingtonbooks.com.**